IF I TOLD YOU,
I'D HAVE TO KISS YOU

ALSO BY MAE MARVEL

Everyone I Kissed Since You Got Famous

IF I TOLD YOU,
I'D HAVE TO KISS YOU

A Novel

Mae Marvel

ST. MARTIN'S
GRIFFIN
NEW YORK

First published in the United States by St. Martin's Griffin, an imprint of St. Martin's Publishing Group

IF I TOLD YOU, I'D HAVE TO KISS YOU. Copyright © 2025 by Mae Marvel. All rights reserved. Printed in the United States of America. For information, address St. Martin's Publishing Group, 120 Broadway, New York, NY 10271.

www.stmartins.com

Designed by Omar Chapa

The Library of Congress Cataloging-in-Publication Data is available upon request.

ISBN 978-1-250-89470-0 (trade paperback)
ISBN 978-1-250-89471-7 (ebook)

Our books may be purchased in bulk for promotional, educational, or business use. Please contact your local bookseller or the Macmillan Corporate and Premium Sales Department at 1-800-221-7945, extension 5442, or by email at MacmillanSpecialMarkets@macmillan.com.

First Edition: 2025

10 9 8 7 6 5 4 3 2 1

For spies like us, which is to say, in love and learning how to love more with every mission

IF I TOLD YOU,
I'D HAVE TO KISS YOU

CHAPTER ONE

The Ritz-Carlton, Toronto

Yardley Whitmer held her champagne flute aloft, wondering if her smile looked natural or like the grimace on a French revolutionary's death mask.

It felt like the latter.

"But in the end, my darling Tommy, the number of guests, the number of flower arrangements—even the number of bridesmaids doesn't matter. The only number that matters to me is three thousand five hundred and seventy-two." The bride reached up to press a finger to the corner of her eye and give the groom a convincing, nongrimacing smile. "That's nine years, nine months, and seventeen days," she said. "How long I've had with you so far. And now, my love, the only number that matters is how many thousands of days we'll have together next."

Tommy leaned over and kissed his beloved, then pulled off a very tasteful clink of his crystal lowball glass against her champagne flute while the crowd of rich white Canadian guests went wild.

Yardley took a sip to rinse away the involuntary burn of tears in the back of her throat. She was the worst kind of sucker for romantic declarations. Childhood fantasies of crystal-and-taffeta weddings had trailed her into adulthood like a heartbroken ghost.

Never mind that she was a lesbian, an orientation that had barred her from the ostentatious nuptials of her dreams until the Supreme Court finally came to its senses in her early twenties. By then, it didn't matter, because Yardley was well on her way to achieving another childhood dream by becoming a case officer for the Directorate of Operations at the U.S. Central Intelligence Agency.

In other words, a spy.

The life of a spy was incompatible with long-term romantic commitments. Yardley had known this from the outset, but with KC she'd made the mistake of letting herself get sentimental. She'd started to believe she could have a home and a woman all her own to come home to. She'd helplessly surrendered to her childhood dream by falling for a pint-sized redheaded computer nerd, and what did she have to show for it?

Six weeks of rolling over on the stiff guest-bed mattress to find the sheets cold and no KC whispering a little something in her ear, that was what.

"Security has moved off the east stairwell." Atlas, her handler, interrupted her reverie.

"Got it," she murmured into her champagne flute.

Sliding the long blond waves of her wig off her shoulders, Yardley subtly surveyed the ballroom. "You have entry into the suite for me?" She flicked her gaze away from an immaculately groomed man in a tuxedo whom she'd accidentally made brief eye contact with.

"Negative," Atlas answered. "You'll have to get in the old-fashioned way."

The man was now strolling in her direction, smoothing both

hands over his dark hair, seemingly certain of sexual conquest. She could work with that.

"Hello there." He took a flute off a passing tray and tipped it in Yardley's direction. "You must have been sitting in the back during the ceremony. I hadn't noticed you until now." There was the tiniest smear of brow gel above one of his eyebrows.

"I snuck in late." She gave him an adorable nose wrinkle and a hint of dimple, wanting him to see her as just another moneyed, winsome blonde. "I've actually been dying to pop up to my room for ten minutes to freshen up before the dancing starts, but, silly me, I lost my key card." She touched her earring to tip her camera toward the man so Atlas could get a picture.

The eyebrows drew together in a deep furrow. "Didn't they send you the app download?"

Shoot.

"Copy that," the voice in Yardley's ear said. She fumbled with her clutch for her phone, buying herself a moment to listen while she tamped down a blaze of anger. The fact that this hotel's rooms were keyed with an app ought to have been part of her briefing, but to call the preparation for this short-notice operation "scant" would be generous.

Yardley wasn't feeling generous.

Atlas's voice returned with a crackle of static. "Get us a device loaded with a key to any room, and tech can do the rest."

"There it is!" Yardley sounded awestruck as she pulled out her bejeweled phone. "Oh my gosh, I've been traveling so much lately, I completely forgot they do the app thing for room keys here. No wonder I couldn't find it." She winked at the man.

"I could follow you up and show you how it works." He knocked back the rest of his champagne, and, like an unearned promotion, another tray passed by to receive his empty just in time.

"Why don't you save me a dance?" Yardley stepped forward and touched his lapel. "I really do need to freshen up."

His expression went through a series of independent verifications of the likelihood her request was genuine before it smoothed out with a bland smile. "Of course."

Atlas spoke again. "The target's in line at the bodega, but it's only a five-minute walk. You've got ten to get the job done. Fifteen, tops."

"I'll be back in a jiff." She smiled, brushed against the man's jacket as she distracted him with a quick arm squeeze, and sighted a path to the east stairwell as she slipped the phone she'd just stolen from her would-be lover into her clutch.

"Can you break the suite's lock with the prize I got you?" she asked, safely out of earshot.

"Affirmative." The faintest hint of feedback accompanied Atlas's reply. These earpieces liked to kick up a fuss about being underground or deep in the interior of a vast building like the Ritz-Carlton. Presumably because the agency knew there was nothing that provided quite the same rush as the mortal fear of running a black bag operation on skimpy intelligence with no link to the outside world.

Or it *could* be Yardley was getting cynical. Project Maple Leaf had her overexposed.

Ten weeks ago, just as the leaves were turning red on the oak tree outside the window of the bedroom Yardley used to share with KC and there had still been a chance, however faint, of salvaging their three-year relationship, Toronto became the testing ground for a completely new kind of digital weapon. When deployed, it killed every cell tower, internet signal, and communication line in a thirty-mile radius around the city. For forty-seven minutes, the device grounded planes, imperiled hospital patients, and shut down electronic systems of every imaginable type and function, causing not a little panic.

No one took credit for the stunt, but the word on the street was that the weapon hadn't worked as advertised. Something technical had gone wrong. Still, the promise of a digital device capable of delivering mass chaos came through loud and clear, and the agency was desperate to lock it down before it could be perfected and sold.

Yardley had spent two months chasing leads around the globe, with ever-diminishing returns. Today, her mission was to break into the suite of a woman whose web activity suggested to the agency's analysts that she might be involved in the weapon's development.

"Status update on the door?" Yardley leaned down to ease off her heels so she could take the stairs more quickly. The target's suite was twenty flights up.

"Tabasco's working on it."

Dang it. If Tabasco was handling the tech, that suite's lock would be hacked in no time. Less than no time.

Tabasco was a technical agent, one of dozens who worked in the bowels of the headquarters building. To a field agent like Yardley, the techs were largely interchangeable, known to her only by their code names, but Tabasco was the exception. According to the rumor mill, Tabasco was a child genius who'd hacked the red phone on the president's desk. The director was said to ask for their reports personally, eschewing all other technicians.

Yardley started to run.

Growing up, she'd loved nothing more than to drive around the Piedmont with her granddaddy, listening to his stories about the years he'd spent spying on the Russians. No question, those stories hooked her but good, and they were absolutely the reason she was currently barefoot, quads burning, trying not to pant as she flung her body up flight after flight. Unfortunately, not once in all those stories he'd told her, over all the years she'd made him tell them, had Yardley Whitmer Senior of Cary, North Carolina, bothered to mention how much time spies spent running.

Yardley never remembered this when she let herself sleep late instead of going for a run.

She stopped on the tenth-floor landing, chest heaving, and gave herself over to self-censure. KC *never* skipped a run, and she wasn't even a spy. She was a web marketing freelancer for companies that sold things like health supplements and sustainable T-shirts. In fact, KC had been running a lot in the six weeks since they broke up.

Not that Yardley could blame her. Miles running the Glade Stream Valley in Reston, Virginia, was a thousand times better than the miles of awkward silence between them as they lurched side by side through the death of their relationship.

She made herself start climbing again, ignoring the burn in her throat—the same burn that returned whenever she thought about weddings and empty, cold sheets and what KC used to do and didn't anymore.

Or how fast she'd fallen for her at that backyard picnic where they first met. How much they'd laughed, especially the first year, when Yardley's life was a whirlwind of missions and covert ops and briefings in between trying out food trucks with KC, exploring the city, walking in the summer heat, and kissing like it was the only reason to keep breathing.

Not now, Whitmer.

She rounded the final landing. "Second suite past the fire door," Atlas said. "We've almost got the code. Tabasco's impressed. It seems either the target or someone working with them reprogrammed the lock with their own layer of security."

"That's fantastic," she panted. She stopped in front of the suite, keeping her head down and away from the hallway camera. "Not easy to impress Tabasco. So glad to know there's a new and exciting barrier to the successful completion of this op."

"Hold on," Atlas said, chuckling. "Almost there."

Yardley retrieved her phone from her clutch and leaned against the wall, gazing and poking at the screen to give the impression of mindlessly scrolling as she waited.

Her own phone was back in Virginia, but Yardley's texts and voicemails forwarded to her field phone when she was on assignment. If she were captured, everything would be wiped remotely to prevent the sensitive details of her personal life from falling into the hands of the enemy, but there was nothing compromising on the screen cradled in Yardley's palm. The only human communication she'd received all day was a single text from KC.

> guy in a big truck came by to pick up your moving pod, gave me attitude because i told him it's not ready & you're not here. maybe deal with that

KC worked from home. She didn't like being interrupted. She'd barely looked up from her computer when Yardley lied and said she had to take a last-minute trip to New York for work.

It used to be that when she was in the field, Yardley's phone would fill up with messages from her girlfriend. Memes KC thought were funny. Videos of baby pigs—Yardley's favorite kind of animal videos. I love you's. I miss you's.

She sighed. She'd forgotten to change the pickup date on the POD. Most of her things were boxed up and loaded into it, but the apartment she'd leased wouldn't be ready to move into for another two weeks, and both her presence in KC's house and her absence from it seemed to irritate KC equally.

She never smiled anymore. When they first met, KC's elfin smile was the first thing Yardley had noticed about her. It was a tricky one, curled up at the edges, and it came with freckles and short strawberry hair that had made Yardley feel like she'd been handed a bouquet of fancy spring flowers.

"Anything?" she asked Atlas in a low voice.

Obsessive spy craft provided such an excellent distraction from the quivering pulp left of her heart.

"Thirty seconds."

She blew out a slow breath.

"That should be it," Atlas said, just as Yardley heard the soft whirr of a tumbler. The lock plate lit up a green LED. Tabasco had done it again.

She turned the brass handle. "I'm in. What do the Sisters have to report about our target?" Canadian intelligence—CSIS, known in the trade as "the Sisters"—was handling surveillance.

"She left the bodega, but it looks like she's going to take a break in the park to feed the ducks. Yeah. She's settling in with . . . yep, that's a sleeve of crackers. Nonstandard choice for recreation, but it helps us out."

"Good." Yardley scanned the enormous luxury suite and whistled. "*Double dang.*" She walked over the marble floors toward the windows that looked out over the CN Tower and Lake Ontario. There was a five-seat banquette table with glove-leather-soft chairs, a lot of muted, expensive drapery, and the remains of what appeared to be a multicourse seafood lunch on a side table. "You guys ever think we're working for the wrong side?"

"You'd couch surf and eat nothing but beanie weenies if it meant you could be a patriot for the agency," Atlas said. "No one's ever going to turn the Unicorn with fancy penthouse suites. If someone did, I'd know it was time to defect."

Yardley rolled her eyes while she used an electronics meter to scan as many square inches as she could in the vast suite. They'd started calling her "the Unicorn" on her first mission, when it became clear how her background as a Southern debutante and sorority princess enhanced her capabilities as a CIA officer. It was a combination hard to find among the usual recruits.

Yardley was glad her queer friends only knew her too-boring-to-ask-about civilian cover as a Securities and Exchange Commission compliance consultant. They'd have a field day if they ever found out she was actually an infamous international lesbian spy known as "the Unicorn."

Her meter flashed. "The safe," she said.

"That's disappointing. So obvious."

Yardley leaned closer to the hotel safe, discreetly tucked behind the door of a tiger maple credenza. "Boring one, too. Biometric lock. No fun to crack." She paused, looking closer. "But maybe she does have a few tricks up her sleeve. We have an Elizabeth Bentley fan on our hands."

"A what?" Atlas's voice was a little faint. "We've almost got a profile you can use to open it. Stand by."

She crouched to the side of the safe where the light just caught the thin black thread stretching across the fingerprint screen. "No one knows their spy history. Elizabeth Bentley. Soviet spy who defected to the FBI after the Second World War. Our guys were constantly tossing her place in Brooklyn to make sure they weren't being double-crossed, so she protected her secrets by placing black threads over the openings of trunks and boxes to tell her if they'd been disturbed."

"You obviously paid a lot more attention to your history coursework during training than I did."

"I read history as a hobby." Yardley kept her voice low and her senses alert as she spoke. "Military, spy stuff, a bit of dabbling in archaeology. Did you know it was women who identified Roman artifacts that had been misidentified for decades? It had never occurred to men that the ancient toys they were digging up might, perhaps, be miniature versions of ordinary household items. We've found a lot more brooms and saucepans than cool weapons, it turns out. That story is what inspired me to build that one-twelfth-scale model of a Roman domus I told you about. I have an order of scale Cornish stone coming from the UK."

"You're a strange ranger, Unicorn." Atlas said this with a smile in their voice.

Yardley Whitmer, I love you, but you are a lot. That was how her mama always put it. "You should've met me as a kid. I spent half my time shooting and fishing with my granddaddy and the other half pretending to be one of the Founding Fathers. I used to write letters to General Washington in code, just in case the British intercepted them. My parents despaired."

"You're exaggerating."

"I most certainly am not." She finished photo documenting the room and the safe, then got to work easing the black thread away from the fingerprint screen. "Everything coming through okay?"

"Yeah. We put your fingerprint profile into the hotel system. Go ahead."

Yardley pressed her finger against the screen, and the safe door's lock *chunk*ed, allowing the door to open a quarter of an inch.

"Move your hair back so I can get a better picture."

Yardley brushed aside her wig hair and surveyed the contents of the safe. There was an EU passport, a thumb drive, and a greeting card envelope, its corners furred and soft. She slid the thumb drive into one of the input slots on her agency phone so her team could pull the data. Then she opened the envelope. "Well, that's interesting." Yardley held the black-and-white ultrasound photo up so the camera could see it. The date on the photo put the person at least six months into pregnancy.

"Huh. All right. We got the drive, you can disengage it."

Yardley slid the device out of her phone and set it back in the safe. She flipped the cover on the passport and began photographing the pages. "Parent-to-be is Kris Flynn," she said. "Female. Irish citizen. Thirty-two years old."

"Target's on the move," Atlas said. "ETA under three minutes."

Yardley closed the safe, did her best to replace the thread, and started toward the suite's entrance.

Then she stopped.

The side table with the seafood lunch had caught her attention. Something about the way the discarded dishes were shoved aside to make an open space.

She crossed the room for a better look.

The corner of the table closest to a comfortable chair was clear, with two empty plastic bottles of herbal iced tea nearby. On the wall, she noted a four-outlet plug. Two cords lay abandoned on the ground, one for a laptop, the other a phone. The woman, Kris Flynn, must have taken the tech with her to the bodega. The third plug charged a battery backup brick.

The last one held a charger cord that snaked behind the buffet with the minibar.

Yardley extended her electronics scanner along the path of the cord, watching the meter carefully for a reading. Nothing.

She got down on her hands and knees and followed the cord. Crackling static told her that Atlas was trying to speak—probably to tell her again to get the hell out—but Yardley's stomach had swooped with déjà vu. The adapter on that fourth charging cord looked eerily familiar. She reached behind the buffet, following the cord, and then felt what she'd been hoping for.

A second laptop.

"Hurry," Atlas said.

"Mm-hmm." Yardley thought of KC. *That* was what the state of the tabletop and the mess of cords had reminded her of—when KC was up to her neck in her freelance work and set up a command station in the living room. Food shoved out of the way, laptop balanced on the edge of the remaining surface, empty drink bottles everywhere.

The size and weight of the boxy black laptop pinged a similar memory. She opened the lid, already half certain what she'd see. The screen lit up with the icon of a dragon eating its tail.

"Bingo." Yardley clicked the computer shut. "I don't think Kris Flynn's a wild goose chase, everyone. I don't even think she's an intermediary. I think she's the person we've been looking for."

Once, on a rainy Sunday afternoon when Yardley and KC were still on naked Sunday morning terms, KC was working on a big project for a blue-chip brand. Their app had been hacked, and their engineer fixed it, but they'd wanted KC to check their security. Yardley vaguely knew KC sometimes dabbled in internet security, but when she'd dragged a couple of laptops into bed, Yardley started asking questions. She liked to keep up on her tech. It came in handy.

KC had explained the basics—mainly, that she kept a special computer for jobs like this. The heavy, boxy laptop had enough capacity to allow KC to remotely load the contents of a server over a private network she set up. Yardley had lazily watched her connect the client's servers one by one to run the laptop's program, searching for holes in the servers' security.

"Flynn's either a network security specialist with the Irish equivalent of two weeks' vacation and a 401(k), or else she's a hacker," Yardley said. "Like, a hacker's hacker. And this laptop was cloaked against scanning, so she doesn't want anyone to know."

"Something's wrong." Atlas's tone was suddenly urgent. "The Sisters are scrambling. Get out of there."

Yardley shoved the laptop back behind the buffet. She knew from KC's lesson that there wouldn't be anything on it but the program and a lot of drive space and memory to run it. "Going."

"Use the elevator. Drop your cover before you hit the lobby and wait for my okay to leave the building."

"Copy that."

Yardley slipped on her shoes, and then she was out the door, making sure to show the camera her waist-length beachy waves, a practiced walk in heels, and nothing else. The elevator doors shushed closed as soon as she stepped inside. "Status?"

"The target's gone."

Yardley's scalp prickled. "Meaning what exactly?"

"Meaning disappeared. She turned a corner, and the Sisters didn't pick her up on the other side. They're checking their cameras, but likely she caught on that we had eyes on her and took evasive maneuvers."

"Or someone picked her up off the street," Yardley said. "Could be a hit. Anyone on their way up?"

"So far, you're clear. We have multiple angles on the lobby."

Yardley ran a fingernail under the lace front of her wig where it was adhered with hairspray. It was the work of a moment to twist the wig into her clutch, loosen her own dark layers from the braids she'd pinned them up in, swipe on a deep red lip, put on Ray-Bans, and drape her shoulders in a dark brown silk scarf that covered her black minidress enough to render it unremarkable.

"Car's waiting," Atlas said. "Lobby's clear."

She breezed out the front doors into a cool early November afternoon and slid into a black sedan parked near the alley. "Hi there, Joe." She unzipped the bag on the seat next to her to retrieve a pair of soft joggers, a T-shirt, a cardigan, and—bliss—socks and tennis shoes. When she'd finished changing, she rested her head against the back of the seat and watched urban Toronto roll past the window, briefly wondering if Kris Flynn really was the person who'd made that terrible device. Where had she gone? Had she run or been captured?

It was a setback. The agency needed, desperately, to know what Kris Flynn knew.

But then, drawing on the hard-won wisdom of a hundred-plus field missions, Yardley made herself stop. Her work was done. She'd made it out in one piece. The rest of that mess was for the analysts to figure out.

"What's next, Joe?" she asked.

"Your plane's ready at CFB Trenton. It'll land at Dulles en route to taking some Mounties to Vancouver."

"Tell me it's not a Skyvan, though."

"I could." He expertly wove through traffic. "But that wouldn't mean it's not a Skyvan." He laughed at his joke.

A small military passenger plane, the Skyvan was the equivalent of riding in an airport parking lot shuttle, except thirty thousand feet in the air. Not exactly comfortable.

But it wasn't comfort, really, that got Yardley out of bed in the morning, or put her on planes, trains, and buses and sent her all over the world, risking her blessed hide for information. It was faith that she'd been born with a particular combination of talents and grit, and she had an obligation to use them to make the world better. Working for the agency was how she transformed her purpose into action.

Also, call her old-fashioned, but she truly did believe that putting her own self in peril kept other folks, civilians—good people—safe. People who were loved. People who loved others.

People like KC.

That was what Yardley thought about on the Skyvan between dozing on and off, wiped out from what had been a thirty-six-hour sprint.

KC.

How every single time KC Nolan had smiled in the eleven hundred ninety-seven days since they met, Yardley felt the same way she did the first time.

Like she was coming home.

CHAPTER TWO

Reston, Virginia

Newly fallen leaves crunched under her running shoes as KC Nolan flew over the narrow streets of her neighborhood.

No matter how fast she ran, the beat of her soles on the pavement wasn't loud enough to drive out the only two words in her head.

Kris Flynn. Kris Flynn. Kris *fucking* Flynn.

As she came up on a set of stone pillars marking the entrance to the parking lot of Glade Valley trailheads, her way was unexpectedly blocked by a dark sedan rolling slowly through the entrance onto the street in front of her.

The headlights flashed once, but the car didn't move. She couldn't see who was inside it.

Jesus, fuck.

KC stopped in the middle of the road, heart in her throat, scanning for an exit. The headlights flashed again, and she wondered if the element of surprise would be on her side if she parkoured off the sedan's trunk onto the closest stone pillar and then dropped into the brush by the creek that ran alongside the park. From there, she could run through the middle of the creek for a few hundred feet—it was shallow this time of year—then scramble up the bank to meet up with the trail.

She bent her knees and made her shoulders go loose, calculating the distance between where she stood and the back end of the car.

The driver's door opened. "For heaven's sake, get in. I want a breakfast sandwich before I have to report to headquarters. I don't have time for your shenanigans."

The car door shut.

KC looked up at the moon, already fading, and let out a sigh. She wished she didn't have a reason to be so cagey and hypervigilant. She wished it wasn't her own fault she was jumping out of her shoes at every noise, shadow, and communication.

She wished she hadn't felt like she had so much to prove to Dr. Brown that she'd agreed to develop the demo of a digital weapon that was suddenly very neatly turned in her direction—thanks, apparently, to *Kris Flynn*, a hacker she hadn't run into since they were both teenagers breaking into government databases for the LOLs.

She glanced at the time. Last night, she'd barely had a chance to regroup from handling tech for the Ritz-Carlton mission before she heard Yardley sneak in and shut the guest-room door behind her, coming home late from her last-minute work trip to a brokerage house in New York. Those trips meant hours of meetings with tedious corporate men.

Tedious men loved Yardley. They couldn't resist her cultured North Carolina accent, Snow White gorgeousness, and easy charm.

KC, on the other hand, had not won any pageants. First of all, the talent portion never involved tech expertise, deadlifting, or arguing. Secondly, she said what she thought, often betraying the remnants of one of those *not*-cultured Virginia accents. As a child, she'd been saddled with nicknames like "Half-Pint," "Firecracker," and "Red." The word "trash" had also been bandied about, mostly by tedious men of the type who adored Yardley.

She jogged around the front of the sedan, opened the passenger door, and dropped into the seat. "It took me all night to crack the encryption on the data from that thumb drive you got out of Flynn's safe. I turned in my homework. Can't a girl have an hour to clear her head before dealing with you bird-watchers?"

Gramercy pointed the car down the road, keeping the headlights off. KC had never seen her new handler wear anything but a crisp suit, and this was true now, at five forty-five in the morning.

Sometimes she tried to imagine what Gramercy must have been like in the field twenty years ago—a literal ghost, deep undercover in the Russian president's cabinet—but she couldn't imagine him without his slim-cut suits, wildly patterned pocket squares, and stylish glasses. Although the deep grooves bracketing his mouth hinted he might be *capable* of using it to express something other than exasperation. "There's a bottle of water in the glove compartment," he said.

KC took a look. "And a Glock with a silencer. You know I hate guns." She grabbed the Fiji and closed the compartment.

"I removed it from my holster in deference to your sensibilities." Gramercy turned down a dark alley that he probably thought was clandestine but was actually just the access road behind a row of houses where three sets of parents of her elementary school friends still lived. She'd carved her name into the brick half-wall in this alley when she was eleven.

The car finally rolled to a stop behind a detached garage with an ancient Toyota pickup parked beside it. The wheels were gone, its axles sagging onto cinder blocks.

"I kissed a girl for the first time behind this garage," KC said. "Back then, it was as pink as my grandma's denture glue, but I like the way it's faded to more of a coral."

Gramercy did not smile. "There's a situation."

"You don't say." She crossed her arms with false bravado, wishing he'd caught up with her five miles into her run instead of when she'd just started to hit her stride. KC desperately needed to unwind the tension in her shoulders and neck. She'd spent too many long days and sleepless nights in front of a keyboard the past few months, trying to save the world while waiting for the other shoe to drop. Or, failing that, waiting for Dr. Brown to emerge from whatever safe house he'd been stashed in and explain everything.

All while weathering the worst breakup in the history of the D.C. metro area.

The one way KC knew to get the grit out of her eyes and come down from what was becoming a habitual state of cranked-up hyperfocus was to run and keep running. It was only when her quads burned and her lungs hurt that her body and mind finally snapped back together and let her feel like herself again. Like she *had* a self.

The agency didn't care if she had a self, but KC did. The descent of her life into a calamitous hellscape of loss and lies had made her perversely protective of what little belonged to her. Her opinions. Her unique abilities, such as they were. Her relief that she hadn't yet received a burn notice.

The last time she spoke to Dr. Brown, he'd made a point to remind her of what he'd told her when he was first given the black op to develop the device. He'd chosen KC to make this piece of technology because she kept her eyes on the higher truth, even while her mouth had to lie. He'd told her not to let one bad day expose a mission.

The strain in his voice was audible even over the crackling comm connection. He'd been injured, and it was entirely her fault. The controlled test of KC's weapon in Toronto had gone as bad as worms in cheese, and now her mentor and friend was recuperating somewhere, unable to reach out to her for risk of exposing the mission.

Without orders to follow, KC had taken the weapon apart into hacked-up pieces of code, which she'd stashed on the dark web. Safe as houses, she'd thought.

She'd thought wrong. Days later, the agency began picking up whispers that the device was being reassembled. Those whispers told KC that somehow, despite her precautions, her hidden pieces had been located by someone who knew where to look.

The only thing she'd been able to do was dedicate herself to helping the agency track down whoever had it. She needed to keep the technology safe, and to keep people safe *from* it, without revealing that she'd been the one who made it—at least until Dr. Brown returned and told KC who in the agency they could trust.

"You're in a mood," Gramercy observed. He turned toward her, his blue eyes assessing through the lenses of his glasses. "Trouble in paradise?"

No, no, and nope. KC never asked Gramercy questions about how things were going at home with his husband. She and Gramercy were not on a personal-questions-asking footing. In fact, KC wouldn't say, strictly speaking, they liked each other.

"That's not a work-appropriate question," she bit out. "Also? You already know the answer because we work in intelligence. I had to file a report when Yardley moved in last year. I'm sure you know I put a moving POD on my credit card, and you probably also know my girlfriend bought a stack of retaliatory moving boxes the very next day, because you clowns see fit to monitor her every move, even though the CIA promises the American public it doesn't spy on its own citizens. But I'm going to be understanding and pretend you're not prying out of a purely ghoulish impulse to pick over the bones of my love life."

"Kind of you." Gramercy stared through the windshield at the alley. "I forget how much more difficult it is when your partner doesn't have security clearance."

Anger fired in KC's gut. Gramercy's husband, Lucas, was a three-star general. "Sure. *Sure.* Naturally, privilege is the answer, privilege I don't have and never will. She's a mere civilian, so I can't tell her anything when she's *just* my girlfriend. Maybe someday if we got married, if I got permission, if she got clearance, but you know what? It turns out that when half of what you tell your person isn't true and the other half skates the surface lest you inadvertently put her in mortal danger, she starts to think you're shifty as fuck."

Gramercy made a noise in his throat that KC couldn't interpret.

That was fair. KC didn't know how to interpret that outburst herself, except as an expression of the unburned adrenaline flooding her system, pressing in on her chest, trapping all the things she couldn't say in her throat.

She'd been like this ever since Atlas told her over the Toronto comm yesterday to start pulling background on Kris Flynn—the name of the one person who could *definitely* have found where KC concealed the code for the weapon. The person who could reassemble it, because once upon a time KC and Kris Flynn had come up with the idea together, and they'd known each other before either one of them had anything to hide.

And now Kris could expose her.

She wondered if Yardley, an old-fashioned rule follower who made sure finance bros followed Uncle Sam's regulations and didn't hoard outsized pieces of the pie, would have any sympathy for a woman who wasn't a good enough spy to keep weapons out of the hands of the enemy.

Probably not.

Gramercy adjusted his tie. "Speaking of what was on that thumb drive."

"We weren't." KC glared at him, but his face revealed nothing, and he didn't respond to her aggression. Fatigue crept in as her anger drained away. "What, then? What."

"The analysts have been working with the data that you, as you said, stayed up all night to provide a decryption key for. It seems the target, Kris Flynn, who we now assume was the maker of the device, was collecting intel about her employer."

KC sat up straighter. "Who?"

"One Devon Mirabel. A nationless criminal whose accomplices are known to acquire and sell gray-market tech to the highest bidder."

"Never heard of him."

"The agency's had a file on him for years. Here's the critical piece. Mirabel's shopping the weapon to buyers."

KC's heart filled with ice. "I thought it was nowhere close to being ready for sale."

Could Kris have found, assembled, and made the weapon market-ready so quickly? What did she have? Who had she shown it to? How careful had she been? How many copies existed?

And why the fuck hadn't anyone heard from Dr. Brown? KC

had never needed him more in her life. He was far from a perfect man, but he'd never let her down like this before.

"We've confirmed the intel," Gramercy said. "We already had an asset make contact with Mirabel's people. We'll be sending in an agent posing as a buyer."

KC lapsed into stunned silence.

This was it, then. This was what they'd been working toward—a clear shot at capturing the weapon before it left Mirabel's hands and they lost any chance of controlling where it ended up or how fast it proliferated.

One of the things that kept KC awake nights was the running list in her head of the ways this cyberweapon could disrupt the world as she knew it.

It wasn't supposed to have been a weapon at all.

It was *supposed* to have been a digital skeleton key, a program that unlocked doors and learned as it went. That was what she and Kris had imagined all those years ago. With Dr. Brown, her mentor and the agency's counterterrorism specialist, KC had talked about using the program to stop blockades against aid in war, or deploying it to arrest a train derailment or a fatal traffic pileup before it happened.

When she'd figured out it could cause panic and harm as easily as it could help, she'd explained this to Dr. Brown. That was why he'd suggested the controlled test in a relatively small area with robust infrastructure. A Toronto neighborhood on a sleepy Sunday afternoon with full permission from the prime minister.

But it had gone so wrong.

"Where's this happening?" she asked.

"Mirabel landed at Dulles from Heathrow this morning."

"Oh, happy day." KC took a drink from her water bottle, thinking hard, every muscle in her body locking up as she put together what she knew, what Gramercy wasn't saying, and the sudden development of a new and dangerous mission in her own backyard. "When's the meeting?"

A muscle in Gramercy's jaw flexed. He checked his watch.

"Christ in a chicken basket, it's happening today?" KC looked through the window at the formerly pink garage. "All y'all are spies, right? Just tell me you're not sending the Unicorn in for the meet. Maple Leaf has been playing catch-up for two months. Our analysts are as confused as a fly in a fan factory, and the Unicorn's overexposed. You send them in, they're bound to get made."

Gramercy pretended not to have heard her. "Our agent will make contact, posing as the buyer. We want you in the van."

She whipped her head around. "No fooling?"

She'd never been asked to participate in a mission from the field before. Dr. Brown always said the agency wanted KC for one thing and one thing only. For years, they'd kept her alone in a room full of monitors with her headphones on, talking over an encrypted channel to someone she couldn't see, whose real name she didn't know, or at least wasn't supposed to. They called her "Tabasco"—the worst code name ever, considering Tabasco sauce wasn't even made in Virginia.

An emotion that KC couldn't interpret flitted across Gramercy's face. He rubbed his temples, silver against his dark hair. "We need you to capture as much intel about the device as you can. You know how important this is. It has to happen."

Yep. It absolutely did. It had to happen, because, in an unavoidable, persistent, and very chillingly *real* way, the fate of the world rested on—

Well, not on KC's shoulders. Not exactly.

But a little bit. A little bit it did, and it was enough of a burden that she hadn't been able to think about anything else in her life, any*one* else in her life, since the grid went down in Toronto and Dr. Brown dropped off the map.

She had known him since before she was a legal adult. Sixteen years old, her noodle arms barely strong enough to carry her textbooks at MIT and the tendons in her forearms already three-quarters of the way to her first carpal tunnel surgery from the clandestine shit she'd taught herself to do with a keyboard. The agency had caught her building a backdoor into the EPA system so she and a group of climate activists could move up the dates on industrial site inspections. Dr. Brown was the man who showed up at her dorm room door and announced he'd been sent to either arrest or recruit her.

He wasn't the first person to tell KC there were better things she could do with her powers, but he was the first to make an argument that KC found compelling. His vision for her future had fueled KC straight through training.

He knew her better than most.

KC stilled her bouncing knee. "Tell me it's not the Unicorn, though."

Gramercy sighed.

"What the fuck? I mean, I get why you used them at the Ritz. Rumor is they're slick as butter, and they must be something to look at, because Marie-Claire in forensic accounting, who says she's met them in person, turns red as a fire hydrant whenever the subject comes up, even though she won't say if they're a he or a she or neither one. But, Gramercy, if the CIA had an official mascot, it would be the Unicorn. You're going to get them killed."

"It's not my decision."

"I'm sure that will be a comfort to you when the time comes," she said. "And the meeting has to be today?"

"This afternoon."

"Bring me in for the briefing, then." Dr. Brown had never let her sit in on a briefing, not even when she told him she needed to be included to understand the scope of what the black op required. But if KC was going to be made—or ruined—risking her career to keep the secret of Dr. Brown's op, she wanted to feel like she'd done it as a part of something good.

And she wanted to see the Unicorn with her own eyes before she sat in a van and did what she could to keep them alive.

"You'll be provided with the information necessary for you to—"

"Let me go to the briefing!" She yanked at her seat belt and twisted to face Gramercy. "I have a better chance of not fucking this up if I know the players and the stakes."

"You won't fuck this up."

"No, because you're taking me to the briefing."

"Because you can't." Gramercy's voice had gone hard. There was nothing to argue with when he used that tone, and KC didn't bother. She opened her car door.

What a waste of a day. She'd thought after her run, after she'd blown off some steam, that she might check in with Yardley. She regretted sending her that text yesterday, essentially telling her to get out, already. There was no reason for acrimony.

No reason when the end of their relationship was completely KC's fault.

"KC." Gramercy had opened his window.

"What."

"Figure out what you can put together in advance, but then we'll need you in the van at thirteen hundred."

KC lifted her hand and gave a sharp salute, knowing she'd log in within the hour. She would be in the Unicorn's ear for this op. She never had before. She'd handled only the very barest of the Unicorn's data—their fingerprints, their location—because silos and separation meant safety. It was one of Dr. Brown's mantras and the reason he usually gave for why, for so many years, he'd kept KC with him in their silo of two.

Still. The Unicorn was a legend, and KC had admired the finesse of their work for some time. It would be exciting to partner with them, even for moments.

She headed out of the alley.

"KC!"

The volume with which Gramercy spoke her name in a dark alley at dawn compelled her to turn around. He was leaning his forearm out the open window.

"For what it's worth, I know it's hard. Maybe you'll be surprised, and it will work out. Can't tell you how many times everything went right up to the line, looking bad, and in the end, there was rescue. Don't lose hope."

"Are you talking about my love life, my career, or the fate of our country?"

Gramercy shrugged, and the tinted window went up.

She turned around again and started walking, shoving surprise furious tears off her face. As soon as she got to the end of the alley, KC began to run.

She kept going, faster and faster, until she was a block from home and her shoe caught a slick pile of wet leaves, dropping her down to the asphalt, her knee grinding into the road.

"Mother*fucker*." KC heaved herself up and looked up at the sky and stomped her feet, feeling blood trickling down her shin.

When she limped into the house, she was surprised to discover Yardley at the kitchen table, wearing the extra-short navy-blue robe that murdered KC every time she put it on. The morning light made her skin glow, and her ordinarily shiny, perfectly perfect inky hair was messed up everywhere.

KC's stomach soured. She'd loved morning Yardley. Morning Yardley had been entirely *her* Yardley. Messy, sexy, gorgeous in the raw.

But she wasn't KC's anymore.

She knelt down to untie her shoes, grateful for the sharp sting in her wounded knee. Glad to be able to look at the damp knot of her shoelaces so she didn't have to look at the woman she couldn't stop disappointing.

They'd met at a backyard barbecue. Yardley was a friend of a friend of a roommate, and KC had heard her very memorable name a few times in passing but never run into her until that blistering-hot summer day. She turned around from laughing at a joke and spotted Yardley Whitmer in a white strapless sundress, her bow-shaped lips painted red, dark hair braided and pinned up, looking exactly like the illustration of the goddess Athena in KC's favorite childhood collection of Greek and Roman mythology.

I'm going to marry that woman. That was the thought KC had. Only it wasn't a thought, it was more like the voice of her actual ancient and immutable soul, speaking aloud the purest desire it had ever felt.

KC kicked her shoes off and started toward the bathroom.

"Why are you bleeding?" Yardley stood, her soft alarm and prettiness like another world from Gramercy in the alley.

"Bit it."

"It looks like it hurts."

It did hurt. It never stopped hurting. An uneasy silence filled the space between them.

"It's fine." KC hated this—the awkwardness where there used to be endless conversation. The anxious stomach ache she got every single time she tried to talk to Yardley now. "I'm going to grab a shower."

Yardley's gaze was fixed on KC's knee. "Let me look at that first. It might have gravel. Sit down, and I'll get something to clean it up." She hustled out of the kitchen to the bathroom cabinet in the hall, leaving KC to hunch over in the warm seat of the chair Yardley had vacated.

Her hands were shaking.

They hadn't been able to talk to each other since KC had spite-ordered the POD after finding out Yardley signed the lease on an apartment. When it got delivered, she'd watched Yardley's blue eyes fill with tears that spilled over her blotchy cheeks while she stared at KC, not even wiping them away, and it became perfectly, horribly plain that they weren't going to be "taking a break" or "taking time to find their way back to each other."

It was over.

Yardley's extensive travel, more and more extensive all the time, followed by KC's overwork and lies—those were the first blows. But KC had taken apart the rest with her failure to act on the knowledge that Yardley desired and deserved more. More romance. More gestures. More confidence in their commitment.

It wasn't that KC hadn't wanted to, it was that she couldn't. She *couldn't* talk to Yardley about forever when their past and present wasn't the entire truth. And even if she had been able to, she couldn't live with how much she couldn't give this woman who deserved to have every single thing she wanted.

Yardley came back into the kitchen with a huge brown bottle of hydrogen peroxide and a bag of cotton balls. "Sit up straight." She knelt down on the floor in front of KC. The placket on her robe fell away to reveal the soft, luminous skin of her throat and shoulder. When she looked up, her deep blue eyes were crinkling at the corners with concern that made KC's chest feel tight. "It's pretty deep, actually."

"It's but a flesh wou— Yikes!" KC jumped at the unexpected cold sting of a cotton ball soaked in antiseptic touching the scrape.

Yardley dabbed one more time and then—dreadful—leaned forward and softly blew on KC's knee.

It completely stopped the pain. Mainly because of KC's overwhelming and instant horniness.

She gripped her uninjured knee against the sudden impulse to grab Yardley's wrist or to say something, anything, to tighten this unexpected thread of connection between them.

But what could she say? Nothing had changed. Yardley wasn't even paying attention anymore. She'd stood up to stare out the window at the driveway, where the white hulk of the POD waited for the last boxes to be loaded in.

"I have to remember to call those guys back." Her voice was flat.

The coffee maker beeped, loud in the quiet kitchen. KC's knee hurt three times as much as it had before. She squeezed her hands into fists to stop the trembling, listening to the coffee maker hiss and gurgle.

Coffee. That was why Yardley had been sitting at the table. She hadn't been waiting for KC. She'd been waiting on her coffee.

It was just a few minutes after six. KC had never known Yardley, when she was home, to get up before seven thirty. Certainly not when she had the day off. "You're awake early," she said, breaking the heavy silence.

Yardley tightened her robe. "I have a work thing."

"I thought you had the rest of the week off."

"I thought so, too, but my boss called. There's paperwork we have to finish up for the mortgage brokerage in New York. Then, after, I'm meeting someone." Yardley gave KC a small shrug.

KC didn't permit herself to react, even though this—the small shrug, and the way Yardley held her mouth when she was doing the small shrug—was a blow. Not because she believed Yardley would be unfaithful even now, when there was nothing left to be faithful to, but because KC had heard her say this kind of thing too many times.

I'm meeting someone. I have a work thing. I'll be late, I'm getting together with a friend in the city after.

Every time, it hurt a little more what Yardley *didn't* say.

I wish I could stay home with you.

Do you want to come with me?

Mostly, KC couldn't even go with her, and if Yardley happened to decide to stay home, KC would have to make up a reason to explain why it was necessary for *her* to leave so she could drive herself to Langley. It was pointless and stupid to care about Yardley's solo friendships, her excessive work hours and endless business trips, when they were precisely what made enough room for KC to carry on her secret life.

But she did care. Because she was a fool.

"When will you be back?" she asked.

"Not sure, actually." Yardley waved her hand. "You know how it is when a friend's in crisis."

Just a few hairs lifted at the nape of KC's neck, the way they did when she was on the trail of something and her hindbrain noticed an anomaly in a hot mess of code. "So it's work on your day off and then a friend in crisis? Who?"

Yardley frowned. "Not really *crisis*-crisis," she said. "But you know."

That "you know" was a bald cue for KC to pick up. *Agree and let me go*, it meant. *You don't want me here with you any more than I want to be here.*

KC didn't know if it was the sting in her knee or her early-morning tête-à-tête with Gramercy making her obstreperous, but she refused to say her expected lines. "I don't remember you having a friend who has problems."

Yardley coughed. "Who doesn't, right?" She looked away from KC again. "It's kind of a friend and kind of a work thing. Hard to explain."

"I'm pretty smart. You could try."

KC watched color climb from under Yardley's hand up the sides of her neck. Finally, she turned her head to meet KC's eyes. "It's not really your business, is it? Anymore."

Awful. Hopelessly, desperately awful. KC had to pinch the bridge of her nose to keep the sting in her eyes from turning to tears. "Yeah," she finally choked out. "Right. Not like it ever was."

Civilians weren't supposed to know anything about KC besides her cover. Dr. Brown had made it clear when she joined the agency: from that day forward, she was a smart, precocious kid who'd been raised by Dad and Grandma after Mom died, who went early to college, then set up her own freelance tech business. KC's cover's life was an easy-breezy one, without a lot of money but with enough of everything that mattered. Nothing to worry about or dig deep into.

That was who she'd been with Yardley. Who she'd had to be.

Maybe KC could've, *should've*, shared with Yardley more of the emotional truth of her life—the benign neglect of her upbringing, the anxiety and loneliness, how her idealism had led her to the community she'd always needed but also to the illegal activities that threatened her entire young adulthood.

But for KC herself, her shallow cover story was more comfortable. It made her feel equipped for a relationship with someone like Yardley, who'd grown up surrounded by family and friends, entered private schools and sororities, and could navigate a career in finance with grace.

KC's decision to stick to her cover had killed any possibility that she and Yardley could share the joyful fantasies and dreams of an ordinary couple three years into their relationship. They'd walk past a school during recess, and KC would squeeze Yardley's hand and nearly ask, *So have you ever thought about kids?* But then she'd bite her tongue, knowing it wasn't possible, and she didn't want to get Yardley's hopes up. Or Yardley would tell a story about her beloved childhood cat, Okra, and KC would stop herself just short of saying, *Should we get a pet?*

There were so many words arrested in her throat, frozen and unsaid. It meant that every sweet nothing came out a little more strangled until Yardley inevitably noticed, and then KC didn't have an answer for, *What's wrong with us? How can we fix us?*

The only thing she ever could say to Yardley that was the full truth was *I love you*. But that didn't matter when Yardley could never really know the woman who was saying it.

The scrape of the kitchen blind on its track was jarring in the silence between them. Yardley yanked the slim rope until the blinds were partially closed, obscuring the view from outside. She was always getting after KC about turning lights on early, transforming the house into a fishbowl. "I have to get ready," she said.

And then she was gone, leaving KC in an empty kitchen with no choice but to make herself forget about her heart for now. Forget the waste of the best three years of her life, and forget the dark, narrow feeling she got in her chest when she thought about what living here would be like without Yardley.

KC had to focus on the Unicorn.

Whatever she could dig up, whatever advantage she could give the Unicorn for this shitshow the agency had decided to fling its best agent into without adequate preparation, had just become Priority One.

CHAPTER THREE

CIA Headquarters, Langley, Virginia

Atlas leaned back in their chair at the conference table. Their leather blazer was so fine, it didn't make even the softest creak when they shifted position. They'd recently grown out their hair from a deep burgundy, and now their short, rich brown Afro set off the golden tones in their dark skin.

They nodded at Gramercy, dashing as usual in one of his three-piece suits with a green-and-white paisley pocket square. It was Gramercy who coordinated the analysts and tech for Project Maple Leaf. Atlas took point on operations, while Yardley hobnobbed, flirted, infiltrated, and developed assets as she could. There were others assigned to the team, but the three of them formed its core.

Gramercy slid a briefing file toward Yardley, fat with all of the need-to-know details of today's op.

"Aren't we waiting on Tabasco?" Yardley glanced toward the door.

Instead of responding, Gramercy looked at Atlas. Though Atlas's expression remained as still as late summer, the two of them were obviously engaged in a silent but heated argument.

"Really?" Atlas finally said.

Gramercy lifted his shoulder one millimeter. "Not my call."

"Care to tag me in?" she asked.

Gramercy leaned back, his expression easing into what Yardley privately thought of as his *congenial boss of everything* face. "Tabasco doesn't have the opportunity to join us at this time."

Sometimes Yardley really hated spies.

"I'll start," Atlas said. "Devon Mirabel's trip to the District has been planned for a couple of days. Tabasco has accessed lines of communication among people in Mirabel's network that we've used to develop the Unicorn's credentials as a potential buyer."

Despite a morning with KC that had made Yardley feel like her heart was full of tears ever since, she was a little bit excited that the mysterious Tabasco would be in her ear today. She'd tried to get more intel about this silicon mastermind late last night after remembering that an officer she'd partnered with to visit a squirrely asset in Paris a year ago had claimed to have once been in Tabasco's lab *with* Tabasco. Yardley had put in earbuds and FaceTimed her colleague, Delaney, from under the scratchy guest room sheets, and though Delaney enthusiastically answered Yardley's call from a café in Bern, she only shook her head when Yardley asked about Tabasco. *I'm under orders to keep their identity undercover,* she'd said. *That's straight from Dr. Brown with counterterrorism. I will say I tried pretty hard to get Tabasco under covers*—here, she'd winked at Yardley—*but I got the sense I had absolutely no chance. It was fun to try, though.*

This was not helpful. Delaney's type was inclusive, to say the least.

Yardley flipped through the file for today's mission. It wasn't hard to figure out what she'd be doing. Charm and awe in equal measures. Make sure the salesman didn't have a chance to think. Let the dorks in the van pick up intel off the various devices they would plant on her body. Yardley was always more interested in the people part of the assignment. "What can you tell me about Mirabel?"

"He's from money," Atlas said. "Got his start as a London-based lobbyist and slithered his way into a special advisor position to the prime minister before being ousted for unstated reasons."

"Never great."

Atlas grimaced. "After that, he opened a consulting firm, began dabbling in arms and antiquities of questionable provenance, and the past few years he's been comfortably situated in banned, stolen, and dangerous tech."

Gramercy tapped on the tablet in front of him. The large flat-screen at the head of the table lit up with a gallery of images. "This is Mirabel."

Fiftyish, with a full head of blond hair and a gleaming mouthful of veneers. "He looks like a talking head on cable news." She turned her attention back to the folder in front of her. "So I'm . . . ?"

"You're a real estate financier from Queens with aspirations to represent New York in the U.S. Senate," Gramercy said. "You've been behind the scenes, working for your father since college, trying to steer him into running for office, but he's always had cold feet. He's now stepped aside, and you're filling the family's power vacuum and getting political." As he spoke, Gramercy flew through several more slides to offer Yardley a visual sense of her cover.

"Baby Jesus and his fishing pole, where do you guys come up with this stuff?"

"It's not difficult, actually," Gramercy said. "Davis Sterling-Chenoweth, your cover's father, is a former operative and current actual financier. Old money. He's perfectly willing, in this case, to claim a daughter from an extramarital relationship heretofore unknown to most."

"When I retire, please don't approach me with a dossier on my fake love child that I have to vouch for in order to reassure an arms dealer." Yardley raised an eyebrow at Gramercy. "Won't do it, and just try to find me on the deck of my boathouse in the Outer Banks."

Gramercy didn't smile in response to her joke. Yardley had never coaxed a smile from him. He must have been *brutal* in Russia.

"Our friends downstairs will complete your cover with photo documents and disguise," Atlas said. "We're not going too deep on this. We're mostly interested in if Mirabel has tech on him that Tabasco can pull anything from. If he warms to you, there's always the hope of completing a sale. I'm sure Uncle Sam would be happy to pay through the nose for the privilege of putting this threat to bed."

"What you're telling me is that once again, this op is thin and messy. I hope I'm going in there looking like Margaret Thatcher's kid sister, because I have to tell you, I am right on the end of the diving board, hovering over the pool of getting made. I haven't loved being sent all over North America and Europe with little more than a fake ID and sunglasses. I at least want a good prosthetic nose."

Gramercy picked up his gold fountain pen from the conference table. "Your New York boroughs accents are impeccable." He rose to his feet. "Go downstairs. There's a lot of tech for them to sort. I need to check in with my people."

She gave him a sharp salute. After he'd gone, she turned to Atlas. "Where am I headed for this?"

"The Starbucks on Pennsylvania and Third."

The bottom dropped out of her stomach. "Make it easy, then. Starbucks on a gorgeous afternoon in the fall, in the middle of a district of thirty thousand people, half of them with a hankering for a Pumpkin Spice Latte. The president wasn't available to drive by in a motorcade? Because I'm not sure this is challenging, honestly."

"It's what Mirabel requested."

"Well, if it's what *Devon* wants." Yardley pushed her chair back from the conference table and crossed her legs. She'd lodged her protest, but there was no real conviction behind it. Her heart was too sore.

Atlas wore a gold band on their left ring finger. Once, when they took the ring off to rub their finger during a meeting, Yardley had noticed a tattoo on the same finger with the initials MW. It made Yardley wonder who Atlas went home to.

This morning, when KC had come into the house from her run, her bloody knee had caught Yardley off guard. It was just a scrape, but the small path of blood tracing down KC's shin made every moment of danger Yardley had navigated in her career flash through her mind in a nickelodeon of horror.

She'd always worried, but it was worse since they moved in together. Coming home to see the blue light of the computers glowing through the windows of the room KC used as her office made Yardley sick with fear. There were woods in the back. Anyone could see in and know KC was alone, wearing headphones, distracted. Who was going to protect KC when Yardley was out protecting the world?

She reached across the table to tap Atlas's ring. "How do you do it?"

Atlas lifted their hand up with a small smile and rubbed the ring with their thumb. "Slow. With a soundtrack."

Yardley snorted.

Atlas put their elbows on the table, leaning in. "Do you have something you need to get off your chest before this mission?"

Yardley received the very faint implied rebuke in Atlas's question. Her head was not in the game.

"Nothing I didn't bring on myself," she said. "You know I never thought of any other choice than to do this work since I was a preschooler begging for one more spy story on my granddaddy's knee. It's just . . . Have I ever told you my Nana Nancy divorced him?"

Atlas shook their head.

"It was after he got declassified. She learned the truth about where he'd been going all those years and kicked him right out. Hired a crackerjack divorce attorney, took half the savings, and kept the house besides."

Yardley paused to unfasten the clip on the slim gold watch KC had given her, loosening the band so she could flip it around her wrist.

Out of all the mistakes she'd made, one of the biggest had been to take KC with her to North Carolina. In that world, among everything and everyone Yardley loved, she'd listened too hard to her heart, bonging with recognition, telling her KC was her person. Her home.

Drunk on that feeling, Yardley didn't hesitate to accept when KC presented her with her mother's gold watch and a key to her house, but she also didn't tell KC that what she really yearned for was a ring, forever, and to give KC every part of herself.

Yardley could have a watch. She couldn't have a wife.

"When I asked my granddaddy about that time in his life," she told Atlas, "the only thing he could say for himself was, 'I kept her safe.' He told me that, and I felt something I couldn't put a label on." She closed her eyes. "Admiration for his patriotic sacrifice, mostly. But then I asked my nan to give me her side of the story, and she said, 'Every time your granddaddy left town on business, he took off his wedding ring and left it on a dish on top of the bureau. I thought he had a second family in Atlanta. I was convinced he had a different ring, one his other wife had given him, and he wore that when he was with her.'"

"Aren't they married, though?" Atlas asked. "Your grand-parents."

"That's right." Yardley fastened the watch back onto her wrist. "She let the ink dry on their divorce agreement, and then she invited him to stop by sometime for a glass of tea. She made him sit in her wicker chair and drink sweet tea and prove to her there'd been more to their marriage than her loyalty and his lies." She met Atlas's eyes and smiled. "A year later, they got married again, only this time she made him pay for a wedding at the Biltmore, and if you don't know what all that means, I'm not sure how I could explain it to you."

Atlas laughed. "My people are from southern Georgia. I know what that means."

"They are? You don't even have an accent!"

"I'm a spy," they deadpanned. "But Marla sees the real me." Their accent rolled out like a pearl from a fresh bay oyster, and one of the knots in Yardley's middle loosened at the connection to her handler.

She'd hoped it would be enough to share a house with KC, even if it wasn't the life she wanted, but it only created more distance between them. It got harder to tell KC what she felt. Yardley's solution was to pretend as hard as she could that everything was okay.

It turned out *that* was the lie that swamped their emotional intimacy so utterly, it broke her heart.

And no matter what she did, there was nothing to fix the fact that if she'd ever told KC the truth and demanded what she dreamed of, she'd be putting the woman she loved in danger for the rest of her life.

"Thank you for understanding," she told Atlas. "And for listening." She stood to leave. Her entire body was sore with feelings, like one word or noise could make her cry. "I should get downstairs."

"You know, Whitmer." Atlas gave her a small smile. "Secrets aren't the only way to keep a person safe. There are ways to share this work with a family or a partner. They aren't easy. There are no guarantees. But my mama lost her husband, my dad, when she was only thirty-nine, and he was a schoolteacher. *Life* isn't safe. You understand?"

Yardley nodded, swallowing back tears. She understood that Atlas was a kind person and an excellent mentor. Maybe if she'd had this talk a few months ago. A year ago.

But the doc had already called this one. She and KC were beyond help.

Yardley's New York driver's license was still warm when she stepped into the sleek black Lincoln.

Her gray trousers were tight, the tech disguised as a push-up bra taking the girls up and over, and her gray suit jacket was a puff-sleeved, lace-appliqued confection. The wig she'd been given was so high, it was kissing angels, and frosted besides. There was no chance she would blend in at a Capitol Hill Starbucks full of black cashmere sweaters and designer strollers.

But she was pretty sure that was the point.

Her driver pulled over to the curb. "The van's a few blocks to the northeast. I'll be circling, listening on your channel. Should be able to get here in three to five if you need me."

"You bet," Yardley said with a shiny smile as she climbed out of the car, drawing her voice into her nose as she tapped on her comm. "Don't you fucking take a break." She slammed the door shut, startling a woman with an oversized fuzzy scarf, and minced to the Starbucks entrance, cleavage bouncing.

Atlas's voice came into her ear. "He's by the merch. Black suit. Tabasco's standing by, monitoring your front-facing video and audio. They'll let you know what you can do for them."

Yardley met Devon Mirabel's eyes while wealthy mothers and college students looked on in ill-concealed shock. She gave him a sharky smile and a brusque wave, obviously unbothered by the attention. "I like a man in a suit," she said by way of greeting, reaching her arms out and stepping into a New Yorker's version of a Continental embrace, which involved a lot of personal-space-bubble violation. "And you wear it well, buddy. I'm Ashley. Feels like I'm meeting a celebrity."

He wrapped his hands around her forearms a smidge too tight. She forced herself to relax into his grip like she enjoyed the threat of his dominance. "Ashley. We've managed to catch each other. I wasn't sure this could happen."

He meant that he'd never heard of her before this morning and therefore was suspicious, but his entire world was suspicious, and he liked money, power, and drama, so here they were. Also, it would be hard for her to plunge the business end of a

hypodermic full of poison into his neck in the middle of Starbucks.

Not impossible. Just hard. She'd once had a shoulder cannon
pointed at her in the middle of a market in Marrakesh, so anything was possible.

"Oh, I can make whatever I want happen, Dev. Hey, you
there!" Yardley lifted a hand into the air, addressing the startled
barista, who was steaming milk. "What does it take to get a coffee? Do I have to hike up a mountain in Jamaica, what?"

The barista stared at her, but she slowly moved away from the
steamer and grabbed two paper cups.

"All right," Yardley said. "Let's sit. Turbulence was a fucking
nightmare out of LaGuardia."

Mirabel gave her a reserved smile that nonetheless made his
veneers glint. He was attractive in person, which caused Yardley
to doubt he was all that smart. She could count the number of
attractive, smart evildoers she'd encountered in her career on one
hand with fingers left over.

"I must say, Ms. Thompson—"

"Mrs. Thompson. I don't send Marshall's shirts out and lie
awake listening to his CPAP machine at midnight to lose my hon-
orific to political correctness."

Someone snorted with laughter in her ear. Not Atlas. They
never betrayed their feelings about Yardley's performance in the
field. *Tabasco.*

Yardley felt her chest puff out. It surprised her, the little jolt
of validation that Tabasco's laugh had given her. She hadn't felt
little jolts in a long time.

"Pardon. Mrs. Thompson. I was surprised to hear from our

mutual friend that you'd like to discuss business." Mirabel said this lazily. "I believe—"

The barista knocked into his elbow, interrupting him to put two coffees on the table with a look Yardley translated as *Ma'am, this is a Starbucks*. Yardley opened her Chanel chain bag, pulled out a twenty, and slid it in the barista's direction. "That's not a tip. We need some of that lemon pound cake." She blew on her coffee and took a sip. "You were saying?" she asked.

"I was saying I'm surprised I don't know anyone who's met you."

"I'm not." This was the part of the encounter where she would figure out if it was an audition to make another meeting or the meeting itself—the only aspect of these things that could get tricky, primarily because the men Yardley met with usually had a business agenda, a paranoia agenda, and a seduction agenda. It was easy to misinterpret the cues. Yardley leaned in and gave Mirabel a smile. "I like things to happen when I say they happen, I'm not a fucking Amtrak. It turns out you have something to keep me on schedule."

"That's another thing." Mirabel picked up his coffee, took a sip, and winced. "What's your plan, precisely?"

She brayed out a laugh. "I like a sense of humor. I sure as fuck have your number, so I assume you have mine. Look." The barista appeared to put the paper bags with pound cake on the table. Yardley opened her palm, and the woman huffed and shoved the dollar and change in it before flouncing off. "I'm young, but my money's not, and the way things went in Toronto, I should be doubting you, not the other way around. I've talked to people who say that was all you had and all you've got. So far, I'm the only buyer young, cracked, and rich enough willing to risk a lemon."

Mirabel's eyes widened only slightly. "Perhaps we should have dinner," he said.

Dang it. This was an audition.

"I'm having dinner with Daddy in New York, and I don't stand the man up."

Mirabel's eyes darted around the Starbucks. The tables were mostly full. The laughter, conversation, and kids begging for cake pops provided plenty of camouflage for their conversation, but they also made Yardley aware that her work was the only thing keeping these people safe right now. If she had backup, so did Mirabel. "My sources tell me your interest is impulsive."

Yardley smiled, opened up her body language, and channeled every bit of Cyndi Lauper's easy authenticity with her accent. "So was the Boston Tea Party."

Another abrupt laugh from Tabasco over the comm—thrilling, and too fleeting—but Mirabel's expression had soured.

"You're losing him," Atlas said in her ear. "Tabasco's picking up something. Stay—"

Yardley had to keep smiling past the sharp prick of feedback against her eardrum.

Seriously? What she didn't need was a comm issue. Again. She scooted her chair closer to the table so she could lean her spy bra into Mirabel's arm. Gazing into his eyes, she cocked an eyebrow like the daughter of a mobster. "Another time, hon, I'm more than happy to split a good bottle of merlot with you and yak over a steak, but that's not why you set this up, and I don't see any other American citizens with barrels of cash taking a meeting. Like I said, Toronto was cute, but not cute enough that I have more time to give you than it takes to finish my coffee." This kind of bluff, in her experience, usually worked. Yardley felt Mirabel's hand on her thigh. Good sign. She inched closer. "What have you got for me?"

Another knifelike squeal attacked her eardrum, followed by an exclamation that sounded either like *bad intel* or *bombshell*—neither option good—and then Mirabel's hand was replaced by the very distinctive sensation of the business end of a gun.

Shoot. She hated guns.

"I see." Yardley smiled, trying to keep her eyes from crossing while her comm exploded in her ear. "Is that all you have in your pocket? I bet you've got something bigger."

The gun pressed itself hard into the tender skin over her femoral artery. "Fucking shut up," Mirabel whispered, his accent no longer posh. "I just got some information that very much ends this meeting."

There was a scream by the door, and answering squeals from various Starbucks patrons as a small, sweater-clad form barreled across the dining area, bounced over a chair—and then Yardley was on the ground, the wind knocked out of her, and Mirabel was already on the move toward the counter, probably heading to the back exit.

Her training took over. She flipped the body that had tackled her and lunged at Mirabel, fitting the meaty part of her palm over the back of his wrist and bending it the wrong way while using the leverage to lift herself up.

He grunted, and she scrambled to her knees.

She was vaguely aware that the person who'd tackled her was fighting with another patron—or security?—while people emptied out of the Starbucks, but she didn't have time to wonder who her attacker was because Mirabel had yanked her to her feet, snatched her against his body, and shoved his cursed gun back into her side hard enough to leave a bruise.

"Walk with me," he hissed.

Yardley dropped her body weight and slammed her foot on his instep, then rose back up to collide the back of her head into his face, thankful her closer-to-heaven wig blunted the contact. She felt another hard yank on her waistband, and the person who'd tackled her managed to pull her back down and behind their body, using it to shield her.

Then, the last voice on earth Yardley had ever thought to hear in this situation said, "Back the fuck up."

KC?

Her KC?

Yes. Katherine Corrine Nolan of Reston, Virginia, wearing huge sunglasses and a hideous lime-green ball cap that featured the distinctive logo of the Lynchburg Hillcats, was using her own body as a shield and pointing Devon Mirabel's gun at his face in a very competent grip.

Absolutely not.

Yardley took a hold of KC's waistband and yanked her back two feet so that *Yardley* was the shield, then unarmed her to point the gun back at Mirabel.

Just in case her cover wasn't completely blown to bits, she smiled at him. "You gotta learn to trust more," she said, faintly gratified that her wig hadn't slipped and her Queens accent remained intact. "But I like you. I'd love dinner sometime. Let's keep in touch."

Then she fisted KC's sweater and towed her along behind her to the back of the room, keeping the gun on Mirabel until they were through the service door and down the hall that spit them out behind the building.

She headed east at a dead run, dragging KC behind her until they nearly collided with the agency's van, disguised as an Amazon truck, which she had no choice but to pull KC into.

Even if her cover stayed intact with Mirabel, there was no way the brown contact lenses Yardley wore or the makeup designed to make her eyes look a little closer together could ever manage to fool KC.

Why in the world had she had a sudden hankering for Starbucks on a Wednesday, anyway? KC never came to the Hill. Couldn't she have put her pink drink order into DoorDash and had it delivered?

Yardley just hoped the town where the agency set up her new identity was nice.

As she slammed the van's door shut, she glanced at KC, who had lost her hat and removed her sunglasses and who, predictably, looked surprised. Her color was up, her eyes bright, giving Yardley an instantaneous sense memory of the power behind that tackle.

She blushed hard under her makeup.

It had been a minute since she'd blushed like this from only *looking* at KC.

Dang it.

CHAPTER FOUR

The van was moving at a good clip, Atlas talking low and furious into a sat phone. The techs had gone wordless, probably because they didn't know what to say.

Understandable. KC had blown their cover.

KC, more accurately, had stolen Atlas's hat and sunglasses from the dash to wear as an impromptu disguise, flung the van's doors open, burst out of the back, and sprinted away at full speed toward the Starbucks to save the Unicorn.

Who was Yardley.

Yardley was the Unicorn.

A bead of sweat rolled down her neck. Her brain felt like a device that wouldn't boot.

She kept reliving the queasy seconds after the comm dropped out. Her recognition—*Someone's jamming the signal.* The other two techs had scrambled to deploy countermeasures, but KC hadn't been able to find a whit of patience for that, not when the woman who'd been witty and brash in her ear, so funny she made KC laugh out loud, was down the block with a gun on her.

She'd only recognized the woman as Yardley Whitmer when they were hauling ass to the van and it hit her with a percussive clang.

The way she held her arms. Her long legs pounding the pavement. Even in a tight suit and an improbable wig, she'd shoved KC behind her and taken control of their physical encounter with Devon Mirabel with the same habitual elegance that she used to slide a pan of vegetables into the oven to roast, fold a stack of towels, or shimmy out of a dress.

Because she's the Unicorn.

KC winced.

"Are you hurt?" Yardley was staring at KC with her hands clasped between her knees.

"I'm fine." *Flooded with adrenaline and panic, but fine.*

KC hadn't decided to save the Unicorn. She'd just gone to her, driven by a demand so outsized and urgent as to be a compulsion. Because *Yardley* was the Unicorn.

And some part of her, hidden from herself, must have known that.

"I'm sorry." Yardley's eyes were bright with unshed tears. "This must be so difficult for you, all of this"—she gestured around the van—"but when we get to headquarters—god, you don't even know what I'm talking about, *headquarters.*" She wiped her hand over her mouth. "I'm *so* sorry, but I'm sure they have someone who can explain—"

"You don't understand." KC dropped Atlas's sunglasses into her lap and rubbed her temples. "You think I—What, I just wandered into Starbucks? *That* Starbucks? Versus the one two blocks from our house. Is that what you're telling yourself right now? You're the *Unicorn.*" She couldn't look at Yardley, so she studied her own knees, covered in black high-performance fatigues she hardly ever wore except for required training. Her boots. The hem of the black ribbed sweater that Yardley had given her for Christmas last year.

"Would it help if I had a name tag that said, 'Hello, my name is Tabasco'?"

KC looked up just in time to watch Yardley go pale as wax. "What did you say?"

This was a nightmare. Her stomach was stuck in a slow, woozy roll. "No wonder you wouldn't tell me where you were going this morning. You were in fucking Toronto yesterday?"

"KC? You're Tabasco?" Yardley's voice rose up at the end. The color was coming back into her face from the neck up. "But you've been in the middle of that rush job for *Rolling Stone*'s website." She cocked her head. Blinked a few times. "Except you haven't. Right? Am I catching up now? You've been hacking door locks and manufacturing identities and credentials and whatever else tech gets up to where no one else can see them and *we don't know who they are*."

Yardley's voice had taken on the clipped annoyance of her mother's, deep in a pique, each syllable delivered like a precision jab. KC couldn't deal with angry Yardley *and* the Unicorn, not when she couldn't even deal with Yardley *being* the Unicorn. Not when her brain wouldn't stop rapid-scrolling through a list of the places the Unicorn had traveled in the last six months, an itinerary as wide-ranging as it was hazardous. A six-month period that had witnessed the slow strangulation of their relationship, and during which KC had believed Yardley's extra work trips to routine and domestic places like New York, Philadelphia, Kansas City, and Omaha were about taking a look at some bank's compliance with fee practice and, as a bonus, keeping herself away from another argument with KC.

Which the CIA fucking *knew*, but they'd purposely kept KC and Yardley in the dark. No wonder Gramercy hadn't let her attend the briefing. She rubbed her palms down her thighs, knocking Atlas's sunglasses to the floor in her restless fury.

But as soon as KC's anger flared, she remembered that Mirabel wouldn't have pointed a gun at *her Yardley* if KC hadn't made something that a lot of shady actors were willing to pay for with a briefcase full of diamonds.

This, right here, right now, just like everything else that had upended KC's whole fucking life, was her own damn fault.

"Tabasco isn't even made in Virginia," Yardley said, her voice remote and hard to pin down. "You're not from Louisiana. Unless you *are* from Louisiana? No, we live in your grandma's house. Or you do. I used to. I'm crashing in your horrible guest bedroom. But you're a website marketer."

KC shook her head. Her throat hitched, searching for words. She couldn't find any that weren't prayers for a time machine.

"You work for the agency," Yardley whispered.

"I do. So do you."

She'd spent three years dating a spy. In love with a spy. Not just any spy, either. The *best* spy. It was the Unicorn who she'd given a gold watch to, along with the key to her house. The key to her heart.

And then she'd ruined it.

The van pulled into a gated and disguised tunnel that led to a garage at Langley. When KC had sometimes fantasized about the time there would be a way to tell Yardley everything, she had imagined something like this—driving to this facility and using her key card to admit them to the hidden tunnel. She would be nervous, but also self-satisfied at the opportunity to finally impress the most beautiful woman in the world with her secret identity and coolness.

She looked at Yardley, gazing into the middle distance with a stupefied expression. Yardley, who spoke god knew how many languages and knew how to disarm someone in a fight. Who had rappelled from the Eiffel Tower and parachuted from a helicopter, and who was rumored to be immune to poisoning via having subjected herself to some secret CIA protocol.

KC worked in front of a screen in the basement and was currently embroiled in a black op that could very well lead to her forced transfer to the satellite office in South Dakota.

"Whitmer," Atlas said as the van pulled to a stop. "Nolan. Follow me. We've got bigger problems."

The lobby outside the director's office was emptied of everyone but KC and Yardley. Still, KC felt distinctly like she was being observed.

Maybe it was the ring of eleven-by-seventeen portraits of white men hanging in a long, unending line on the dark paneling. KC wouldn't be surprised if the portraits *were* observing them, via concealed monitoring devices. She wouldn't be shocked, even, to learn they were being observed by the subjects of a few of these portraits from beyond the grave.

This was the CIA, after all.

Yardley sat with her arms crossed in a leather armchair with Ashley Sterling-Chenoweth Thompson's wig like a small dog beside her. She was determinedly studying the line of portraits. A tech had taken her bra for analysis, and she'd buttoned her jacket to the collar for modesty. She wore her black hair pinned in a crown of braids against her head, a style that KC thought of as very Yardley and had never—not one time—put in the category of *useful hairstyle to wear under a wig.*

KC still couldn't reconcile everything she'd heard about the Unicorn—everything she'd observed firsthand about the Unicorn this afternoon—with *Yardley.*

Yardley and her soft palette of soft clothes, and how she squealed when she found a spider in the shower. The way she shoved her cold feet under KC's ass on the sofa when they watched a movie together and loved rom-coms, the more rom the better. The way she took care of KC, bringing her something to drink when she was working. The way her eyes used to flutter shut as she sighed and pushed up her hips when KC gently held her wrists above her head, *just* pressing them against the pillow, and kissed her neck with a little bit of teeth.

"How bugged do you think this lobby is?" Yardley's voice sounded thick, like it did when she was upset.

"The usual amount."

"So they'll know I sneezed before I do."

"And why."

KC wanted to smile, but the mutual acknowledgment of *spying,* making a joke about it, had swamped her with a new wave of disbelief and . . . yes. Betrayal.

Hers. Yardley's.

She'd imagined this day would come, the day she confronted the enormity of the lies she'd told Yardley once and for all. *If I just told her,* she'd thought, like a mantra. *If I told her, she'd have to believe me. She'd have to forgive me. She'd have to still love me.* But KC had never once imagined the enormity of the lies Yardley had told *her.*

It was not fair to hold Yardley to account for those lies. KC could acknowledge that. But her heart was a fickle bitch, and it was holding Yardley to account regardless. Her heart was reliving their entire relationship, sifting through it for what was actually true.

The venom of hurt inside her made her knees unsteady. She wondered if Yardley had ever respected or loved her for real. If any of it, any of what they'd shared in three years, had been *real*.

KC tried to stop herself, but the spiral had well and truly pointed itself downward. The Unicorn was known to be able to convince anyone of the veracity of their cover. So what had Yardley convinced KC of? Who was Yardley when she was with KC? Why was she with KC at all?

Yardley suddenly turned to face her. "I don't care if they can hear us. We have to talk about this." Her voice broke on the last word, not with tears. Probably with the same hot, dry disbelief that KC was currently swallowing over.

"Okay," she said. Or didn't say. Her feelings were so loud inside her body, it was hard to maintain her connection to reality.

Yardley leaned forward. Her eyes were brown, not their natural blue, rimmed by false eyelashes and sparkling shadow. Yardley almost never wore makeup. "Because we haven't *talked* about this."

"We're not supposed to!" That was what burst out of KC's mouth. And then, appallingly, without warning, she had so many words, she couldn't stop them. "We're *not supposed to*, Yardley, and I don't mean because of the agency, I mean because that's how it is with you and me. I'm not supposed to ask you why you're crying in the shower. I'm not supposed to tell you the real reason why I can't sleep. We're not even supposed to talk about why we're not talking anymore or why you're sleeping in the guest room or moving out, not beyond 'this isn't working,' 'I miss us,' 'maybe we moved too fast'"—KC stopped just long enough to suck in a shallow breath—"which, if I ever said it or agreed when you did, that was a lie. I would've moved in with you after the first day we spent together. The first time you talked to me at that party. I felt like we had everything with each other, and then everything wasn't enough." She shoved her hands into her hair and pulled to keep herself from crying. "*Yes*, I held myself back because I had to keep the agency's secrets. Yes. Yes. But then I think I just got in the habit of holding myself back. Maybe you did, too, I don't know, but I don't think I know *how* to talk to you, Yardley, not anymore. If I ever did."

When she stopped, another thought sheathed her skin in icy prickles. Had Yardley been pretending in the van? The Unicorn would be able to do that as easily as breathing. "Did you *know*?"

"No! I didn't. Did you?"

"No."

"But *how* didn't you?" Now Yardley's disconcertingly incorrect brown eyes searched her face. "Doesn't Tabasco know everything, isn't that their whole deal? Whenever I had a problem and Atlas told me, *Tabasco's got it*, I would relax. Tabasco could solve any problem, figure anything out. But you didn't know it was me? I can't square that."

"Says the superspy." KC's heart was pounding in a way that made her think it could stop any moment. "You're the expert in body language and observation. Though it bothers me less to think you might have *made* me than the idea that everything we had, you made up. Isn't that what you're good at? Convince people to believe what you tell them, like some kind of Jedi mind trick?"

KC knew that wasn't fair. She'd felt her entire soul shy away from her mouth as soon as she said it. But *god*, the hurt. It was an entirely different magnitude than what she'd felt in the middle of the night, burying her face into Yardley's side of the bed for a single breath of her.

Yardley stood up, then sat back down again. She looked away from KC for a long minute, and when she looked back, KC knew for sure that the passionate furor in her face was one hundred percent real.

"My heart has been *broken*." Yardley pulled off her false eyelashes and snapped off her sparkling earrings. Her hand dove into her pocket, emerging with a tissue she used to roughly erase her lipstick. "I have stayed up into the middle of the night with you, crying, begging, talking, arguing, holding your hands and trying to find the words to give us a chance. I knew I couldn't show you my entire self, and I had gotten in too deep, just like my granddaddy, but the fact is that every single lie I told you wasn't about *you*, KC. It was about the cruel sacrifice required by duty to my country."

KC couldn't avoid thinking of the nights Yardley was talking about, nights of circling, desperate conversations she tried to leave behind when they came to nothing. She'd been close to telling Yardley the truth so many times, wanting nothing more than to boil down those tangled and confusing talks to a single problem they could tackle together. *If I just told her. If I told her, it would fix us.*

"But we know everything now," she said, wildly, "so that means no problems anymore, right? Because that's how I thought it would work."

Yardley tossed her head. "You just told me keeping secrets means that all you learned from us was how to hold yourself back. Here's where I tell you that I was fool enough to think when we moved in together, that was you asking for more. Now I think it was life support for something that was never meant to be. So does finding out *one* of the secrets we had from each other really fix anything?"

KC knew it wasn't a genuine question. Even if it had been, she couldn't make herself push any more words out of her battered, tender throat. Yardley was right. Knowing the truth couldn't fix it.

And Yardley didn't even know the truth.

KC didn't have any anger left. There was a numbness that made her want to get up and start walking until she had walked to the dark other side of the earth. "I guess we'll never really be sure what was real and what wasn't."

"So it's over. It's really over." Yardley's jaw was clenched, but her words were barely audible. She reached down and sank a hand into the wig lying on the chair, and her nostrils flared as she took in a huge, shuddering breath.

Before KC realized what she was doing, Yardley had hurled the wig at one of the portraits on the wall. It zipped through the room like a malformed duck and hit a particularly smug-looking balding agent who appeared to have been active in the sixties, square in the face, tilting the frame and knocking the canvas out of it.

They both watched the portrait slide to the ground, the wires of a listening device nearly as ancient as the painting following like a tail.

"They knew," Yardley said, staring at the downed agent and the wires. "They knew this entire time." She pushed her hands flat against her crown of braids. "I'm so boneheaded, I could laugh if I had any feelings left at all."

The hallway went silent for a full minute, and KC sat in the numb quiet, waiting for whatever came next.

"Project Maple Leaf."

KC wouldn't have thought anything could shock her, but it made her cringe from her scalp to her toenails to hear the code name of the absolutely secret, dangerous antiterrorist mission come out of Yardley Whitmer's mouth.

"I want to see it through," Yardley said.

"So do I." KC didn't have a choice.

"We've never interacted in our work before now." Yardley clasped her hands in her lap. Her neck was blotchy, but she looked regal and determined. "Clearly the agency made its own decision to keep us apart, but there's no reason to assume we'll have to interact on this, going forward, beyond the minimum. I assume we're both capable of putting our personal feelings aside in favor of service."

"I can persist. Assuming they don't remove me for exposing the mission at the Capitol Hill Starbucks. And they don't remove you because everyone in the world who's interested in this thing has already dealt with you twelve times in the last six weeks."

"Then I'm game." Yardley nodded. "If not doubly motivated to put this project to bed in short order and then never think about it again for the rest of my life."

Never think about you. That was what KC heard.

At least, if they weren't tossed out of Maple Leaf, they could see each other for a little longer. Now and then. Sure, it would be because they were working together, but it might make the landing softer at the end if they had the chance to gracefully say good-bye as coworkers. Once KC recovered herself enough to pretend to be someone with grace.

"I'm in, too. If what the agency wanted was for our relationship not to interfere with their shenanigans, then for sure our not-relationship won't, either."

Just then, Atlas walked into the lobby from the hallway that led to the director's office. "Officers," they said. "There's a new wrinkle to this clusterfuck of a day. Come with me."

KC stood, wondering if the floor had tilted or if her entire brain was just reorienting itself once and for all to this new, terrible reality where she would have to relearn to walk and breathe without Yardley.

They followed Atlas down the carpeted hallway, but before they made the corner that would take them to the double doors of the director's office, Yardley halted abruptly, settling her hands on her hips. "First things first."

She waited for Atlas and KC to come to a stop, her eyes on Atlas. "I can understand why none of y'all made a peep when we were dating. You took a wait-and-see approach. But you knew we moved in together a year ago, and you kept the truth from us all this time. I deserve an explanation, and so does KC. Right now. This instant."

Atlas put their hands in the pockets of their tactical pants. "I didn't make the decision, and I didn't agree with it, but I can tell you the reasoning I was given from the director's office. Our intel was that your relationship was not . . . in a secure status."

"Rough seas," Yardley supplied. "Rocky. That's what you mean."

Atlas pressed their lips together. "It wasn't in the interest of the agency to get in the middle."

"Not if your problem was about to work itself out," KC interjected. Her anger tasted like battery acid at the back of her throat. "Let us die a natural death, am I right?"

Atlas closed their eyes. "Once Maple Leaf became a priority, the decision was made that disclosure would compromise the agency's ability to make the most of your talents."

Yardley had gone red from her throat to her cheekbones. "That's shameful."

KC thought of what Dr. Brown liked to say. *Silos and separation meant safety.*

Whose safety, though? That was the question that was really coming to bear for KC at the moment.

"Shall we?" Atlas pointed down the hall. With a *hmpf* and a toss of her head, Yardley took off at a brisk pace that meant Atlas had to walk faster to hold on to the lead. They navigated KC and Yardley to a second lobby that KC knew led to the transportation bay.

"Whitmer, if you'd like to change, that's been arranged for you in the locker room adjacent to this area." Atlas indicated the direction Yardley was meant to go. "Once you're finished, we'll be taken to the White House to be briefed."

KC stopped short. "The White House?"

"Everything will be covered at the briefing."

With this, Atlas strolled away to the double doors, already open and letting in cool air and the chemical smell of the transportation bay.

"Do you know anything about this?" KC asked Yardley.

"No." Yardley tipped her head and seemed to scrutinize KC. She still had color in her cheeks, but her eyes were sharp and assessing. "You covered me pretty quick in that Starbucks."

"I've been trained. And I don't skip workouts."

There was a time Yardley would have laughed at KC teasing her, but her assessing expression didn't change. "You don't. Ever. In fact, you're really strong. Decisive. You've always been observant, but you haven't worked as an operative. Have you wanted to?"

"Who doesn't?"

"That's a nothing answer. Lots of people don't want to be in the field. Do you?"

KC remembered too late that the Unicorn was a notoriously exacting and ruthless interrogator. "I don't run for my health," she hedged.

"Officers," Atlas said to the transportation bay. "If we could."

Yardley strolled in the direction of the locker rooms in stocking feet, moving in a way that was so arrogantly unconcerned, it made KC think of seeing her for the first time at the barbecue.

The way she carried her shoulders in that diaphanous white picnic dress. The intelligence in her gaze that pinned KC in place right before she smiled. Like she'd planned that moment. Like it was happening exactly the way she wanted it to.

I'm going to marry that woman, she'd thought, as though Yardley had put the desire in KC's body herself.

If absolutely everything had been different, they could have been so, so good.

CHAPTER FIVE

Situation Room, the White House

Typically, Yardley enjoyed meeting the president.

Ada Williams had a presence that filled every room she was in with easy warmth punctuated with intelligence and gravitas. Yardley was fascinated by how she managed to invite her colleagues to bring their best selves to the table, encouraging collaboration while still maintaining the personal force field necessary for America's first Black woman president to command.

And she mixed a mean old-fashioned.

In ordinary circumstances, the tense mood in the Situation Room would have fired up Yardley's delight with strategy as she sorted through the subtle power dynamics and social hierarchies at work. This was the type of once-in-a-career gathering her granddaddy called "a quilting bee," and on any other day Yardley could have counted on her central nervous system to be as relaxed as a lizard on a desert rock.

She was the Unicorn in large part because she paradoxically enjoyed a wrench tossed into the works. Her brain held plans B through Z in reserve like a full house in Vegas.

The Unicorn had not arrived, however, to solve the problem of KC Nolan. The Unicorn had tossed her rainbow mane at Yardley and insisted she deal with this disaster that she had so spectacularly caused.

KC was a spy. Yardley was a spy.

The world was still in danger because today's mission had failed.

She was still broken up with the only true love she'd ever had, but now she sat across the table from the president of the United States of America, who had undoubtedly been briefed about all of this, including everything Yardley and KC had said to each other less than an hour ago, possibly accompanied by photographs or video.

Yardley suddenly remembered she'd thrown a wig at a portrait of Officer Byron Davis, an unsung hero of the Cold War whose quick thinking avoided a nuclear disaster. This fact would be dutifully recorded in her file, waiting for declassification in some unknown future.

She bit the inside of her bottom lip to stop herself from bursting into tears, because her dry self-talk was *not working*. The five stolen minutes in the locker room at Langley during which she had choked on stormy sobs, curled up in a ball on a locker room bench, thereby startling another operative as they came out of the showers, had been insufficient. She needed a landscape big enough to take her sorrow, shock, and bitter disappointment. She required a moor. Or a heath. Or the shore. A very big cliff over all three where her sobs and screams would be taken by the wind.

She stole a look at KC. Her jaw was tight, her beautiful auburn hair stark against her pale face.

KC did not sit in her chair like she'd never been invited to a table like this. She sat in her chair like Tabasco. She was five feet of coiled muscle with the kind of mind shining behind her eyes that made people not want to be the first one to talk, just in case they weren't as smart as they thought. She had lighted into her seat like one of those small, compact birds of prey that could dive toward its target at a hundred miles an hour, talons first. No one in the room had managed to look straight at her yet, as if attracting her attention meant certain brutality.

Yardley's *heart*. How absolutely ludicrous it was to believe they could work together, assuming this meeting wasn't some sort of dramatic sacking that would result in exile, when everything she had ever loved about KC were the same things that made her Tabasco.

Yardley was very neatly fucked. Truth was a stiletto in her heart. She swallowed so that she had room in her throat to breathe.

"Everyone," the president said. Her voice dissipated the tension with genuine power. "Let's begin."

It was the first briefing Yardley had ever sat through that she struggled to give her full attention. She half listened as the president and CIA director Michael McLaughlin tag-teamed their way through the background on Project Maple Leaf. Mostly, Yardley watched KC.

I guess we'll never really be sure what was real and what wasn't.

She squeezed the hands in her lap into fists.

"Kris Flynn." The president looked from Yardley to KC. "An Irish national with a legitimate job in network security and, it seems, a side gig in digital weapons development, has seemingly coded a sequence capable of unlocking and disrupting digital communications and information transfer between systems as huge as a city's power infrastructure and beyond. Certainly, we can appreciate the implications. How a weapon like this could harm vulnerable people or potentially—"

"—destabilize democracy."

Everyone looked at KC, because she had just interrupted the *president*. She was leaning forward, her forearms stacked and balanced on her crossed legs. Yardley recognized this as her scary deep-listening pose. "The demonstration in Toronto managed to fuck with the grid and some of the medical infrastructure. Concerning, but chaotic. It didn't inspire a lot of confidence or respect. But what Flynn was holding on that thumb drive—intel that I decrypted yet was not invited to review or analyze—must have been impressive enough to motivate a contact with Devon Mirabel in broad daylight. And now here we are, at the White House." KC didn't take her eyes from the president. "Clearly something about the situation has changed."

Gramercy cleared his throat meaningfully in KC's direction. KC ignored him. The president answered the stunned silence that followed with a small smile. "A very concise summary of a rather complex global threat, Ms. Nolan. Particularly given what I've learned this morning."

KC didn't waver, but from Yardley's angle she was able to observe the slight stiffening of her upper spine.

"Madam President. I work in the basement at Langley. I'm not even officially assigned to Maple Leaf. Tell me, what am I doing in this room?"

KC said this with what anyone else would hear as polite confidence, but Yardley had spent a lot of time analyzing the smallest shifts in KC's tone, hoping to avoid an argument or see a way in to fixing one, and she could hear KC's fear.

Interesting.

What else had Yardley missed?

"I understand Flynn is not unknown to you, Ms. Nolan," the president said. "In fact, I've just learned that the two of you have a significant history."

Yardley's middle dropped away, replaced with electric anxiety as she waited for an explanation. Unbidden, one of her granddaddy's stories hijacked her attention. He'd been at a party in Saint Petersburg, dealing with a new asset. His most trusted colleague, Levi Petrov, who also happened to be the godfather of his children, had secured the woman as his asset because she gave the agency access to the director of the KGB. The asset was agreeable to Yardley Senior's plan to sneak away with her during the party to see the chairman. Too agreeable. But Levi was known for his deft handling of assets, so her granddaddy had ignored his gut. He followed the asset to the kitchens and down a hallway, where she said the chairman had a secure office. At first, he was confused when they encountered Levi, who had been tasked with distracting the minister who was hosting the party. The gun in Levi's hand, pointed at her granddaddy, cleared up the confusion.

That had been Yardley Senior's first encounter with a double agent, and the agent was his very best friend. It took weeks for him to devise an escape. When he arrived at a safe house just on the clear side of the Iron Curtain, he was near-starved and raging with fever.

Yardley didn't pray as much as she should, but she started praying right then, watching KC's face as the president waited on her to speak.

"I met Kris Flynn when I was thirteen years old." KC's voice was matter-of-fact. Easy. "Well, I met her online, not in person. We never met in person. But we were both essentially unsupervised, and we had been entertaining ourselves with computers for as long as we could read. We got to know each other in a chat room we called"—KC raked one hand through her hair—"um, the Daisy Dukes."

There was a surprised huff that might have been laughter from Atlas. KC sent a very discreet glare in their direction. "Like I said, we were *thirteen*. We wanted to save the planet. It was supposed to mean we were, I guess, *dukes* for the daisies. Protectors."

Another huff.

"Look, we barely knew what dukes were, and I'm pretty sure *I* didn't know we were referencing a character in short shorts from a long-ago television show we'd never heard of. At the time, it sounded very cool."

"We'll trust you on that," Gramercy said, without a speck of amusement.

"Continue, please," the president said.

"We did things like send memos from local governments to large cities telling them they were required to initiate a recycling program. Once, we hacked into the Orange County public works project database in California to create a work order so a construction team repaired beach-safe trails instead of spreading asphalt at a state park. Stuff like that. Stuff kids thought would make a difference. From there—"

"Did it?" the president interrupted.

"Did it what, Madam President?"

"Make a difference?" The president smiled.

KC blinked, and Yardley watched the color come back to her cheeks. "I hope so. I mean, we didn't have a way to get a lot of confirmation our, um, seeds were planted." KC got redder. "That's what we called a completed mission."

Now Atlas didn't even try to disguise their laugh. Yardley sat back in her chair. This was getting less scary and more interesting by the moment.

"We were teenage computer jockeys, and we meant that we were planting daisies. We had no other referent. Come *on*."

"My apologies," Atlas said.

"As time went on, our projects got a lot riskier, and we started attracting attention from environmental fringe groups. I was at MIT by then, meeting the kind of students who rented camper vans to go to anti-globalization protests over spring break. I can understand now that we didn't have great judgment when it came to the jobs we took on. We didn't understand the nuance of shutting down worksites and lumber supply chains."

"So you stopped." This interjection came from the director, McLaughlin, who'd been keeping himself in reserve.

"No, sir, we did not. Like I said, we didn't understand the nuance. Or even the obvious implications. We took a job for a group that wanted action from the EPA on industrial pollution."

"You and Flynn hacked into a federal agency," the president said.

"We did, yes."

"With what outcome?"

Yardley leaned forward, breathless to hear the rest. All she'd known was that KC went to college early. She had a general impression that KC had messed around with hacking in a recreational sort of way during the part of her youth when Yardley's central preoccupation was the outcome of Rush Week.

"That's how I ended up in the CIA," KC said.

"You were offered a deal." The president gestured to an aide standing along the wall, who handed her a brief in a leather folder.

She opened it. "Immunity from prosecution in exchange for your commitment to be educated and prepared for the academy."

"Yes, ma'am."

Yardley was astonished. She knew there were operatives who found their way to the CIA by nontraditional means, but she never could have imagined this was KC's path to the agency. Yardley herself had competed for and won a college internship, which she parlayed into an entry-level job. Her rise to the role of field operative was considered meteoric, but it wasn't half so impressive—or, she could admit, flashy—as KC's story.

There was no chance she and KC were about to be fired. No, they were being conscripted. For what, Yardley didn't know, but she guaranteed it would be the kind of operation she'd be able to tell stories about once she got declassified.

"And Flynn?" the president asked.

"I never heard from her again," KC said. "The first time I caught a whiff of her since the EPA hack was in Toronto, when I looked at the code she'd added to the digital lock on the hotel room door. It had her signature. Impeccably clean. Impossibly efficient. It's hard to explain, but imagine you watched someone solve a complex math problem with a single equation." KC sifted her fingers through her short hair, her eyes on the ceiling. "I've come to understand over the years that she was legitimately a genius," she said. "Obviously, she still is. The only reason I was able to unlock the door was that I knew her once, so I still know her well enough to think like she thinks. Even so, it took me hours and hours to pick apart her encryption on the thumb drive. If anyone thought the passport or ultrasound photo were a plant to frame her, the lock code and encryption would be proof Kris herself is actively involved."

"Does she have the capability to code this device, this sequence that was used in Toronto?" The president didn't look up from her perusal of the brief in the folder, but the rest of the room went still again.

Because it was a room full of spies.

Yardley couldn't speak to what the director, Gramercy, and Atlas had been privy to in advance of this meeting, but she could read the way the wind was blowing here. The president didn't like that the agency had failed to lock down this device, and she had something in mind to get the job done—a plan that included KC and Yardley.

Her guess was that whatever that plan was, it would be both as smart and grim as the mood at a shootout, because President Williams had been on both the House and Senate domestic and international intelligence committees for years before running for office. She knew what was what.

"Yes," KC confirmed. "Kris is more than capable of making a device like this."

The president leaned in, her attention steady on KC. "Do you think that she *did* make it?"

Oh. *Oh*, Yardley had not expected that, and it took her breath away for a moment. KC was swimming deep here, in ways that Yardley absolutely didn't understand.

But she would, it seemed. Whether she wanted to or not.

"No," KC said. "I don't think Kris Flynn made this device."

Her surety was utter. Nonetheless, the statement plucked the strings of Yardley's intuition with a warning.

"And why is that?" the president asked.

"If Kris had made it, Toronto would still be in the dark, relying on forty-year-old analog tech pulled out of basements."

The room found yet another level of silence.

"What do you believe Flynn's involvement with the sale of this device indicates, then?"

KC's muscles flexed under the fine merino sweater Yardley had bought her last Christmas. If Yardley hadn't known her and her body so well, she would've missed it.

KC was hiding something.

"If I knew what Kris was capable of," KC said, "I would hire her to fix it."

The president leaned back and looked around the room slowly. "And tell me, please, who here knows what Flynn is capable of?" Her voice bit off every word. They had gotten to the headmaster's lecture part of the program.

KC's expression shifted from nearly unreadable to surprised in a moment. She looked at the director. "I would assume every single one of you do. I disclosed all of this when I was recruited in extensive interviews with Dr. Brown. It should be in my file."

The warning from Yardley's intuition got louder as she examined each person at the table in turn. If Flynn had been in KC's file, then Maple Leaf would have been looking at Flynn months ago, not trailing her once she popped up in a weapons bazaar on the darknet. Yardley didn't get any weird vibes off the president or the director. Gramercy's face was a closed book. But Atlas met her eyes, and there was something there.

"That is an excellent point." The president's gaze snapped to the director's so fast, Yardley watched his hair blow back. This was not a good look for him. Then Ada Williams returned her attention to KC. "And in your association with Flynn, had you ever discussed or worked on this device or anything similar?"

The question was a bald one, following a series of bald

questions. Yardley felt like her entire soul was ripping in two as she tried to keep a grip on what she and KC had agreed on—pure professionalism—while watching the woman who had been more important to her than anyone on earth be interrogated by the president for what seemed like a good reason.

It turned out it wouldn't be luxury that would tempt Yardley to abandon her post. She was a fool for love. Even the kind that didn't belong to her anymore.

"Madam President, we had a lot of conversations at that time about how to use tech to solve problems. Yes, some of those conversations were about how to make systems like the grid more efficient and accessible and safe. Listen, though." KC leaned forward. "With Maple Leaf, we're in the trenches holding on to our helmets. I blew the Unicorn's cover, so you can't put her out there on this—not when Mirabel's seen her, and someone on his team jammed our comm channel, and I crashed the party and made it even more obvious than it already was that U.S. intelligence is close enough to smell their cheap cologne. They're gonna bolt the door and check ID from now on. No way they'll let the Unicorn close. But Tabasco is another matter. I had a half-assed disguise, sure, except Yardley smashed his nose pretty good, so I'd be shocked if Mirabel got a good look at me. That Starbucks was chaos. He and his cronies might know who Tabasco is as an entity, but according to the world we're talking about, I could be anyone. I could be more than one anyone."

"Concise." The president had leaned back in her chair. The rest of them should have had their mouths hanging open, but they were spies, so every face in the room had gone vacant as a three-week-old litter of coonhounds.

"No one knows me," KC said. "And, even better for you, I

know Kris. I'm guessing I'm at this table because it's our top priority to secure her as an asset, and to hunt down every scrap of code that could conceivably belong to this device before it's purchased and secure it, too."

The president put her elbows on the arms of her chair. "You have anything else to say?"

"Only to ask when I can get started."

She gestured at the director with her index finger. "McLaughlin, you want to take this? For example, what potential reservations the United States might have about assigning your officer to do exactly what she suggests, starting ten minutes ago?"

KC's expression hardened. "There's no call for reservations."

"Not if you're handled strategically for this mission," Director McLaughlin said. "Keep in mind, if you had any field experience whatsoever, you'd be in custody right now while we sorted out what is or is not in your file and filled in your history with Kris Flynn more completely. But since we're not concerned you have the skills to evade the agency, we've decided it's worth the risk to put you on this. With appropriate supervision."

KC looked at Gramercy. In his first sign of life since the meeting got started, he shook his head and pointed his gold Montblanc at Yardley.

That was when the room went dark, because Yardley closed her eyes in the hope she would be rendered invisible.

The CIA had kept her granddaddy assigned to tracking and cultivating a relationship with Levi Petrov for years after he went over to the Soviets. *No one knew him better than I did*, Yardley Senior had explained with a shrug. *You know how the agency is.*

She knew how the agency was.

"You were listening to us," KC said, her tone flat and hard. "Earlier. In the hallway."

No one acknowledged what she implied—that the people in this room had just had a front-row seat to the official breakup between the Unicorn and the last hope of Project Maple Leaf. So why not leverage everything the Unicorn knew about Tabasco at a moment when she might be a little less biased than usual?

The director shrugged. "Time is a factor. We need this device located and secured as soon as possible. We need Flynn. We need to know what Mirabel's plans are for the sale, or for detonation. We can't use the Unicorn in the usual way. As you've said, you're uniquely qualified to find Flynn, and, so far, a basement full of techs with analysts breathing down their necks hasn't been able to dig up any connection between the two of you since you left MIT, so we're willing to take this risk and tip the odds in our favor as much as we can."

Yardley heard her voice before she thought about speaking. "I can still access Miller. I've been to London several times to make brush contact with him for intel relevant to this mission. He's deep enough undercover that he no doubt knows more than we do about the sale."

"No," the director said. "Better to go straight to the source if we can. It has to be Nolan."

Gramercy shifted in his chair. "Our options are our options. Nolan, we expect Whitmer to guide you every step of the way. Atlas and I and our strongest team will be behind you." He tapped the tabletop once with his first finger, his focus entirely on KC. "This is an opportunity. Quite honestly, it's an opportunity you should have had long ago. Be grateful you'll be mentored in the field by someone of Whitmer's caliber. If your personal relationship gets in the way of your ability to feel that gratitude, set it aside."

"I understand, sir."

Yardley couldn't take her eyes off KC. Gorgeous, dazzling, brilliant KC, who was more than Yardley had ever imagined, and shame on her.

"It looks like for the first time in a long time, we're starting on the same page," she said. "Shall we?"

KC got up without a word, and they left the room together.

Just like she had in those weeks after they met, Yardley was diving headfirst into the unknown. She could be betrayed. She could fail. And, no matter what, in the end, she would say goodbye to Katherine Corrine Nolan.

She couldn't help but think they were taking the first steps toward a day they would be strangers to each other.

If they weren't already.

CHAPTER SIX

CIA Headquarters, Langley, Virginia

KC waited in the hallway as Yardley snapped on a light to reveal a closet-like room adjacent to a tech lab. They were in a mysterious and apparently abandoned wing of the headquarters building.

"Ignore the wear pattern in the carpet." Yardley gestured at a bare spot about the length of a person pacing back and forth. "I promise no one has ever been kept prisoner in here."

"Isn't that exactly what you would say just before you locked the door?" Reluctantly, KC made her way inside and sat down on a creaky rolling chair opposite another broken-looking rolling chair. There was a small metal table between them. The room was otherwise empty.

"No locking, I promise." Yardley pulled the door halfway shut behind her. "This was the best I could do on short notice before I organized a few things. I'll be back."

She exited without further comment, leaving KC to her own devices.

On the way from the Situation Room at the White House to this dilapidated and abandoned office, Yardley had said nothing. Secret Service had escorted them to the helipad, they'd flown and landed, KC had trudged behind her new mentor to a familiar tech lab where Yardley got a comm earpiece and took KC's cell phone, and now she was here, with no debrief after the briefing.

She jiggled her leg, staring at the door. She'd already heard Yardley walk down the hall and bang through the double doors at the end. Likely to be gone a while yet.

"Keep it moving, Nolan." Her voice fell flat against the acoustic tiles and hard-wear carpet. She looked for and found the security camera, mounted in a discreet corner. It was a TaborView wired continuous feed cam that looked more than a few years old. No way to tell if it was recording without a specialized scanner.

She gave the dark lens a wave. Even if they were watching, she wasn't going to sit here like an obedient child. She left the room and stepped into the dim hallway.

The door on the dark tech lab was locked. She keyed in a door code she'd established for herself in her first week at the agency, one she used when she didn't want her movements—physical or digital—to be tracked.

The lock clicked open. Banks of overhead fluorescents blinked slowly to life. KC stepped out of the doorway, her back against the wall, and waited a moment, listening.

No footsteps. Nothing.

She slid a laptop off of a metal cart and returned to the room she was supposed to be in. It took her a few minutes to wipe the computer and cloak its signal.

Very little had happened to her in her life that she hated more than sitting in a meeting with the president of the United States and her ex-girlfriend-slash-peerless-spy and telling them 90 percent of the truth.

Especially considering the remaining 10 percent that was a lie was a *big* one.

In fact, I made the weapon, Madam President. I pinky swear it was for a legitimate reason that will be explained at a later time.

As the president herself was now fully aware, KC had gotten into some messes, but she'd never been in this deep. She didn't know what Ada Williams knew about Dr. Brown's black op, much less McLaughlin, Gramercy, Atlas, or Yardley. No question, the president *should* know everything. The CIA's entire purpose was to gather intelligence and present it without bias to the president, so nothing should be happening at the agency that the executive branch was unaware of.

But just because things were supposed to work a certain way didn't mean they did.

She would have liked to inform the people in the Situation Room that Dr. Brown was hurt and off the grid, and he would explain when he was able to reemerge. She hadn't been able to do that, however, because he'd been injured in the course of the very same black op she couldn't talk about, which meant even his injuries were a secret to anyone outside of the op.

Which was everyone, so far as KC had been told.

All she'd been able to do was remind herself over and over again that Dr. Brown had said to keep the op a secret until she heard directly from him.

Directly. He had been explicit.

So KC would just have to be grateful that the president and the director hadn't asked her any questions about Dr. Brown's whereabouts or his involvement with the weapon.

What the president had given KC was an opportunity, as Gramercy pointed out—the opportunity to find Kris Flynn, figure out how bad the mess was and how many copies or versions or pieces there were of the weapon, and clean it up in time for

Dr. Brown to answer the SOS that KC had left for him in his encrypted inbox.

With one ear to the hallway, she got to work. It didn't take her long to track down a couple of Canadian hackers who owed her a favor. Almost as soon as she posted her request to them, she got a message back from one and heard a noise from the hallway at the same time.

Footsteps. Still far off, but KC needed to move.

She decrypted the message.

Take a look at this, it said.

There was a small package of code that appeared to have been transmitted from a household smart device. KC scanned through it as fast as she could until she heard the doors clang open at the end of the hall. Then she wiped the laptop and leaned it against the wall on the far side of the room as though someone had left it behind after a meeting.

Yardley appeared in the doorway. "Did I give you enough time?"

"For what?"

She glanced at the computer. "If you weren't quite ready for me, I could step out and get us something to drink."

"Were you watching me on the camera?"

Yardley narrowed her eyes. "No, but I was certainly hoping that *Tabasco*, if left alone for the first time since her run this morning, would engage in a bit of tradecraft. You surely haven't been sitting there this whole time waiting for me."

"Maybe I took a power nap."

Yardley sighed. "Where's Flynn?"

KC sighed back, but her heart rate hadn't slowed down. "Probably in trouble. After she bounced from the Ritz, she hacked a smart device, some kind of appliance that's connected to Wi-Fi, to send a signal."

"To whom?"

"Hard to say. Anyone who would know it was her, looks like."

Yardley tapped her finger against her bowed upper lip. "If she's talking to the world with a toaster oven, that means she doesn't have her phone on her. Or access to a computer."

"Probably not."

"Her phone and computer weren't in her suite at the Ritz. I assumed she'd taken them with her. Then she drops momentarily out of the Sisters' eyesight and disappears, but she doesn't have her things with her anymore. That says 'kidnapped' to me."

"Or on the move and not interested in being located by the wrong people."

"Where did she send it from?" The easy cadence of Yardley's fast-paced questions was pleasantly familiar.

"I can't tell, but it doesn't matter. It's an old signal, I think. If it were actionable, I doubt my source would've given it to me."

"But you don't know for sure? Do you want to grab that laptop and take another look?" Yardley issued this challenge with a raised eyebrow. Sassy.

"Don't you have to teach me how to waltz and wear emerald earrings that double as poison darts?" But KC walked over to retrieve the laptop. A few seconds, and she restored the message she'd wiped. It took a few more to rapidly scan through the rest of the package she'd been sent. Then her eyes crossed. "Holy *night*."

"What?" Yardley sat down on the broken chair across from hers.

KC double-checked what she was looking at. "Weren't we all

just at a briefing? It was my understanding that at a briefing, information is shared."

"KC." There was a warning in Yardley's voice that KC usually only heard when she flipped through the streaming menu options for too long, searching for the perfect show.

"Like." KC exported everything she could to her own private server, because fuck the agency. "Come on."

"Katherine Corrine Nolan, if you don't tell me what you're going on about, I will lay you out."

"You and what upper body? That whole set of pink-and-aqua dumbbells in the corner of our room has dust on it."

"Hey!"

KC looked up from the laptop to Yardley, knowing she'd see laughter in her face—the laughter they always shared when they fake-fought.

Of course, now KC knew what their real fights were like.

Yardley seemed to remember at the same time, and it made KC's stomach hurt to watch her school the amusement in her eyes and retreat behind her new, professional *Unicorn* expression.

She forced herself to focus on the laptop screen. "So Flynn sent this message, and within a few hours, it was picked up."

"By whom?"

"That's what's making me spin. By us."

"Us, as in—"

"Looks like Corsen saw it. Corsen reports to Gramercy."

Yardley pointed the toe of her crossed leg. "But you said this message must be old, or your contact wouldn't have given it to you. So she sent it, we saw it, and we went after her? Stashed her away somewhere?"

KC thought about it. "That's more than we can infer. All we

actually know is that at some point after she was last in our sights in Toronto, Kris Flynn broadcast a message from somewhere, and Corsen intercepted it and may or may not have reported it to Gramercy."

"All right." Yardley wound a strand of dark hair around her finger while KC savored her agreement. *All right* wasn't a term she'd heard much from Yardley recently. "You're right that it's the kind of intel I should've been given. How do I know what's hinky if I don't know where she's been or who would lock her in a room with nothing but a toaster oven? Or why she would pass a note to the agency?"

"We don't know for sure she was locked up, she didn't send it directly to the agency, and it doesn't have to be a toaster oven. It could be one of those fancy refrigerators I wanted to get but you talked me out of because you said it was just a fridge with a giant iPad—though, for the record, that is not an uncool thing to have."

"No? Agree to disagree." Yardley reached across the table and turned KC's laptop toward herself. "Can you see anything else?"

"You mean do I know where she went after the Ritz? No. Could I find her? Depends. If she doesn't want us to find her, we won't. What this tells me is she's smart and resourceful, and she knows she has a reason to keep herself as far out of the way of trouble as possible. Not to mention she's pregnant, so now she's probably ten times sharper and has grown fangs and claws."

"You're right. She's smart. Maybe smarter than us. What that tells me is that you recognized Flynn's work on the hotel lock because Flynn wanted to be recognized." She rolled her squeaky chair around the table and pulled up close to KC, who rotated to face her. At some point in the minutes she'd been gone, she'd brushed her hair shiny and put on lip gloss. "How likely *is* it that Flynn's work wouldn't change after years and years?"

"Unlikely, unless she wanted someone specific to notice her." Her eyes were the right color again—the fathomless dark blue of an underwater dive. KC could smell her lip gloss, mixing with the familiar lavender of her soap.

"Someone specific like you? Like your old Daisy Duke contacts?" One corner of Yardley's mouth quirked into a smile.

God. How long had it been since Yardley smiled at her like that?

How long since they'd teased each other, or worked together even on something as simple as placing an order for dinner? It was more potent than KC had counted on, with Yardley so close—her sticky lip gloss and full mouth and bluer-than-blue eyes—and the rush of intimate associations swamped KC's focus so completely that she didn't even try to think. She simply let KC-and-Yardley take over. Their way of communicating that had never failed but that they hadn't used in so long.

She reached out and slid her hand under Yardley's hair, gripping her nape at precisely the same moment that Yardley threaded both of her hands into KC's hair, and *god*. What a relief to touch her and be touched. Her arms broke out in gooseflesh so fast, she had no choice but to squeeze her eyes shut tight again so she could just *feel*.

Feel Yardley's lips against her own, the softest pressure, only asking.

Feel the sound she made, such a good sound from her throat that it skipped over KC's brain like a bad needle on the best record ever, anticipation and frustration all at the same time.

Feel her heart bang in her chest, throb between her legs in time to Yardley's breath panting against her mouth.

Feel the way her entire body went still in warning.

"Oh," Yardley breathed. "I didn't mean to."

It would have been a funny thing to say if KC couldn't feel Yardley's lips against her upper lip and her thumb circling over her ear, sifting her hair.

Her touch, her nearness, her tenderness, her want, kept it from being funny.

It wasn't funny because it had been so long that even those things—Yardley's breath, Yardley's fingers in her hair, her lavender skin—were enough to set off aching, insistent, reckless desire, the kind only sated by skin against skin.

It wasn't funny because Yardley's nape was hot, and because Mirabel hadn't fired his stupid gun, and because KC had been crushing on the Unicorn for ages, and she could almost taste Yardley and knew just how she melted and went hot and alive when KC softly bit her bottom lip.

So she bit it.

Yardley's legs laced between hers with a soft moan that sounded like a prayer.

"I didn't mean to," KC whispered.

Yardley smiled against her mouth. They hadn't even really kissed, only touched their lips together. But if KC didn't do something quick, she was going to really kiss Yardley, and that wouldn't be fair.

She wasn't being fair.

She didn't want to be fair.

She didn't want this blackmailed job, one arm wrenched behind her back by the people who were supposed to be her colleagues. Didn't want to lie anymore. Didn't want everything she'd been foolish enough to hope for to be reduced to this miserable, flaming bag of shit.

She wanted to want, and get what she wanted, every urgent grind and gasp leading to more, more, more.

She wanted a kiss that would force their love back to life, a kiss that would take them back to that party and give them a chance to start completely over and not fuck it up.

Everything she couldn't have. That was what KC wanted.

She eased back, everything hurting, her body protesting leaving Yardley's body with pain. "Hey."

Yardley shook her head, just a fraction.

"No," she whispered. She'd begged with only that word so many times in their fights, when they didn't have any more words left—*no, no, no.*

"It's only because of the day." Her voice rasped over the lie, a barbed hook in her throat. "Because of being scared earlier, the adrenaline. Being in a room with one of the most powerful people in the world. Maybe the helicopter." It definitely wasn't because of the helicopter, but she needed to convince herself so she could convince Yardley.

Sooner or later, Yardley would find out about the secrets KC had been keeping. It was safer, better, to put anything but a professional relationship behind them.

Yardley's hands were still in her hair. KC made herself remember the POD in the driveway, pushing mental fingers against the bruise until it hurt enough to give her the resolve she so badly needed.

"We've never worked together before." She managed to say it with some conviction. "We forgot. We forgot because we haven't been doing anything but arguing or crying or not talking for weeks, months, and then suddenly we were doing something new together."

"It's not real," Yardley said.

"It's definitely not. How could it be?"

At last, Yardley dropped her hands from KC's hair and pushed her chair back. KC did the same, the sting of bare truth washing away the throbbing ache of what was gone and couldn't be recovered. "We'll get used to it," KC said. "It'll get easier."

Yardley almost looked like she might say something in response to that—KC couldn't imagine what—but she didn't. She took a deep breath that seemed to smooth the color from her cheeks and make her eyes cool.

"The point I was making," she said, with that same crispness leaching into her voice, "is that Flynn's skills must also have developed over the years. So if she's leaving an old calling card in her code, it's likely because she wants old contacts to see it. Is there anything about what you saw from the door key code in Toronto, or even this toaster oven message, that speaks directly to you or to anyone you could identify?"

The question snapped Tabasco into focus. "Not directly to me, though it's definitely her old signature. But you have a point. Word gets around. She might know I'm with the CIA."

"Do you think the toaster oven message was for you? Given that you cracked the hotel door code and she knows that you, specifically, could do it as quickly as you did?" Yardley had eased her chair all the way to other side of the small table. The distance helped.

"Maybe." KC gently shut the lid of the laptop. "What's the plan for this mission?"

"They want us to fly to Dublin on a military jet and shake down Flynn's partner, assumed baby daddy, for where she may be. Find a cover for you at his workplace. Or surveil him, et cetera."

KC wrinkled her nose. "That is very—"

"Predictable. I know. But I don't take their initial offer. If I'm supposed to be your mentor, that's my first bit of mentoring. Never accept their original plan. Too many people already know what that plan is, talk too much, and usually they've put less than zero thought into your personal safety. An officer in the field is an expendable officer. They can always cut you loose, and they know it. Also, I hate being made somewhere inconvenient and having a lethal weapon pointed at me by some petty terrorist's understudy when I've got weekend plans with you."

KC winced as this collision of worlds caused her to rapidly shuffle through every mental image she'd ever had of Yardley at work—sitting on the edge of a mattress in a stuffy Holiday Inn Express, for example—and replace it with her curated catalog of mental images of the Unicorn.

Sprinting away from an explosion in black leather. Clinging to a balcony to escape detection in a Lisbon flat. Stealing a tuk tuk to chase a target through the traffic-thick streets of Phnom Penh.

Yardley had done those things.

The lump in her throat felt like a boulder. KC wiped her hand over her mouth, leaving her palm sticky with a trace of lip gloss. "What do you suggest?"

"Let's not go to Dublin. I want intel that carries us right to Flynn's front door, not intel that leads us to someone else who *might* have intel, and so on. Maple Leaf has been too much of that. I'm over it."

"I can keep looking for her here." KC tapped the lid of the

laptop. "She's bound to either pop up or run into someone who gossips about her. Could take a while, though."

"That would require more patience than I have. I'm thinking we need a mean girl. Mean girls are incredibly efficient if you give them what they want." Yardley turned her full attention to KC, looking her up and down with detached assessment.

"Why are you doing that?" KC crossed her arms over her chest.

"It's nice to work with someone who literally no one has ever seen in the field. It means you can mostly be yourself, except with higher heels and less clothes."

"You're talking in spy. I'm tech, remember? You have to explain. Why can't I wear clothes?"

"Because no woman wears very many clothes at Wally's, and all the men there are mean girls. By which I mean they're professional gossips. Powerful. Tech will have to build you a profile, but you barely need a cover story." Yardley glanced at her wrist, checking the time on the gold watch she'd worn every day since KC gave it to her. She stood up. "Let's go, Eliza Doolittle."

"Who's that?" KC asked, rising from her seat at the table. "Eliza Doolittle?" She had to jog to catch up to Yardley striding down the hall, cutting into a tunnel that opened up after they passed through the double doors' biometric lock.

"It's a story about a linguist who proves he can transform a flower seller from the streets of London into a lady. Eliza is Henry Higgins's protégé. Henry's the linguist. You're Eliza. I'm Henry." She stopped in the middle of the tunnel. "You know it's a love story?"

"I graduated from high school when I was fifteen. I can't be expected to know this kind of thing."

But Yardley was already on the move again. Her reply drifted over her shoulder. "It's a Greek myth originally. This sculptor makes a sculpture of a beautiful woman and falls in love with her. Then the goddess Venus brings her to life for him." She turned and tapped a code into a door KC didn't recognize.

"Revolting."

Yardley flung the door open. The overhead lights illuminated a vast carpeted room filled with racks of clothes. The wall opposite the door was mirrored, creating the illusion of endless space in front of changing cubicles. Yardley walked to a rack in the middle of the room, near the front, and began flipping through the hangers. "I concede your point. But also, Henry and Eliza are from the stage version of *Pygmalion*. The fancy British linguistics expert who tries to teach a Cockney-speaking flower girl how to talk and act like a lady? He does it on a bet with a friend. Eliza doesn't know about the bet. She thinks he's a good guy who's going to help her crawl out of poverty."

"Class bias, power imbalance, and barefaced lies are such a good foundation for a love story," KC said.

"They are, actually. The problem is always the ending. No one knows how to pull it off."

Yardley gave a lot of niche-knowledge speeches like this. It was weirdly calming to listen to her deliver an impromptu lecture on an obscure subject while preparing KC for an experience she had in no way anticipated when she woke up this morning. "Explain."

"Well, in the original ending, she doesn't fall for Higgins. There's a different guy." Yardley paused, removed a hanger from the rack, and held up a red dress. "Too obvious." She put it back and continued flipping. "But nobody likes that ending, because clearly they've got something, these two. There's a connection, it's kind of hot, and the audience hates being told it's impossible and Eliza has to stick to her own kind. So when Lerner and Loewe wrote a screenplay for a musical version, which got turned into a movie later, they changed the ending. Now, every time the story's retold, they use the love story ending where Henry and Eliza waltz off into the sunset together."

She stopped again, slid a gold dress off its hanger, and dropped the hanger on the floor. After shoving the dress at KC, Yardley made her way to a rack of shoes, her blue eyes rapidly scanning through rows of open boxes. "I mean, obviously, the discovery of the bet is quite the third-act dark moment. But the romance of it all manages to survive. It takes some hand-waving, though."

"Because, again, class difference, power imbalance, and lies. Tough to overcome."

"Yep. Audrey Hepburn plays Eliza in the movie, which helps. Turns out it's mostly a casting issue. Julia Roberts in *Pretty Woman* is another example. Irresistible."

"And yet I am feeling so much resistance." KC turned the dress in her hands. "Which is the front and which is the back?"

"How adventurous are you?" Yardley's smile was too familiar. "I'll turn around."

KC shucked out of her clothes and looped her body into the garment in the most likely configuration of gold straps, limbs, and areas that needed to be covered to avoid arrest. The dress exposed her underboobs, she supposed in lieu of her nonexistent cleavage, as well as her legs starting from the hipbone, and—going by the breeze—at least an inch of her ass.

Yardley handed her a pale pink bobbed wig, which KC dutifully put on. It matched her footwear. She couldn't bring herself to call the impractical four-inch stilettos with laces that crisscrossed up to her knees "shoes."

When she was done dressing, a woman knocked on the door and handed Yardley something, which she gave to KC. Matte black eyeglasses packed with tech. "DC loves glasses on a beautiful woman," Yardley said by way of explanation.

KC slid them on, struck again by déjà-vu as her mind tried to smash together her life as a spy—she'd written the lion's share of the code that could package, encrypt, and transfer raw data from these glasses—and her life with Yardley, on whose nose the very same glasses had perched more than once as she tipped her head, batted her eyes, and tricked a target into telling her more than they should.

It was a lot. This was a lot.

KC sat down, then sat down a different way when she realized that sitting her normal way flashed everyone. While she'd been getting ready, agents had slowly filtered into the room, bringing things Yardley must have requested. There were a number of murmured conversations.

Yardley handed her a tablet, awake and preloaded with KC's cover. There was a photo of her in thumbnail with the pink hair and the glasses, so KC could only assume the mirrors in this room had cameras. She read over the name they'd given her, the background, the objective. Surreal. KC had compiled cover documents like this for other officers. "There is absolutely no way this is going to work," she said, mostly to herself.

But when she looked up, she was startled to discover Yardley smiling the big, nose-crinkling, double-dimpled grin that signaled she was on the verge of breaking into laughter.

KC's breath caught. She hadn't seen that smile in forever.

"Is it so strange, really?" Yardley's voice had dropped below the murmur in the room, for KC's ears only. "Are we that surprised right now to find ourselves here? Even when I thought you were a web developer and told you I was a finance bureaucrat, we've always respected each other's competence."

KC couldn't disagree. However much their connection had been stress-tested and warped beyond bearing by the lies they'd told in the past, Yardley was right that it didn't feel *strange* to be here with her, doing this. They knew and respected each other. It wasn't everything they'd had, but it was something.

Although, from what KC had heard earlier, it sounded like Eliza Doolittle and Henry Higgins had formed a pretty tight bond, too.

"If you truly don't think it will work," Yardley said, "now's your chance to call it off."

"No." KC rose to her feet, aware of every muscle in her legs as they adjusted to the sensation of four new inches of height tipped forward at a forty-degree angle. "It's never been the *challenge* that's kept me from trying to convince straight older men that I'm a lusty coed."

Then Yardley did laugh—her best laugh, with the tiny third dimple that sank in at the top of her cheekbone—and KC took a deep breath and let herself relax.

The mission would be fine. KC would do her best, and so would Yardley. Together, they were more than the sum of their parts. Like Henry and Eliza, they had something.

KC wished she didn't already know they could never pull off the ending.

CHAPTER SEVEN

Wally's Steakhaus, Navy Yard, the District

Sitting with her legs crossed in the comms van, Yardley entered Wally's Steakhaus through KC's eyes.

Reaching forward, she adjusted the view on her monitors to lighten up the gloom of the dim interior. She hadn't appreciated that these cameras and biometrics were so good. She could practically smell the Wally's mélange of too-sweet sandalwood colognes, malbec, and charred steak.

No wonder Atlas was always so in control. They knew *everything*. She opened her display to include face recognition scanning of anyone KC ran into, in case it was useful, and also because it was cool.

The sleek tech and how well KC was doing so far made Yardley feel extremely fat with confidence. She had never fumbled a mission, and she wasn't going to start now.

KC had never even heard of Wally's Steakhaus, but Yardley was a regular. Wally's was where the power-mad and morally centerless denizens of politics and espionage liked to broker, plan, and gloat. After what had gone down with Devon Mirabel in the Starbucks, Wally's would be buzzing. Already while monitoring KC's cameras, she'd spotted the son of a KGB double agent who had a very loose job description as a "consultant," two lobbyists with horses in the arms race, and a billionaire who was on MI6's watchlist.

And every one of them—along with several others—had noticed the fresh-faced Georgetown undergrad leaning against the bar.

KC. Aka Caitlin Parr, a poli-sci major in her sophomore year and a budding indie fashion influencer. Her false eyelashes kept bonking into the lenses of her glasses. She'd told Yardley she felt like one of those spindly, dying crane flies that drifted around the porch light in the summer, but she looked like a runway model in those heels, and she'd absorbed Yardley's crash course on the dynamics and players at Wally's with impressive speed.

"Who's taking care of you?" Mr. Son-of-a-KGB-agent made the first bid for KC's attention, leaning next to her at the bar and signaling the bartender. He was a bit over six feet tall, obnoxiously lantern-jawed, with a thick, unmovable swoosh of chestnut hair. Over the years, Yardley had witnessed him work his wiles on any number of young women, but KC's pulse did not pick up a single beat when he brushed against her upper arm.

"I think the tender's checking if he has any prosecco in my price range for the Aperol spritz I ordered." Yardley could hear the winsome smile in KC's voice. Hilarious. KC could deadlift two hundred pounds. She was the farthest possible thing from winsome.

"The sun's down. Spritzes are for picnics." The man snapped his fingers at the bartender. "Pour a flute of that 2014 Roederer Cristal for this girl." He rested his arm on the wall behind KC's head and leaned closer. The picture was so clear, Yardley could've counted the pores on his nose.

"Maybe I don't like champagne." KC laughed but accepted

the skinny flute from the bartender like she was born to the club. She took a sip. "Of course, that doesn't stop my roommate and me from stealing bottles from her dad's events for girls' nights. He used to be a congressman."

Okay, that was impressively smooth. Tabasco had some tricks up her sleeve.

"Who's your roommate?" The man pulled a sterling-cased vape from his suit jacket's inner pocket and tipped it toward her. She shook her head.

"Elizabeth Corners." This was the name of a college-aged senator's daughter who attended Georgetown and kept a low profile. KC had dropped it to showcase her cover's insider connections.

"Senator Corners doesn't know his ass from his elbow." KC's mark blew a vapor ring. "He took two mil in donations from Big Pharma and then voted to put a price cap on specialty medications. Didn't get a second term. Fucking idiot." The man laughed and slid his vape away.

KC set down her phone on the bar. It had a faux marble case and Swarovski charms, and it immediately began transmitting several more angles of Wally's dining room with multifocal laser cameras. "Huh." She scooted closer, letting her hip nudge him. "I'm Caitlin Parr." She held out her hand, and he shook it, holding it a little too long. KC smiled. "You're?"

"Kyle Bornakov."

She smiled again, without even a flicker of recognition at the consultant's name, though Yardley had told her that she hoped he'd be at Wally's, given his penchant for gossip. "Here's where I admit I'm really into this stuff, despite what the bling and the shoes might be advertising," KC breathlessly confessed.

"I like the shoes." Kyle grinned. "Into what, baby?"

"The insider politics." KC laughed again, a confection of naive sex appeal and intelligence. Yardley was not unaffected. "Stuff I'm not supposed to know."

"There's all kinds of things a girl like you isn't supposed to know."

Lord.

"Tell me *one* thing," KC said. "Over the clothes only."

Yardley laughed, forgetting the sound would go straight into KC's ear, and *that* was when she watched KC's heart rate do a small rumba.

One of the techs looked at her with disapproval. Oops.

"You're doing amazing," she whispered, trying to make up for her handler gaffe. Was this compliment something she whispered to KC at other times? Maybe. She was a little caught up in the high of KC's unexpectedly self-possessed performance.

"Do you read more on that thing than just Instagram and Snapchat?" Kyle gestured at KC's giant phone sparkling on the bar.

"I read there was some kind of incident at the Capitol Hill Starbucks today. A witness said an assailant knocked down a woman. This witness had overheard the woman say she was running for Congress."

Oh, nicely done. Yardley watched Kyle straighten up, his gaze sweeping over KC's body from head to toe. "You're a tiny thing, aren't you?" It was a question that betrayed his growing appreciation for KC.

"But my mind is huge." KC widened her eyes. "Tell me about Starbucks. Unless you don't know anything?" She took another sip of the champagne but kept her full attention on Kyle.

"No small talk?" Kyle put his hand on her shoulder, covering more square inches of bare skin than was necessary for the purpose of polite attention. Yardley had to bite the side of her cheek to stop herself from making a comment that would prevent KC from living truthfully in these imaginary circumstances.

She should be embarrassed to be jealous of Kyle Bornakov. Her moves were so much better. If she spotted a woman like KC by herself at a bar, she wouldn't waste time with champagne and generic game. She'd state her intentions immediately and clearly, with solid examples of the pleasures on offer, along with the receipts she could deliver.

Men didn't know how to do this, bless their hearts.

"Did you walk over here for small talk?" KC asked.

Kyle laughed. "You're not one of those Capitol Hill gossips, are you?"

"Who *isn't* one of those Capitol Hill gossips?"

"Follow me, hon. We need to take this somewhere more discreet." Smiling, he beckoned KC to the dining room. When KC picked up her phone, the cameras swooped and blurred before coming back into focus.

The dining area was packed with circular booths filled with men too old for the women sitting next to them. White-coated servers darted between them like pinballs with trays of steaks and bottles of wine. Kyle stopped at a small booth with a discreet RESERVED sign, and KC scooted herself in.

The view tilted to one side as KC angled her head. Kyle had gotten close again in the dark dining room.

"So what happened?" KC asked. "Did a future congresswoman actually get knocked over on her ass? Who did it? Was there really a gun? I mean, *something* happened. But it's confusing because it's Starbucks, not Cafe Milano."

Good. She'd dropped the name of the spot for District intrigue that Yardley told her about. It telegraphed to Kyle that she knew the scene, and her thirst was serious. It also made Kyle laugh. "What I heard was that Ashley Sterling-Chenoweth Thompson was meeting with a goddamned spy."

"Ashley Sterling-Chenoweth Thompson?" KC repeated. "That is a lot of name for someone I never heard of."

"Big money. Her daddy is in finance, and she's quietly held down the farm, but now she wants a seat at the table."

"So why would someone like that meet with a spy? You're telling me stories."

"Is it working?"

"Ha!" KC rubbed the rim of her champagne flute. "A little. Show me your work on this one so I get it right when I impress my international diplomacy prof. He's such a wannabe, and I got a C on the last term paper. I need some meat to feed him."

Kyle leaned closer. "You can tell your prof that this spy's selling something Miz Ashley thought could help her win a seat. Of course, she could buy a seat, but this would reduce the price. A power coupon, if you will."

"Information?"

Kyle shrugged. "Someone knows, but not me."

"But can you tell me whose spy it was?" Excellent. KC was probing to find out how much Kyle could tell her.

"Devon Mirabel. British-born, but he's a free agent."

"Never heard of him."

Kyle took a drink of whiskey a server had placed at his elbow. "Used to be a high-level government advisor. No credentials. Shows up in too many rooms and at too many meetings." He waved his hand around the dining room. "There's a dozen spies here right now. Anybody who speaks Russian. Foreigners who live in hotels. Men who call themselves consultants."

Kyle was showing off. The only spy in the room at the moment was KC.

"So who was the dude who tackled our future congress-woman?"

"I'm guessing a Swede."

"What?" KC's voice rose an octave in her surprise. Yardley winced, but Kyle only reached over to drink from KC's champagne flute, having drained his whiskey.

"What I heard is Mirabel headed to his mansion in Lidingö—incredibly gauche, by the way—and he was in a hurry. He was supposed to be staying in the District for a while, but not anymore. So there must be business."

Lidingö. Stockholm. "Bounce," Yardley said.

"Gotta find the ladies," KC purred.

In the alley on the way to the comms van, KC picked up speed. "That was embarrassingly easy," she said over the comm as she walked. "You sent me on a baby mission. For babies. Itty-bitty spy babies."

"Wally's is tedious, but it tends to deliver."

"Do you have to play solitaire in your head to keep yourself entertained? Because I've seen men offer you free appetizers in exchange for a single dimple—the good kind of appetizers, with things like truffle oil and individual table smokers. I have to imagine the men in there have handed you a great deal of useful information for our country."

Yardley watched an agent help KC into the comms van, her dress shining madly, her cheeks flushed and eyes bright.

Mission high. It looked good on her.

"Kyle Bornakov is one of my favorite mean girls," Yardley said as the van pulled away from the curb. "He'll talk behind anybody's back, which means he hardly has to watch his own, because no one knows who they'd piss off if they stabbed him in it."

KC pulled a face. "His breath is one of the worst things that's ever happened to me. Like the breath of a leathery old tortoise."

The laughter burst out of Yardley before she could stop it, loud enough in the small van that everyone turned to look at her.

"And that place stinks," KC added. "Same as your hair after you've come back from your book club night."

Then, KC went still, staring at the ceiling of the van. When she looked at Yardley again, her mouth was grim. "There's no book club, huh? That's a shame. You loved the idea of that book club when you brought the flier home from the library."

"I do think I would love it, if I were ever able to go." Yardley slid off her bench and reseated herself next to KC as the van moved through the dark streets. She was dimly aware of the background chatter that had taken over her headset, arranging transportation and a route to Sweden. "Look. Doesn't it make you wonder . . ."

"What?" KC's profile was half in shadow, the pink bob covering too much of her face for Yardley to tell what her expression was.

"If it might do us good." She cleared her throat. "Give us closure, maybe. I mean, if we tried looking more at what was true instead of everything that was a lie."

When KC turned to her, her brown eyes were fathomless with a sadness that made Yardley's heart pinch. "The truth is a lot." She turned away. "And we're spies. Not a good idea to stop searching for the lies."

That stung. Yardley could feel her mission high draining into the rubber mats on the metal floor of the van.

"What's next?" KC asked.

The way she said it—her eyes darting away to look around the van, her shoulders tight—Yardley knew for sure she didn't mean for them.

"They're readying the Darkhorse at Andrews."

After that, KC started talking to one of the techs while they pulled everything from KC's cameras and audio, and Yardley watched the streetlights go by for the rest of the half-hour ride to the airbase.

Ninety minutes later, they were doing Mach 5 over European airspace, and Yardley was reviewing an updated briefing document on her secure tablet when she noticed the time.

Just past midnight in Virginia.

When she'd woken up this morning in the guest room, she never would've imagined the day would end with her strapped into a leather jump seat across from a sleeping KC in the metal-and-black cabin of a military aircraft so new and fantastically expensive that Yardley assumed its use must have been authorized by the president.

Everything she knew about KC—and Tabasco—kept shuffling around and coming back into focus like patterns in a kaleidoscope. KC's strength and cleverness and technical brilliance were the same color for this KC and the woman Yardley thought she knew, but the KC in the Situation Room was a different color. So was the KC at Wally's.

The KC who knew where all the zips were on a flight suit and how to do a preflight check was six new colors Yardley had never seen before.

What about the KC who used to bring Yardley coffee in bed, who still had a stuffed purple cat from childhood that she kept on her reading chair? The one who told Yardley gossip about the bros in her sweaty gym, giggling, and liked to use a brand of teen deodorant that smelled like cotton candy?

What about the one whose thighs trembled and toes curled and throat flushed when Yardley touched her?

The critical work that intelligence agents did, 99 percent of the time, boiled down to reading people. It bothered Yardley that she couldn't get the KC she knew so well to integrate completely with the colleague she'd known by reputation but met in person for the first time less than twelve hours ago.

Then again, when it came to KC, Yardley had never figured out how to get her personal and professional impulses to balance.

KC was supposed to be . . . not a fling. An *affair*, Yardley had told herself at first, knowing a night or two wouldn't be enough to get this glorious woman out of her system. An affair was something glittering and wonderful, but with a short season. Yardley had thought she could have that, at least.

She'd probably started to catch feelings as soon as KC talked to her at that party and Yardley found herself memorizing the freckles dusted over her cheekbones and the bridge of her nose. The black halter top she wore showed off the smooth, curvy muscles of her upper arms. The sun lit up the intense red of her messy cropped hair, and the corners of her big eyes squinted a little, her intelligence washing over Yardley like a midnight breeze off the ocean.

They didn't leave the bed for a week. Each other's sight for two. Then Yardley had gone on a mission, telling herself as she boarded the plane that she was letting KC fade into a gorgeous memory.

But the moment her traitorous feet met the tarmac in Virginia again, they were walking themselves to KC's front door.

Three years. And then, today—no, yesterday—after they'd broken up all over again in the hallway outside the director's office, they'd had that incident. The almost-kiss-and-definite-bite at Langley. KC was probably right to say it had only happened because there had been so many long and august moments between them without tension or crying or cold silence. Just that, all by itself, had been enough for Yardley to move her body close to KC's like they both had rare earth magnets embedded in their breastbones.

"Where's your watch?"

Yardley startled and checked the seat opposite her. KC still had her eyes closed and her head tipped back, but her voice was crisp over the comm—and, if Yardley wasn't mistaken, faintly accusing. The Darkhorse flew higher and faster than any aircraft Yardley had ever been transported in. The headphones were the same noise-canceling kind Yardley had used in military helicopters. They gave KC's speech a crystalline quality.

"It's safe. I don't usually wear it in the field." This was not untrue, but definitely evasive, given that the watch was currently zipped into the pocket of her flight suit. Yardley hadn't wanted KC to remember she had it and take it back.

She forced herself to take a deep breath. She didn't want to argue, and she didn't want to talk about the mission. She could accept that her impulse to carry the vision of KC in her flight suit to her bunk was only a delusional response to the fatigue of an emotional day, but she wasn't going to waste a chance to talk about *something*.

Yardley needed them to have a conversation. More than anything, she needed to get to know this woman across from her in a new way—a way that would let her smash together all the KCs and Tabascos in her head into a single person whose behavior she could understand and predict.

"You know," she said, "when my granddaddy finally got declassified and told my nan he'd been a federal intelligence agent for the whole of their marriage, she kicked him out of her house. Wouldn't return his calls. She'd always thought he cheated." It was the second time in as many days Yardley had brought up this story, and the second time she wasn't sure what she hoped to gain by telling it.

"And yet you made up your mind you wanted to have his career," KC said. "Fully aware of the consequences that came along with it."

"I wasn't going to let myself fall in love." It tightened Yardley's stomach to consider how shortsighted and naive she'd been. She'd really believed that her foolish romantic constitution would be made immune by the power of a resolution.

Who had she been protecting with that noble resolution, exactly? Not the eligible women of the Southeast. It seemed like she had been trying to avoid the exact spot she now found herself in, broken up with someone she'd break the world for, with nothing left but a gold watch zipped up next to her bewildered heart.

"On the other hand." KC opened her eyes. Her steady gaze on Yardley's was full of wry humor. "You told me never to accept the first plan."

"I did say that." Yardley gave KC just enough of a smile to

keep her attention. "So here we are. Tell me what I don't know. What you could never say."

KC looked down and rubbed her fingertip over her thumbnail. She wouldn't. That was what her body language meant.

There was nothing new about KC refusing to share, but the disappointment that Yardley would never truly know this woman rolled through her in a bigger, blacker wave than she'd anticipated.

She had already turned her face away to master herself when KC spoke.

"My dad was never around. Not really. He was a quality control inspector for a company with a bunch of vegetable canneries. His territory ran from Virginia all the way up to Wisconsin. When he was home, he didn't say much. About anything."

Yardley had never met KC's father. She knew he lived in the Florida Panhandle in a modest retirement duplex. He rented out one side for income. At the holidays, he sent KC a card with a fifty-dollar bill taped inside, but he never called, and KC didn't call him.

She wondered if the things she and KC couldn't tell each other had hurt them more than the lies.

"My mom died of an amniotic embolism when I was born," KC said. "I told you that, and it was true. But they weren't married, even. They'd met in a bar. Her mom fought with my dad for my custody for a couple of years, I guess. I have a vague memory of her. But then my dad moved in with *his* mom, and having her around plus his salary meant my mom's mom lost out. Or maybe she just lost interest. I'm not sure. She never reached out again, and I always felt like I couldn't ask."

Yardley had listened to a lot of stories from colleagues in this field that started like KC's. Stories that told about how a person became self-sufficient and observant. Often they were stories of neglect.

Once, when she and KC cleaned out the garage together, Yardley had found an envelope of miscellaneous snapshots. There was a picture of KC in jean shorts and a Power Rangers T-shirt, just old enough that her permanent teeth had come in and looked enormous, her hair bright as a new penny, sitting on the concrete steps with a pair of sunglasses on. Another showed KC's grandmother in a recliner in the living room, the oxygen tank for her COPD parked on the green shag next to her.

There were no pictures of KC's father. No friends or relatives.

Yardley had never seen those snapshots again. Probably if she hadn't been the one to find them, she never would've seen them at all.

"My grandma was a nice woman, and I think she did okay for a long time. But when I was in sixth grade, I started finding the door to the house unlocked, or no food in the cupboards, or the stove left on. I'd get called down to the office because there had been a paper sent home that parents were supposed to fill out and return that never got done. Bills were coming in the mail with my grandma's name in red through the plastic window. When I was in eighth grade, she hit a kid on a bike with her car. Broke his leg. She lost her license. We were supposed to be using the city bus, but it didn't go everywhere we needed it to. My dad was . . . more gone."

"You became the grown-up."

"I figured it out." The way KC said this did not invite pity. "I started driving because I was good enough at it that a kid driving attracted less attention than an older woman making too many mistakes. By the time I got a license, I'd gotten as interested in driving as I was in other kinds of machines. Tech. Finances, even. I can drive anything. I figured out how to get what I needed."

Everything she needed, she had supplied for herself. That was what KC wanted Yardley to understand—that she was someone who'd drawn on her own resources to figure out a way that she could meet all of her needs and the needs of her grandmother.

Never mind that she never should have had to do that.

Yardley held her body still, hoping to get more from KC by suppressing her reactions to what was, objectively, a much smaller, sadder story about KC's experiences of home and family than Yardley had ever been told.

"It was because of the counterterrorism investigation into our EPA project that Dr. Brown found me." KC's speech was precise now. This, too, was a sensitive subject, but also, Yardley guessed, a difficult one. "He did his job and secured me as an asset. He offered me a way to take care of everyone at a time when I didn't know how I was going to keep doing it, which had the bonus of being an attractive alternative to federal prison. Helped me find a nice assisted-living apartment for my grandma. All through my last few years of college, he was the one who'd call to see how my exams went. If I needed anything. He was there."

He was there. It wasn't the same thing as *He loved me.* It wasn't *I adored him*, or *He made me feel safe*, or *His mentorship meant the world to me.*

He was there.

Yardley didn't love that KC's primary person, for so long, had been an officer of the CIA, or that he'd been introduced into KC's life when she was so young.

She also didn't love that Dr. Brown hadn't been in the Situation Room, deflecting the heat from KC, who was his direct report.

As soon as Yardley had stashed KC back at Langley, she'd chased down Atlas and asked them directly about Dr. Brown's whereabouts. The only thing they'd been able to tell her was that the counterterrorism director was in the field and could not be contacted at the moment. Yardley had been able to hear that what Atlas meant was the agency was keeping tabs on Dr. Brown, but they weren't about to share information with her.

That could mean almost anything.

She studied KC's tight body language in her jump seat. She could tell that KC was trying to keep her expression extra neutral.

Yardley didn't blame her. They were exes, brand-new exes, and Yardley was asking her personal questions after the fact. But she needed to know.

"Tell me," she said, and the words came out more desperate than she'd meant for them to. *Tell me every single thing you never told me.* That's what it sounded like she was asking. *Tell me everything I deserved to know, everything that could have built bridges between us where our secrets made chasms.*

Her poor, stupid heart.

KC raised an eyebrow. "That's what I'm doing."

"I'd like to hear more about what your dynamic with Dr. Brown is like now." Yardley forced herself to inject indifference into her voice. "I don't know him well. When it comes to counterterrorism, he exclusively works with tech. I would have thought he'd be on Maple Leaf."

Something minute and extremely terrible happened behind

KC's face—a suppressed emotion that, if Yardley hadn't known KC, hadn't loved her, she would have missed.

But a question like that shouldn't have made CIA officer KC Nolan uncomfortable.

When KC shrugged, her arm lifted with her shoulder, indicating the gesture was false. "He's on medical leave."

Yardley's throat squeezed. *That was a lie.*

Before she could take a breath, a hard wall of pressure pushed her into her seat. The impossibly young pilot's voice came over the comm to let them know they were descending and would be wheels to ground in five.

KC pulled out her tablet and tapped it awake, as though their conversation had reached its natural conclusion.

Yardley spent the five minutes to landing deep inside her head, racing through everything she knew and didn't know about KC Nolan, Tabasco, Dr. Brown, Kris Flynn, and Project Maple Leaf. She pictured the way KC's back had stiffened in the Situation Room when the president made it clear she'd come into possession of game-changing information. She considered how much bravado KC had shown in that meeting, which seemed to disguise significant fear.

But fear of what?

When they landed, she unbuckled her harness and stood up at the same time KC did. A soldier opened the cabin door. On the tarmac, two men wearing black fatigues with no visible insignia maneuvered the stairs into position. A black BMW sedan sat twenty feet away, the engine idling.

Freezing-cold air rushed through the opening in the plane, blowing through KC's fiery hair. Yardley thought again of the snapshot she'd seen of her on the steps of her grandmother's house.

What KC had been through were the kinds of experiences that made a person hypervigilant, careful, observant. The kinds of experiences that made spies.

And traitors.

The cold air was blissfully numbing. Where they'd landed, on an isolated runway at the Air Target Sweden AB, could be anywhere with scrubby trees and a few armored military vehicles parked in tidy rows in a covered lot. As KC climbed into the car beside the driver, Yardley tried to remember the last time they'd really kissed.

She couldn't.

That was a tragedy. She'd *loved* KC Nolan. She hadn't known everything, but she'd known enough to love the girl who KC had been, with skinny legs and knobby knees, big teeth and huge sunglasses, sitting on the concrete steps of her grandma's house and smiling big over the loneliness in her heart.

She'd *loved* that pint-sized twelve-year-old sitting on a cushion, steering a Lincoln slowly through the streets of Reston, Virginia, and she'd loved the teenager who'd taken up service to her country when what she'd really needed was support, mentorship, and a chance to relax and actually be her age.

They'd kept too many secrets—that was obvious—and the agency had put KC in the basement, maybe for too long. Maybe for long enough that bad actors had reached her or she'd reached out to them in order to solve a different problem. Yardley didn't know why KC was afraid and concealing information, but her instinct told her KC was in more trouble than the mission was.

The CIA would do anything to its officers it suited them to do. Her granddaddy had been more than clear about that.

So it was a good thing Yardley was the Unicorn. KC needed someone willing to get to the bottom of things before anyone caught on—either the bad guys *or* the good guys—and fix it.

Keeping KC safe and out of the line of scrutiny so that she could thrive would be the kind of parting gift that might make it possible for Yardley to put her broken heart back together.

She just needed to come up with a plan.

CHAPTER EIGHT

Ulrikagatan Street, Östermalm, Stockholm

KC took a seat at the small table in the galley kitchen of the flat. It was downright tatty for this address in the posh Östermalm neighborhood. How did the agency find these places? Was there a top-secret registry of properties all over the world with one working tap and painted-over light switches?

Although she couldn't pretend there wasn't still a small part of her that was actively being bowled over by these surroundings. She'd never been to Europe. Never taken a transcontinental flight, much less on a top-secret military jet that traveled at near-hypersonic speed. She'd been to Stockholm in surveillance footage and on body cameras, had familiarized herself with significant traffic patterns and landmarks, but seeing it with her own eyes hit different.

Travel was one of many promises Dr. Brown had dangled in front of her that had not materialized.

"Hmm." Yardley was walking in a small circle, her hand over her mouth, her eyes focused on something that was definitely not in the room. She sat down on the foot of an iron-frame bed in the corner of the studio and whipped her dark hair into a ponytail with an elastic on her wrist.

She'd been like this since they landed. As soon as they arrived at the flat, KC had collapsed on top of the bed's lumpy mattress and dropped into a dreamless sleep. She woke up four hours later to the sight of Yardley still pacing.

On the Darkhorse, when KC had been caught off guard by Yardley's question about Dr. Brown's absence from Project Maple Leaf, Yardley had noticed. And KC had noticed her noticing.

No one else could have seen the way a single muscle at the inner corners of Yardley's eyes tensed, or known that muscle *only* tensed when Yardley was attempting to independently verify one of KC's claims, like, *Of course I wiped down the kitchen counters after I made myself an everything bagel.*

At this point, it was starting to seem downright laughable that KC had never guessed Yardley was the Unicorn.

She couldn't be sure when Yardley would strike. It set her nerves on edge, which meant she had devolved into old patterns whereby she attempted to distract Yardley from whatever bone she was gnawing.

"Is it bad I slept so long? I had no idea I was that tired." KC unscrewed the top of a water bottle she'd found in a well-stocked mini-kitchen area. "Ordinarily, I'd go for a run now, but obviously that's not a great idea, as much as I'd like to see the city firsthand instead of through a monitor." She took a big gulp of water.

"Mm." Yardley was tapping her knee, thinking.

"Weird that this safe house is an apartment in a regular building. I mean, I knew that's how it works sometimes, but it was still strange to pass by those kids downstairs."

Yardley nodded, crossing her legs. Still, terrifyingly, thinking.

"Maybe I *will* go for a run. Probably there's a disguise somewhere in here, right?"

"Third floorboard from the front window is hinged. Pull up. There should be a basic street disguise. Better than a ball cap and sunglasses, at any rate." Yardley crossed her legs the other way.

In a completely different time, place, and life, KC would have stalked her across the room, accused her of brattiness while possibly biting the cap of her shoulder, and a few hours would have passed that culminated in panting, dehydration, and lassitude, as well as full distraction.

She had no idea how to get the Unicorn's attention without detonating something.

"Or I could just wear this." KC grabbed a hooded sweatshirt from the enormous standalone wardrobe and pulled it on. She'd swapped her flight suit for joggers and a T-shirt before she fell asleep.

Yardley finally looked at her. "It says 'CIA' on the back in big yellow letters."

"Ironic, right? A spy would never. Perfect cover."

Now Yardley's expression had shifted, and her attention was fully on KC, but with scary flames in her bright blue eyes. She leaned back and crossed her ankles, holding up her body on forearms like she'd just taken direction from a fashion photographer. "Where would you go if you had to take cover near Stockholm?"

"Hålet," KC said without hesitation.

"The Hole?" Yardley tipped her head.

The effortless translation reminded KC that the Unicorn was a polyglot. That *Yardley* was a polyglot.

Which, sure. Yardley could accurately and delightfully mimic anyone. But KC had believed that was an artifact of her having survived a childhood without siblings and with an opinionated mother who obviously adored her but absolutely did not under-stand her. Maybe childhood was where Yardley's facility with languages had begun, but clearly there was a great deal more to it than that.

There had been so much more to everything.

It made KC feel hopeless not to be able to turn the clock back and claim the right to a do-over, knowing what they knew now. She wasn't sure what would happen if they could, but she didn't think they'd end up like this—suspicious and guarded, afraid of fucking up and getting hurt worse than they already were.

She forced herself to pay attention. The Unicorn was mid-interrogation. One wrong step, and KC could find herself trapped.

"Yeah, the Hole. Hålet. On the E18. Eskilstuna. It looks like every other internet café near a medium-traffic train station, but it's not. Or so I've heard."

"Where?" Sometime while KC was sleeping, Yardley had changed into a black sweatshirt with a blue-and-yellow-striped heart to represent the Swedish flag, which she must have found in the wardrobe. With the ponytail, she looked like any one of the Swedish millennials they'd seen on the street, walking into a shop or pushing a pram.

"Where have I heard? In the backroom forums, forever. I think I first learned about it when I was fourteen."

"And it's still there." Yardley sat up.

"It still generates a lot of chatter. Questions. Requests. Has its own servers."

"Why would you go there? If you needed to get gone, it sounds like too many of you know about it. You'd be made instantly."

"It's hacker Switzerland. Or, like, a church. You know, sanctuary. It's always been that way. You don't sell anyone out who's in the Hole. It's never been compromised in that way."

"But if you walk out the doors?"

"You're fair game, I would imagine. But, look. The movies make it seem like hackers are either very glamorous or constantly running through urban streets wearing moto jackets. Really, we're what you've seen in my office—regular dorks in Patagonia fleece complaining that their new ergonomic setup isn't hitting while we look up how to code something on YouTube. If someone burst into the Hole sweating through their clothes, looking over their shoulder, and furiously making copies of a floppy disk while muttering, my guess is that whoever runs the place would call a doctor, not Interpol."

Yardley smiled. "There's a lot out here in the field the movies are missing out on, actually, that would make for great tension and visuals."

It took a second for KC to understand what she meant.

Peril. That was what she meant.

"I think that's supposed to be a joke," KC said, "except it makes clear how often you haven't been safe when I had no fucking idea, because I thought you were at a Courtyard Marriott in Columbus, Ohio."

She wouldn't have said that, and certainly not in such a scathing tone, if it weren't for the fact that her palms had broken out in pins and needles, and her stomach was churning in the familiar way it did when she felt especially anxious.

"And I thought you were underestimating your potential," Yardley bit back, "making social-media-integrated shopping carts and branding packages. But it turns out you were breaking into Russian server farms."

The return serve hit harder than it should have. *Wasting her potential.*

KC *couldn't* fight with Yardley, feeling all the terror she'd missed out on in the years they'd spent lying to each other, *and* worry about figuring out a way to locate Kris Flynn before something awful KC had made ruined the world, all while she kept Dr. Brown's secret even from the president and lacked any certainty she was doing the right thing. She couldn't feel this many feelings at once and survive.

"We can't do this here," she croaked. "We just have to get through the mission."

Yardley's full mouth had a way of getting so small, it nearly disappeared. "Absolutely, that is the way to go if you'd like to die in the field. Stuff your feelings down, ignore your instincts, don't—super duper *don't*—deal with your shit, and watch it get both of us killed."

"Jesus Christ, Yardley."

"*Well.*" She put her hands on her hips. "How's this? You said back at Langley that you don't know how to talk to me, that maybe you never did, and then we're going Mach 5 and you're telling me things you never told me in three years together, even when you could have. So here's a truth I never told you, KC. I didn't know a nerdy woman in a Patagonia fleece who's a WordPress jockey, gamer, and dreamed of illustrating for *Magic: The Gathering*. Maybe that's your cover, but closer to the real truth—even more the truth than the one where you're a spy—is a woman who forgets to eat, sits in front of her computer all day long, and runs for miles and miles and miles until she collapses into bed without talking about any feelings she has at all. That is the KC Nolan I know."

KC gripped her elbows, hard, and swallowed. "You're not being fair."

"No. I'm not! But it doesn't make anything I said less true. In fact, it makes it more true. I'm certain the agency has been waiting to see if you'd ever demand something. That's the only way you get out of the basement. I've been waiting for you to demand something. I've been waiting for you to demand *me*."

KC had never figured out what to do when she got punched besides punch back harder. "Let's talk about that, Yardley. How exactly was I supposed to demand your attention when I couldn't even get you to answer a text until the end of the business day? It got so that every time I heard the squeak of that one wheel on your carry-on bag, I felt sick. And you know what? I don't even think it was ever just about the agency! When I had you, I didn't really have you. You always want to get together with friends, go to the bookstore, there's something you read about we need to see at the Smithsonian, you're shopping for a contractor to redo our bedroom. It's like a simple conversation with me isn't enough!"

"Is that what you think?" Yardley put her hand over her chest, got up, and sat down hard on the chair next to KC's. She started shaking her head. "That's not it, it's not. I've had so much I want to . . . that I just *want*. For us. I wanted you to design a monogram of our initials so we can decorate every room in the house with it. I dreamed I'd take you to a Whitmer family reunion, which is an experience no one should have, they are on the Gulf Coast in high summer and they always reserve blocks of rooms in hotels known for their cockroaches. If anything wasn't enough, it was *us*. I have been obsessed with work, I have, because I didn't think there was anything else I had *permission* to be obsessed with. I've been hurting. *Yearning*, KC."

That was when she had to turn away, her hands gripping the edge of the table, because she couldn't think of anything to say in response.

She'd thought she knew why Yardley smiled when they caught each other's attention at the picnic. Why they'd gone home together. Why their bodies fit against each other so perfectly, why kissing Yardley felt so right that KC had been brave enough, finally, after Yardley invited her to North Carolina to meet her whole family, to ask her to move in.

She'd thought they *fit*. She'd thought they were fated. That it was right. They were made for each other.

She'd honestly believed that if she could just tell Yardley the truth about everything, it would fix what was wrong, and they could have that feeling back from their very first hours together, before KC started to lie and fucked it all up.

"Eleven hundred ninety-nine days," Yardley said into the silence.

KC made herself turn to look at Yardley. Her eyes were tired. "What?"

"Eleven hundred ninety-nine days. I went to that wedding. At the Ritz-Carlton." She glanced at KC. "The bride said how many days it had been since she met the groom, how it was the only number that mattered. It's been eleven hundred ninety-nine days since I met you. I thought I'd do anything for another eleven hundred ninety-nine. For all of them. But I never could figure out if it was what you wanted, KC. If what you ever wanted was me."

Eleven hundred ninety-nine days. That was how long she'd had with Yardley. That was as long as she'd ever have her. Putting a number to it made KC feel unruly, smothered by a fate that was choking the breath out of her while she kicked and screamed in a futile struggle. "I was going to fix it," she said bitterly.

"Excuse me, ma'am, what?" Yardley crossed her arms.

"I was going to fix it! I needed to get through Maple Leaf and then resign, or get reassigned to something completely unclassified, because I wanted things, too! Maybe not a monogram in every room, and the reunion sounds awful, but everything else. I did what I *could* do. I asked you to move in, even though that was the worst idea and didn't change anything, and the agency hated it, obviously."

"That was the worst idea." Yardley nodded, her jaw tight. "The worst idea. The watch and that key and the speech at my mama's house? The *worst* idea."

"That's not what I meant! I meant because of this." KC whipped her hand back and forth between them, then around the apartment. "The spy thing! Of course I wanted to move in with you, it's just that it made everything more complicated."

"Complicated?" Yardley lifted up her chin. This meant KC was in danger, but she didn't care. She didn't have Yardley. She was still embroiled in the middle of Maple Leaf and could be tossed into one of the CIA's dark holes anytime with no one to talk to but an interrogator named Bradley who had no emotional regulation. What did she have left to care about?

Yardley crossed her arms with an audible huff that was more like a suppressed scream. "*Complicated.*"

Causing an ear-splitting screech, KC scooted her chair toward Yardley and leaned forward into her face. She could smell her skin, her French lavender soap, and it was outrageous for Yardley's smell to be so arousingly familiar, still, in the middle of this mess, thousands of miles from home, after they'd lost everything. KC gripped the arms of Yardley's chair. "I said what I said," she bit out. "Sometimes things are complicated. Sometimes there isn't a debutante's stack of silk pillows to fall back on. Sometimes things are hard. Sometimes you're getting six different directions from twelve different sources and no time to think. Sometimes you're surprised your chest hasn't split open with a bloody squelch from all the secrets you're stuffing in it. But none of that has to mean I didn't want to give you a fucking watch and a key! For fuck's sake. That was the only thing I'd been sure of for a long goddamned time."

She was *right there*. It made KC furious to be stonewalled and disheartened when Yardley Whitmer was right there, close enough to touch, close enough that KC could count every single one of her ridiculous dark, thick eyelashes against the clear sapphire blue of eyes that KC had spent nearly a thousand days memorizing. They'd given up, and the agency had screwed them over, and the actual fucking president had made it so KC had to be here, where she could almost *see* the temperature of the place under Yardley's jaw where it curved into her neck, how warm it always was against her lips, then sanded with goosebumps as she would kiss back up to her mouth.

"*Dang* it," Yardley said, but so softly, it meant something entirely different.

KC hit the end of her rope and let go. There wasn't anything to do but skip the apology on the tip of her tongue and whatever else she'd spent three years failing to say in favor of grabbing two handfuls of Swedish sweatshirt.

Yardley hooked her hand into the collar of KC's hoodie and yanked, and it was all the permission KC needed to start in the middle.

They both knew how good the middle was.

She pulled up Yardley's shirt just as Yardley slid her arms out of it, and KC grabbed Yardley's waistband to drag her to the wool rug so it was easier for Yardley to slide her hand straight down the front of KC's joggers.

Her fingers were fast and rough and speedily slick where she found KC ready, lifting her hips to ease the way. "Fuck." KC tipped her head back as Yardley's fingers, her palm, found just the right place at the same time she bit KC's neck. Had she been this hot and wet the whole time they were fighting? Were they fighting or saying good-bye?

KC didn't know, but whatever this was, she was taking it. She needed it.

Yardley shoved up the hem of KC's sweatshirt and applied her tongue to KC's aching nipple while she pushed two fingers up and down alongside KC's clit, building a rhythm that forced KC's hips to plead for just a little bit more than she was getting. More pressure. More speed. More. And when Yardley closed her teeth around KC's nipple and pushed her wicked fingers a fraction harder, KC knew, she *knew*, that this was penultimate to a move between her legs that would force her up and over into a fast, furious orgasm that would fist her hands and cord her neck and barely take the edge off. But if they were going to bad-idea-sex their way out of this fight, she was determined to wring more than thirty seconds of pleasure from it.

She hooked her leg over Yardley's and rose up over her, pushing her thigh between hers, caging her with her forearms, looking into her eyes.

This gorgeous, imperious, singular woman. KC had never, ever known what to do with her, but she sure as fuck knew how to make her come.

She pressed hard with her thigh where Yardley was hot, damp through her jeans, and watched Yardley's eyes close as she bit down on her lower lip.

KC freed that lip with her thumb. "You're not going to look at me?"

Yardley's mouth came open, her hips lifting in a grinding movement so explicit, it made the seam of KC's joggers slick over her clit where Yardley's knee was applying constant, exquisite pressure. The hit of that pressure forced a deep pulse through her clit and sent her right to the edge, and they both made a noise she knew meant that one hot, open kiss would put them out of their agonizing, fucking perfect misery.

"Please," Yardley begged against KC's mouth, and KC didn't know what would make her hesitate on this precipice, but she did.

She was.

She wanted to kiss Yardley more than anything—her entire body was enraged with her that they weren't kissing right now—but a part of KC that had kept quiet since she and Yardley hit the floor had picked this moment to remind her of all the times, when she and Yardley had been together like this, they'd said how much they loved each other.

That wasn't what this was.

This wasn't anything they'd ever done. It felt like it was, her body knew how to move as though it was, but her heart was hitching, aching, and, worse, the corners of her eyes had started to burn.

Then, three pounding knocks rang against a door no one in Sweden was supposed to know was there.

No one anywhere.

CHAPTER NINE

KC pulled up to all fours, her blood gone cold in an instant. Yardley rolled silently across the floor and leapt up to press herself flat against the wall to the side of the entryway. She signaled to KC to move out of the path of the door, and KC crab-stepped over, fear and confusion so crowded in her body that she could taste blood at the back of her throat.

Yardley caught KC's eye and signaled confidently with a hand. *Stay back, say nothing, but be ready to fight.*

"Vem är det?" Yardley sounded like a harassed Swedish mother of three trying to change a diaper while soothing a toddler, but not remotely suspicious. Not afraid or even concerned. "Om du har mitt paket, lämna det vid dörren tack!"

Everything went quiet.

Yardley reached up and pulled a few locks of hair from her ponytail, scrubbed her hands across her face, and, to KC's dismay, undid the bolt and chain on the door and opened it a crack. "Jag försöker få bebisen att somna, kan du komma tillbaka senare?"

"Sorry, I thought—" KC heard a woman's voice, a little husky, neither old nor young. British?

She tried to very silently breathe so she wouldn't pass out.

"You've got the wrong flat?" Yardley replied in accented English.

Then silence again. KC straightened to her full height as everything she'd ever been trained to do in hand-to-hand without a weapon dropped like a warm blanket over her body.

Yardley would not get hurt. She would not. There had been times she might have, times she'd been within a hair of losing her life for her country that KC hadn't known about, but *this* time KC had a say in it, and it was not fucking happening. She did not run forty goddamned miles a week and work on gains in her stupid gym to let some morally bankrupt bottom feeder so much as leave a bruise on Yardley's body.

KC eyed a sturdy table opposite Yardley. She could be on it and sting from above in seconds.

"Look, I'm here to talk to, um, KC Nolan?"

Oh, god. Not a British accent. *Irish.*

Unless KC was very much mistaken, Kris Flynn was at the door of their top-secret safe-house apartment.

"I believe I've got the right place?" the woman said. "I doubt someone else has been following me halfway across the world and breaking into my hotel rooms."

Yardley opened the door a little wider and leaned against the frame, crossing her arms. "Flynn, I presume?" She'd dropped the accent.

"Yeah." The woman sounded relieved.

Yardley turned her head to look back to KC. "Your friend's here." She pulled open the door wider, and KC scanned to the woman's right and left first, unconvinced she'd come alone. But there was no one but her.

Kris Flynn was a heart-faced woman about her age with short, thick blond braids under a stocking cap. She wore a man's coat. The arms were too long, but the coat wasn't big enough for her to fasten around an obvious baby bump.

Kris clocked her standing behind Yardley and grinned. "KC, at long last." She pulled off her hat while Yardley shut and bolted the door behind her. "Us keyboard jockeys are usually bringing up the rear, aren't we?"

When she wiggled out of her coat, it was easy to see that Kris hadn't come here from a good meal, warm bed, and stroll through a rose garden. The circles under her eyes were deep, her sweater had a rip at the shoulder, and there was mud on the hems of her jeans.

KC forced herself to push what Kris had interrupted into her darkest periphery. This was the last moment in her life she needed to be flooded with hormones and reactionary behavior. She'd hoped to get to Kris first. There had been an undefined plan to beat Yardley at her own game and find out what Kris knew before anyone else did. In the best-case scenario, generated while she pretended to nap on the Darkhorse, KC had imagined swearing Kris to secrecy and convincing her to cooperate with the project of decommissioning the weapon. Then, later, she could report to Dr. Brown that all was well. Problem solved.

But Kris had found them first. KC had not prepared for that possibility, and so she was utterly fucked.

Given that she had no idea what she was doing on this mission, it didn't surprise her. What did surprise her was that, beneath her fear and apprehension, KC was glad to see Kris.

She'd always wanted to meet her.

"Sit down." Yardley pulled out one of the chairs. "And you won't mind if I—" She held up a tiny scanner that checked for digital devices and signals.

Kris held out her arms. "Go for it. Don't have so much as a mobile."

When she'd completed the scan, Yardley put the device back in her pocket and nodded at KC. "She's clean."

"But how are you here?" KC shook her head. "Our driver took evasive maneuvers and triple-checked for a tail. This apartment doesn't exist. You disappeared off the street an ocean away from here two days ago."

"I've got a few friends yet." Kris shrugged. "Long story short? I recognized your work in Toronto, and I knew you were with the CIA."

KC's heart stilled. What work had Kris recognized?

"It's a right mess, I'll admit." Kris yawned. "I tried to be a good girl, but enough didn't add up, and I missed Declan."

"Declan?" KC's spinning brain couldn't place the name.

"Baby daddy. Dublin," Yardley supplied.

"Cor! Jesus. We've been together for six years. I'm not doing this with any dickhead!" Kris pointed at her belly. Then her eyes filled with tears. "And god, don't I miss him. He likely thinks I took off on him. I'd been such an absolute bloody knob lately. Hormones. He was taking good care of me, making me feel beautiful. Fixing up the nursery. And here I am talking to you lot, and it's cold as fuck here, and I don't have my good coat. I got this out of a charity box." She touched the sleeve of the coat she'd taken off and put in her lap. "I don't have anything, actually, thanks to that puffed-up wanker, Devon, and this ridiculous mess. I've missed two appointments, you know that? What if this baby's growing a second head? I won't know. I'll be in some international prison with a two-headed baby in my lap."

KC laughed. She couldn't help it. The real-in-person Kris sounded so altogether like *Kris*.

"Let me get you something to eat," Yardley offered. "This flat is terrible, but there's nice food."

"And a cuppa?" Kris asked. "Sweet and light, please."

"Sure thing." Yardley went to the mini fridge in the corner that had a basket and a kettle perched on a board on top. She raised her eyebrows at KC, pointing the spoon she held at Kris.

There was something way, way too *attentive* about Yardley's whole demeanor. It was terrifying. How many bad guys had picked up on this vibe before the Unicorn crushed them under her heel?

Yardley lifted her eyebrows higher and double pointed at Kris with the spoon.

Right. Time to interrogate their potential asset. In front of Officer Whitmer, superspy.

"Could you start from the beginning?" Yardley continued to make tea with her hands while, with everything else, she watched KC.

Maybe she should've been watching Flynn, but if an obviously pregnant woman without identification, money, or even a good coat had found a CIA safe house with two spies in it, then Flynn—no matter what she'd done or what side she was on—would be working for the agency shortly, at least for the duration of this mission.

Nothing to be concerned about there. Yardley was a lot more keen to find out what information Flynn's presence would extract from KC.

"Did I interrupt something?" Flynn twisted around to look at Yardley. "I'm feeling like there's an undercurrent."

Yardley turned her attention to pouring hot water over the tea bag and let herself smile, even as the question made her throat tighten with navy-blue sadness. She could still see a mark on KC's neck where she must have bitten her. She was going to have to put her unabated horniness for her ex-girlfriend to work in the service of sharpening her ability to observe her.

All's fair.

"Why?" KC asked. "What makes you think you interrupted anything?"

Yardley was impressed with KC's tone. It was *almost* uninterested in Kris's answer. If Yardley hadn't spent the last months scrutinizing every shift in her expression and all of her spare energy trying to figure out how to save them, she might have believed KC wasn't freaked out.

Flynn showing up here was obviously what had her freaked out the most. Freaked out on a personal level, if Yardley was reading her right—and not because Kris shouldn't have been able to find them. It gave Yardley more evidence there was something about KC's involvement with Project Maple Leaf that she didn't know.

She *would* know it, but she didn't know it yet.

It was a good problem to keep at the center so that the yawning pit of denial and grief currently squatting in the spot where her heart used to be didn't swamp her focus.

"I thought I heard you arguing as I came up the stairs," Flynn said. "It sounded personal. And there's something in the air." She waved her hand around. "I've been a lot more sensitive lately because of the baby."

"We're colleagues," KC said, like she was holding ice in her mouth.

Ha! No. Not the best way to win the trust of a critical asset. "We broke up," Yardley said. She plucked a bright red packet of Ballerina biscuits from a basket near the kettle, selected a banana, and carried them to Kris Flynn.

Flynn accepted the snack, meeting Yardley's eyes. The steady intelligence in her gaze confirmed she was not a woman to underestimate.

Yardley enjoyed meeting people like this on a mission. Regardless of what side they were on, they became part of a network of wildly unusual and smart people who were all very useful to each other when it came to balancing the humors of the world.

"Colleagues is how I met Declan," Flynn said. "We had cubes right next to each other in the same firm. He specializes in software architecture. Extremely excellent work. He was absolutely dead hot, but I couldn't look because Aisling, my assistant, said he had a girlfriend. But then I found out Aisling only wanted a crack at him herself." Flynn pointed a biscuit at KC. "That's when I moved in, or I would've, but Declan moved first. Shagged me in the unisex."

"Oh my god." KC shot Kris the small, crooked smile that Yardley thought of as her warmup smile. It meant she was starting to like someone, or find a conversation too tempting to resist participating in, even as she held herself in reserve.

It made Yardley wonder what kind of mentor Dr. Brown had been to KC, if his intercession in her life meant she'd ended up with a career at the agency but no Kris Flynn. No one close.

And she'd struggled to let Yardley close.

Flynn was smiling back at KC. "It wasn't the story I told my da, for sure, but Declan and I haven't been able to keep our hands off each other since, so it wasn't just an impulse. He'd been hint-ing he might propose, and I'd had fantasies of a wedding before baby comes. Don't know whether that will happen now, do I?" Flynn shook her head. "So what's the trouble with you two, exactly? Don't say there isn't chemistry. That's plain."

KC coughed, her hand covering her mouth to conceal what Yardley was certain would have been a bark of surprised laughter.

"You two not permitted? Are you fighting your attraction while saving the world? Tell me, I'm tired and pregnant."

Yardley carried the steaming mug of tea to Flynn, who immediately took a long drink. "That's perf, thank you."

"We just found out we both work for the agency." Yardley heard the caution in KC's voice as she confessed this to Kris. "After being together three years, the last one after she moved in with me. But, like she said, we broke up. Weeks ago. And again yesterday."

"Oh, I've been there, I have," Kris said. "Though your situation is a bit like Mrs. and Mrs. Spy. Well, don't stop now, I'll be needing the whole tale. I already know your secret names. Heard you calling her Yardley from the corridor."

Yardley retrieved a chair from next to the wardrobe and sat down with the two women.

"Can I have a cup of tea, too?" KC asked.

It was a bold question. One of Yardley's little love bids had always been bringing a drink or a tea to KC. Had KC asked it out of habit or to test her feelings?

Clearly, she was going to spend this whole mission perseverating on everything non-mission-related that KC did like she was a seventh grader nursing a crush on her lab partner.

"Chamomile?" she asked.

"Please."

KC turned back to Flynn.

Yardley almost missed the tell—one long second of meaningful eye contact shared between Flynn and KC, after which the tension in KC's shoulders eased by a degree.

Whatever secret KC was hiding, Flynn had just taken up part of its burden.

Wow. She hadn't reckoned that KC would send her for the tea in order to telegraph a message to Flynn unobserved. Project Maple Leaf was finally getting interesting.

And very dangerous for her heart.

"I don't think we have the time it would take to get into Yardley and my story right now, unfortunately. Or fortunately?" She smiled. "I decrypted the data on the USB in your hotel safe, which led us to Mirabel. But we need to hear the story from your perspective."

Flynn blew out an exhale. "You know I was near yanked out of my office in Dublin."

"When was this?"

"End of August, the twenty-sixth. You lot turn up, your mister suit-and-tie, who told me that I had to go with him or be arrested and detained by the U.S. government for my role in an act of terrorism from our Daisy Duke days. He had an arrest warrant and an ID, the kind in a little black leather case."

KC didn't react. Yardley, now desperate to hear the rest of this story, was not about to interrupt.

"I wasn't permitted to go home," Kris said. "He took me in a car to an airfield. All of my personal belongings were confiscated in a hangar except for what I'd grabbed and shoved into my bra before he made me leave my office. Mirabel was there, too."

"Who was the agent?" KC leaned forward. Likewise, Flynn

had put all of her attention on KC. They were friends again. Friends trying to figure something out.

"Don't I wish I knew? Can't tell the men in black apart, and he only flashed that ID at me for a second. In any event, I didn't see him again after Mirabel took me to that hotel and told me I had to help him with a job or they'd go after my Declan. So of course I start questioning if it's really the CIA who's got me. You lot don't put Irish nationals in a Canadian hotel, do you, and threaten to hurt the people we love?"

"No," KC said.

"It depends," Yardley murmured.

KC and Kris looked toward the kitchenette.

"Sorry. Don't mind me. But in this case, no, I don't think it's the CIA." Not because the agency had scruples, but because Flynn had been picked up so soon after the demonstration in Toronto. Even the Sisters hadn't known much yet, and what they knew, they weren't sharing. The CIA hadn't had enough intel to act on. If they had, Yardley would've been briefed. Probably.

"What did Mirabel want you to do for him?" KC asked.

The kettle clicked off, and Yardley let her attention split as she poured hot water and stirred honey into the warm mug on the countertop. Part of her listened to what quickly became a mind-numbingly technical conversation between Flynn and KC, but the part that made her the Unicorn—that kept her alive and two steps ahead—was more interested in the big picture.

Someone claiming to be CIA had come for Kris Flynn right after the weapon's demonstration in Toronto, taking her into custody ostensibly for the same long-ago hack into the EPA that brought KC into the agency. According to the story Flynn was telling KC, she'd escaped her kidnappers, been recaptured, and escaped again before finding her way to this CIA safe house. Flynn did verify that she'd been the one who sent the SOS message the CIA intercepted—via a smart thermostat, not a toaster oven—but she'd been put on a plane shortly thereafter, and nothing came of it.

There was no reason to assume Flynn hadn't been followed here, or sent by Mirabel or another actor close to the device. No reason to take her story at face value.

Nonetheless, Yardley's instinct was to believe her.

"Could you tell who made it?" KC asked.

Flynn wiggled another biscuit out of the packet Yardley had given her and took a bite before she answered. The hesitation was so obvious that Yardley couldn't be sure it wasn't an act.

"A ghost, looked like to me."

Flynn and KC held eye contact as KC tried to keep any expression off her face. But Flynn wasn't a spy, so she didn't know how to give KC what was obviously a shared codeword without inflection.

A ghost. Who or what was the ghost?

"Did you rebuild it?" Yardley carried the chamomile over and dragged her chair close to KC's. When she sat, KC's auburn eyelashes fluttered, and she looked briefly down.

Composing herself.

"I tried to refuse," Kris said. "That was when they showed me my last ultrasound picture, which Declan had pinned up in his study. They'd been in our home. They wouldn't tell me if Declan was all right. So I did what they asked, but I also tried to find out everything else I could to save myself, the baby, and Declan."

"That's what you had in the safe," KC said. "All the information you could find about the project and who was involved."

"It is." Kris stretched her arms over her head. "Not difficult to track down, to be honest. More difficult to track down who I could trust to report it to."

"Dang." Yardley whistled. "I have to give it to a girl who's thinking ahead."

Flynn shifted in her chair to look at her. "Not just about me anymore, is it?" She stood up and lifted up her shirt, where there was a black band wrapped around her belly. Before KC could reach Kris, Yardley had her restrained from behind.

"Take it off her." Yardley directed this to KC.

But she could already tell it wasn't necessary. Flynn was compliant, and she didn't have a gun or a bomb, which Yardley's scan would've picked up anyway. It was a passport belt, the cheapest kind, like you'd get at any souvenir shop. KC gently unbuckled it and unzipped the pocket as Yardley released Flynn's arms and helped her back to the seat.

A sage green thirty-terabyte micro hard drive gently clacked into KC's palm.

"How didn't I catch that with the scanner?" Yardley sat back down.

Flynn's expression made it clear that she didn't think too highly of Yardley's technical prowess. "It has a silencer, doesn't it? Like how noise-canceling headphones work because they're actually making sounds that exert silencing pressure on your ears. This emits a signal that makes it invisible to devices looking for a signal."

KC rubbed her thumb over the smooth plastic. "If it's what I think it is, how do you have it?"

"Better question," Yardley said. "Where, exactly, have you most recently come from, and how many people are looking for you?"

"That's two questions." Flynn took a long drink of tea. "I escaped a few hours ago from a fancy row house. My guess it's a place Mirabel has use of, not where he lives. I was able to upload a signal to my friend using the chip in the silencer case. It was only Morse code, but they got it. The electronic lock on my door released a few minutes later, and I got a lift directly to the Hole. My friend has a friend who's obsessed with planes. They've got drones with telephoto lenses filming at Bromma, the Air Target base, and Arlanda. Your Hermeus came in this morning. This drone fella had never seen a plane like that, so it's a bit of a flap for him. Two women get in a car, and he follows with his robot. I knocked on four doors before I found you."

Kris pulled another biscuit out of the packet and ate it in two bites with the rest of her tea.

Yardley wondered if, when this was all over, Kris would consider relocating to the States to take a job at the CIA.

"What's on the drive?" KC asked.

"The whole wheel of cheese. But it's a copy. Mirabel doesn't know I have it, but he knows what *he* has, which is the new and improved version of the weapon he wanted. If I'd had more time, I could've miscoded it to do nothing more than turn off the freezers in every Aldi in Europe, but the best I could do is make sure you lot can take a look and see what you're dealing with."

"And it's only on two drives—this one and the one Devon has?"

"Correct. Cleaned up behind me."

Yardley's proximity to KC was doing what she'd hoped it would. KC couldn't stay cool knowing Yardley was monitoring her reactions. Two hot pink stripes had emerged on her cheekbones, indicating high emotion—relief? fear?—in response to Flynn's news.

"You're sure that everything is on these drives, this one and Devon's?" KC asked. "The code wasn't captured when it was deployed in Toronto? Or at the time you retrieved it?"

"I told you, I cleaned up." Flynn gestured at the drive in KC's hand. "That and its twin are it. And here's something that may provide a little breathing room. I also managed a teeny, tiny failsafe, just in case someone uses it before you get to them. I tried out what Simsenshi came up with a couple of years ago. It was theoretical. Now it's not."

"The Fuse," KC said with a nod. "That would mean you could upload this weapon into any infrastructure or machine, and it would burn the evidence of itself up right behind it. If Mirabel did use it, it might be bad, but it wouldn't be bad again and again. Do I have that right?"

"Works a treat," Flynn said. "No notes."

KC finally looked at Yardley, her cheeks scarlet. "We can kill it. We get that other drive, dump them both in the Söderström or burn them in a fire, and it's over. Even if Mirabel uses it before we can do that, the damage is contained to the city it's deployed in. Bad, but not an ongoing threat. And then, as long as we keep this one safe or destroy it, it's over. For good."

Yardley held KC's gaze as a thought sank its teeth into her brain.

How had Mirabel known to grab Flynn, of all the code jockeys in the world, to find and reassemble the weapon?

This weapon was absolutely connected to KC. Maybe KC had been involved in Toronto, maybe KC and Flynn had never stopped working together, maybe it was only that a bad actor knew enough about KC and Flynn's connection from back in the day to exploit it. But Flynn had never been a coincidence, and even the president of the United States was surprised to learn that KC knew her, despite KC's claim that Flynn's name was in her files from the EPA hack.

This mission was finally cooking with gas. All it had taken was unraveling the massive lie that Yardley and the love of her life had been telling each other and breaking up almost three times. Didn't feel like a fair trade.

"I vote for getting into Mirabel's place and finding the thing," Yardley said in the doomed silence that had settled over the three of them. "Before someone else does."

KC let out a long breath. "Yeah."

"That sounds impossible." Kris bit into her banana. "Best of luck there."

"Easy." Yardley smiled at the woman next to her—complex, secretive, brilliant, in-over-her-head KC. "No one else has Tabasco."

CHAPTER TEN

Street corner, Norrmalm, Stockholm

In the wee morning hours, Yardley pulled her stocking cap down over her ears and adjusted her round, dark-framed eyeglasses, stomping her feet against the cold.

She'd done her best impression of a cat burglar when she snuck out of the dark safe house, leaving KC asleep in the same room with the asset it was Yardley's shift to guard—all so she could make a phone call over an unsecured international long-distance line.

She listened to the long series of hums and clicks from the black receiver pressed against her ear. She'd found it dangling from the round, red, coin-operated housing of what was probably the last functioning Swedish pay phone, but thankfully it still worked.

Yardley had used this phone before, tucked around the corner from one of the newer, automated twenty-four-hour convenience stores that were popping up everywhere.

When the call connected, her heart grew warm at the familiar voice. "I was just getting ready to sit myself down with a sweet tea, Miss Yardley, so it's a good moment for a yak."

It was very late in North Carolina, but Yardley hadn't been worried about waking up her nan, who was a night owl and liked to sit outside in the dark with a glass of tea, taking the air.

"Nan." Yardley breathed out tension she hadn't known she'd been holding. "I can't talk too long."

Her nan laughed. It was a laugh that could have just as easily come from an eighteen-year-old debutante as from a tiny senior lady—feminine, musical, and schooled, but warm enough to make anyone smile. "Well, I don't imagine you can. You're not dodging gunfire right now or hanging from a wire somewhere?"

"No, ma'am." Yet Yardley could not claim to be exercising immaculate judgment.

She didn't think the pay phone was bugged, any more than she thought a pregnant woman who was wanted by multiple international interests but had deliberately sought out both KC and the CIA was likely to take off, but she couldn't be sure.

What Yardley *was* sure of was that she didn't have a prayer of working through the mess in her head without help. She'd told KC it was dangerous to bottle up her feelings on a mission, and she'd felt that same danger building inside her all through yesterday afternoon as they'd pumped an exhausted Kris Flynn for every scrap of useful information. By nightfall, Yardley had made up her mind to call her nan for a private talk at the earliest opportunity—even if she had to make one.

"Well, get to it, buttercup."

"KC," she said, squeezing the receiver.

"Is a peach. Smart, makes a nice income, treats you right, doesn't annoy me, can deal with your mama."

"Yes." Yardley bit her lip and poked at the coin slot.

"What's got you twisted up? You're going to have to tighten your girdle and come out with it."

Yardley had never told her nan she and KC were having trouble, much less that they'd reached the end of their road. Telling

Nan something was what made it real. "I found out we're in the same line of work."

"Well. You didn't know that?"

Yardley forced herself to look up, survey the area, and count to five. She couldn't have said for sure what she was feeling—a mix of irritation, anger, and something deeper than both. Shame, probably. It was usually shame when she hated what she felt but didn't know what to call it. "Nan, I had no idea."

"You met this woman at a picnic practically in the backyard of Langley. She once visited with my Brazilian gardener in his native Portuguese. She's hardly taller than me, but she could lift your granddaddy over her head if she wanted to. You really thought she made websites?"

Yardley tightened her mouth, feeling the first blast of resistance to being wrong. "I trusted her and believed she was who she told me."

"Did you? Then what part of what she told you did you believe, what came out of her mouth or what has been coming from her, from KC, all this time? Her focus and her competence, her sense of service, the way she can put together a whole library of information as pretty as one of those college-educated preachers? Have you seen that, or have you been too damn busy saving the world in fancy outfits?"

"Well, *you* didn't know that granddaddy—"

"Yardley Lauren Bailey Whitmer the Third. You weren't raised to sass at me like that."

"I'm sorry, ma'am." Yardley squeezed the receiver. Her throat had begun to ache. "I only meant when we love someone, we don't question what they tell us."

"Let me tell you something, then. I actually don't think I *did* love your granddaddy like I should have, nor did I muster up the curiosity and interest I should have felt about the man I married. I have regrets. I wasted time. I centered myself so much, buttercup, that I couldn't see past my own fiction that he must be stepping out on me when he was gone like he was. That's because I was hurt."

"Because granddaddy never should have lied to you," Yardley said. "He should have trusted you."

"Not my point," her nan said briskly. "Hormones and infatuation got me to the altar, but what should have deepened and mellowed into love got stuck on fear. And let me tell you, did I let it fester. By the time he did tell me about himself, what my feelings had deepened into was anger. I thought I had never been so angry at another human being in my life. It took me a long time to understand I was angry at myself."

"He kept so much from you, though," Yardley said, a few tears leaking now. She'd been telling this story—to herself, to Atlas, to KC—but she hadn't been telling it right. "You can't put that completely on you."

"No." Nan laughed. "I can't. But I can't tell you his side of the story and his regrets. That's for him to say. I can tell you that man loved his work and might've had a talk with his supervisors about my level of classification. It wasn't unheard of for a wife to understand more than I did, even then. But, my love, can't you see how a man like your granddaddy, who had so much to offer, wouldn't have given more and more of his big heart and his big love to his work if it wasn't true that I wasn't making any space for him to give it to me? His commitment and heart had to go somewhere. I made myself someplace he couldn't get to."

Oh, shit. Yardley's diaphragm jerked hard, pushing the breath

out of her body as she thought of KC with one hand on her ergonomic mouse, a bank of monitors lit up bright in front of her
while Yardley wheeled her suitcase out the door.

She'd done that. She'd made herself someplace KC couldn't
get to. Her friends. Her book club. Her business trips. Her secrets.

It's like a simple conversation with me isn't enough.

She slumped against the side of the payphone enclosure, tracing a path down the enameled red metal with one fingertip. "I
have messed things up but good."

"I bet. More important, what are you going to do about it?"

"What did you and Granddaddy do? It would be helpful if
you could give it to me in an easy-to-remember saying. You know,
one of those ones with an animal and a rhyme in it."

"*Yardley.*"

"I'm desperate, Nan." Yardley felt the truth, the real truth,
start to crack out of her chest the way it always did when she
talked to Nan. There was a reason her grandmother was the person she had come out to in middle school, who knew she was
the Unicorn, and who was the first one Yardley called when her
private school headmaster threatened to suspend her for making
out with Amy Truebill backstage during the school's production
of *The Crucible*. Because her nan had always made space for her,
listened to and understood her, and that meant that whatever
truths Yardley had been hiding from herself, they came bursting
out of her when they spoke.

"She's it for me," Yardley said in a rush. "And I didn't tell you,
but we've fought, and then we broke up, and then did that again
after we knew we were both spies, and right now, well, what I can
say is that we're not in a kiss-and-make-up kind of circumstance."
Yardley forced herself to scan the street for irregularities or a tail

to rule out the possibility of being killed in a phone booth while choking out a litany of stupid mistakes to her nan. "But I don't want to feel like this even one more minute, even if it's also true that I'm not sure about the precise, let's say, entanglements that KC may have in this mission."

It made her feel better to confess this. If it had been true that KC was a double agent, and Yardley had felt that truth inside her heart, she definitely would have said so to Nan. But she didn't feel compelled to tell about her secret mission to figure out exactly what KC was hiding. According to the rules of magical thinking, that meant the universe wanted Yardley to understand that KC Nolan was no traitor.

She heard her nan sigh. There was a soft clink Yardley recognized as the sound the iced tea glasses made when they were set down on the patio table.

Yardley would have given a lot to be right there right now, on a dark patio in North Carolina with her nan, and with KC beside her. In this fantasy, she had already figured everything out, and it was easy, and no trouble would ever come to her again.

"The only thing I can tell you, Yardley, is you're still breathing, so it's not too late."

"For what?"

"It's not too late to do whatever it is you should've done in the first place if you hadn't been afraid. What you would have done, every minute, from the first moment you knew you wanted this woman, if you had no fear."

Yardley relaxed her vigilance for just a moment so she could ask herself what that was.

Be with her all the time. Tell her everything about me. Ask her everything about her.

But she hadn't done that. She'd held so much of herself back that KC had felt rejected. How much had Yardley contributed to that feeling over their years together, breezing in and out of KC's life between missions, maintaining the illusion of a busy social calendar so she would have plenty of excuses for why she had to walk out the door?

KC had held back from her, too, beyond what she'd had to do to keep her cover intact. Yardley had been truthful when she'd said she'd never been completely sure that she was what KC wanted. But what reason had she given KC to be vulnerable when nothing she'd done had communicated what *she* really wanted?

No reason at all. Probably because Yardley had been telling herself all along that it didn't matter. She couldn't have it.

"Oh, damn," Yardley whispered. "Excuse my mouth, but I don't know how to fix this, Nan." How was she supposed to manage loving someone the way she wanted to love KC? In *her* life?

Her nan laughed. "God help you. But you are no shrinking violet, as much as your mama's always tried so hard to get you to act like one. I think you're up to it. And if you're not, well, KC will have no problem finding someone to mend her up. She's a firecracker and an affecting flirt."

"Nan!"

"Just a warning to keep you motivated, my dear. I'm guessing you better go."

"I'd better. Thank you. I love you the whole ocean."

"And I love you every fish in it. Be careful."

Yardley set the receiver in the cradle. It was still dark, but the city was moving from its preoccupied nighttime hum to the energy of a new day. She didn't have much time to get what she and KC needed and return to the safe house.

Something to make this mission successful and, Yardley hoped, to get to the bottom of what KC was hiding.

She took the alley behind the building with the market, then walked briskly off the main roads until she was on a small road parallel to Strändvagen that had a pedestrian tunnel underneath the busy street and would spit her out within a block of the Hotel Diplomat.

None of the bellhops and valets under its red awning paid her any attention as she strode into the lobby and straight to the women's restroom. At this time of the morning it was serenely quiet, with not even a faucet dripping in the marble-clad, cavernous space. She locked the hydraulic hinge on the door, then counted the oversized pink-and-black marble tiles on the wall until she found the ninth one, three up.

She pulled out her pocketknife and rammed its blade along the gap in the grout. The tile eased out. She grabbed the metal case inside and pulled it down onto one of the vanities, wheeling the number combo lock around until it clicked open. From it, she took a comm set, a laptop in a Hello Kitty shell with a cross-body strap, and a signal kit, then locked up the case, shoved it back in the hole behind the tile, and replaced the marble.

Yardley had hides like this all over the world, but this was one of her favorites because the Diplomat's bathroom always had a dish of tiny Marabou chocolate mints. Yardley grabbed six, unlocked the door, and slipped out, putting the sparkly strap of the case over her shoulder and unwrapping a chocolate as she waved at the valets.

The fifteen-minute walk back to the safe house took forty-five due to Yardley's various evasive maneuvers. By the time she was approaching the flat, she knew there was no way everyone wouldn't be awake and angry with her, despite the box of pastries she balanced by its string on her finger.

She'd altered her typical posture-perfect stride to mimic the antisocial scuttles of the black-clad Swedes heading into work. She took the main pedestrian walkways instead of skulking in the alleys—skulking attracted attention this early in the morning— and blended with the purposeful crowd.

All of this meant that as she approached the safe house, she immediately noticed the man standing in the street.

He wore expensive-looking wired headphones. She might have dismissed him as an urban music lover pausing to adjust the sound mix on the player cradled in his hand if it weren't for his utter stillness.

When the man reached up to adjust his headphones, Yardley caught the quick twisting motion of his wrist as he flipped open the dish of a disguised parabolic microphone.

Spy.

Dang it. The pastries in the box were still warm.

She hadn't worn a comm set because the one provided by the agency was hidden in a hole in the box spring of the bed KC and Flynn were sleeping on, and she hadn't wanted them to wake up. The comm she'd just retrieved from the hotel would have to be set up before it could connect. She couldn't signal for backup. Or warn them.

Yardley wove backward through the crowd as unobtrusively as possible, mentally setting her view above the man so she could anticipate where his associates might be.

In front of her, leaning against a set of building stairs, she spotted a woman stopping to smoke a cigarette whose lips were moving between every fake puff.

Yardley marked the silhouette of a sniper's stand on top of a bakery on the corner.

Headphones was crossing the street now, and Cigarette had stubbed out her cover and started toward the apartment building.

Absolute focus sparked at the base of her skull, slowing her heart rate and sharpening her vision. She approached Cigarette at the steady, purposeful pace of the crowd until she could clearly see her face.

Yardley didn't know her.

Cigarette briefly made eye contact with Yardley.

Cigarette didn't know her, either.

Good.

She changed the trajectory of her walk, speeding up when she noticed Cigarette murmuring into her comm. Yardley brushed past her, blocking out the rest of the street noise by pure will, nearly tripping and calling attention to herself when she caught the word Cigarette had spoken as Yardley passed.

Tabasco.

Her higher cognition dropped out, and she turned around and ran toward the alley alongside the safe house. When she got there, she reached up to yank down the ladder to the fire escape. No doubt they'd seen her, and certainly they'd heard the screech and clang of the ladder, so she didn't worry about the rubber-on-metal noise of her boot soles. She just climbed to the third floor as fast as she could.

They were after KC, and they knew her code name. A spy with a laser-assisted sniper aiming at them and their code name in the wind was a dead spy, so Yardley didn't care to think through why any of this would be the case until after she had protected KC's precious body.

She wrenched open a window and threw herself into a random apartment. A young woman immediately started screaming.

"Get out! There's a fire!" Yardley yelled in Swedish.

She ran out of the apartment with the woman, and as she reached the door to the apartment where KC and Flynn were supposed to be safe, she heard the voices of an American man yelling in the stairwell and a British woman yelling back.

Cigarette and Headphones, on their way up. They knew where to go.

Flynn hadn't, but they did.

Before she opened the door, she yanked down the fire alarm in the hall.

She slammed the door behind her and found Flynn already standing up in distress at the sudden noise.

"Get down! Curl up in the bottom of the wardrobe."

Flynn moved fast and shut herself in, but Yardley was already shrugging off the laptop strap and disentangling the mangled box of pastries from her wrist, focused on locating KC.

There she was—crouched in a fighting stance in the space behind the door, eyes alert.

"Man and a woman in the hall in less than ten seconds," Yardley shouted over the wail of the fire alarm. "Probably armed. Looking for you, so put that hood up and keep your head down while we fight."

"You laughed and fell down all the way through that trial kickboxing class we took, and we're going hand-to-hand with two armed hostiles?" KC yelled.

Yardley put her palm on the doorknob and looked over her shoulder at KC. "Don't worry about me. I fight dirty."

With that, she smashed the door open into Cigarette's shoulder on the other side, pulled the door back and smashed it again, and then leaped out and tripped her as she reared back in pain.

"Got it," KC said, and as Yardley stomped on the small of Cigarette's back, she watched KC crouch and swing her legs across Headphone's ankles, bringing him to his knees for just long enough for KC to stand up and wrench back his arm, grab his gun, and drop out the cartridge, which she stuffed in her pocket.

Yardley wished this was a date.

It would've been one of the best they'd ever had.

CHAPTER ELEVEN

KC lay on her back and panted, trying to find her breath. The grit in the grotty hallway carpet pressed into her shoulders. Her thigh was screaming with a giant, throbbing bruise, and the ear-piercing bell of the fire alarm rattled her teeth.

They'd gotten away.

KC had been running after the man and woman she and Yardley disarmed and nearly subdued when Yardley caught her by the hips before she could stop their descent down the stairwell, knocking her backward.

Now, Yardley was breathing hard, on her knees but getting ready to stand up. The alarm cut out with one last sharp trill.

"Why the fuck did you stop me?" KC peeled herself up off the floor. She could hear shouting residents at the bottom of the staircase and the sound of a siren nearby.

"Because they were running away." Yardley reached her hand down. "I don't chase anyone or anything unless it's absolutely dire. Which is almost never. What would we do if we caught them, torture them with snacks until they told us what we wanted to know? The CIA is not law enforcement. Let the FBI chase people. They have to pass physicals."

KC accepted Yardley's outstretched hand and got to her feet.

"Shouldn't we jet before the fire crew comes? They'll sweep the building."

Yardley was already on her way back into the apartment. KC brushed herself off and followed in time to see her tap on the wardrobe. "Clear for now."

Kris opened the wardrobe and stepped out.

A lot of chemicals had flooded KC's system in the last three and a half minutes, the kind that would probably leave behind a few gray hairs as they broke down inside her body, but it hadn't occurred to her to be angry until she saw Kris attempting to discreetly wipe the tears off her face.

"What the hell were you doing?" KC scanned the room, noticing a partially smashed bakery box on the floor. "Did you sneak out without leaving a note or way to find you just to buy *pastries*?"

Yardley bolted the apartment door, then went to the kettle. She pulled down a mug from the shelf. "Of course not. I left to get tech." Her face was pink from exertion and as serious as KC had ever seen it. "Listen, you can be as mad at me as you want to." Yardley's posture was debutante correct, her voice scratchy. "But I'm going to get hot tea into our asset, and you need to reach into a hole in the left side of the box frame for the comm set so you can tell Gramercy to call off the firefighters and whoever else might be on their way. We need the cover to stay put for about a half hour without anyone else on us or the local emergency squad making problems. Someone needs to check for a sniper on the roof of the bakery on the northeast corner of this block. Gramercy should get transpo ready for Evenes Air Base. Don't tell him about the micro drive yet. Give us a minute before we have to deal with Mom and Dad."

KC had already found the comm set ten minutes before Yardley crashed into the apartment. She froze as she sat down on the floor to take the components out of the case to activate it. "You *don't* want me to tell him about the microdrive."

Yesterday afternoon, interviewing Kris while Yardley closely watched them both, had taught KC the difference between concealing the whole truth to keep herself and people she cared about safe and muffling vital information into silence for reasons that didn't sit right. Back home, KC had become weary from the lies she told Yardley to protect Yardley, herself, and the agency, but she'd never felt like she had swallowed a razor.

She didn't know how deep cover and black ops officers like Dr. Brown overrode their own intuition, the strong urge inside them to trust someone who could help, in favor of a much bigger picture.

KC didn't like it. It wasn't her thing. Not at all.

Yardley had crossed to the window to look through the blind. Now, she turned around, and the light drew a golden glow around the outline of her body. "It's always a good idea to hang onto your pocket nuke. If something comes up and you have to use it, you still have it to use. Or you can trade it for something else you need. As long as you're in the field, it's your mission. Your decision."

KC took a moment, fiddling with the comm set, to absorb Yardley's perspective.

She'd thought it would be a relief for the drive to be taken out of their hands. To give up control to the agency, come what may. The truth was, she was scared. The people she'd fought in the hallway scared her. KC hadn't recognized them, and, thank Christ, she didn't think they'd recognized her.

If KC was a mark, it likely meant Dr. Brown's op wasn't a

secret anymore. It might mean Dr. Brown wasn't safe, or even still alive.

When he had sworn her to secrecy, he'd told her that maintaining the covert nature of a black op was a matter of life or death. But what if this secret KC kept was what got Kris or Yardley killed?

KC wasn't sure how much Yardley suspected at this point, but she owed it to the three of them to make smart decisions. She wanted to honor Kris and the terrifying risks she had taken to get here. Kris knew KC had built the device—she'd made that clear when she told KC it looked like a "ghost" built it. It was what they used to say when one of them had made something secret, often something risky. *I'm going in as a ghost.*

KC cleared her throat. "You're in charge," she said. "I'm just making sure I've got my orders clear."

Yardley squatted down in front of her, bringing her face closer to KC's level. "Here's another field lesson," she said gently. "Don't let them tell you when the mission's over, and as much as you want to go home or save innocents, don't let it end too soon."

KC could feel her heartbeat in her ears. Maybe if they'd had more time apart, she would be able to tell the difference between her feelings for Yardley and what was best for this mission.

But they hadn't.

She couldn't.

All of it—Yardley, the pain of losing her, the futile scraps of hope that something of their relationship could be salvaged, alongside the fragile and explosive mission that was Project Maple Leaf—had stripped away any but the most immediate decision-making capabilities from KC.

"Good advice," she said. Yardley raised her eyebrows, maybe

surprised KC hadn't argued with her. "Along with don't chase anyone," she added.

"Not unless they're really hot."

A morning sunbeam caught motes of dust in the air, lighting up a halo around Yardley's smooth, dark hair. There was a rip at the knee of the black trousers she wore—clothes she must have pulled out of the wardrobe in the dark, so stealthy that KC hadn't heard her.

Before, KC might have said the Yardley she knew was incapable of waking up before dawn to carry out a secret mission and return with breakfast. That the Yardley she loved was a soft, intimate creature who liked to snuggle deep under piles of blankets, exclaim over baby pig videos on her phone, and take hot showers until the bathroom mirror dripped with steam.

She was different in the field, but she wasn't a stranger.

KC knew this woman. She was the Yardley from that backyard picnic, the woman KC saw and fell in love with in what felt like the same breath. KC knew how this woman kissed, how she begged, the way her hands felt sliding up the bare skin of KC's back. She knew how to make her laugh and how to make her moan and how to make her burst into angry tears.

She also knew how to hold herself back from this woman until she withdrew, gave up, walked away. KC had done it and done it. She'd made excuses. She'd made herself wretched.

But she'd never really trusted Yardley—not with the stories that made her vulnerable. The fears that made her sick.

She wondered what would happen if she did.

And so she smiled at Yardley's joke, and watched as Yardley was surprised by the congenial olive branch. KC put in the earpiece and only reported what Yardley had told her to, ignoring the rest of the rapid-fire questions Gramercy put to her. Then she disconnected and set the comm on the mattress.

Yardley had put a hot mug of tea in front of Kris and deposited the crushed box of pastries on the table. She carried over a short stack of plates to serve them on.

"Even if you don't want to eat these"—Yardley plucked a plastic Hello Kitty case from the floor by its shoulder strap—"I do have something you like."

She set the case on the table and opened it to reveal an extremely sophisticated bit of machinery that KC had, in fact, more than once yearned to get her hands on if the agency would ever let a tech have anything like it.

They wouldn't, lest a tech take over the agency.

"I got this from a Ukrainian gentleman who I played cribbage with on a train." She stacked a signal booster and comm set on the table. "I thought if we were going to hit Mirabel's place, you might need a higher caliber of toys to play with. I'm certain, given this morning's events, there's plenty of chatter among people like you two who know where to find it. It would be helpful if we had schematics of Mirabel's properties and holdings, and if we could get intel on whether he'll stay here now that Flynn's given him the slip."

Yardley pushed the pastry box in Kris's direction. "Don't skip meals. We'll have long days before there's even a minute to rest. The bakery these are from is unreal. It's run by a Nigerian couple who trained in Paris, and their semla buns are made with a sweet-potato dough."

Her voice had dropped into the hospitable and soothing cadence of her mother's. If KC hadn't seen it for herself, she would have no way of knowing that moments ago Yardley had dropped an agent and stepped on her back.

She thought about the deliberate stress she'd been put under in agency training—learning to lose a tail and failing repeatedly, learning to fight, to secure an asset, and most of all, to separate her own interest from the nation's.

Yardley seemed quite literally born to the trade.

With a deep, centering breath, Kris untied the string on the pastry box and pulled out a bun overfilled with custard. She took a big bite. Her hands shook.

"How's baby?" Yardley asked softly. "I'm sorry we didn't have more notice and you were frightened."

"Kicking away." When Kris smiled, her face looked a lot clearer. "I don't know where I stand with you lot, but I'd like to take a crack at pinning down those schematics you're interested in. I understand that my predicament means that I am more or less the CIA's lapdog at this time, but the sooner the other drive's in your hands, the quicker I have a chance to get home to start forgetting this ever happened."

"Yes," Yardley said. "Do that. We should have about twenty minutes before we'll hear where to meet a driver."

"Give me a second." KC retrieved a small plastic case from the box that had been in the mattress. "I need to reconfigure this router so we can plan without the agency seeing what we're doing before we want them to."

"Sure," Yardley said. "We'll get what we need unless we're overridden and they decide to go with a raid."

Kris shook her head. "If Mirabel suspects a raid, he'll deploy the device in order to create chaos."

A few quiet minutes passed. Kris was on her second pastry and had already jumped onto the signal KC set up, efficiently pulling packets of information from different civic and backroom sites, when she looked at Yardley with her eyes wide. "A *sale*. Bloody, feckin' arse! Mirabel's decided he's going to put the weapon up for auction."

Motherfucker. KC pulled her chair next to Kris's. "He's finished with subtlety. He's been spraying this invitation around on the dark web like it's an Evite to a church fish fry."

Yardley came over to stand behind them. "That's the guest list?" She pointed at a column of names that had just unscrambled itself on the screen in front of her.

"Looks like it." Kris downloaded the list.

Yardley whistled. "I can't go in. There's not going to be a soul in that room I haven't tangoed with, and half of them probably have a standing order to slip plutonium into my teacup the next time we cross paths. The operative has to be KC."

KC's stomach flipped over.

Not in a bad way.

She was starting to feel . . . better. Less like a hunted animal, more like a predator. Kicking ass side by side with Yardley had gotten her blood moving. Could be it was just the adrenaline making everything feel sharp and clear and a little bit easier, but KC didn't think so.

She thought it might be that she'd come up against a bad thing and, for the first time in a long time, made a different decision.

"On the other hand"—Yardley was still studying the intel Kris was putting up—"spies change sides. I know how to disappear in a room. There's at least ten rivalries on that list I could exploit in an act of diversion."

But she turned and looked at KC with a question in her eyes.

"I think it should be me." This was an auction for tech, so KC had a lot of experience with what would be important in this sale. And as soon as Maple Leaf was over, and Dr. Brown did what he needed to do to sweep up, she didn't want to be in a basement anymore, where her circle was so small there was no hope of collaboration or sharing the very real burdens of projects and secrets.

She was going to need something like the distraction of field work to heal after she and Yardley said good-bye.

"How certain are we that the micro drive is *on* the premises?" KC looked at the schematics and blueprints Kris was pulling up of what she assumed was Mirabel's estate.

Yardley snorted. "Mirabel's probably going to have it on a silver platter surrounded by a garnish of bullets. We'll need a bidder plan A that comes with a briefcase full of gold bars, a plan C, the one with the helicopters, speed boats, and soldiers rolling out of vans with tactical gear—which, so far I have never used plan C and would rather keep it in the 'never' column—and a plan B that involves stealing and getting out alive."

KC watched Yardley scan the intel Kris was finding, the day already careening toward an evening that would have to be the end to all of this. After so many months—after the horror of the demo in Toronto—it was hard to believe. The stakes were so enormous to depend on a single night.

KC was still contemplating that when Yardley murmured into her comm, then looked up. "Grocer's van in the west alley in five."

Kris and KC stood to retrieve their things while Yardley gathered up KC's comm set and pulled the one she had been using out of her ear. Then she piled them on the table, picked up Kris's empty tea mug, and smashed them to bits, twisting the mug over their remains until they were obliterated.

Kris had stopped packing up the laptop in its case mid-buckle. KC couldn't seem to make her thoughts move past the horror of two twenty-five-thousand-dollar comm sets reduced to silvery shards on the table.

Yardley put the mug down and brushed her hands together. "Before we're on that van, then on a plane to Evenes to plan this mission, and while we still have some privacy, I do have a question."

"Okay?"

"When were either one of you going to tell me that the architect of the weapon used in Toronto—the one that you, Kris Flynn, just made even better—was Katherine Corrine Nolan?"

Yardley raised one perfect inky eyebrow.

KC had been Unicorned.

CHAPTER TWELVE

Even as Flynn sat back down, her hands settling instinctively over her belly, KC kept her chin up. She didn't look away.

Her expression gave Yardley nothing.

Yardley depended on what she knew about people to complete operations at a high level in the field. What she had learned was that there were no coincidences in intelligence, to keep her eye on the women, and that a whole bunch of lies tended to eventually add up to the truth.

So far, she had worked out that KC seemed to be hiding and lying the most, even though, between KC and Flynn, Flynn had more to lose—unless her baby bump was a con, but when they'd taken the micro drive off her, that inside-out belly button looked very real. Not to mention that a pregnant woman had gone through a lot of danger and trouble to get to her old friend.

KC started to open her mouth. Yardley held up a finger. "Before you answer, keep in mind that my options are significantly more vast than yours are. You can lie, but I can report my suspicions."

She hated saying that, but she didn't have a choice. In the aftermath of the assassination attempt—and Yardley had no compunction about calling it what it was—she was desperate to protect KC, whose situation had become untenable. Worst case, the people trying to find her would get to her and take her out. That outcome was unacceptable, so Yardley had put it out of the question by bringing in the agency. They'd move to Evenes, where fences and guns would keep them safe.

But that meant they'd be under the CIA's purview. Soon enough, the agency would figure out the same things Yardley had, come to its own conclusions, and Yardley would never see KC again.

Just as unacceptable. That outcome would force Yardley to go rogue to find where KC was on the planet, and, yes, that was exactly what she would do, which meant she understood what her nan had been trying to tell her. Finally.

She was still breathing, so it wasn't too late.

She had to act as if she had no fear. She had to do what she should have done from the beginning.

Right now, that meant it was time to demand the truth from KC.

Yardley didn't much care what the truth was. Once she had it, she would do whatever she needed to do to keep KC from harm. Anything. And knowing *that* provided not a little clarity about what she wanted in the uncertain future on the other side of this mission.

"I'm aware of what I am gambling by answering your question." KC shoved her hand through her hair. "Are you aware of what you're gambling by asking it?"

"Not even twenty-four hours in the field and full of vinegar, I see."

KC, possible *double agent*, rolled her eyes. "I wouldn't call fighting off hostiles you lured to the door where we've been holed up since yesterday and were tracked down by our target being 'in the field.'"

Her color had come up, and for the first time Yardley noticed she had changed into some jeans she'd likely retrieved from the wardrobe, because she'd had to cuff them at the bottoms. Those cuffs were hitting her black boots, and paired with the T-shirt that was a little small and showed off the muscles in her arms, KC looked like a darling, white-hot, redheaded James Dean. It made Yardley dizzy to think of what she could do to her if every single circumstance were different.

"Don't look at me like that." KC's tone was as stiff as her jeans.

"Like what, like I'm applying the necessary pressure to do what's right for your country?" Yardley ignored her own blush.

"More like you want to work this one out on the horizontal." Flynn sucked custard off her thumb. "But I'm interested to hear Nolan's answer."

KC closed her eyes. "This isn't about you, Kris."

"Ah-ha!" Yardley pointed at KC. "That answers at least half of my questions."

"Unless she meant the screaming sexual tension wasn't about me," Flynn said. "Versus your spy-guy conclusions."

"We're losing the plot." Yardley took a deep breath. "KC, did you make the weapon deployed in Toronto?"

KC also took a deep breath, and then, thank god, she met Yardley's eyes, and Yardley could really see KC in there. The KC she knew. The KC she had faith in when she was talking to Nan— the one who she'd never truly *stopped* having faith in, even when it would have been better, smarter, safer to give it up. "Yes. I did."

Yardley's stomach yo-yoed with a sick little drop.

"But it wasn't a weapon."

That was when Yardley remembered something KC had said in the Situation Room. *We wanted to save the planet. We didn't have a lot of nuance.* "Is this device something the two of you had talked about when you were kids?" She directed this question to Flynn.

Flynn looked at KC. She waited for KC to nod before she turned back to Yardley.

Yardley liked this terrifyingly genius Irishwoman. She had integrity.

"We'd talked about how technology could be used to create fail-safes, but it almost never is," Kris said. "What if CCTV cameras scanned the environment for events likely to result in an accident? What if they could identify a vehicle whose driver is blind drunk behind the wheel and talk to traffic lights or patrol cars to shut him down? But then we started thinking bigger, because that would mean technology could also be used to override the cruel decisions made by politicians. Satellites could send a signal to stop drones and bombs that would harm noncombatants, for instance. What if you could connect things in just this way so that less people were hurt in the crossfire of global conflict? Or there was simply even more warning for things like earthquakes and whatnot, because more of the tools we already have could talk to each other?"

"We called it the Butterfly Wing device." KC's tone was sober. "After the idea that the flap of a butterfly's wing on one side of the world could result in a hurricane on the other."

Yardley's heart squeezed painfully. The Butterfly Wing device. Two girls trying to save the world. *Dang it.*

"Did you make it?" she asked.

"We didn't," KC said. "We only knew some of the ways it could be coded, and we were teenagers and easily distracted from a project so big. But I never forgot it, and I mentioned it in passing, as idle conversation, to Dr. Brown. I wasn't proposing it. It was more like, 'When I was a kid this is a thing I thought about, and wouldn't it be a great counterterrorism project if it could be real?' He asked me if I'd actually be interested in giving it a try. I didn't see the harm in researching what it would take, but by the time I was talking to Dr. Brown about what the code would have to look like, he told me he had approval to proceed with the device. He called it the Guardsman. He said it would have to be a restricted, Sensitive Compartmented Information, special forces project."

"A black op?" Black ops were vanishingly rare, and she'd never heard of one this extensive.

"Just until it could be confirmed to work. Then, information would be shared more widely, and from there it would be up to the executive branch to decide how to use it."

"And Toronto?"

A familiar calm had settled over Yardley's shoulders like a warm blanket. This was more complicated than if KC had been secured as an asset by a foreign agency. At least in that case the CIA would simply find a way to steal her back and get their hands on what she'd made.

Yardley had thought she would be minimizing the fallout from something like that, finding a way to largely pin it on some-one other than KC so she could keep KC in the District and mov-ing up in the agency. But if this situation had been generated *by* the agency and then discovered by stateless chaos agents, the level of difficulty in resolving it became incredible. And rescuing KC would be much harder.

The agency protected itself first.

"After I had coded the beta version of the Guardsman, I raised significant concerns to Dr. Brown," KC said. "I could see too easily how it could be used as a weapon. How it could hurt people. So he had it independently analyzed. He informed me that a controlled demo was arranged in Toronto under the guise of a planned power grid reset. But something went wrong. Really wrong." KC's voice was rising, making her sound younger and more vulnerable than Yardley was used to hearing her. "It was just me in the control center. Dr. Brown sent through a message he was hurt. I haven't heard from him since. He made it clear before then that my priority had to be to protect the op."

KC inhaled, harsh and choppy. "I couldn't tell anyone. All I could do was break up the device and stash it where no one could find it. I didn't have a secure hard drive big enough to dump it onto in the control center. I was going to do that as soon as I returned to the lab."

Yardley's ears were ringing with distress. Imagining KC—and, she had to be honest with herself, she was imagining *her* KC—embroiled in such a nightmare, feeling such sickening accountability, was breaking Yardley's heart in a brand-new way. How was anyone expected to be okay in a situation like that?

How could any relationship have been okay?

"That's when I was snatched," Kris said. "Mirabel knew what kind of thing to tell me to look for. It sounded so much like the Butterfly Wing, I started there and got lucky. Well, *unlucky*, really. I couldn't imagine how KC had knit herself up with such a thing. I did my best to focus on minimizing the damage and getting to her if I could."

Yardley tried to keep hold of the thread of all this, barely pinched in her fingers. "Was there enough time after it deployed for anyone to make the connection that it was similar to what the Daisy Dukes had talked about making back in the day, and so assume you and Flynn were involved? And then take Flynn because, why, she was easier to find?"

"I've been running it and running it," KC said, "but I haven't nailed down how it's come to this, and to the auction tonight. Dr. Brown is definitely off the grid, and I can't think of why that would be the case unless he's—"

"—a shifty pickle?" Flynn interrupted.

"Compromised." That was how Yardley put it.

KC rubbed her temples. "I was going to say . . . dead. But I don't think he is."

"You trust him?" Yardley didn't. Atlas's response to Yardley's question about Dr. Brown's whereabouts had suggested the agency knew where to find him, but that didn't mean he was doing what he ought to be doing, wherever he was at.

"I've never had a reason not to."

Yardley drummed her fingers on her crossed forearm. Despite KC's faith, she couldn't ignore her own suspicion. She didn't like that he'd recruited KC when she was underage, or that everyone knew Tabasco was his pet agent, or that KC had never made it out of the basement. It suggested Dr. Brown might not be approaching his work with empathy for the people he encountered, and agents who became jaded were easy to lure off the narrow path of justice with the kind of temptations that usually worked on men. Sex. Money. Power. "So you're thinking there must have been a leak?"

"I can only assume. I don't know who, because it truly was just Dr. Brown and me until the analysis by NSA and the clearance for the demo."

"That's more than enough margin for a leak."

KC took the laptop from Flynn. "Look, when the president

asked me those questions about Kris, I assumed it was because at some point at the beginning of the Guardsman op, Dr. Brown must have pulled any mention of Kris out of my file to protect the project."

Yardley doubted that Dr. Brown's motives had been anything so pure. But it didn't matter. They had a micro drive to retrieve from the middle of a snake's nest, and if the agency got confirmation that KC had been the one to make it, she'd be sequestered in a holding cell in the unmapped part of the headquarters building before she could squeak out a protest.

Maybe the intelligence KC could provide from her years of association with Dr. Brown would give the agency what it needed to find him, but it would be considerably more efficient to get their hands on the device now, when they knew where to find it.

"No doubt our ride's here." Yardley stepped toward KC.

If the agency had treated them fairly, or if they had been brave enough to tell each other everything, she and KC would have years of experience with a professional relationship by now.

They hadn't been given that chance.

Without it, all Yardley had known how to build between herself and KC was the energy of their connection—those invisible signals that passed between them and told her how KC felt or what she might need. She didn't want to have to use that in this setting, but she did need to know how KC was doing.

For every kind of reason. But mostly because she hadn't gotten over the part where she loved her.

She touched KC's wrist with the tips of her fingers, stroking the bone with the side of her thumb, watching KC for any trace of evidence that Yardley could affect her, transform her, take her from one state to another.

KC's fingers curled into a fist. Her throat hollowed out. Yardley could feel that something had unbuckled inside of her that had been cinched way too tight for way too long.

When their eyes met, Yardley knew what to hope for. She didn't know if it was what KC hoped for. She wasn't brave enough to even whisper it aloud. But if she could get KC out of this mess, then she would figure out what to do next. Not for the agency, but for them. For a shot at a future between them that wasn't just professional.

So this mission had better go smoother than a creek pebble, because Yardley was not in the mood for surprises from bad actors, general delays, or peril. In and out, democracy wins.

She was going to Unicorn this so hard.

The three of them went to the door, and Yardley opened it, showing Flynn what stairwell to take, but before she locked up behind her, every possible feeling in her body crowded up and filled up her heart and pressed into her ribs at once.

She turned to KC, who was set to follow Flynn, and said, "Don't."

KC cocked an eyebrow.

Yardley bit the inside of her cheek, trying to think how to express the surge of overwhelming feelings, but there was nothing elegant here. She put her hands on her hips. "Don't you dare tell anyone what you told me. Not one person. To hell with your integrity. To hell with anything but the protection of every single red hair on your person. Do you hear me? No one. Nothing leaves that room, and I'm locking it up right now. Not even Gramercy. Do you understand?"

Yardley tasted tears.

KC gently took the keys from Yardley's shaking hands and locked the door. "Nothing leaves that room. I'll tell Kris."

Yardley's chest opened, and air whooshed in.

She didn't say another thing on their ride to the airport.

There were only three words left she could tell KC, and she likely wouldn't get a second chance to say them.

CHAPTER THIRTEEN

Evenes Air Station, Norway

Gramercy was on a video call with the president of the United States.

The comm swallowed his voice into silence, so KC could hear nothing of the conversation. They were in the basement of a Norwegian military installation. She and Yardley and Kris had arrived via helicopter shortly after noon.

She didn't know where Gramercy had been when she spoke to him on the comm this morning, but it definitely wasn't Virginia. Possibly he'd already been here. Evenes was the only military installation in Northern Europe with the capacity and resources to plan and equip tonight's mission. It also had the advantage of being far enough from Stockholm to keep them dark from whoever might be looking for her, or Kris, or her and Kris, for a few hours.

KC caught sight of Yardley entering the room through a sliding door that KC hadn't been permitted to use. This was her chance.

"Yardley." KC touched her elbow after Yardley had given a tech a file. "A minute?"

Yardley looked around the room. "You wanted me to run you through how to use the specialized comm set for tonight?"

"No." KC was confused. "I helped make the comm set we're using tonight two years ago. I wanted to ask—"

Yardley stopped her by telling her to shut her mouth with lasers shooting from her eyes. "I know you wanted me to walk you through it someplace quiet." Yardley widened her eyes so she could speak to KC telepathically. *We can't talk here, dumbass.*

There were at least ten agents in the room, most of them tech, quietly working at different stations. Having participated in many ops from where they were sitting, KC couldn't fail to appreciate the vast reach of international intelligence behind her own bank of monitors.

Or what terrible, incorrigible gossips techs were.

"Right." She sighed. "Let's go someplace so you can teach me how to use the comm set I helped redesign."

"I forget about your ego," Yardley said as she started walking toward a door behind the monitor bank where Gramercy was taking his call. "Until it rears up like one of those tiny but lethally venomous snakes." They walked to a vestibule that led out to the airfield. "I have four minutes before one of these very humorless, very tight Norwegian intelligence officers decides I've gone rogue. You'd think the brisk weather and relative peace would infuse a certain amount of cheer, but they've always been like this. I think it's the lack of sunlight."

KC made herself focus. Yardley, in this moment, was so very *Yardley.* Funny, with prissy complaints, radiating intelligence with a disarmingly femme affect. This kind of woman was very much, generally, KC's type. She was helpless to such a woman, and never more so than when she met Yardley, who epitomized the type and had long legs, besides. It was all KC could do not to fall into their old, delicious pattern, where KC teased and feigned grumpiness so Yardley would flirt her out of her grump, and then they would both enjoy the resulting canoodling.

She missed her so much. God. She hadn't spent this much time with Yardley in months. Longer. But they weren't on vacation, and Yardley wasn't *hers*, and even if she might kiss KC back if KC made a move, it would be out of habit, not because of . . . anything else.

"Don't look at me like that," Yardley said. "I definitely don't have time for that."

KC's laugh sounded shaky. "I just wanted an update on Kris. On the micro drive."

"You're not gonna love it. I don't love it. Flynn's in custody, of course, but the kind of luxury custody reserved for people the agency wants to keep for itself. However, she's threatening to notify The Hague because they won't let her contact her boyfriend. I insisted it be Atlas who interrogate her, one, because that's their thing—they once interrogated the leader of a bloody coup while in a tank and stopped a war—and two, because I have very few options for sympathetic operatives. I haven't been debriefed since, but I've gathered Flynn immediately gave everything up that she will ever be willing to give up."

Yardley gave KC a significant look. *I have made myself clear about what you are permitted to give up, which is nothing whatsoever.* That's what her look meant.

KC had to steel herself to keep from taking a few steps back in an instinctive bid to escape thinking about what Yardley had said to her as they were leaving the safe house. She hadn't felt a feeling that passionate from Yardley in a long time, if ever, and she didn't know what it meant. If it was about the mission, or about her, or them. Or something altruistic related to Yardley's professional trust in her.

There were dozens of ways it made KC uncomfortable. Not even her relief in knowing the black op was temporarily protected helped alleviate the churning worry and guilt.

"The drive?" she asked.

"I told Flynn to hand it off, and she did. I couldn't work out a reason to hold on to it now that I'm the mission lead and I have the agency's resources at my fingertips. My recommendation, and Flynn's, as well as yours—which I told them—was that they take it right out to the airfield and rocket it into the sun."

KC nodded in adamant agreement. "Destruction is the ethical choice."

"However, this is the agency, so—"

"—they want their shiny new toy. Sure." KC looked at the overcast sky. The agency's behavior didn't surprise her, but she did hate it.

"And Flynn made it clear to them that the drive *is* the device. As soon as it's plugged in, it's a lit fuse, and it won't stop until it runs out of fuel, at which point it's burned up and useless to everybody."

"But what if they *want* to light the fuse?" KC sighed. "I don't love these moments where your own side is being as big of an asshat as the alleged enemy."

"Mm-hmm. Of course, we have the maker, so it's actually worse, because even if we do light the fuse, we also own the factory."

KC's blood ran cold. "You're certain she's safe? Flynn."

"Yes. But we need the other drive. We need to take Flynn off the grid. We need Dr. Brown found and this black op shut down."

"You have people looking for him." KC should've known she would.

"People, drones, hacks, assets both dirty and clean, shop-keepers all over the world who I make a point of tipping hand-somely. My dragnet is utter." When Yardley pressed her lips together, her angry dimple made an appearance.

"Okay," KC said. Yardley was powerful, and her view of Project Maple Leaf was sharp. KC had to admit it was nice to have a boss willing to take care of things.

"I have to go. Look." Yardley took a step toward KC. Her voice had dropped to a whisper. "I know we haven't had a chance to take a minute."

KC looked into Yardley's eyes, wide and blue and kind, and let her see her more than she usually would. Mostly, she let Yardley see that she was sad. KC knew they probably wouldn't get that minute, at least not until they made it back to Virginia and Yardley was handing her back the house key.

Not the watch. KC wanted her to keep that. She'd given it to Yardley to be hers forever.

"I'm good," KC said. "I know there isn't time for personal stuff." She had to ignore the shine in Yardley's eyes. There was a lot ahead of them tonight, and KC could only deal with it if she tackled her problems in order of their destructive potential. She started back down the hall, then thought better of her exit and turned. "Hey, Yardley?"

"Yeah?"

"Do you think you could get some kind of Norwegian military

base doctor to take a look at Flynn and the baby? So she feels better?"

Yardley smiled. "Already done."

KC returned to the tech room and dropped into the seat where she'd been told over an hour ago to wait for Gramercy to give her instructions. Moments later, his monitor shuttered to black. He turned around in his chair, unlooping his earpiece and mic combo. He wore a beautifully tailored suit with polished wingtips. The matte shine of his dark tie was knotted in a perfect Windsor.

No smile, though.

Do something different. That was what KC told herself, contemplating Gramercy. This was a veteran agent sitting across from her, a man who'd been so deep undercover that his cover's name still made lists of powerful Russian oligarchs. A man whose husband was a three-star general.

He wasn't Dr. Brown. He wasn't warm and immediately forthcoming. He couldn't be counted on to share with her everything he was thinking, or dress her down, or give her a tech task that he dared her was impossible. But he also had been unfailingly respectful, and there was no manual for handlers. Nothing required Gramercy to call for a car to take him to Reston in the wee hours so he could wheedle and cajole KC into doing her job.

If she didn't count the baby mission at the steakhouse, tonight's op would be the first time the agency actually tasked her with the kind of work she'd trained so many years to do. Maybe she couldn't wipe the weapon she'd made off the face of the earth, but she could make sure it was only in the hands of people she more or less trusted to do the right thing.

"I can do this," she told her handler.

"I know you can."

She nodded, noticing that even this mild vote of confidence made her feel like she'd won a medal. "I *want* to do this."

Then Gramercy did something *he* had never done before.

He smiled.

It was a great smile, not at all like KC might have expected. His bottom teeth were a little crooked, and his thin face creased along all the lines KC had noticed, but the effect wasn't actually dapper or dashing. His smile made him look real. She'd never really thought of him as real.

KC smiled back. "So."

Gramercy leaned back in his chair and crossed his arms, barely creasing his suit jacket. "I want you to know that I asked to be assigned to you. There was a bit of a bet going, actually. Whether anyone could succeed in the position. Dr. Brown had kept you to himself, some thought with good reason, others took issue, but certainly the exclusivity of the relationship was commented on."

KC adjusted her shoulders, noticing that what Gramercy told her made her uncomfortable. "Any perceived exclusivity to Dr. Brown wasn't coming from me."

"I didn't think it was. I'm telling you it seemed he was keeping you to himself. And, powerful men being what they are, the only reason why one would sequester one of the agency's best talents was in order to, by association, *become* one of the agency's best talents."

She appreciated the compliment, but there was a KC inside of her who yowled in protest at the idea she'd only meant to Dr. Brown what she could get for him. It was the same KC inside of her who had immediately protested Yardley and Kris's speculation that Dr. Brown was either a bad actor or the source of the leak.

She hadn't lied to Yardley when she said Dr. Brown had never given her a reason to believe he was dishonest. But there were things she hadn't said. Dr. Brown hadn't been her father or her friend. He hadn't even been much of a mentor. But he'd been the one person who was clearly on her team, and everything KC had ever learned or known about this work—hacker, MIT student, agency intelligence tech—had always been, to a greater or lesser extent, about fighting.

Fighting to keep her head above water after the agency blackmailed her into going to work for them. Fighting for the bros to recognize her code was good. Fighting to contribute to the conversation. Fighting to make the world a better place.

Her red hair wasn't the only reason they called her Tabasco. She got spicy. She'd learned how to do that when she was young, struggling to get what she needed for herself and her grandma. And it had worked. She'd survived. She'd made it this far. But there were consequences, not least that fighting kept her separated even from people she wanted a deeper connection with.

People like Yardley. And Gramercy.

The situation KC found herself in wasn't entirely about Dr. Brown. It was about the choices she'd made. The things she'd done wrong.

So maybe she should stop waiting for Dr. Brown to save her from it.

Maybe she shouldn't have waited for Yardley to save their relationship by telling KC exactly when it would be okay to be more vulnerable and stop fighting her own life.

Maybe.

"You're right," KC said. "He used my talents to make himself and his division look better. I was sequestered, without the opportunities to experience what it means to have colleagues."

"My god." Gramercy smiled again.

"That's all you get, right there," KC said. "You have to understand that I not only got started on the wrong foot with you, I didn't have a first step to take with you. I literally don't know how to work with you. At all."

Gramercy looked at her for a long moment. "You are not the only tech," he said. "You're not even the only tech at the agency with your level of talent or potential, and I am very sorry, on behalf of the agency, that you've carried the weight of believing that you didn't have colleagues or peers. I'm sorry you haven't had more opportunities to see for yourself the positive impacts of your work. In the protection of our Constitution and the sovereignty of our country, it's easy for us to forget those that protect values and concepts are *people*."

KC couldn't help it—she shrugged, just a little. That had been a very sincere and earnest speech, and she was KC. "I mean, colleagues sound nice."

"Colleagues *are* nice." Gramercy tipped his head. "Mostly. Taken on the whole."

KC laughed. It was the first time Gramercy had ever made her laugh. "I can't imagine you being anything but coolly magnanimous."

"I have hollered at you out of an open car window in the middle of the street."

"Hmm. *Hollered* is what my grandma did. You gave an oppressed shout." She leaned back. "But you wouldn't have done even that if you didn't care."

"No." Gramercy pointed at her. "I would not have. And now I can appreciate that you also care, which is good timing, because succeeding at this mission is going to be harder than jumping out of an airplane in a tuxedo and landing undetected in the courtyard of a Russian palace and stashing the parachute in time to give a toast to the president that distracts him long enough for his chief advisor to parlay with a diplomat and defect."

"But you did do that, is what you're saying."

"It wasn't *easy*. That's my point. And this auction tonight will be many times more complex."

"All right." KC rubbed her hands together. "I'm listening."

"First, I want to talk about some other stakes," Gramercy said. "There hasn't been a good opportunity to debrief."

KC's brain scrolled through the events Gramercy might know about that required debriefing. "The fight at the safe house?"

"If you survive a fight, the debrief's built in. I was thinking more about Starbucks. And the conversation you had afterward outside the director's office."

KC glanced around the room. Nobody seemed to be paying attention to them, but KC knew it was an illusion. Their talk was definitely being recorded, for starters. Probably at least half the techs in the room had known she was dating the Unicorn before she did, and all of them knew now. She tightened her grip on her elbows. "No one likes to feel ridiculous."

He shook his head. "It wasn't my decision."

KC swallowed. "Sure. I could've guessed as much. What I keep thinking about, though? When I was sitting in the van a few blocks from the Starbucks, listening to the Unicorn with Mirabel, and the signal dropped—that ten seconds of silence was the longest ten seconds of my life. And nobody in the van said a word. Everyone else *knew* the love of my life had a gun on her. Everyone but me."

"The reason—" Gramercy cleared his throat. His words had come out a little hitched. "The reason you're going out there tonight is because you listened to the part of you that did know. Without being told. You acted, overriding protocols, likely saving an officer's life, and absolutely handing the agency more information. I will tell you that I believe you will keep listening to that part of you, at work and with Whitmer."

KC tried to think of something to say that would sound like agreement, but her stomach felt like she'd swallowed a rock, and she couldn't tell Gramercy that *she* didn't believe it.

There was such a big difference between knowing what she wanted and believing that what she wanted was possible.

He leaned forward to rest his elbows on his knees. "Lucas and I. I told you it helped that he's a general, and he has the security clearance to know about my work. I didn't say what I meant to."

KC searched his eyes. They were blue, like Yardley's, but lighter, with flecks of green. He'd seen things she couldn't imagine. He'd lived a whole life before she was born.

"Go on, then," she said.

Gramercy clasped his hands together. His wedding ring was a thin gold band, dull and nicked. "I don't imagine you're going to like it."

"I mean, on the list of things you've done that I don't like . . ." But KC smiled. Her stomach buzzed with nerves, uncertain she wanted more insight into a relationship that had taken so many hits at a time when she was still hurt.

"All right. Lucas was deployed seven times in the first fifteen years we knew each other. A lot of that time, I was embedded, undercover, and sometimes didn't get home for six months at a stretch. When I became . . . preoccupied with thinking about how dangerous his work was—or he did the same—we told each other, 'Someone always has to be the first to leave.'"

"*Jesus*, Gramercy." Her lungs felt tight, her heart hammering in her ears.

"Death is inevitable. It's the only certainty. We don't know when. We don't know how. It's possible you won't make it through this operation. It's also possible you'll be taken out by a rogue Pacific wave on a well-deserved vacation. Or you'll outlive every one of your forebears and die holding hands with your beloved on a porch rocker forty years into your retirement."

KC didn't let herself paint that picture with Yardley in it. But god, she wanted to.

"Given the utter inconsequence of our opinions about when and how the end comes for us and the people we love, there's nothing to do but surrender. Then, and only then, can we ask ourselves what we want to do in the meantime. Who we want to be. And, if you have the good fortune to love another person who loves you, you ask yourself what you can do to make space for them to *be* the person you love, for as long as you have them."

KC wiped at her damp cheekbones with both hands. "That's awful. You're right. I hate it."

Gramercy stood up. He unbuttoned his jacket, reached into the interior pocket, and retrieved a crisp white square, which he offered to her.

She took his fancy handkerchief, but only balled it in her hand.

"One more thing," he said. "Before Lucas and I learned to appreciate the gift we had both been given, we were, as I said, preoccupied with the danger and the complexities of our relationship. There was a long stretch where we might see each other for a few days every three or four months, and when we did see each other, we either fought or we . . . made up for lost time." Gramercy shrugged one shoulder. "In other words, every time we saw each other, we were mostly afraid."

KC made herself breathe, because what she wanted to do was curl up around the rock in her stomach and go to sleep. Or cry. "I never had a chance to be afraid for Yardley."

"I didn't know how not to be afraid for Lucas, but I knew I didn't want him to be afraid for me. It was suggested to me by my mother, as it happens, that what we were missing wasn't love, and wasn't time together. It was trust. We didn't trust the other's intention to use our talents to stay safe, and we didn't trust the world that had brought us together. I was so angry, because she was suggesting I do the hardest possible thing to be with Lucas. Loving him wasn't hard. I loved him enough to bear up against the time we lost to our work. But trust?"

KC recalled her mortal fear for Yardley at the Starbucks.

She thought of the two of them arguing outside the director's office, her throat choked with hurt. Yardley throwing her wig at the bugged portrait when KC told her she didn't believe they would ever know what part of their relationship had been real and what part a lie.

But she also remembered how it had helped to tell Yardley about the black op. Gramercy wouldn't be sharing any of this if it didn't seem to him—this veteran agent, this husband with decades of practice loving another man whose life was dangerous—that KC and Yardley had something worth saving.

Or at least *trying* to save.

"Trust," she said. "Like parachuting to a teeny-tiny target."

"More like a free fall." Gramercy smiled again, a sad smile of understanding. "But when it's love, you won't hit the ground."

He stood up and held out his hand. "Come on. It's going to take the time we have left to get through what we need to cover."

She stood, accepting his hand and holding on to the sensation of his firm, dry palm against hers for a moment. "Thank you."

"No thanks required, but appreciated." He started walking toward a set of double doors at the back of the area they had been in, which KC had thus far seen only high-ranking uniforms and somber-faced people in suits exit. No one had entered.

She followed him to the three-phase lock, which involved a fingerprint, a retinal scan, and a code. He completed all three before looking at her. "Are you ready for your first field briefing?"

She was surprised by the whisper of anticipation that suddenly rushed up through her body like Christmas, like hearing Yardley hum in the shower before they went out, or the moment before a heavy lift when she knew she was going to jerk nearly twice her weight over her head and make it look easy. "Gramercy, I've been ready forever."

That was the first time she made him laugh.

Turned out, Gramercy preferred good old-fashioned, earnest joy over a joke.

Maybe she could learn something from that.

CHAPTER FOURTEEN

U.S. ambassador's residence, Östermalm, Stockholm

Yardley strode out of a ballroom full of CIA operatives. She had a problem.

In advance of this evening's op, the team had returned to Stockholm in order to be closer to Mirabel's compound. They'd settled on the ambassador's residence because it was one of the most fortified structures in the central city—essential for protecting the micro drive and Flynn, both of which Atlas and Gramercy refused to let out of their sight, by order of the president—and also because it turned out that Amanda Berg, U.S. ambassador to Sweden, had a great deal of personal and professional ire directed toward Devon Mirabel. The presence of his compound in her assigned country kicked up a lot of unsavory characters she was obligated to keep track of.

This left Yardley to direct a team of eleven field operatives, analysts, and tech from inside the confines of a beautiful Swedish rådhus in one of the most delicate and terrifyingly vital intelligence missions in U.S. history.

That was not her problem.

One of her eleven operatives, a certain KC Nolan—currently in a helicopter somewhere between Norway and a top-secret helipad from which a car would whisk her back to this very rådhus—had done so well in the Evenes briefing that Yardley had spent the entire two hours she'd observed over the comm link awash in goosebumps that were not one hundred percent professional.

Even that was not her problem. It was inconvenient to have a crush on a—technically—subordinate who she was—technically—broken up with, but not a *problem*.

Her problem was that she needed to talk to KC.

Not about tonight's mission. Yardley felt the same way about tonight's mission that she'd felt about her debut at the Cherry Hill Country Club when she was seventeen years old: overprepared and very powerful.

She needed to have *the talk* with KC.

Tonight, KC would walk into a four-acre semi-rural compound, accessible by one narrow road and facing a canal, to attend a party stuffed with some of the slipperiest eels Yardley had dealt with on the global stage. Those eels were going to be more than suspicious of a newcomer. Yardley's intel didn't put Cigarette and Headphones at the auction, but there was no way to be sure. KC would be unarmed, except for the guns she tended to so lovingly at her sweaty gym, and it would be her first time in the field.

Yardley was scared.

But she was the Unicorn, as she kept reminding herself, and she was *not* her granddaddy. Or her nan. She was a capable, creative queer woman with excellent instincts who had made her way to the highest echelons of trust and service.

It's not too late to do whatever it is you should've done in the first place if you hadn't been afraid. That's what her nan had told her, and Yardley's nan was always right. So she'd asked herself, if she hadn't been afraid of never having the chance, what would she have done by now?

They would have sat down and talked. That was her answer. They would have taken ownership of what went wrong—and not the Mrs. and Mrs. Spy business that Flynn had pointed out, but their real problems, the ones they'd argued about at the safehouse, the ones her nan had put her finger on so precisely and without having to think hard or write a list down on a piece of paper, so conspicuous were these problems.

Holding back. Failing to say what they wanted. Never learning how to have the emotional intimacy they needed and craved, and filling the void with work and sex.

Yardley was scared, because she didn't know what KC wanted or if there was any hope for them. But she was not afraid of this talk anymore. She was only afraid, in the bustle of this time-sensitive mission, she wouldn't figure out a way to have it.

She braced herself in the doorway of a guest bedroom and leaned inside for a rapid survey. It was a poem of blond woods, thick rugs, and a pillowy duvet. If she used this room, they would not have the talk they needed to have. They would do the other thing they liked to do instead of talking.

She closed the door on a fantasy of red hair on linen pillowcases.

Every hall, stairwell, and nook of the rådhus was beautiful, spare, very Swedish, and covered by discreet cameras and agency security. In her snoop around, she was stopped no less than six times by officers who wanted to ask her a question or show her how clever they were.

It was only after she'd rejected yet another inviting bedroom that she started to feel an involuntary haze of desperation and preoccupation with how KC kissed her, which was bossily, passionately, and with little interest in stopping.

Overtaken by this ardent mental image, Yardley started telling herself she *needed* it. She needed how one of KC's kisses obliterated her busy mind while also making her feel acutely alive. Not just alive, but hungry for life, like wildflowers would start sprouting through her hair, and searching roots would find the earth from her toes.

She pressed her hand against her stomach, wishing it would stop flip-flopping along with her convictions.

First, talking. Then, if it was natural, mature, and called for, perhaps a kiss good-bye. Couples did that at the end. It was tender. A kiss could smooth the artifact of the relationship into the scrapbook of one's life, to look back upon fondly.

Yardley found a settee in the hallway outside the ballroom to sit on and silently cry. The low Scandi design of the furniture meant that she felt awkward and oversized, but possibly that was simply a manifestation of her emotional state.

As she stared down the quiet blondwood hallway, the fancy bench made her tailbone ache almost as much as her heart.

"Do you have everything you need?" Ambassador Berg stepped into the hall from behind a silent pocket door that concealed a study, wearing flawlessly cut slim taupe slacks without a single wrinkle and an asymmetrical sweater in precisely the same color that set off her warm white bob like it was jewelry. "I could certainly find you a more comfortable seat. Ole Wanscher was a genius designer, but he was not concerned about the health of his countrymen's spines."

Yardley looked at her for so long without being able to formulate a response that it became obvious, and then embarrassing. The Unicorn was famously unflappable. Yardley, by contrast, had been torn to pieces, the scraps of herself flapping in the wind.

"I don't want to disturb your planning." Ambassador Berg smiled fully. "Please excuse me."

"That's very kind, but you haven't disturbed me." Yardley swallowed.

It hung between the two women. The acknowledgment of heartbreak.

"Well, now I must know." The ambassador leaned in, her eyes very kind. She glanced toward the closed ballroom door. "It's one of them in there? Tell me who so I can peer at this person in the cameras."

Yardley answered with a watery laugh, visualizing the assembled agents in the ballroom. "No. It's—"

A door opened suddenly at the far end of the hall, and Yardley and the ambassador turned to see who had come in.

KC.

The light from the bulletproof clerestory windows picked up every single shade of her improbable hair, chestnut against her neck, bright as a copper kettle where the sun had bleached it, rich mahogany where Yardley had watched her raking her hands through it during the briefing, leaving it in untidy wisps and curls. Her heavy black jump boots, issued with her flight suit, moved as silently over the glossy floor as the feet of a feline creature who lived in the deepest part of the forest.

Dramatic, yes.

But no lies detected.

"Ah," Amanda said with a laugh. "I see."

Yardley sighed helplessly.

"Good luck," the ambassador said. "There isn't a camera on the entrance to the linen storage room on the east side of the ballroom."

And with that helpful bit of intel, she disappeared behind the door she'd emerged from.

Before Yardley had a chance to take a deep breath, KC spotted her.

She watched KC pull her shoulders back infinitesimally. To Yardley's credit, she didn't run down the hallway and tackle her to the ground. She did sit up straight and cross her legs and stick her bosom out. Once KC started walking toward her, Yardley threw in a hair toss. She was going to need every bit of what she'd learned from cotillion class, her sorority sisters in Chapel Hill, and at her mama's knee.

"Ma'am," KC said when she'd stopped in front of her, recognizing Yardley's superior status in a clipped, neutral voice.

Oh, so it was going to be like that.

"Nolan," Yardley returned, rising to her feet. "I trust you had a good flight."

"Uneventful. What service should I report to?"

With that question, Yardley picked up on what KC was trying to hide, which was her excitement. Her hyperfocus. Yardley knew that feeling of arranging every bit of intelligence from a good briefing into multiple configurations, like it was a puzzle, in order to look for possibilities, options, opportunities—or maybe *missed* opportunities.

"You should report to me."

That was fun to say, but she should probably be clear.

"We should have a preamble to official report," she said.

KC's brow furrowed. "A preamble? Is there a pre-report step?"

Yardley shook her head. "What I mean is, can we talk?"

"Talk?"

Yardley glanced down at her gold watch. They had time. KC

already knew more about the schematic of Mirabel's estate than the rest of the officers in the briefing put together.

She looked up and realized KC had noticed the watch, which Yardley had strongly implied she'd left at home. Her heart skipped a beat.

She really didn't want to give back this watch.

"KC." Yardley ignored how her thigh muscles went weak and her vision had zeroed in on KC's mouth, her breathing, and every bit of skin visible on a fully dressed woman in a coat.

"Ma'am?" That question was accompanied by the tiniest quirk at the corner of KC's lips.

"Follow me." Having crammed all the haughtiness she could manage into that command, Yardley began walking down the hallway. She couldn't quite pull it off and had to check that KC was following her. Twice. But she was, so it had worked. Yardley took a small passage she'd noticed earlier, probably for caterers and service people, and followed it until she spotted a brass handle fitted into a door that was hidden in the wall. "In here."

She opened the door. A light automatically clicked on, harsh in the small room lined with shelves stacked with dozens of folded white linens.

KC let the door shut behind her. Yardley reached over and turned the lock, then smoothed her hands down the front of her thighs, nervous in a way she was not accustomed to. She'd walked into some of the diciest possible situations in the world, but she had never been nervous. The stakes had never promised so much and had so much power to take everything away.

"I just thought before tonight we should say something." But her nerves had made this statement sound like a question.

Say something about what, Yardley Lauren Bailey Whitmer?

She closed her eyes, trying to find words that would put her and KC in a place that they could come back to after this mission, a place different from the one they'd started in after KC had pulled her off Mirabel's gun in the middle of Starbucks.

"About us. About what went wrong. A talk where we don't blame our work, because we've both acknowledged there was more hurting us than our secret lives."

KC leaned against a linen shelf. "You want to officially break up."

Yardley did not. She'd have liked to stipulate they already had, repeatedly, but it seemed too direct to say any such thing at such a delicate moment. "I want us to try to agree to what we had, name our part in it, good and bad, and I want to"—Yardley looked around the tiny room—"try to leave this linen closet on terms we agree are kind and fair, so we know what happens when we touch down at Dulles."

KC studied Yardley for a long time, making her stomach flip and flip, making her feel so many things at once, she couldn't breathe. "Okay. You start."

"I don't have to. You can start."

KC smiled. Cataclysmic. "Absolutely not. This is a terrifying plan, but I concede it is a very mature one."

Yardley's legs felt dangerously weak. She looked around frantically, and then saw a rolling hamper with a wooden lid and yanked it over to sit on. "All right. Okay. I will start by saying that we never had a plan. I never made a plan that had you in it, KC, and that was doing us a disservice."

KC shoved over a tied-up bale of towels and sat on that. "You're saying we just let us happen to us."

She wondered if the linen closet had a radiator in it somewhere, because her lower back had broken out in sweat, and she could feel her hair curling at the nape of her neck. "Yes. That. And it meant there were conversations we didn't have. The kind of talks I think other couples, couples who make it, must be working through constantly, about what kind of home they want to make together and how their love will grow."

"Yeah. Some of those walks past the playset in the park were more than a little fraught."

Yardley let out a nervous laugh. "Yes. Sure. Kids. I mean, not that I wanted to have a conversation about kids, but I mean, yes, kids were at the park that we walked past, and kids have a way of making one think of the future." That had been unbearably awkward and difficult to say. Yardley congratulated herself on managing it.

"Because they're young. And we'll die first." KC had a very small tone of teasing her. Fair, but enraging. This was incredibly difficult, and Yardley didn't remember KC having initiated this talk. No sir. That would be Yardley Whitmer who'd brought them to this moment.

"What I *mean* is that I can understand in retrospect why we both may have avoided that conversation. But this mission, and the things you told me on the Darkhorse, and the argument we had at the safe house, the briefing—I think I'm getting a glimpse of what it would have felt like to really plan something with you. I wish we'd had a chance to do that."

The teasing look on KC's face mellowed into kindness. "I wish we had, too." She brushed her hands over her knees. "You're right that I should've shared more with you. There was a lot more margin in my cover to be honest than I pretended. I guess I'd say that not one person I've known has asked me to share my life with them or indicated that sharing or being there for each other was even a thing people did. Even if they loved them." KC nodded. Nodded too much. She was doing the nod that meant she was trying not to cry. She rubbed her hands hard beneath her eyes, which was even worse.

"You can't cry," Yardley said in the voice of an autocrat. "Because then—"

"You'll cry." KC laughed. "I know. For the record, I think we had a lot more good than bad, Yardley Whitmer. I'm a better person because of you. I can't regret any of it, even how it . . ."

"Exploded? Collapsed? Fell apart like a pier in mud?"

KC pointed at her. "Yes. In the end. And, listen, I know tonight's mission is delicate. But I don't think it's impossible, or even difficult, to have a good result, and that's because of you and your skills and your planning, which I admired before I even knew you. I also admired it when it was directed at one of the miniatures you put together in the basement, not just when you were trying to keep the world safe. I look forward to working with you in the future." With this solemn declaration, KC's smile returned. "Look at us. Talking about the future."

Yardley laughed, but she had to press the heels of her hands against her eyes. She was too hot, too worked up, too sad, too grateful. "I wouldn't have anyone but Tabasco on my team."

There was a click, and the closet went pitch black.

"Dang it," Yardley said. She couldn't see a thing. The automatic light must be on a timer.

"Maybe it's got a motion sensor," KC said. "Wave your arm around."

When Yardley did stand and lift her arm, however, it was

captured halfway up by fingers around her wrist, circling her gold watch, and then gently lowered but not let go of.

KC's body had somehow gotten close, *very* close, to hers. Yardley could hear KC breathing, but her eyes hadn't adjusted to the total darkness of the closet, so breathing was all she had to go by. KC's breath, the petrichor-like whiff of ozone mixed with herbal shampoo, and how firmly KC held her wrist.

So firmly that Yardley realized KC was guiding her backward.

She'd only said half of what she wanted to. There were other things that felt like they really must be impossible to say aloud, at least without some encouragement from KC, but she couldn't not try. "Listen."

"Shh," KC breathed. Yardley could hear the smile in her warning, and then she was so elated in the dark with KC's body almost pressing against hers, with any choice she had taken away from her by KC's wildly erotic hold on her wrist, that she was certain she would shatter into a million glowing pieces.

It was more encouragement than she'd hoped for.

"*KC.*" Her back hit something—soft, starchy linens by the feel and smell—and for a moment she was at her nan's, at a party, hiding under a table with a long tablecloth, looking at everyone's fancy shoes. Then KC's cheek was against hers, immediately transporting her to a different familiar place, every one of her senses so turned up that there was very nearly feedback, electric static, everything an ache or a throb or a hot pulse.

"I promise," KC murmured against her cheek, as her other hand, the one not holding Yardley's wrist, was suddenly raking through her hair, sending delicious prickles over her scalp, "I have things I want to say, too. I want to talk about trust. I want to talk for a whole day. Maybe more. I want to see if we can even do that."

Oh. Oh, if that wasn't the most romantic thing anyone had ever said to her. It turned out Yardley had been *longing* for KC to talk about the future. It meant they had a future, or at least that they might.

It meant she really could start to hope for something different than the ending they'd been headed toward.

"I can do that," she said. "I may need to take a few breaks, but I will try my hardest."

"Probably this isn't a good idea," KC whispered. The word *this* was punctuated with a small press of her hips against Yardley's.

"It's true," Yardley said, letting the feelings in her body melt against her overwarm skin, "that generally this kind of thing can confuse a woman. So let's get any confusion out of the way."

"About?" KC asked this question with her lips against Yardley's neck.

"Your intentions." Yardley couldn't say this without infusing the phrase with prim tartness that made KC ease back.

"We just broke up again. I thought, this time, with a lot of emotional intelligence." There was laughter in KC's voice.

"But we also implied that we would like to give more talking a try. And I should correct myself, because I *don't* think we've done this before. We've let ourselves get caught up, but we haven't gone in fully knowing how we both feel."

"Which is?"

Yardley bit her bottom lip. There was something serious in KC's voice, and there should be. She was still holding Yardley's wrist, which had the gold watch on it, reminding Yardley that her own intention wasn't to hang on to the keys KC had given her but rather to trade them for something that did a better job of encompassing what she thought she could feel for KC Nolan, given the chance. "I think we feel like there's more to our story."

"Yes," KC said. "I think we do."

"So our intentions . . ."

KC put her lips on Yardley's neck.

With one warm, open-mouthed kiss, she dissolved every word from Yardley's head. Her hands were at Yardley's hips, sliding over her sides, up her back, and it had been so long since she'd felt KC's body against hers like this—the way she surrounded her and teased her, asked her and promised her—that Yardley had forgotten how much everything inside her turned on in response.

It made her want to rush it. She wanted to press her thigh between KC's legs and fit her mouth over her bottom lip. She wanted to get so hot, clothes were nonsensical, and she wanted to let the sweet ache sharpen between her legs until there was nothing to do but rub herself against it.

This wasn't like their almost kiss in the conference room at headquarters, or when they'd tumbled to the rug before Kris knocked on the door of the safe-house flat. Those moments were echoes, old responses to tension and silence.

This was new. This was *new*.

But she had to ask. Even if she only wanted this long, private moment to go on forever, she had to know. "What do we call this?" She swallowed over a noise in her throat that KC provoked with a gentle scrape of her teeth against Yardley's neck.

"This is for tonight." KC's voice was gentle and, for the first time in this space, uncertain. "If you can. If you want to give us this."

KC's mouth, and her want, and their promise to talk, felt like it could be more than enough for tonight. It was more than Yardley had hoped for.

"I want to," she said, and KC's grip moved from her wrist to her hip. Her other hand slid from Yardley's hair to her jaw, and Yardley tasted KC's thumb on her bottom lip, so unexpected that she opened her mouth to take more. She would give KC whatever she wanted.

Their mouths met in a kiss, and the thud of desire that hit through her body was the surprise, because she wouldn't have believed she could want KC *more*.

She might have whimpered at the touch of KC's tongue against hers. She thought she must have, but she wasn't embarrassed. Her gift of that whimper to KC was what made KC press her body fully to Yardley's and grip a fistful of hair at her nape. Their kiss tasted like a lazy summer morning in bed, filtered sunlight on bare skin, KC's hard grip and her slow, explicit kissing that made the boundaries of Yardley's body unwind.

She'd missed this. Summer was the last time they'd had this.

The zippers on KC's jacket pressed into Yardley's skin, drawing her attention to the urgent problem of the stupid, stupid clothes they were wearing and reminding her she had hands, too. She traced her fingers down the front of the jacket. "Take this off."

KC kissed her again, open-mouthed, distracted. "You take it off."

They fumbled, kissing, breathing against each other's lips until Yardley found the tab and pulled the zipper down, shoving the jacket off KC's shoulders right before KC got a grip on her sweater and yanked it up so that Yardley was forced to lift her hands over her head so she could be stripped to her bra. They came together, KC's mouth on her breasts, Yardley's hands taking apart the fasteners of KC's flight suit, pushing it out of the way so that as much of their skin as possible could touch.

The furrow between the muscles of KC's back, knobbed with her spine, felt explicit in the dark. With her hands flattened against it, Yardley could almost predict how KC might touch her next by the way her muscles moved. KC's attention was committed to finding every hollow of Yardley's body with her tongue, making Yardley shiver and forget to breathe.

Their mouths met again. Yardley could feel each sure stroke of KC's tongue in the hot, urgent heartbeat between her legs. Her head filled with everything she wanted to say at once. *I love you. I missed this. Don't ever stop.* But the silken blackness swallowed her words, and there was only touching this miracle of a woman with all the feelings she had ever felt for her and the hope that KC would hear.

She'd guided Yardley back to something firm, something she could lean against, and rested her forehead against Yardley's. They were both panting. KC's hands hovered over the button of Yardley's jeans. "Do you want to?"

"I want to, god." Yardley reached down, accidentally tangling her fingers with KC's. She pulled at the button, hitching up her hips. Yardley couldn't see, she only felt when her waistband went slack and the burr of her zipper came down with a hard enough press of sensation to bring her right to the edge, more wet than she could ever remember being.

"Do you want to come?" KC's voice was hashed, her skin hot against Yardley's.

"Do you want me?" Yardley wanted to hear how much KC wanted her and for that to be what made her come too soon, as soon as KC touched her, so KC could see what she did to her and

Yardley could get to her knees faster and shatter KC's composure with her tongue.

"I always want you." KC's fingertip pressed and worked Yardley's clit in one soft stroke, focusing every speck of Yardley's attention on her inevitable orgasm, poised to send her into luxurious free fall.

"God, god." Yardley hitched up her leg and rested her foot on KC's hip. She knew it hadn't been longer than a moment but she was one hot throb, close to coming, seeing colors in the void.

KC's fingers slid inside her, slow enough Yardley could protest if she wanted, but she loved the deep fullness, the heavy thrust, and even more she loved how it was going to send her, slippery and senseless all over KC's palm.

"That's my girl." KC bit her neck, working her, still holding that wrist with the watch on it.

"I'm so close." Yardley pushed her hips up, the blackout sliding over her hot skin, KC's teeth and tongue in every place that made her shiver, she was *right there*. "So close, so close, so close."

Then KC was quiet, focused on fucking Yardley with her fingers, putting just-right pressure on her clit the way she liked between each stroke, and Yardley didn't know how long they went on like that but she was panting, reaching for something she couldn't catch, and then she was crying.

KC kissed her neck. "Sweetheart." Slowly, she slid her hand away, and the loss was like a missed heartbeat, unsettling and frustrating. KC kissed her forehead.

"But it's what I *want*." Yardley pulled her knees to her chest, her tailbone throbbing, everything else achy and unspent. "It's what I want. I want it."

It was the truth. But it felt like one more lie.

KC's arms came around her, and Yardley grabbed on. She held KC tight. For the first time in weeks—for the first time when it was real—she wept.

"I'm sorry," she sobbed. "I'm so sorry."

KC's lips were tender on the crown of her head. The tenderness made another sob hitch in Yardley's chest.

"You can't," KC said. "I think if you knew it was the last time you'd ever be with me, you could. And I think if you knew I was with you forever, you could."

"But I don't know one way or the other, so it's not . . . so I can't." Yardley wiped the mess off her face with her palms, grief-stricken with the loss of KC's body, KC's skin, KC's everything.

She heard her shrug into her flight suit and fasten it. Yardley did up her jeans. "KC?"

She wasn't sure what to ask for. She needed something, something she'd never known how to request, from this woman she'd never been able to be completely, totally sure of. Even as she'd loved having KC's arms around her, as certain as the clasp of her mother's gold watch. "Promise me something," she said. "Whatever you can."

"I promise we'll figure it out," KC said, as though she'd had those words at the ready, a gift to hand Yardley. "I promise we'll know."

It was enough for now.

Yardley was about to speak, trying to formulate a promise of her own, when she heard a hesitant knock at the door. Soft enough to pretend it was nothing, nothing.

"I'm so sorry." The voice drifted through the hardwood. "It's Amanda."

The ambassador. The blood in Yardley's body cooled a degree, and she reached out until she felt KC's hand and grabbed it. KC squeezed back. That squeeze returned the breath to her body, smooth and even.

Yardley thought, as KC moved away for good and turned the lock to open the door, she ought to have been able to say *I love you*. It was in her throat. In her heart, she felt it.

She'd said it to this woman thousands of times, idly and passionately and tearfully and laughing, but in this split-second pause between the return of wild hope and the cold place they'd been living in, she couldn't. She actually put her hand against her throat to accuse it of failing.

But maybe their kiss in the dark was like a seed they'd planted together. Safely tucked in, ready to grow up into the world where they could say everything they had ever wanted to.

The door opened. The light clicked on like a slap, making Yardley squint her swollen eyes. Amanda was in the doorway, an apology written all over her face.

"I am genuinely sorry. This is absolutely the worst timing, but you're being looked for." She must have seen something in KC's expression, because she shook her head. "They have no idea where you are, I only made a good guess. But I'm obligated to tell you they've detained someone outside the residence who's asking for Kris Flynn. A Declan Byrne?"

"*Dang it.*"

But KC started laughing, and she turned around, directing her laughing face at Yardley—her full smile, her big brown eyes with their illegal copper lashes and her kissed lips and her extra-super-messy hair—and Yardley started laughing, too.

"He's the love of her life," KC said. "We should've seen this coming."

"We should have." Yardley felt a sudden burn of tears in her eyes despite the laughter. "But we didn't this time."

"We'll figure it out," KC said, reaching her hand out for Yardley's. "Come on, before Declan's thrown into Swedish prison."

Yardley took KC's hand, pressing their damp palms together, and it felt like maybe they had gotten somewhere new after all.

"It's nice, actually," Yardley said as they left the room and went to another hallway Amanda pointed out to them.

"What's that?" KC let go of her hand, but slowly, with another smile.

"Swedish prison. I'd have to take off a star or two on account of it being *prison*, but the food was excellent, and at the time I was hungry and incredibly tired."

"Put a pin in that," KC said. "Later."

Later.

Yardley let herself believe it like it was their first truth.

CHAPTER FIFTEEN

Lidingö, Stockholm Archipelago

The last thing KC had reviewed in the ballroom before she ducked into the back seat of the BMW X5 was drone footage.

Now, as she traveled through the city of Stockholm and over the New Lidingö Bridge to Devon Mirabel's private compound, her mind's eye kept pulling back and away, zooming out to consider the shape of Northern Europe hunched over the Baltic Sea like a protective parent. Water breaking against coastline had left behind a low landscape riddled with lakes, canals, and islands.

Mirabel's compound sat on just over four acres of pristinely kept woodland and rolling green lawns. KC had been briefed on the locations of public land and parks, access points on the electric grid, propane reserves, power lines, and cell towers. She knew where the agency had land, air, and water support stationed for the mission and the locations from which more support could be called in.

All of this, KC imagined on her mental map as pinpoints and outlines superimposed over access roads and highways, canals and bridges, sea lanes and air traffic routes.

Mostly, though, she thought about how, from the air, Stockholm looked like northern Minnesota, where the fertile farmland fragmented into small lakes, breaking apart until, at the Canadian border, there was nothing but blue.

She'd gone with Yardley on vacation to those boundary waters the first year they were together. They'd flown to Minneapolis and driven a rental car north until they ran out of land. An outfitter supplied them with canoes and bags of equipment and food, and they'd spent five days paddling, reading maps, learning what loon calls sounded like. They'd laughed and slept in late and eaten fried trout. She'd discovered that Yardley had a beautiful singing voice but only knew the lyrics to maudlin English ballads. That she had no compunctions about putting a minnow on a hook. That her head was full of random and delightful facts, and she could sit on a rock without moving, watching the sunset until it had completely disappeared below the horizon.

That trip was when KC had known that the first thought she'd had upon seeing Yardley—*I'm going to marry that woman*—wasn't something she could pretend was anything but the voice of fate.

The kind of fate she'd never really believed in.

When Yardley moved in, she set up an area in the basement to make her dioramas. She had magnifying lights and a Dremel. She kept her supplies stacked in Sterilite organizers full of moss, dirt, and bitty rocks in various sizes and colors. KC had asked for a tour, and Yardley—pink-cheeked, talking too fast—showed her a diorama of the Boundary Waters. It had a little canoe, with two tiny figures. The figure at the back of the canoe had red hair.

KC couldn't look at Stockholm from the air and not think of Yardley. She couldn't look out the window of the agency's black car, purring slowly over the winding island road, and not think of the layers and layers of maps in her head. Sea lanes. Air support. Escape routes. Yardley's enthusiasm, making the world glow. How she was quiet and unguarded in sleep. What had gone wrong.

Every map had a red dot hovering above Mirabel's teal-roofed compound, which KC had committed to memory. The main house, three outbuildings, the pool, the stables. Thirty bedrooms. Thirty bathrooms. Four levels, a wraparound driveway, a firepit, a boat launch, walking path, garage.

The guests. Their dossiers. Their security. Their motives, objectives, weaknesses, pet peeves, histories. Who would have weapons, what kind, how to disarm them.

A hundred things that could go wrong. A thousand errors KC could make that meant she failed to achieve the mission's single objective.

Get the drive.

But when she closed her eyes, what she heard was the faint, whooshing white noise of her comm and what she liked to pretend was the sound of Yardley breathing, even though it probably wasn't. She slowed her own breath down to match it, the same as she used to do when she wrapped her arm around Yardley's middle and closed her eyes in their bedroom, letting the warm, breathing aliveness of the woman she loved lull her to sleep.

That kiss. That kiss in the closet that smelled like towels fresh out of the dryer, like the sheets at an expensive hotel in the District where she'd splurged on a date with Yardley last year.

The way, when KC found her mouth, Yardley had made a noise like it hurt in the best, brightest way, and her skin was so hot, everywhere, against KC's palms, and she couldn't get enough even as she couldn't quite convince herself it was happening.

But it had happened, and it had done something to KC like it did to see her mother's gold watch on Yardley's wrist after she'd implied she left it in Virginia. It meant she'd never taken it off except when she had to. It meant she hadn't taken it off *yet*, and so there was more than just that encounter in the dark to work with. There was the conversation they'd had, halting and difficult, but real.

Trust.

Tonight, KC had decided to let the heavy fabric and loose neck of the sequined, oversized black satin T-shirt she wore tell her body how to move. The woman she was pretending to be was young and insouciant. Spoiled. Sharp. The dress was so short, KC wore black briefs and fishnets essentially as pants, but she liked the knee-high, patent leather Docs. Their platform soles changed her gait, changed her attitude, and cloaked an arsenal of tech.

No one will look too close, Yardley had said, tapping through a tablet, double-checking mission details. *They'll be insulted you're not packing a gun.*

I hate guns, KC had said, which made Yardley laugh.

So do I.

It was funny. When KC had imagined Yardley Whitmer in her role as a financial consultant, she'd pictured her gliding through airports in a silk blouse with her roller bag, distant but polite with the tedious finance bros. She'd told herself that her Snow White princess saved her fullest, most secret, weirdest self for KC and KC alone.

But the Yardley who built dioramas in the basement, who snorted at KC's most juvenile Monty Python references and made herself caches of salty, slightly revolting snack foods in case she suddenly needed them for fuel because she burned even more calories being alive, being *a little too much*, than KC did running forty miles a week—

That Yardley did not belong only to KC. That Yardley was the Unicorn.

In the ballroom, coordinating the mission, she talked fast, and she was always two steps ahead. She moved constantly, pacing, gesticulating, throwing off beams of energy. She absorbed dossiers and details, briefing documents and updates from the analysts, from tech, from Atlas and Gramercy, like they were KC telling her a story—her round chin balanced in her hand, her long legs crossed, nodding her head, taking it in.

The first time KC had kissed her, it was because Yardley asked her to, after hours at that party talking, flirting, eating, finding ways to touch KC's hair, hand, arm, and shoulder. KC had slowly wrapped her hand around the bodice ties of Yardley's white sundress. She'd pulled her mouth close, and through the silky cotton of those ties, like they were wicks pulling melted wax, she felt Yardley go entirely still.

She'd asked Yardley against her mouth, holding her to a wall hidden from the partygoers—the smoothest KC had probably ever been—if she still wanted the kiss, and Yardley had closed her eyes and begged *please* in such a broken voice, KC knew that the kiss was going to lead to their first everything.

It was a lot, how it was between them. In the beginning, KC had been where Yardley could put it all.

They'd hurt each other the most by holding back, because KC was who the Unicorn came home to. KC was Yardley's person, her respite, her soft sheets and hot mugs of coffee and long, lazy mornings in bed. Just KC. Even when she hid the truth and didn't give Yardley everything she deserved, she'd still been the person the Unicorn chose, the person Yardley Whitmer took to meet her family, and that meant their relationship had always been real.

Real, and messed up, and imperfect, and falling apart.

But things that failed could be put back together. How many times had KC taken her own lines of painstakingly assembled code and cut them into pieces, rearranged them, rewrote them, so she could fix them and make them work?

She'd made Yardley a promise in that linen closet, and she intended to keep it.

"Confirmation from Atlas, the device is onsite." Yardley's voice in the comm was buttery and tart at the same time. It was the same voice she used on the phone with her mama. That made KC smile.

"Does it include confirmation the product is for auction?" Out the car's window, she could just see the lights from Mirabel's compound, curving along the long driveway. There were two cars in front of them and few more trailing behind. Some of the guests would be arriving by water, others landing at a private helipad a mile away on the far side of a forest preserve to be shuttled to the property by Mirabel's staff.

"Affirmative." Atlas's voice came in. "This is a one-stop shop."

"Tech is reporting at least one more RSVP." Yardley exhaled. "No intel."

"Copy." KC had a sinking feeling about that RSVP, but there wasn't any point articulating it. They'd prepared for every contingency that could be prepared for. "Sidebar. Has Absolute Tosser finished interrogating the asset's unexpected visitor?"

Absolute Tosser was not Gramercy's code name, but it had been enthusiastically taken up in the last hours of the mission, as Gramercy had been the one to take Declan Byrne into custody at the ambassador's residence to determine if he posed an intelligence risk. It had made Kris pretty touchy, which wasn't a great combination with her current stage of pregnancy and her desperation to see Declan.

Yardley laughed. "Indeed. Our lovebirds are sequestered in monitored custody."

"I think he's a fine young man," Gramercy came on. "With a lot going on at the moment."

All of this, of course, was simply chatter. A way for KC to test if she had nerves, if she was thinking clearly, if she was focused. But she felt good, as calm as she did when she settled in around the third mile of a long run and everything smoothed out.

She knew what to do. She trusted Yardley.

The car pulled up out of a copse of trees. The circular drive was lined with lights and guards with AKs. KC counted them, cursing guns, noting the sight lines because one thing it was hard to get clear intelligence about in advance was how a location looked from the ground.

She spotted, with not a little surprise, an armored personnel carrier parked in the grassy expanse ringed by the drive. A U.S. Stryker. It had a cannon mounted on the top. "Do you see this ride?"

"Whoa," Yardley said. "Settles my bet with Atlas about what Mirabel's been keeping in the horse stable. I told you he didn't have horses. Also, are there used military vehicle lots everywhere now? With those waving inflatables and prices written in shoe polish on the windshields?"

"Maybe he's going to use it as a flower planter," KC said as the car pulled to a stop. The covered entrance to the home had crystal chandeliers lighting the path, three liveried valets who KC recognized as part of Mirabel's second-ring security detail, and a young Russian oligarch smoking with a discarded Italian cabinet member who had been lately dabbling in opium import-export.

"Hey, losers." KC hopped out of the car the moment her driver opened the door. "Where's the party?"

She strode up to the two strangers while they pretended not to be interested in her. KC was beginning to understand that there was a lot of showmanship in spy craft. Also rules, cliques, gossip, and grudges. Yardley had told her that going to Vienna, the spy capital of the world, was like showing up at an endless debutantes' coming out ball. KC had only attended a year of high school, and she definitely had never so much as received an invite to a coming-out ball, but she'd been a short, scrappy, queer redhead from birth. Theater came pre-installed.

"I didn't believe it when I heard Daniel had a kid." The woman took a very long drag of a bright pink cigarette. "But it makes sense now." She raised an eyebrow at the man beside her, who laughed.

"Daddy issues," he said, with a knowing nod.

KC's cover was that she was the reprobate daughter of a well-known California-based arms dealer who was actually a CIA operative. They'd kept the background simple. Invitations to tonight's auction hadn't been difficult to come by.

"You don't know the half of it," KC said. "I don't even answer the phone unless he's already told me I'm a good girl." She finger-gunned them. "Later." One of the uniformed henchmen gestured her inside. "Cool friends," KC murmured. "Definitely going to add them on Snapchat when I get home."

"Isabella can be fun," Yardley replied. "She actually got me out of a jam in Ulaanbaatar once, but then she stopped answering my texts."

"That is tragic."

She passed into the entryway, where a bored-looking man

stood with his arms crossed, supervising a second bored-looking man who waved a wand over the guest who'd arrived in the car in front of KC's. He wore a paisley smoking jacket and T-posed for the guards, exposing a shoulder holster that held a large-caliber pistol. When the wand passed over the pistol, a monitor beeped. Both guards ignored it and waved him through.

"Don't talk to me on the comm," Yardley reminded her as KC held her arms out for her own scan. "Oh! To your left, just past Paisley Jacket? That's the guy from the wedding in Toronto! I did not make him for one of us. Or one of them."

"Canadian intelligence," Gramercy supplied after a brief pause. "Jack Tremblay. Just got the courtesy notification a moment ago."

"Oh ho!" Yardley said. "So the prime minister did not trust us to pull this off. I should have known that guy was a Sister. They all think they're 007 with their fancy haircuts and abs." Yardley sounded peeved but amused, like she did when KC took them on a route that would add mileage to their run after promising to keep it short.

"I have abs and a fancy haircut," she replied under her breath, but barely attending because the entry hallway opened out into a vast space, and she needed a moment to integrate what she knew with what she could see.

Which was a long wall of windows overlooking the patio and lawn to the water, shiny inlaid flooring, rows of enormous chandeliers that appeared to have birthed the baby chandeliers she'd seen outside, and a glittering array of people whose cocktail attire and bling put the lights to shame.

In the middle of the room, she noted neat rows of wooden folding chairs, a few already occupied by guests. The last chair in each row had a number on its side. At the far end, there was a dais with a podium. A projection screen mounted behind it displayed an enormous image of a round blue velvet pillow encircled with gold braid.

"I called it," Yardley said. "That's where they'll put the drive, reclining like a painted lady on that sexy pillow. None of these men are creative. I would've gone with something more like when you unbox a new iPhone. Lots of custom packaging and concealed magnetized clasps."

Someone touched KC's elbow, and she turned to see one of Mirabel's security detail—*Harry Davies*, her memory from the briefing supplied, *thirty-one, hails from the dodgy part of Leeds, bit of a thing for off-track betting*—holding something out to her.

A paddle. Her paddle, for the auction. They'd assigned her number sixty-nine.

"Niiice." KC took the paddle and pulled a lascivious face for Harry, who immediately started huffing with laughter, one hand on his waist. His laughter surprised her into her own, and then, in the middle of an island mansion in a ritzy island neighborhood near Stockholm, at a party for every henchman around the globe poised to purchase the most destructive nonincendiary weapon currently known to the international community, KC was sharing what was undeniably a *moment* with a petty criminal whose background, after all, was no better than her own.

He put his hand on her shoulder to support his belly laugh. "Oi, that's what I said, wasn't it? But these boys can't take a joke." He snorted a final time, giving her shoulder a pat, and then leaning back. "Phew, I needed that." He scanned the room. "Bit uptight here for such a do, don't you think?"

"Maybe we should spike the punch." She gestured to a champagne fountain by a French door open to the vast patio.

"Oh, it's spiked. I'd stick to the bottled beer at the bar." He nudged her with his elbow. "Good luck, then."

He melted back into the crowd as KC started across the room, marking every face she recognized, all the exits and obstacles, expected and unexpected.

"You made a friend," Yardley purred in her ear. "Good job, you."

"Useful friend," Gramercy said. "There's an Interpol Black Notice on him. Seems he was the last to speak with a woman who went missing in the Lake District. Former mistress of Mirabel's, but no doubt that's a coincidence."

"You can take him hostage and promise not to turn him in if he cooperates," Yardley said. "Assuming he wouldn't sing like a bird if you gave him a good smile and asked if he wanted to do lines in the stable, which I'm entirely certain he would."

"Too many spies in the kitchen," KC whispered. "Simmer down."

"Tech wants you closer to the stage," Atlas told her. "They want to see what they can pull."

KC headed in that direction, pausing to set her paddle on the chair with her number on it. There was no one to her right, but the seat to her left was occupied by none other than Jack Tremblay, Canadian spy. He nodded collegially. He wore an Armani suit with a bright shirt unbuttoned to the navel. She rolled her eyes and made her way to the dais, where a few very serious players were loitering.

Including Devon Mirabel.

He saw her. KC had to remind herself he'd never gotten a good look at the Starbucks.

He shouldn't be able to recognize her. But if he did, there was always plan B.

KC stepped closer and extended her hand. "Daphne Sullivan. Thanks for the invite."

Devon accepted her hand. His gaze lingered on her face for a long moment, searching her features. "You don't look one bit like your father."

She sent a silent apology to Daniel Sullivan before she replied. "Not anymore, thanks to the baby Jesus and the miracle hands he gifted to a doc at her discreet Beverly Hills clinic. Have you seen the nose on my dad? No, thank you. Bought this one as soon as I had access to my trust fund. Where's this piece of plastic you've got us all so excited about?" She stepped closer to the empty pillow, hoping it was close enough for her tech support to pick up something useful.

"I'm surprised he sent you this evening," Mirabel continued as though she hadn't asked the question, searching her face.

KC didn't want to suffer through one of this man's endless personal auditions. She'd watched a lot of tape of a lot of encounters with Mirabel, and where her team saw a boss to beat, she simply saw tedium.

"Fucking kick me out," she said cheerfully. "I don't care." She looked around. "But everyone else here will treat this tech like a toy to destabilize events literally no one will give a shit about in a single news cycle." She pointed at Mirabel's stupid face. "My dad didn't send me. I edged him out with a set of steel basement window bars, a few friends who have automatic weapons and poor impulse control, and genuine millennial ambition, which is a combination of astrology and white-hot rage at the capitalistic, heteronormative, boomer-bred patriarchy that forces us into anxious complacency. I'm here because I want to burn it all down. The question is, are you ready for a new world order?"

"Yikes," Yardley breathed.

KC was gratified to see rage flare in Mirabel's eyes. She did have a gift for repelling male dominance. He reached into an inner pocket of his suit coat and pulled out the micro drive, hushing the ring of buyers at the dais. Still looking at her, he slammed it on the pillow and strode away.

"Can you—" Gramercy's voice.

"She's already on it," Yardley said. "Don't bother my protégé."

KC sidestepped, mashing the toes of a woman who'd made the mistake of wearing sparkly high-heeled sandals, and got to the pillow first. She put her hands on her hips, elbows wide enough to play defense against anyone who might be thinking of pushing her out of the way. Then she took a look.

Shit.

She strode off the dais.

"Tech requests another few moments with the device," Gramercy said.

"That's not it." KC stalked away, waiting to say more until she'd found a spot close to the windows where she could contemplate the view unobserved. "I was really, super hoping for Plan A."

"Tech didn't quite—"

"The material that kind of drive is made of is an old-school casein-based plastic. It looks a way. The sage green color is distinctive. I didn't touch it, but I know that if I had, it wouldn't feel right. It's a dupe."

"You're going by color and . . . anticipated feel of the drive case?" Atlas broke in.

"I have been looking at buying one of those adorably minuscule drives to play with for two years, but the agency doesn't pay me enough. I know what's in my unpurchased online shopping cart. Those are sacred items."

"Affirmative," Yardley said with a satisfyingly stern tone. "Plan B it is."

Plan A had been straightforward: KC would win the bid. The U.S. government would transfer whatever obscene number of dollars KC spent, or convincingly pretend to—that was for the money guys, not KC's department—and she'd put the drive in her briefs, tuck herself into the back seat of the agency's car, and hand it off to someone who she would advise to take it to a secure room and incinerate it in a small, security-cleared kiln.

Simple.

Plan B was a lot more like trying to knock a hornet's nest off the shed on a hot day while covered in pancake syrup.

"Please take your seats." The blonde with the sparkle shoes was circulating through the crowd. Portuguese accent. *Lorena Fonseca.* "The sale will begin in twenty minutes."

"No updates from the analysts on the location of the safe," Yardley said. "Still a toss-up between the carriage house and the master suite, so you'll have to go by your gut and be ready to pivot."

KC mingled her way toward the Portuguese woman. Fonseca had been deep in the hacker scene for the Russians a few years ago, and her code was enviably efficient and flawless.

"E aí?" KC asked. "Tudo bem?"

Fonseca narrowed her eyes. "Your accent isn't bad. Nanny?"

"One of them." KC had actually honed her Portuguese to a fine point during a lonely period her first year of college. She'd run across an access door to stream the Portuguese telenovela *Ajuste de Contas* and had gotten hooked after watching a few episodes and catching a blistering parasocial crush on the actress Paula Neves, who she'd wanted to be able to talk to on Tumblr.

"We begin in twenty. Why are you bothering me, vagabunda?"

"If you wanted to transfer seven hundred Bitcoin over a firewall that Kate 'The Hackmistress' Mason built around the National Australia Bank," KC asked, leaning in close, lowering her voice, "and your cover was to powder your nose during a weapons auction, what power outlets would you use in this house? I don't want to flip a breaker."

"Why are you little pestinhas like this? This party is for grown-ups."

"I know, I know. But I really like the sensation of my face attached to my skull, and I don't want to look at it hanging from some guy's finger just because a teeny-tiny item on my pre-auction to-do list slipped my mind."

"Caralhos me fodam," Fonseca swore. "Mirabel has a private grid on the carriage house. After ten minutes, I'm sending someone to tie you to a chair and throw you in the canal."

"Perf! Brigadinha!"

"This is why you send tech into the field, ladies," Yardley said as KC hustled to the patio. "They can go on more than their gut."

"I hate this view," KC said as soon as she'd made it outside. There were quite a few people on the patio, most of them men clumped in small groups, smoking and trying to impress each other. "Dudes in formalwear, dark as fuck, slippery surface—it's like homecoming all over again."

"I went to queer prom," Yardley said. "Lots of light and color. Gramercy, do we have anything decent from the cloaked drone you can give her?"

One of KC's contact lenses showed her an image of the grounds from the air. She had to blink and take a moment to adjust, but she'd practiced with this tech, so her brain only glitched for a moment. "Much better. How live is this feed?" She made her way toward the edge of the patio.

"Bit of a delay," Gramercy said. "Five to seven seconds."

"I'll let you know if anyone's coming," Yardley assured her.

"Copy." After checking the feed one last time, she slipped off the porch and onto the damp lawn. The cold raised chill bumps over her bare arms.

"There are seven armed guards along this pathway. Copy?" Yardley's speech had sped up, but it remained unbothered, like she trusted KC to handle the guards. It warmed KC's muscles up without stretching.

"Yep." She scanned the landscaping along the path, checking it against the drone feed. "It might be nice if our Canadian buddy made himself useful and distracted those three clustered together at five o'clock closest to the French doors."

"Copy," Atlas replied. "We'll get that done."

KC went still until she heard what she assumed was the Sister's voice greet the three guards, asking for a light and making a gross joke about the champagne fountain attendant. As soon as she saw the group move off, she somersaulted between two trimmed shrub rows that had guards on either side, her focus moving down to what felt like one vibrating point.

She moved up to a crouch and made a standing jump onto a stone pillar that put her body above the last guard she had to pass, standing only a few meters away. Before he could turn around (in the event he heard the soles of her Docs hit the granite), she crouched and leaned toward the carriage house until her palm hit rough wooden trim, then swung her body in a tight circle to the small side vestibule over a door.

"*Parkour*," Yardley whispered.

Smiling, KC reached into a slit in the leather of her boot to pull out a lockpick set. "I'm going to need help with the alarm system. I can see the light bank through the door window. It's a KorenSur 30x, so we don't need to get fancy, we can just jam the fuck out of it. Tell tech to use the two-step code I wrote, but not the new one. We want that sweet vintage version that's all power and no finesse."

"Copy," Gramercy said, with a smile in his voice. After a few seconds' delay, he reported back. "We've got it running. You're good to proceed."

Most of the other students in KC's training cohort at Langley had been recruited through the traditional channels, and none of them had picked a lock prior to their arrival in Virginia. It was one of the few units KC had completed in her training with top marks.

"Gramercy issued that acknowledgment," Yardley said, "because I was still recovering from the sweet move off that pillar. I had to dump a bucket of ice over my head."

KC's cheeks were hot when the tumblers fell. She reached up as she opened the door and, before the tongue could disengage from the strike plate, pressed down on the button on the top of the door that would've sounded an onsite alarm if she hadn't.

After three seconds, she let go, held her breath, and finally exhaled when she did not, thankfully, hear the piercing wail of a siren.

She was glad for the platform soles. Without them, she never would have been able to reach the button.

She watched the KorenSur's light bank until all the lights had blinked from green to yellow, then stepped into an open-plan room containing a lot of antique Scandinavian furniture painted with flower motifs. "I need a power scan—" KC stepped forward into the room and heard, from the light bank of the KorenSur, the soft, nearly inaudible click of a connecting circuit. "No." She bit her lip.

"No, you don't need a power scan? Confirm?" Yardley asked.

"I do, but first I have to know if there is a laser field or a heat-sensing field in this room before I take another step. You probably have another twenty, twenty-five seconds to figure it out."

"Copy," Yardley said, and then, a second later, "Both. What do you need?"

"I'm going to have to finish tripping it, and what I want tech to do is just silence the alarm and block the notification to whoever has it set up on whatever device. This is KorenSur's app-based system. Kind of cheap on Mirabel's part."

"Like what Tabasco did for me in Berlin a couple years ago?" Yardley said.

"Exactly that. I'm going to proceed to where I am assuming the safe is, based on what kind of laser and heat fields cover this room. Don't love that it looks like my Portuguese friend set me up. I'm guessing my time here is limited."

"Copy, clear to proceed. We'll have a fat twenty seconds before the notification goes out. Easy. And Lorena is power mad. Don't take it personally."

KC walked through the room, holding her breath, mentally counting down the seconds as she strode through the invisible field that was changing the voltage of every sensor and thereby tripping the alarm, even as she couldn't hear it. Once she crossed the room, she came to a pony wall that looked strange, given the open plan. "I assume I'm good?"

"So good," Yardley said. "You get any better, I won't survive this mission, and I'm safely tucked away in a warm van, not eluding henchmen and lasers."

KC's helpless grin in the empty room was the only thing about her reaction to Yardley's flirting on an open comm channel that she could safely assume belonged to her and her alone. It felt precisely like one of the dozens of times Yardley had flung a bit of sass her way in the middle of a run, stopping KC dead in her tracks to laugh, or to protest, or to grab her by the waist and kiss her.

It had been a long time.

"I've been thinking," she said, running her fingertips along the pony wall and making sure her cameras took in every inch of it, because the agents in the van could pick up more than she would.

"I already like what you're thinking," Yardley said. "See if there is a door somewhere to the left of you."

"Should we all reconsider 'Tabasco'? Because Tabasco's from Louisiana, as you pointed out." She found the invisible seam and pressed two fingers into it. She heard a soft pneumatic hiss, and then the hidden door, thick and heavy, came open an inch. "And it's kind of insulting? It implies a certain heedlessness normally associated with men who have friends everyone calls 'Rooster.' Or 'Jug Belly.'"

"Absolutely not my associations, but I take your point," Yard-ley said. "Unfortunately, you're stuck with it. You can open that up. We have around seven minutes until the auction begins."

KC opened the heavy door to a panel with an embedded com-puter console. Not the safe—another layer of security in front of it. She put her fingers on the keys, waking up the computer into standby mode.

"You need tech?"

"What do you think?" KC ran through a few opening lines of code just to see what she was dealing with, overriding the screen view so she could see the source.

Damn it all to hell.

"I need our asset to join us on the comm link," she said.

"Negative," Atlas broke in. "The asset's authorization is limited to confirming we have the right product."

"I thought we were authorized to save the world. Look, Mirabel locked this with, for lack of a better term, a riddle he got from the asset. These are kind of her thing. My hope of cracking it and making time are less than zero. I can't torch my way in. If I blow it up, we lose what's inside. So I either get the asset on comm, or I'm going to have to belly crawl out of here and swim home."

"I have the asset on comm link," Yardley said. "Please don't get in the water. It's forty-one degrees Fahrenheit, and you're wearing boots. Bride, you can go ahead."

"You catch my code name, then?" Kris's cheerful, extremely loud voice made KC touch her ear as though she could turn down the volume. She could not. "You're going to want to start with running a regular password request. Doesn't matter what kind."

"Are congratulations in order?" KC prompted the system to ask for a password. "Got it."

"Do you remember the Sphinx Questions code from back in the day? Do that. And, yes, Declan showed up here with three juicy carats, and I said yes!"

"Is a proposal less romantic, do you think, when it happens behind bars?" KC tapped the screen. "All right, I've been hit with one of your skeleton key codes, so you're going to have to give up one of your famous secrets."

"Does it matter where a girl finds herself when she's in love?" Kris's voice had gone a little dreamy, and KC's heart softened in response. "Seems to me the only thing you can choose in this life is love or fear. That's it, really. Love or fear. I do hate to give up my secrets, but this one's old. It's just the code to the start screen of the original *Mario Kart*. It will autofill if you give it the first line."

KC felt her heart twist, just a little, at Kris's philosophy. Love or fear. Simple.

"I'm in."

"Ta! There's someone already holding out her hand for my comm link thing. See you soon, love."

"Four and a half minutes left. Let me have a look at what we've got." Yardley's voice had quieted. It made KC wonder if what Kris said about love and fear hit her, too.

KC approached the safe behind the panel that housed the computer. Its depth accounted for the pony wall. Its face was about twenty-four inches square. She was surprised to see a dial fit over another dial on its face. The first was a circle of tiny brass letters, while the bigger dial had numbers, one to ninety-nine.

Her insides went to buzzing, prickling static, and she felt a bead of sweat make its way to the small of her back. She'd been certain she'd be dealing with a digital lock of some kind. So had the team.

She had no hope of cracking a safe like this, absolutely not in a few minutes.

"No worries," Yardley whispered, just like she did, sleepy and kind, when KC would wake up in the middle of the night from a bad dream. KC could almost imagine Yardley's arm coming around her waist, gathering her close to her body. "I love these little puzzles. No one knows how to crack a good safe anymore. I used to check out the books from the library at Langley and mess around with that stuff they archive in the basement. Did you know safecrackers used to be called 'yeggmen'?"

KC had not. But she felt a little calmer.

"There's an international competition," Yardley said. "Of the yeggmen. The same sonofabitch wins it every year, pardon my language. I have fantasized about entering. I would, and kick him off his throne, if I didn't have to keep up my cover. Okay. This safe is French. Here's where this is going to get strange. Are you ready?"

"Yes."

"I want you to put the pad of your index finger on the numbered dial, the larger one. But very, very gently. Just enough to hold it in place. Then, with your other hand, spin the dial with the letters one full revolution, and try to mark the five places you feel something like a ball bearing rolling from one seat to another."

Yardley's voice had gentled, pulling in all the familiar vowels and cadence of North Carolina. It steadied KC the same way that her flirting over the comm link did—which Yardley must know, or she wouldn't be doing it. KC placed her finger and started moving the dial. "Oh. I felt the first one."

"There you go. What was it?"

"E."

"That's it. That's all you do. Let me know what letters."

KC moved the dial slowly, time losing meaning. "V. O. N. D. Are you fucking kidding me?"

"Devon. Mercy. Move the dial to each letter in order after you reset it to Z."

KC did, and then, to her surprise, the lettered dial popped forward.

"So cool," Yardley said. "Take off that dial. Now's the hard part. You're going to have to take out your comm link."

"What?"

KC heard Atlas and Gramercy say it at the same time she did.

"I need her to stick it on the middle of the dial. It's the only way I can hear what I need to in order to crack it. Atlas, Gramercy, buy me whatever time you can with tech or with a distraction, but this is it. Our team's already determined what's in the safe."

"They have?" KC's voice cracked.

"Yeah. I wasn't supposed to tell you in case it messed up your game, but we're inches away from, you know, mission complete. But I'm not even a little worried. It's you. You can do anything. So you'll have to pull out the comm and place it right in the middle of the dial. I'll send you over your visual link what numbers to set the dial to. There will be five. Ready?"

KC took a deep breath. "Ready. Audio comm down." She pulled out the lockpicks again and used the slimmest one to capture the comm, deep in her ear, the size of a screw in a pair of eyeglasses. The world of sound suddenly pressed in on her—the wind off the water kicking up settling noises from the carriage house, her breath, the creak of her leather boots. She pushed the comm into a little space in the middle of the dial and started turning it slowly.

The visual from Yardley appeared as a transparent blue box in her mid-vision. She made a full revolution of the dial, holding her breath, before the combination came up.

72, 3, 16, 35, 8. KC entered the numbers in.

She should've put the comm back in her ear right away.

She should've been watching her back.

Then, maybe, when the safe opened with a silky pop, and she grabbed the tiny, pale green case and prepared to bolt, she wouldn't have been so surprised to turn around and discover Dr. Brown standing behind her with a disappointed look on his face.

CHAPTER SIXTEEN

A quarter mile from Devon Mirabel's mansion

For the first time in her career, the Unicorn had a long and horrific moment in which she did not know what to do and did not know if it was going to be okay.

The moment the face of Dr. Brown filled their monitors, everyone in the van went silent—Gramercy, Atlas, two tech agents whom KC had handpicked, and a marine provided by the embassy.

Gramercy moved first. He left the van, taking with him the comm set that gave him a direct line to the highest decision-makers and was reserved for literal national emergencies.

Atlas started talking to someone at Evenes, snapping at the tech to pull up intel. Their eyes met Yardley's. "Stay with her."

"She can't hear me."

"But you can hear everything going on in the room, you can see it, and you can send messages to the visual comm. Get it together, Yardley. Get it the fuck together."

KC still hadn't said anything. One of the techs was already talking to Kris, likely trying to figure out if there was any way to wipe or disable the drive remotely. They already knew there wasn't, but this was a desperate moment. The other tech was pulling down every mind in the CIA to keep any alarm or notification off KC until it was clear whether she had a shot of escaping with the drive.

Twelve hundred days.

That was what Yardley thought, frantically, and it was enough to start her heart beating again.

They would make it to twelve hundred and one.

She studied the monitor showing KC's visuals. This time, instead of looking at Dr. Brown's face with shock, she started looking at the circumstances and how to get KC and the drive out of there. In that order.

She sent a message to KC's visual display. *Checking Dr B credentials.*

It was the understatement of the year in a year that deserved every bit of hyperbole she could throw at it.

Yardley didn't know for sure why Dr. Brown was in Mirabel's carriage house, but she had certainly prepared herself for the possibility he'd show up. There was always a chance Dr. Brown was here in good faith. In Yardley's experience, however, the good guys didn't suddenly appear where they weren't supposed to be, and they didn't engage with people whose shock at seeing them could potentially endanger their mission.

She'd kept the secret of Dr. Brown's supposed black op from Atlas and Gramercy, despite her reservations. There simply hadn't been any way to preserve KC's safety while also opening up questions about the veracity of Dr. Brown's involvement in the development of this weapon to a wider audience. There were very few "trust no one" circumstances in the trade, despite the movies, but when such a circumstance arrived, it was time to figure out where you were in the web and who you cared about.

KC stood up from her crouch in front of the safe. It had only been moments, but they'd felt like hours. Yardley noted, hated, and ignored KC's biometric readings, which had all been within normal range until she was surprised by Dr. Brown.

"You're here." The comm on the safe picked up KC's voice as clear as a ten-thousand-dollar speaker, for which Yardley was grateful.

"It's much more surprising that you are." Dr. Brown looked around. "I assume we've still got borrowed time from the boys?"

Dr. Brown always called tech "the boys."

"Mm. Has the auction started?" KC's voice was even. Her heart rate had settled into a respectable rhythm.

"You don't know?" Dr. Brown reached up to tap his own ear. "Who's your handler?"

"I didn't have intel you'd be attending."

Good. KC hadn't answered his direct question. Yardley didn't know yet where KC had determined Dr. Brown's loyalties lay, but a careful operative remained circumspect. KC was a careful operative.

"You're not going to be told more than the basics, Tabasco. I can only assume you're in the field because the Unicorn's been compromised. Or turned."

Yardley felt her nostrils flare. *Turned* was bait. Dr. Brown was baiting KC. Dangerous for a handler to fuck with agents' emotions.

Her heart was pounding in her ears. Where was Gramercy with the intel?

"I'm glad you're okay," KC said. "Truly. It was frightening to know you were hurt and not hear from you for so long. It's been difficult to keep my loyalties safe."

Yardley held her breath. She didn't know Dr. Brown well

enough to know whether his ego was such that he would believe KC would keep his secrets above all others, but KC seemed to know him. She held eye contact with him for several seconds, until Yardley watched tension she hadn't known where to look for melt out of his expression.

He wanted to believe KC. If he could, it would mean his hold on her was intact. Double agents had such a problem with narcissism.

KC's gaze flicked to a dark hallway. Yardley's schematic told her it led to a bedroom with sliders that opened to the wide lawn facing the narrow road along the water.

Yardley sent the schematic to confirm KC's escape route, hoping she hadn't read too much into that glance. That glance meant KC was thinking, and thinking would keep her alive.

Then KC's eyes blinked in an odd flutter.

"You've managed to find the drive. What are your orders?" Dr. Brown leaned against the wall behind him. His tone had lost the note of imperious formality. That was promising. Any amount Dr. Brown trusted KC was time bought and paid for to get her out.

Unless KC *genuinely* trusted Dr. Brown, and he could tell, which was why he was so relaxed.

KC's eyes fluttered again.

"C," Atlas whispered. "C! That's Morse code. With military abbreviations."

"C's affirmative," Yardley whispered, though KC couldn't hear her. "My goodness, honey." She directed the drone over the exit area from the sliders and sent the feed to KC to give her the view she'd asked for.

"You know I can't tell you." KC's tone wasn't one Yardley had

ever heard before. "But my time's about up. We'll need cover inside at the auction, or they'll come looking for me."

"Jack with the Sisters has got it handled," he said. "No one
knows I've stepped out. Meanwhile, everyone's wondering where
you've got to. I have a boat waiting and Franklin in my ear has-
sling me over how long this is taking because he's pissed Ada
couldn't talk the diplomats into letting us bunker-bust on Swedish soil."

General Franklin, he meant. And he'd name-dropped an
active Canadian agent and the president. Either Dr. Brown was
operating at a deeper level of cover than Yardley had been privy
to or he wanted to make KC believe that was the case.

There was a flurry behind Yardley. "A burn notice was issued."
It was Gramercy's voice. Thank heavens. "Flynn has ID'd him as
the man who arrested her in Dublin. We have pretty solid intel
from the analysts suggesting we should assume everyone with a
Northern Europe assignment is dirty."

"That's a small army," Atlas said. "Yardley."

"Yeah." She understood the implications of what Gramercy
was saying. It meant that whoever Dr. Brown worked for knew
about and potentially controlled every perimeter, extraction, and
mission unit they had out here. For now, they had no idea how
deep the corruption went.

Plans B through F were out of the question.

This was well beyond KC's experience. Dr. Brown was packing an armory, and KC hadn't even brought a knife to a gunfight.

He's turned, she typed for KC to read on her visual. The hair
on the back of Yardley's neck stood on end.

Not a single change in KC's biometrics, and she didn't give
them another Morse acknowledgment. She sidled closer to Dr.

Brown. "If that's the case, then come with me." She sounded strangely compliant. "We'll do this together."

"I can't." Dr. Brown smiled. It was a nice smile. At a vulnerable time in KC's life, he'd been present for her. He'd opened doors. How could she be expected to think with her head, not her heart, at a moment like this? "You'll have to give me the drive. Report the handoff to your team, and we'll talk at the ambassador's residence."

Their presence at the residence was Sensitive Compartmented Information. Even inside the agency, no one should have known they were there except people who absolutely needed to know.

Maple Leaf was well and truly compromised.

"We have to dump the drive and extract KC," Yardley said. "It's done. He'll kill her for it if she tries to hang on to it, but if she hands it off, she has a chance. We can find another way. He can't have been that careful. We'll infiltrate whoever he's with." She was talking fast, thinking faster, channeling her resources into her innate talent for strategy because it was one advantage she had over Dr. Brown.

All she had to do was keep one step ahead of him. Half a step.

"That's not what they're telling us to do." Gramercy's voice was tight. He still wore the emergency comm link that gave him a direct line to the director and the White House. "They want her to try to hang on to it. I'm sending you the orders now."

Yardley glanced at them.

No.

A robot drone had been deployed to the slider's entrance. It still hadn't been tracked. She was to order KC to toss the drive for the drone to retrieve under what would be a hailstorm of Dr. Brown's gunfire.

They really, truly intended to get KC Nolan killed.

She had *told* them not to do that.

Yardley rose to her feet inside the small van. "I'm afraid our orders have been compromised. Impossible to know how far up the chain the breach goes. Can't risk following directives." This was a blatant lie, but Atlas let out an exhale that sounded distinctly like relief. "My circle of trust is now the people in this van and Agent Nolan. Soldier, get out of the driver's seat."

"Ma'am." He looked at her desperately.

"I will court-martial you right back to the New Jersey suburb that hatched you. Get up."

"Yes, ma'am." He got up and moved to the passenger's seat.

She grabbed her laptop and started the ignition, looking back over her shoulder at Gramercy. "Get cover on us."

He gave her a look, one beat longer than necessary, just long enough for Yardley to see his gratitude. He'd been *hoping* she'd change the plan.

Yardley was so thankful in this moment when KC's life was in her hands to have trusted the right people that she made a small prayer promising she would start going to St. Anne's Episcopalian every Sunday she could. She put the laptop on the dashboard while she peeled out to race down the road through the trees, her eyes burning with her desire to see the lights of Mirabel's circular drive, willing it closer. She could hear a helicopter above, no idea whose.

A line of gunfire spit up gravel alongside the van.

Not their helicopter, then.

She glanced at the screen and watched KC take a step toward Dr. Brown. "I know the asset."

"Flynn?" he said. "Who doesn't?"

"I mean, we've gotten reacquainted."

KC must be close to him, because Dr. Brown's face filled the screen of the laptop, which was why Yardley was able to see his paternalistic affect drop and shift to interest. "What do you have in mind?"

He pulled out a gun, which KC looked at long enough for Yardley to identify it as a SIG Sauer P229. His duty weapon.

"Insurance," he explained to KC. "You have to understand that what you're implying about your close relationship with Flynn throws my trust that you're with Maple Leaf into question."

KC reached down and, to Yardley's absolute horror, grabbed the muzzle of the gun. It swept up in her field of vision as KC guided Dr. Brown to aim at her head. "I trust you even if you can't trust me."

Then KC turned around, her back to Dr. Brown, and pushed the computer panel back into view. She pulled out the drive where he wouldn't be able to see it before looking over her shoulder at Dr. Brown. "Let me close this up, and we'll get this party started. Like I said, I know Kris. She's my asset now. I'm privy to a few tricks no one else is."

Dr. Brown started to say something, but just as the van rounded the last curve and Yardley spotted the lights pouring from the house—guards everywhere, obvious chaos growing among the most dangerous guests in the world—she watched KC connect the micro drive to the computer panel.

"Fuck," Atlas said as another burst of gunfire from above grazed the road next to them. "I am over this."

The house went black.

Then the outdoor lights.

Then the lights over the water across the channel.

Every feed in the van blinked off at the same moment Yardley's comm link to the carriage house dropped out, and all she could hear was the helicopter, the van's engine, muffled shouts, and occasional gunfire from Mirabel's property.

"She deployed the cyberweapon," Gramercy said, somewhat unnecessarily.

But Yardley's vision had narrowed down. She turned off the van's headlights and barreled over the driveway, around the house over landscaped beds, until she spotted the shape of the carriage house. Then she hit the brakes, flung the door open, and hurtled toward the entrance.

She stumble-ran over the lawn, almost tripping over the drone downed in the grass six feet from the sliders. The interior of the carriage house bedroom was pitch black, then lit suddenly with the piercing horror of a muzzle flash when Dr. Brown's service weapon discharged.

"KC!"

She sprinted through the dark, aiming for where the computer panel should be, praying to every deity she'd ever heard about that she wasn't about to discover her girlfriend's lifeless body, when her jeans were snatched from behind and she was shoved back toward the door she'd come in.

"Get down!" KC hissed against her face.

The breath shuddered from her body. Yardley's vision grayed out in her relief. KC was alive. "Are you bleeding? Did he get you?"

"For fuck's sake." Strong hands yanked her to the floor. "I'm fine, but you're going to get the both of us killed."

"I am not." She was. Yardley had forgotten her training and made herself a target for Dr. Brown, who was still shooting at them. She felt woozy, but there wasn't time to put her head between her knees. KC took her hand, pressing her damp palm into Yardley's, and Yardley wanted to bring it to her lips to kiss it.

KC towed her outside. It was literally a circus on fire. Yardley recovered herself enough to remember what to do. "The van!"

KC got them to it, Dr. Brown somewhere behind them. She tossed Yardley through the open driver's door and shoved her into the center space so she could take the wheel. Yardley was about to sing hosannas to KC that she was alive and well and looking so good besides when KC peeled out.

She glanced at Yardley sprawled on the van's floor. "You almost got yourself shot! I knew you'd come with the van, but you were supposed to be getting my Morse code on how to pick me up, not barrel in there like a rodeo bull!"

"What?" Yardley moved to a seated position, peeking out the windows, hoping the second helicopter above was theirs this time and that it wouldn't fall from the sky any moment after losing its computer controls. "Dang it!"

KC swerved around a pair of guards. "What made you lose your mind like that, for Pete's sake!"

If KC was censoring her language, then she was extremely agitated. KC cursed for pleasure. "He's your mentor! He was playing on your emotions! He had a gun on you, KC. And he went bad, but it would be normal if you couldn't believe it! I couldn't believe it at first. You didn't have any comm! That's too much for a first mission!"

KC was swerving around guests, her body low in the driver's seat. "Too much for who, Yardley?"

"God, KC!" Yardley winced as the van grazed something very much on fire. "Too much for me, obviously! You knew enough to know I'd come with the van but not that I'd come and get you my own self?"

"I guess that's for one of our 'later' conversations." KC downshifted and looked back over her shoulder.

She was smiling.

Flirting, even.

"I knew he'd switched sides as soon as I saw him behind me," KC said. "I hated it, but a lot hadn't added up for a long time. I've known him forever. He thinks he knows me, but men always think they know someone, and when have you known any of them to really pay attention to anyone but themselves? No offense, Gramercy."

"Not at all." His voice was remarkably calm for the amount of automatic weapons fire and small explosions going off around them. He'd been here before.

"Oh," Yardley said.

"Yeah. I was playing *him*. I actually had a lot of options in there as long as he didn't shoot me, which I didn't think he really would. Men underestimate their emotional attachments. I'm the same age as his daughter."

"He has a daughter?"

"Gretel," KC said. "She's an architect in Arizona. He dotes on her."

"I did not know that," Gramercy said.

"Me neither," Atlas said.

"Everyone brace yourselves!" KC shouted, and immediately after Yardley gripped the seat in front of her, the van made sickening contact with an immoveable object. "Stay down and follow me. Don't stop moving, even if it gets weird."

KC opened the van door and rolled out of it, and the soldier

Yardley had ejected from the role of driver, obviously recognizing authority when he saw it, ripped open the sliding van door and got into a crouched, sheltering position, leading out Atlas, Gramercy, and the two techs.

"Get yourself back together, Whitmer," Yardley whispered, her usual calm finally starting to return. "KC Nolan is a superhero, and if you play your cards right, maybe she'll take you to dinner."

She crouched down and followed the techs out, the soldier at the rear. That was when she realized that KC had rammed the van into the M1126 Stryker Combat Vehicle. Immediately following this realization, Yardley experienced an auditory hallucination of KC telling her, *I can drive anything.*

Whoa.

She'd already brought down the rear entry to the Stryker. Atlas, Gramercy, and the techs were buckling themselves into the seats that lined each side of the interior. Yardley looked at KC, who directed her to a seat behind the commander's. She put the soldier in the second driver's seat.

"I've only completed computer simulation training, ma'am." The soldier buckled himself in.

"That's enough for where you're sitting." KC got the rear door shut, then reached over her head to turn on orange interior lights. "What's your name?"

"First Sergeant Dhaval Patel, U.S. Marine Corps, ma'am."

KC sat in the commander's seat, pulled down the periscope, flipped off all the lights except one, engaged the parking brake, put the massive gear shift into neutral, and yanked out a knob marked AUX MASTER, turning it on.

Well, then. This was happening. Yardley reached under her

seat and found her ear protection. Everyone else followed suit. The engine was cycling, lights on the command board flashing, when KC leaned over and turned the engine to start. The Stryker roared to life.

KC jumped out of the commander's seat and climbed up a short ladder to the side. "Patel, get on the periscope and set the cannon to the UTM coordinates 10, 5, 25, 270 East."

"Yes, ma'am."

KC flipped a series of latches, letting outside air in. She stood on the ladder looking out over the top of the Stryker. "Coordinates?"

"I've got a large white tank in sight. Point nine kilometers."

"Perfect. Looks good from here. Disengage the parking brake and hit the gas. Aim directly at the tank in your sights. The diesel should be warm enough. Let's hope this beast has been serviced recently and isn't just for show."

"Yes, ma'am." The Stryker lurched forward, and wind, shouting, helicopter rotors, and gunfire rose up from outside the armored vehicle in a cacophony that competed with the Stryker's engine.

"Yardley." KC's voice saying her name made Yardley's heart wrench in her chest with a burst of pained adoration. "Hand me a helmet?"

She felt around under her seat until she came up with a comically large ballistic helmet. She unbuckled it before holding it out to KC, who took it, her fingers sliding over Yardley's. They made eye contact for the first time since they'd parted ways before the mission, and, for a long moment, held it.

I love you, she thought. She didn't care if it was too much to feel, too soon or too late. It was true.

KC smiled her elfin smile.

She put the helmet on. Then, to Yardley's dismay, she stood up on the top rung of the ladder and waved her arms. She did something Yardley couldn't see or understand until she heard the rotors.

She was signaling their helicopter to cover them.

By doing semaphore out the hatch of a Stryker under fire.

Yardley put her hand over her mouth, staring at KC's fishnet-covered legs on the ladder.

This woman. This fierce, talented woman. Yardley would never love anyone else. She would never love anyone more.

"Fire on three, then take a hard left toward the road out, right past the explosion."

"Shit," Atlas said. "I hate explosions."

Yardley laughed, tears streaming from her eyes, the laughter and tears finally melting away every feeling but excitement to see what was going to happen next.

"Yes, ma'am. Ready on your count."

There was a short burst of fire from the helicopter.

"One, two, three!"

On three, KC crouched down on the top rung, and the Stryker jerked with the release of a thirty-millimeter round from the cannon.

There was an unholy boom from the tank.

Oh. The *tank*.

A thousand gallons of liquefied petroleum gas, enough to service the entire complex, had just gone up in flames. KC was blocking their exit. Once the fire got started, the road would become impassable.

"Get us the fuck out of here, Patel!"

"Yes, ma'am!"

KC lifted one leg off the top rung and bent her body completely over the top of the armored vehicle. Yardley waited for fear to fill her up as KC's precious self lit red in the light of the exploded tank of propane, but it didn't come.

She was *elated*.

She got it then, she really did. This was what it felt like to go all in. It was love alongside terrifying risk. Love with total acceptance.

And if Yardley couldn't help but remember with a pang the way her mama liked to complain that her precious only daughter had never learned anything the easy way in her whole life— because it was true—Yardley had to believe that was okay.

Even if it took a big, deafening explosion at the end of the world for her to let herself feel what it meant to love KC with her whole, entire heart, she could simply be grateful to feel it.

If she had to initiate a long courtship from square one, that was what she would do. She did not want to do that, but she would. She would hang out at KC's sweaty gym in those tight leggings that made her booty look bigger than it really was. She would pretend not to know how to use the weight machines and compel KC to help her. She would bake cookies and learn to play RPGs and lower her neckline. She was her mama's daughter. Terrifying, manipulative courtship that dazzled the mark was in her blood. Her daddy had bought a ring for her mama's cousin when they met, and her mama had him in a tuxedo standing before a preacher inside of six months.

KC's boots descended a few rungs, and her head ducked into view. "Goddammit." She looked at Yardley. "Get up here with me. I need your tall . . . everything." Yardley flew up the ladder, squeezing her body next to KC's. The view was improbable—the explosion just behind them, helicopters above, boats racing on the canal. Bursts of light from guns. She took a very sharp mental picture so that she would remember. It was these kinds of failures of the creative potential of the human spirit that were a good reminder to do what Flynn—*Kris*—had said. Choose love instead of fear.

"What do I do?" she asked.

"I'm going to unlatch the cannon, but I can't reach the last— Can you see it?"

Yardley looked. "I've got it." She bent, KC warm and alive along her side, and freed the latch.

Crouching down, KC shouted, "Patel! Tap the brakes!" KC grabbed the back of Yardley's shirt and pulled her down. The Stryker lurched, and a horrible clang banged the top of the armored vehicle.

"Yardley, here." KC stood up. The cannon had fallen to its side, only hanging on by a fat bouquet of wires. KC reached over to unhook them. "Watch that I don't get hit by it as it comes off."

Yardley surrounded KC with her body, the explosion behind them, the empty road ahead. The cannon slid, metal on metal, and toppled over the side, hitting the road hard.

"I didn't want to ride into urban Stockholm in an armored vehicle with a cannon on top during a blackout," KC explained.

"No." Yardley grinned. "You've thought of everything."

"I did, didn't I?" She slammed shut the latch, took off her helmet, and hopped into the commander's seat, pulling down the periscope. "All right. Nice work, Patel. You a gamer?"

He laughed. "Yeah. Nothing like this. More of a *Stardew Valley* guy."

"It's fun, though, right?" KC moved the Stryker along seemingly without effort. From the bumps and multiple turns, Yardley guessed she was doing evasive maneuvers.

"KC, a briefing, if you would," Gramercy said. "Now that the firefight seems to have faded into some distance."

"Sure thing." KC shifted gears and pulled the periscope to a more comfortable position. "We're skirting the edge of the nature reserve until the cover runs out. Fingers crossed the bridge is clear enough we can get through and back to the ambassador's residence to retrieve Kris's copy of the device. I couldn't let Brown have Mirabel's copy, and I didn't want to get shot, so the best plan was to use it."

"Because of how Kris designed it," Yardley said. "The Fuse."

"Yes. It's worthless now."

"You may have created a bigger problem," Gramercy said mildly, "having shut down the power throughout the Continent."

"No," KC said. "Mirabel's on his own grid. The device has likely already jumped it, but even if it did, it'll run out of juice somewhere outside of Stockholm. Northern Europe is a bad environment for this program. Because of the geography and the weather, they don't connect their systems as tightly in this part of the world. The hospitals and trains are safe. I checked. Kris told me everything she could about what she thought it could do."

"Jesus H.," Patel said. "Ma'am."

"That's why, in addition to the cool factor, we're driving this baby. I don't know what we're going to find at the ambassador's residence, but I doubt we're going to like it. My highest priority is Kris. Keep her and Declan out of danger and keep anyone from getting the brilliant idea to put her in a locked room and force her to code this monster all over again."

"Plan A is sound," Atlas said. "What's plan B?"

The Stryker hit smooth terrain. KC downshifted. They must've made it to the road. "You mean if the residence resembles anything like what's in our rearview?"

"Let's say anything that's not plan A," Atlas said.

"The general everything-is-tits-up-and-sideways plan is the Hole."

"I haven't been there in years." Gramercy smiled. "I wonder if they still have the cookies that look like tiny peaches."

"Who's there?" Atlas asked.

"Nobody from the agency, first and foremost. People who will know me. Even better, Kris has a lot of friends."

"KC?" Yardley asked.

"Yeah?"

"You can get this moving without Patel, right?"

"Oh. Sure." She smoothed her hand over the steering wheel and gave it a pat.

Yardley nodded. "Once we're at the residence, then, you're our lookout and getaway car. Patel, you'll cover me and Atlas into the residence. If Declan's as savvy as you think he is, I have an idea where he might have found cover for Kris. Tech and Gramercy, stay here to cover KC."

Yardley paused a moment, savoring the glow of satisfaction that often came over her when a mission went bad as a minnow bucket left in the sun, but she nonetheless knew it was going to be okay. "And by the way. Well done, everyone."

The laughter lasted a long time.

CHAPTER SEVENTEEN

Hålet, Eskilstuna, Sweden

KC dumped the Stryker behind the residence, giving its metal side a grateful pat before she traded it for the SUV the ambassador provided.

When Yardley returned with Declan and Kris, covered by Patel, she reported that after receiving Dr. Brown's burn notice, the remaining team had disassembled the command center and were en route to Evenes.

The information they got from the marines and agents at the residence painted a picture of highly organized evacuation as soon as it went dark, including the removal of evidence from the ballroom that served as a headquarters. Everyone was safe, but Flynn's micro drive—under guard and in a safe—had not been there when the agent assigned to retrieve it in an evacuation scenario went to find it.

The guard hadn't been there, either. He couldn't be accounted for at all.

Plan B it was. The Hole.

Eskilstuna, a small city of sixty thousand people, remained without electricity, but KC was enormously relieved to be right that software incompatibilities and self-isolating systems had kept the power outage from spreading much farther afield. Though the collapse of a major node of the internet had borked a variety of essential services—from banking to air traffic control and cell service—all signs indicated it would be a temporary problem.

Small mercies.

Of course, the Hole had power. Its proprietors, the self-named Batwing and her anarchist aromantic life partner, Zinnia, had banked enough juice in the hidden back rooms of the internet café they ran as a cover to keep the server room running for years, probably, and a combination of fiberglass privacy curtains, tight security, and a well-fortified door meant no one would ever know what was happening there unless Batwing and Zinnia wanted them to.

KC came into the main lounge, where Atlas, Gramercy, and Yardley had just finished debriefing in private on a secure link with the president, the director, and several leaders of the free world. She sat down in a deep leather sofa and gave herself a moment to enjoy the delicious sensations of fleece sweats and a soft cushion.

She might as well be comfortable when she spilled her guts all over the floor.

"Lights should be on momentarily," Gramercy said. "How's Flynn?"

"Batwing has her set up, and she's well into programming the countermeasure."

As soon as they hit the Hole, KC had officially secured Flynn as her asset, and the two of them began brainstorming how to construct a Hail Mary against the device stolen from the ambassador's residence. Kris thought she could do it, but there were a few steps in the middle. Like figuring out where Dr. Brown was headed and generally what his plan was.

KC hoped everything they were trying to accomplish against the clock would turn out to be possible. But even if it wasn't, and despite what she'd promised Yardley, she couldn't keep her part in this mess a secret any longer.

Standing face to face with Dr. Brown in front of the safe at Mirabel's compound, it had been crystal clear to KC that the two of them were not on the same team.

He'd made his choices. So had she.

She scraped her thumbnail over the thin skin beside her thumb. "Gramercy. Atlas. I need to tell you something." She waited until they'd both looked up from the pile of papers spread over a coffee table. "I don't know if I'm supposed to file a report or what. I can do that, I guess. But I need you to know that I made it. The device. I made the device."

She forced herself to keep her eyes on Gramercy, replaying the memory of his crooked smile on a loop to help her remember that he liked her.

These people had saved her life tonight, and none of them seemed to have thought twice about it. They were her colleagues. Her teammates. But they were also her friends, and it was that connection KC had to ask herself to trust right now.

"When I built it, I was following Dr. Brown's orders. He said we had authorization for a black op, top secret to all but a few people, and what happened in Toronto was supposedly a controlled demo. Authorized. He said it went all to shit and he got hurt and had to go underground, but he looked perfectly fine at Mirabel's."

KC glanced at Yardley, worried that she'd be angry. She'd been so passionate when she insisted at the safe house that KC keep these secrets.

But Yardley was twirling a strand of black hair around her

finger, her head tilted at a considering angle. When their eyes met, she smiled just enough to sink double dimples into her cheeks. "I believe you," she said.

Her faith strengthened KC's resolve. With a deep breath, KC plunged back in. "I thought I was doing the right thing, and I won't apologize for that," she said. "I am sorry I didn't push him harder when I figured out how much harm the device could do. It wasn't designed to be a weapon, but I did come to see that it could be used as one. That was the point when I should have put everything on the line to stop it."

A deep sigh escaped her lungs. Confessing all this to two veteran agents was intimidating no matter how much she told herself she had to do it.

"Anyway, I wanted you to know before you included me in any next steps," she said. "In case you need to put it before the director and he yanks me out of the field and locks me up for the sake of national security."

Atlas rubbed their fingers over their chin. "Thank you for your honesty," they said. "I don't see the need for this intelligence to go beyond this room at the moment. Gramercy?"

KC's handler crossed his legs, drawing her eye to the fresh shine on his wingtips. "No. I believe your assessment is correct, Atlas." He turned to KC. "Yours, however, requires adjustment."

"Sir?"

"When we spoke at Evenes, I told you Dr. Brown sequestered you to make himself look good. One consequence of that behavior is that he didn't give you an opportunity to participate in this agency in a way that might have impressed upon you what the most essential component of this work is." He lifted one dark eyebrow at KC.

"Information?" she guessed.

"Relationships," he said. "Nothing we do is possible without human connections. If you'd had more people in your circle of trust, you would have been able to make better decisions in the situation you found yourself in. Including the decision to stand up for your beliefs."

It was a solid perspective, to be sure. KC tested it out against her memories, asking herself what she might have done if she'd been able to trust Gramercy enough to go to him for advice. Or if she'd been able to confide in Yardley.

Her guilt washed away in a rush of indignation at what Dr. Brown had decided *for* her, followed immediately by relief that she still had decisions left to make.

"I understand," she said. "Thank you." The next breath she took was her first in a world in which she no longer had to drag the weight of Dr. Brown's treachery and her own guilt behind her. "I'm very keen to get our hands on the stolen drive," she said. "What's our intel?"

"There isn't any." Atlas sipped something from a giant Pokémon mug.

"Nothing back from my net," Yardley said. "I even recruited a few folks at the party to pitch in, since their fun was cut short. That Harry Davies on Mirabel's security team really likes you, for example."

"Whitmer does have a plan," Gramercy said. "I've lost track of what letter it is. Plan D? F? Where are we at?"

"Let's hear it, then."

"London, baby," Yardley said. "We'll head out as soon as MI6 gives us the go-ahead."

"What's in London?"

"Miller."

KC tapped her chin, reaching to remember where she'd recently heard the name. "Didn't you mention him when you were trying to keep me off the mission in front of the president?"

Now that she understood the game better, she couldn't hold Yardley's attempt against her, although KC did make a mental note to add that conversation to her "later" list.

She was looking forward to it.

"Miller is an agency deep cover embed with a gentlemen's club that counts major politicos among its members," Gramercy said.

"He does almost nothing but drink scotch and gossip," Yardley said, "but I've never been let down by his intel on a brush contact. He's our Obi-Wan Kenobi on this one, because Dr. Brown's his handler."

"Our only hope?" KC clarified.

"Is a middle-aged white guy. Absorb the irony. However"—Yardley turned in KC's direction—"the fun part is that *Tabasco* will get to decide what to do with Miller's intel. I hope it involves a near-orbit space plane. Or parachutes. Maybe a very fast car where I am in the passenger seat while you make improbable maneuvers through narrow streets."

"Are you flirting with me?" KC asked this question, for the first time, right in front of Gramercy and Atlas. They had kept enough secrets from her and Yardley, and they needed to understand she was a death-to-the-patriarchy operative and would not accept anyone's idea of what was best for her anymore.

Yardley went pink. "It's extremely hard not to. My upbringing has taught me to secure power when I see it."

Gramercy rose to his feet, gathering up papers. "That's my

cue. I have two more critical meetings, at least, before I can rest *or* die, so I'm going to remove myself to whatever monk cell Batwing has designated for me. Atlas?"

"I think these two can take it from here." They stood up, and the pair left together.

"How much sleep do we get before we're cleared to go to London?" KC was only asking to say something. To stay with Yardley. To see what it felt like to do nothing but sit on a sofa with her in a dim room.

So far, so good.

"I'm hoping for a couple of hours."

They hadn't been alone together since the linen closet at the ambassador's residence.

An incredibly bizarre lightness entered KC's middle. It took her a second to identify it as joy.

Joy, because she didn't have to lie.

Joy, because, for the first time, she could tell Yardley whatever she wanted.

"Do you want to play a game?" she asked.

Yardley's eyes widened. "I want to play a game more than anything."

"Let me tell you about it before you commit. You know how, in corny spy movies, when the handsome spy in the tuxedo has figured out the beautiful woman in the evening gown is with the bad guys, she asks him what she wants to know right before he kisses her, and he says, 'If I told you, I'd have to kill you?'"

"Yes. I know this trope. I've never been in a situation where I got to use it, but I have a feeling I would relish the drama."

KC laughed. "I'm sure you would. Here's my game. I ask you

for intel. About you. About us. And if you want to answer, you tell me, 'If I told you, I'd have to kiss you.' Then I decide if I really want to know, because if I do, I have to let you kiss me."

Yardley captured KC's gaze for a dark-eyed moment. "There doesn't seem to be a penalty in this game."

"The only penalty is if it doesn't work, and more knowing and more talking doesn't lead to where we'd really like it to. If it *does* work but it's hard, the kissing is a way to make it easier. Positive reinforcement." She smiled.

Yardley's exhale was choppy. "Can we have a practice round? One that's easy. So I'm certain I understand the rules."

"Yes." KC thought about something very easy she wanted to know that she should've known a long time ago. "What's the perfume you wear when you go on one of your trips that had nothing to do with finance? I've never found a bottle that smells like it."

Yardley walked on her knees across the long cushion to sit close to KC. "If I told you, I'd have to kiss you." The pink in her cheeks had spread to her throat.

Well. That sounded as good as KC had hoped it might. The words, combined with Yardley's new proximity, sent a wave of anticipation racing over her skin. "I want to know."

Yardley pushed her hand into her own hair, dropping it behind her shoulders in a way that showed KC the outline of her sports bra and the shape of her breasts beneath the white T-shirt she'd changed into. "It's my granddaddy's lucky cologne. He bought it in Ulaanbaatar after he opened a drop package with intel that turned out to be a bomb, but it didn't detonate. It has santal. And blood orange."

When KC took a breath, her memory supplied the smell, but

instead of it making her feel lonely because the smell meant Yardley was leaving, it made her think about what it would be like to inhale it on her neck knowing exactly what it was.

Yardley leaned forward. "Now I have to kiss you."

She did. No tongue, no teeth. Only their lips, softly fit together, before she pulled away.

"It's my turn," she said. "Maybe this isn't a practice round question, but I've never been brave enough to ask." She put her hand on KC's knee. "Do you think you'd ever want to introduce me to your dad?"

KC's shocked laugh made her eyes sting. There were some feelings there, obviously. Even before Robbie Nolan had retired to the Florida Keys, it had never been difficult to keep him in the dark about her job. Or her life. One of his overarching philosophies was to never ask personal questions if he could avoid it. The last time she'd tried calling him on the phone, he'd offered a series of complaints about the hidden fees for a three-day Margaritaville cruise he'd recently booked and then signed off after seven minutes.

"If I told you," she said, "I'd have to kiss you."

It heated her blood to say it aloud. It sounded like a promise, passed back and forth between her and Yardley, that the only consequence of doing something that had always been difficult for them would be to get more of what they wanted.

Could that be true? Could trust build more trust? Was awkward vulnerability the key to unlocking joy?

"Yes." Yardley sounded like she was answering the questions in KC's heart. "Tell me."

"Well, I think it would be much better for him to meet you than it would be for you to meet him. He's locked himself away from life, and if he met you, he'd be forced to remember how big and lovely it can be, because no one can exchange even a few words with you and not feel like it's important to live more. But yes. I will introduce you. It's about time the different parts of my life got to know each other."

KC took Yardley's hand and pulled it to her chest. It felt like a kiss under a porchlight, the kind of sweet moment filled with butterflies that she'd never had. She pressed her forehead to Yardley's, coming down from the glittery high of it. "That's our practice round."

Yardley leaned away, squeezed KC's hand, and slid off the sofa. "I want to play in my room, but"—she smoothed her hands over her hair—"just this game. Just kissing in my bed and telling each other everything we should already know. No . . . sex."

"Are you sure what you're describing *isn't* sex?"

Yardley laughed. "Let's go find out." She led KC out of the lounge and down a hallway to the room that Zinnia had given her, a narrow space with white-painted stone walls, a simple wooden dresser, and a bed with a white duvet. Sitting on the edge of the bed, she pushed off her shoes. "Lay down with me."

KC was nervous. They'd never had this. They'd arrowed right at each other at that party because neither one of them had a future in mind. It was one reason why the certainty they'd felt at the party had never translated into the relationship the other needed.

They were nervous now because they were telling themselves the truth about what was at stake. Because they were acknowledging that they both needed something, and they didn't know if they would get it.

KC was starting to see that love risked everything.

Gramercy had explained it as knowing that one of you had to leave first. When KC had told him she hated that, it was because she could only focus on the loss. She couldn't see the magic of Gramercy and Lucas's revelation, which was the choice to be together. The choice to accept that your love would extend far beyond life as you knew it and into experiences impossible to imagine.

It meant the willingness to tell someone you would bear the loss if they left first, just to have had the privilege of loving them.

She didn't hate *that*. At this point in her life—when she had uncoupled a canon from the top of an armored vehicle with a remarkable woman beside her—it was the only kind of love that felt remotely big enough. Yardley patted the mattress. "Let's go, Officer."

KC shut the door and turned the bolt. She took off her shoes and crawled onto the bed and wrapped herself around Yardley's waist, smiling, tugging until Yardley fell into the circle of her arms.

Yardley's face was close. She adjusted her position, pushed her knee between KC's, and wiggled until she'd found the spot where she liked to rest her head, cradled in the crook of KC's neck. She sighed. "I missed you. A lot."

"I missed you, too." She kissed the top of Yardley's head. "But we didn't get *everything* wrong, did we?" She pulled Yardley tighter against her. "Or this wouldn't feel so excellent."

Yardley rested her palm on KC's chest, over her heart. "I will admit there were compensations for the grief we put each other through."

"Are you going to ask me a question?"

They didn't have much time. If Kris hadn't insisted KC leave her alone earlier so she could think, KC would be sitting in front of a computer right this minute.

As soon as Yardley's plan fell into place, they'd be on another plane, or a train, or a helicopter, pursuing information that would lead them to Dr. Brown.

But not right now.

"Mmm." Yardley's voice was low but suspiciously alert. "I'm thinking."

Yardley's thinking tended to generate its own weather. This was not Yardley Whitmer thinking. "You're stalling. You already know what you want to ask, you're just working up the courage."

Yardley lightly smacked her arm. "Don't rush me. Do you want to get married?"

KC couldn't be certain she'd heard right. Could a simple question rip the breath from her body?

"I'm not proposing. To be clear." Yardley spoke in a rush. "But I've never asked you about it. Like we said in the linen closet, there was a lot of tense, uneasy silence around future conversations between us. Remember when I suggested the entryway should have a skylight so it wasn't so dark?"

KC did remember. Prior to that moment, Yardley had made a few mild suggestions that KC had accepted gratefully as evidence she'd failed to navigate some part of adulthood correctly. Updating the hand towels in the kitchen, for instance. That had been easy to do. But the suggestion of the skylight fell in a different category, a big and permanent change to the house where—with the exception of her years in Boston at MIT—KC had always lived. The house that had never, in her memory, changed at all.

Yardley hadn't been calling contractors. She'd floated the idea impulsively, but KC had shot it down like a clay pigeon at the rifle range, her heart exploding to pieces in her chest.

She'd asked Yardley to move in with her, but she had never really believed that Yardley would *stay*.

Overfocus, stoic self-sacrifice, aggressive independence, and silently waiting for the worst to happen—that was how KC had gotten through every challenge life put in front of her. But she couldn't love Yardley that way.

It meant that she hadn't asked the right questions. Why, when she met Yardley Whitmer and felt something she'd never felt before, had KC assumed she knew everything she needed to know to navigate what would come next?

She'd never bothered to learn how to do the *work* of loving Yardley—how to make herself weak and vulnerable to their love in acknowledgment that she couldn't love Yardley *by herself*. She had to give herself over to who they were together, two women who adored each other and knew nothing about love, not yet, but were ready to knock holes in the ceilings of their lives to let in the light.

"Also, here's the thing." Yardley pressed her hand a little harder against KC's heart, which by this point was beating madly. "I had grown up believing marriage was special. Sacred. It was also something I believed I would never have, not just because of my conviction to give my life to service to my country, but because when the first of my sorority sisters were getting married, it wasn't legal for me to, and I think my certainty that I never *would* had been a balm on that wound. Then the law changed, and I could get married, and my wound has felt a little raw and exposed ever since." She laughed. "You look so scared. That's okay. It's okay. I've been too afraid to even ask the question, and so here

I am, ripping it off like a Band-Aid, because no matter what you say, I'll get a kiss."

"Yardley—"

"I'm sorry to interrupt, but I made that much breezier than I should have." Yardley frowned. "I want to know if you want to get married because the real truth is, just the *idea* of calling a woman my wife makes my heart fall three hundred stories in my chest, like a runaway elevator, thrilling and terrifying at the same time. I've never said that word out loud talking about myself. *Wife.* My wife." Yardley was bright pink. "I'm working myself up."

"If I told you," KC said, "I'd have to kiss you."

Yardley put both her hands over her mouth and shook her head back and forth. "I don't know. I don't know. I don't know." She moved so close that KC had to adjust her legs as Yardley buried her face into her neck. "Tell me, though," she whispered.

"When I decided to give you my mom's watch, I had to take it to the jeweler to have it cleaned and checked and to have one of the little diamonds replaced. I went to pick it up, and she told me that the maker of the watch also made coordinating jewelry. The pattern of apple blossoms in the gold band and around the face is called 'spring love,' which I learned because she pulled out an entire tray of spring love gold jewelry, and in the middle of the tray was a genuinely enormous engagement ring and a wedding band. Which, of course, were the first items she lifted out to show me."

"Did you freak?" Yardley asked this with a huff of warm breath on KC's neck that made KC laugh.

"Um, no. I took the ring set from her and proceeded to have a thirty-minute conversation about what my girlfriend might like. I played make-believe. It felt . . . well, it felt good. I liked telling this jeweler all about you and your tastes and my thoughts about carat weight. Of course, I liked talking to the stranger about it because I couldn't talk to you." KC threaded her fingers through Yardley's hair. "Come here."

Yardley lifted her face to KC's, her eyes huge in the low light.

"I think I would like to be married, yes." KC said it solemnly, because Yardley was right, this was a sacred thing. And because she couldn't say that she would like to be married *to Yardley* until they got to a different "later" than this one.

Yardley's mouth was velvet. KC held on to the back of her neck like the anchor that would keep her here, in this moment, her tongue sliding between Yardley's parted lips, their bodies pressed together on top of a feather bed in a safe room, hidden away from the world.

It was a whispering kiss, an asking kiss. KC moved her lips over Yardley's, rubbed her thumb over her mouth as if to ask, *Did you like that?* And Yardley sighed over KC's thumb, her tongue just touching the pad, and smiled before kissing KC back, deeper. *Yes, I liked it so much.*

It wasn't like any kiss they'd ever had, but it was one they should have had, if their ignorance and self-protection hadn't kept them from it. If Yardley hadn't always been on her way out the door with her suitcase wheel squeaking and KC hadn't hunkered down and hid behind a computer monitor every time she felt the slightest bit intimidated. If they'd just told each other what they felt. Who they were. What they needed.

Every day they hadn't made it to this kiss had pushed them farther apart, but they were lucky, because this was a kiss with the kind of magic in it that could pull them back together.

Best kiss ever. Best kiss so far.

CHAPTER EIGHTEEN

Greenwich, London

Yardley took a coupe glass of a pale pink cocktail with a breath of foam floating on top from Julia Ketchner, the MI6 agent assigned to the Greenwich Palace Club. She and Julia had been fast friends since they met on a Mediterranean yacht in the midst of a tricky negotiation to convert a Greek shipping magnate into an asset seven years ago.

"If you can believe it"—Julia leaned forward while pulling the bodice of her red evening gown up over the curves that were threatening to escape it—"this is tonight's signature cocktail. These gents are calling it 'The English Robin.' There's no one more sentimental about a Britain that never existed than landed club lads." Julia grabbed her own English Robin, which she'd set down on one of the high tables, and knocked it back in one go. "Fuck, but she's tasty, though."

They were on a patio whose classical colonnade overlooked the Thames. Yardley breathed in the gray, with its cold, oily mist of rain, relishing the brisk air on her bare chest. She wore her tuxedo shirt unbuttoned to the navel. Her short, severely cut salt-and-pepper wig was hot, as were her drapey wool trousers. "How's our girl doing?"

Yardley's London cover, Max Konstantopoulos, was one she'd

used for years. It had been easy for Julia to secure an invite to
tonight's banquet, thrown by Miller's club, for Max, an intimidating lesbian black-market intermediary. It didn't hurt that Julia
had been embedded in the club as its receptionist for the last nine
months. Three-quarters of the members were half in love with her
kittenish-blonde persona, which gave her access to some of the
biggest secrets in the world.

"Do I want to steal her from you, or do I want to *be* her?" Julia
asked. "That's the real question."

Yardley raised an eyebrow. "She's not mine yet."

Julia made a move to grab another cocktail from a passing
tray, then thought better of it when she noticed Yardley's still-
full glass. "Everyone thought you were just making her up. Like
a girlfriend you met at camp and lives far away so you don't look
like a big knob."

"No one thought that," Yardley said primly.

"But you didn't know she was Tabasco! *You* said she only
knew your cover! And here she's one of us. Some spy you are!"

Yardley wondered how many more times she was going to
hear that particular dig. Certainly for the rest of her life. Depend-
ing on what kind of business the agency was up to in its less con-
ventional units, possibly into the afterlife.

"To answer your question"—Julia took Yardley's drink from
her and drank it down between breaths—"Daphne Sullivan is the
belle of the ball."

Yardley was not surprised. KC had performed at a level of
consistent excellence throughout the mission, and today was no
exception. What did surprise Yardley was her reaction to KC's
performance, which was to be just as consistently impressed, de-
lighted, and aroused by her breathtaking competence. Except for

that dreadful moment when Dr. Brown had jump-scared her at Mirabel's, Yardley was having a fantastic time.

Yardley was jubilant that KC was finally out of the basement and getting to do the work she should have been able to do all along.

"These men are so excited to have the salty American who probably stole the device show up at their shindig, they're acting like it was engraved on the invitation," Julia said, glancing over her shoulder at the party. "Watching them swarm around her, likely dumping a war brief's worth of intel into her cute little ears, has got me emerald green with jealousy. Once you go in, Max, it's going to be a mosh pit of piping-hot goss while they try to figure out if you're there to negotiate a deal and who for."

Yardley laughed. "I've missed you, Jules. What about Miller?"

"The driver reports that he's still waiting outside Miller's girl-friend's daughter's private school, where the girl is performing her recital. He'll ping me once they're ten minutes away."

CIA officer David Miller had been ignoring their signals all day. Either he had his own agenda—probably bad—or he was part of Dr. Brown's nihilistic army. Whenever Yardley thought about pregnant Kris in an over-air-conditioned, dim room in Sweden, coding against the wind while David Miller carried on his cushy life as a deep embed in a London social club, her pique dialed up another notch. God help the world if there were ever a general strike by everyone who *wasn't* a white cis-het male. The planet would wobble off its orbit and tumble across the galaxy in free fall.

"Any sign of Dr. Brown?" she asked.

Ordinarily, Yardley loved a good honey trap, but she had every one of her antennae up for this one. If the Palace Club's dinner party drew out Dr. Brown, the only option would be to secure him. Anything else would likely incite him to detonate the device.

After the time she and KC had spent together last night—the questions and the kisses that ruptured Yardley's last shreds of self-protective resistance and left her defenseless against the enormity of her feelings—she felt confident that she would personally take Dr. Brown apart with her bare hands if he attempted to harm one hair on KC Nolan's beautiful head.

"No sign of him," Julia said. "And I haven't heard a thing, either. Makes me suspicious, taken with the fact that Miller has been ignoring you. Something's up."

"Then we find out what it is," Yardley said. "I'm ready, if you'll escort me in, Miss Taffy Burton."

"I love your Eurotrash accent. It makes me feel like a college girl abroad all over again."

Yardley laughed and took her arm.

In the low, incandescent light of the chandeliers hanging from an airy domed ceiling, every woman's jewelry sparkled, and every man's tuxedo blurred into an expensive shadow. The air smelled like champagne and the umami aromas floating off the circulating small bites, with an undercurrent of the Ambroxan, amber, and powdery scents of expensive perfume.

The entrance of Max Konstantopoulos created the desired stir. The murmur of conversation dropped low enough that she could hear renowned cellist Alisa Weilerstein's mournful, postmodern improvisations drifting over from where she played on a marble dais in the corner.

Yardley grounded herself into her polished wingtips and stalked toward the club president, who owned slightly less land than the Royal Society for the Protection of Birds but had a great deal more ready cash due to lucrative investments in gambling apps. He watched her approach under a hedge of white eyebrows while sipping his tumbler of scotch.

"Ms. Konstantopoulos. Rumored you'd be joining us, and I couldn't imagine why until that American strolled through the doors without an invitation."

"Why would you correlate my arrival with your party crasher?" Yardley lifted a finger and was handed a champagne from a server's tray.

"My understanding is she's here to advertise her wares to any resident arms dealers." He lifted a shaggy brow, indicating his knowledge of Max's line of work.

"Always straight to the point." Yardley lifted her flute. "I notice you haven't removed either one of us."

"I've become indulgent at my great age, but behave yourself."

"That's not what you really want." Yardley caught the gleam of KC's silver minidress across the room. "Let me know if you're interested in buying anything."

She strode away, the ambient conversations rising in volume around her. She had nearly made it to a massive bronze plinth holding an arrangement of orchids and roses where KC was talking animatedly to a member of the prime minister's cabinet when she was touched on the elbow.

She turned to see Jack Tremblay, the Canadian spy.

"Oh, for heaven's sake."

He frowned. "I would have thought you would be glad to see me."

"Why?"

"Because we're on the same side! My god. I saved your girl's bacon back in Lidingö when you folks were gagging for a diversion."

"Canadians don't have real bacon."

"Is there some reason for the lack of congeniality?" Jack raised his eyebrows, free of smeared gel this time.

Yardley sighed. Her favorite thing about the Max Konstan-topoulos cover was that she did not have to be polite to anyone, and she certainly didn't have to flirt with Jack Tremblay. "You're right." She eyed him intently. "We're on the same side, and you were useful in Sweden. That nearly makes up for the Sisters' failure to prevent our asset's abduction off the street in Toronto. Nearly." Yardley tilted her head. "So what do you have for me?"

Jack's face fell. "You mean what intel do I have."

Yardley suppressed at least two dozen sarcastic and cutting comments that left her mouth too cold to melt butter. Being Max was so *relaxing*. It offered her the rare opportunity to set aside literally everything she'd learned from her mama about how girls should behave.

"Right," he said. "Not quite yet. Just got here myself. I've not even really circulated."

Yardley started walking away.

"But let me know if you need anything!" he called after her.

The politico who KC had been talking with kissed KC's cheek and moved off, leaving her by the plinth alone.

Gorgeous.

"Were you good at fifth-grade basketball?" Yardley asked, leaning against the plinth, taking in KC's muscled legs in stilettos and how the short, backless silver lamé draped precariously over a very small area of her body and made Yardley, or maybe Max, want very bad things.

"Who's good at fifth-grade basketball?" KC moved closer, and

they both turned their bodies toward the guests as if they were
an audience.

Which they were.

"I was vicious at fifth-grade basketball," KC said. "I yelled at
the refs for not calling everyone's blatant double dribbling, and
I had a long and elaborate free throw ritual involving multiple
hand signs and spitting. But I was a forty-five-pound, three-and-
a-half-foot-tall feral animal, so no. Not really *good*."

"Are you having a nice evening?" Yardley moved closer,
relishing her cover because Max Konstantopoulos would not
hesitate to move too close and look at Daphne Sullivan like she
wanted to devour her.

KC didn't balk. She reached up and touched the diamond
lariat resting on Yardley's bare sternum and cocked a hip. The
room got quieter in some places. Louder in others.

Yardley broke out in shivers.

"It's not a terrible party, but I'm more the backyard barbecue
type." KC flashed her elf smile at Yardley, and the memory of
the Virginia heat when this woman had touched her for the first
time chased the shivers right off Yardley's skin.

Tabasco was fully in her powers tonight.

"Is he usually this hard to pin down?" KC asked, meaning
Miller.

Yardley knew Max wouldn't let the fingertip of a woman like
this fondle the chain of diamonds on her chest without erotic
retaliation. She grasped KC's hand and ran her own fingers down
her forearm and back up again. Then, she lifted KC's hand to her
mouth and kissed it with a flick of tongue that made a woman
twenty feet away gasp.

Yardley found her in the crowd and winked.

"What a sweet gig these gray-templed white dude agents get."
She kept hold of KC's hand and moved indecently close. "Ritzy
cover, fancy flat, intelligence flowing as freely as top-shelf cognac,
occasional soft check-in at your pleasure. Never mind U.S. spies
leaving calling cards around the city like a car warranty salesman, please do enjoy your game of snooker at your exclusive club
that my taxes pay your membership for. His failure to check in
seems more like he *hasn't* turned to me. Otherwise, whoever has
been tapped to clean up behind him would've come for us. I'm
thinking Dr. Brown is keeping his cover with Miller. Probably to
maintain the channel of intel."

"I want Miller. I want to know where Dr. Brown is."

"We'll get him. We have so many excellent people working
together on this." Yardley moved her face alongside KC's. "You're
not alone anymore," she murmured.

"I'm not." KC smiled against Yardley's cheek, making her eyelids heavy at the familiar, fleeting sensation of KC's lips on her
skin.

The last thing Yardley remembered from their conversation
yesterday before they'd fallen asleep in each other's arms, fully
dressed beneath a knitted blanket KC pulled up from the foot
of the bed, was KC saying, *Kittens. Did you ever think we should
have a kitten?*

The question was the first thing she'd thought of when she
woke up to find KC gone, and what rang through Yardley's head
like church bells was that "we."

She'd rolled over. Paper crinkled under her shoulder. When
she pulled it out, it was a note in KC's precise handwriting.

If I could take anything back, it would be when I told you that you never wanted to just be with me and talk. I accused you of this, in a fight, in a crappy Swedish apartment that smelled like a dead plant. I would take that back because I never let you just be with me, and for that I'm so sorry, and that apology is directed at us both. Because if I had known how much more I could feel, for you, for me, for us, I would've found a way like I did with my game.

I have something else that if I told you, I'd have to kiss you.

But I'll wait for another moment that's about nothing but you and me.

Yardley had pressed the note to her chest and then arranged for Batwing to send it securely direct to her nan's address with a request to Nan to keep it safe until she got home.

She was considering if Max, at this point, would press Daphne against the wall and kiss her like a sailor on leave, when KC stepped back. "What the actual fuck," she whispered.

At the same time, Julia's voice came over Yardley's comm link. "Miller's just walked in with his girlfriend. Driver forgot to ping me."

"Come the fuck *on*," KC said. "He is kissing her. Nice, Mr. Miller. Nice. I'm sure Amybeth knows all about this. Oh, and Emma *just* had a baby. You worm."

"Explain." She said this as Max would to Daphne, but her significant eye contact communicated to KC that she needed to catch Yardley up, and fast.

"*Miller.*" KC nearly spat the name. "David Miller. I knew he was David Miller, but I thought it was a code name or his cover. I didn't know he was *David Miller* of Marigold Street, Reston, Virginia."

Yardley glanced at the entry. Miller was sliding a trench coat from a woman's shoulders to give to the valet. "You know him? You're sure?"

"Oh, I am sure. I went to kindergarten through tenth grade with his daughter Emma. We weren't BFFs, but we shared an obsession with this MMA fighter, Josh Matherly. For different reasons, obviously. Doesn't matter. I went to her house after school a lot, and we watched his fights on TiVo that we made her older brother record for us."

"You are a miracle," Yardley said. "Very sincerely."

"My point is that I knew her dad. He was around. He had some kind of job in government, but the hours were all over the place." KC shoved her hands through her hair. "Naturally. And he went on business trips. Probably a lot like the kind of business trips you went on."

Yardley could feel the eyes of a large number of assembled partygoers on them, trying to figure out if Max's deal with Daphne had gone south. "Dang it."

"I am incensed. Emma *adored* that man."

"Listen," Yardley said softly. "We're going to have to—"

KC put her hand on one cocked hip. "He fucking stopped coming home."

"What do you mean?"

"He left for his 'business trip,' and then the next time he was expected back—and I'm sure his wife, Amybeth, had some kind of clearance, at least to know who he worked for and when she would see him—he didn't come. Emma told me that her mother checked in with his work, so you know what that likely means, and she got nowhere, which, we can guess what was up there, too, especially if Amybeth's contact was Miller's handler—"

"Dr. Brown."

"Right. Yeah. Anyway, they got to the part where they were talking to the cops—I'm sure the agency loved that—and then Amybeth got an email."

"From Miller."

"From her *husband*, yeah. Email account she didn't know he had. He told her that he hadn't been happy, and he had tried, but the stress of his work and how few people understood really isolated him. He told her to tell his children he was sorry and to help them understand, and also, he'd transferred half their money to himself, and he hadn't been paying the mortgage. *Then*, Emma's brother somehow figured out that David and a woman from Nottinghamshire, here in England, were involved. A professor. They went back over a year. And get this. She has a twelve-year-old kid, and he's been playing stepdad."

Yardley had already known about the woman on Miller's arm, and the child whose school function they'd attended, but KC's personal knowledge of their target introduced a number of new variables. For instance, Yardley now knew the most likely explanation for why Miller had been avoiding them. Even a CIA agent operating under deep cover couldn't abandon his family without consequence.

Miller had gone rogue.

It meant he was almost certainly in Dr. Brown's pocket, but it also meant—thank the sweet baby Jesus—they had leverage. Sweet, sweet leverage.

"Well, then. New plan, given that we've been dealt this un-expected hand of beautiful cards. I need to parlay with Julia. We have to figure out how to make sure Miller doesn't recognize you before we want him to, especially given that you're the most interesting thing at this party."

"Tell me what to do."

Yardley reached over and hooked her finger underneath one of the teeny tiny straps that held up KC's dress, lifted it up, and let it fall halfway down KC's arm. "Be infatuated with me. Trail me around like my shadow makes you horny. Be ready to follow my lead. I'm Fred Astaire, you're Ginger Rogers."

KC turned the tables and grabbed Yardley's shirt placket be-tween her thumb and forefinger. She slid it through her fingers—knuckles dragging over bare skin all the way down to Yardley's sensitive belly—then looked up through her false eyelashes. "I can do that, Max."

The guests were drinking, sparkling, talking, and trying to pretend they weren't gulping down the drama unfolding right in front of them.

If they only knew that what they were really seeing was what could happen if you weren't afraid anymore, knocked down your walls, and found love on the other side.

"Ready?" Yardley asked.

KC smiled. "I am. Finally."

CHAPTER NINETEEN

KC followed Yardley through the maze of people, occasionally stopping briefly to remind a guest that she wanted to follow up on a conversation they'd started earlier or to wink and touch the shoulder of another. She kept Miller on her periphery, where he couldn't get a good look at her.

From now on, she was going to assume every single person who lived within a seventy-mile radius of Langley was a spy. Surely it would be less embarrassing than the predicament KC currently found herself in.

All they needed was for Miller to tell them where Dr. Brown was. It seemed so simple, but here they were, at a lavish party in a massive eighteenth-century landmark, tipping servers with hundred-pound notes.

A lot of complexity for a single question.

She could say the same thing about the last three years with Yardley. How many simple questions could have prevented their isolation from each other? Their hurt feelings? Their broken hearts?

KC supposed that a lot of people who faced the end of a relationship wondered what the answers would have been if they had thought to ask for them. She was grateful for a second chance.

"Daph." Yardley slid her arm around KC's in a protective grip, her devastating tuxedo shirt pulling open to reveal a little more than only the side of her full breast. The insouciant carnality of the move made heat throb between KC's legs. She'd been tearful with wonder and laughter last night, between questions and kissing Yardley, but cover or no, there was no doubt Yardley turned her on like a radio.

"Max," KC purred, letting Daphne look Max over with no manners whatsoever.

"Meet my friend, Taffy Burton. She's the real eyes and ears of the club."

"We didn't get a chance to officially meet, I just bullied you into letting me crash the party." KC held out her hand for Julia to shake.

Julia laughed and tucked her blond hair behind her ear. "Not at all. It seems everyone was very happy to have you. Max, have you shown Daphne around? It's not every day you're inside the inner sanctum of what once was Greenwich Palace. Not that there's anything left of it but the foundations, but they built some part of this magnificent pile on top of those. Thrifty as can be. Christopher Wren was the architect, you know."

Yardley bit her lip at KC. "We haven't been talking about architecture."

"Don't be naughty, Max. You two follow me, and we'll promenade. There's a piece on the far side of the room that's said to be an uncatalogued Parthenon Marble." Julia drew them to the edge of the room. "What do you need?" she asked at a much lower volume.

"I was wondering if you were up for kidnapping an under-cover CIA agent, taking him to a second location, and tag-team interrogating him for the rest of the evening until he gives us what we want. For democracy."

Julia's face became prayerfully solemn. "Yes, please."

KC hooked her finger into one of Yardley's belt loops and laughed as if the three of them were tipsy. Better if the people sneaking looks assumed utter frivolity. Her only concern was Miller, who she was certain would recognize her on sight.

"Once you secure him, if he tells you what we need to know, walk away," Yardley said, "and we'll have our guys ship him back to the States. If he won't, we'll have to assist with the interrogation. We have something on him, but I like to hold on to my leverage against donkey asses like Miller if I can." Yardley ran her fingers through KC's hair idly, making it harder for KC to think up plans B through Z to use if this one didn't work.

Julia leaned a shoulder against a fluted column, positioning herself to watch the hall. "Leading Miller to a private area and securing him isn't a problem, but even if your lads retrieve him, he'll find a way to blow my cover at the club."

KC shook her head. "Then our plan isn't good enough. You're valuable to MI6 here."

Julia smiled. "No worries. Any operative would be valuable to MI6 here, and if I have to answer the phone, 'Good Morning, Greenwich Palace Club, how can I be of service to you?' one more time, I'll break out in frustrated boils. But I need a bit of time to alert the lads at the office, brief them, and secure Miller."

"How long?" KC pulled Yardley's hand out of her hair and softly bit the end of her middle finger. She was gratified to see flushed pink spots bloom beneath the diamonds on Yardley's chest.

"An hour or two? Maybe a bit longer. In the meantime, you lot need to disappear. I'll have the Sister, what's-his-name, put it out to the guests the two of you are striking a deal. I assume such false intel may serve some of your other goals?"

"Nothing like fake news to bring out the baddies," Yardley agreed. "But does it have to be Jack? He keeps turning up like a Canadian quarter out of the soda machine."

Julia laughed. "He's excellent, actually. Especially in rooms like this one. You two should leave out the southwest emergency exit. I'll disable the alarm. The public areas of the building are closed for the night, so there are plenty of places to wait."

At that, she floated away.

"Using the emergency exit means we'll have to make it across the room without Miller spotting me." KC scanned the guests, who were getting louder as the alcohol took hold. Everyone was going to be completely sloshed by the time the banquet started.

"No way out but through," Yardley agreed.

KC grabbed Yardley's hand and squeezed it. "We know how to do that, don't you think? Get through the gauntlet to the other side? I've been thinking that we never made a plan B. We couldn't imagine a plan beyond doing our best to hold on to each other and hope the entire world changed around us enough to let us make it."

Speaking openly about her feelings with Yardley still made KC feel exposed, but it was getting easier. She curled and released her toes a few times inside her high heels to release the tension.

"What is plan B?" Yardley asked.

KC's knuckles brushed against Yardley's wool trousers. "A year ago or so, I start sharing more of my life and feelings with you, and you start believing you can have what you want."

Yardley let go of KC's hand to cock her arm on KC's shoulder. It was a Max Konstantopoulos gesture, but the deep dimple and the sparkle in her eyes were all Yardley. "Okay, but we don't have a time machine. Plan C?"

"I tackle you in the middle of a delicate intel mission in a Capitol Hill Starbucks, blow your cover, and we have a laugh in the van and start sharing all of our tenderest feelings in front of Atlas."

"Hmm." Yardley scanned the room as the path through it shifted. A new round of servers had arrived with fresh small plates. "We missed the mark there. What plan are we up to now?"

"D through Z. That's where the plan is to be willing to keep changing the plan. You know that sometimes the new plan will be scary and risky, but you're willing to lose everything but each other."

"Yes." Yardley guided KC through the throng like a prize, capturing just enough interest to remind everyone what was going down. "That's the plan that sounds worthy of the Unicorn and Tabasco. Who knew making a relationship work would be harder than driving a motorcycle off a boat ramp to land on a yacht?"

She stopped suddenly, whirling around with a smile that caught KC off guard and made her tumble forward. Yardley's hands found her waist, steadying her in the tall shoes. The warmth of her palms made KC conscious of her wisp of a dress, as though she wore nothing but sparkles and thread.

"Everyone who's lucky," KC murmured.

Yardley wasn't smiling anymore. "We have to move," she said, but her eyes were full of heat to match the hit of desire that gripped KC, and her cupid's bow lips parted.

"You're killing me." The words rasped from KC's throat.

Yardley just pressed her lips together, her eyes sparkling with humor, and towed KC into the crowd.

They were halfway across the room, under a central chandelier draped in what must be thousands of amber crystals, when KC felt a tap on her shoulder.

She had the presence of mind to glance at Yardley, who could see who wanted KC's attention. Yardley gave her a silent nod of assurance that it wasn't Miller.

KC turned. A server handed her a business card with thick black writing on the blank side.

We have business. Don't finalize with M.K. until we can talk.

The embossed side carried a monogram of David Miller's initials.

Sonofabitch.

KC slid the card back onto the server's tray with a little pat. "Tell him to stick around, and I'll see what I can do. No promises."

When she turned back to Yardley, she noticed that space had cleared around them during the interlude with the server. KC couldn't risk scanning the crowd to see if Miller had been watching and, if he had, whether he'd recognized her.

Yardley hooked her arm in KC's and guided her past another cluster of people as if they would join them in conversation, but in fact she was moving them toward the cover of a series of more plinths with flower arrangements. They would only have to get past a final cluster of people to obtain the cover, and then they could weave between the plinths to the door.

An alarm in her hindbrain went white-hot. She risked a glance behind her.

Miller was behind them.

"He's at six o'clock, on a direct course and gaining." KC's heel slipped on the marble floor, making her ankle wobble treacherously. She grabbed onto the sleeve of Yardley's tuxedo shirt to steady herself.

"He saw the server give you the note, but your back was to him." Yardley's voice was smooth as a Carolina breeze. "I don't think he's made you."

A woman moved out of the way in her periphery, looking offended. Miller was right behind them.

KC started imagining all the plausible lies she could tell him that would explain the presence of his daughter's childhood pal in a London banquet hall full of bad actors and spies while also preserving her cover, but before she could come up with anything, she felt the presence of someone directly behind her. Yardley looped her arm around her waist as KC started to hiss in warning, "He's—"

Then her back was pinned to one of the plinths, roses draped in her hair, and Yardley's mouth was over hers.

One hand cupped her face. The other splayed over her throat, holding her in place.

KC's mind went black. Hot-black. Was that a thing? Hot, silky darkness that sluiced into her vessels, turned her breath to vapor

and her pulse to a slow throb from the spot where Yardley's fingertips rested against the hollow of her throat to the wool of Yardley's trousers pressed against her bare inner thighs. Her palms
rested on the cool bronze of the plinth, and she curled her fingers
into the grooves in the metal while Yardley's mouth worked over
hers.

It was for show. She knew this kiss was to keep Miller from
knowing Daphne's identity before he was secured. She knew this
kiss was technically necessary to the mission.

But *god*. KC slid her leg around Yardley's and moaned into
her mouth as she bit her bottom lip. This was worlds different
from the near kiss at Langley, full of hurt and their mistakes, or
the frantic search for connection in the safe house, or the desperate eroticism of the linen closet, or even the endless kisses they
used to share between everything they never said.

This was the kind of kiss that a person could recall into
great old age and laugh with joy that it had happened. A kiss
that kept nothing in reserve and spent everything on heat and
sensuality.

Yardley's lavender fragrance bloomed in the air around them,
mixing with the apricot-tea smell of the roses. KC felt naked already, her skin overwarm and soft, moments from glazing over
with sweat to slicken every involuntary jerk of her hips toward
Yardley's.

"Fuck," Yardley breathed into KC's mouth, and she *never*
swore, so KC felt that helpless *fuck* in the arches of her feet.

But it broke the spell. KC chased Yardley's bottom lip as it
pulled away, and the centimeter of distance that opened between
their bodies was the vacuum reality sucked into, yanking KC un-
comfortably into the present moment. "Is he gone?"

"Extremely. Jack diverted him." Yardley pulled back and smiled ruefully. "I guess we owe him one."

"Before we owe him more, let's get out of here." Most of the crowd had started collecting around the twenty-foot carved wooden doors that opened into the dining room as the dinner hour approached. "You trail me this time."

KC moved completely behind the row of plinths and followed an electric cord taped to the floor where it seemed to disappear behind a wall.

"It's an old servants' passageway," Yardley said. "Often they're filled with junk, but this one is clear. There will be a door at the end."

They ran down the passage to a service door. A sign warned it was armed with an alarm.

"Let's hope Julia took care of this, too." KC pushed open the door—mercifully silent—and when it closed behind them, the relative quiet and dark soothed her frazzled nerves.

Yardley reached up to tap her comm link, activating her connection to Julia as they made their way across a smaller, empty hall. "CCTV?" This room was more Regency and less lush than the one they'd just left. Lights from the river came through a skylight and lit up the duck's egg blue walls and polished wood floors.

"Disabled." Julia's voice was crisp in KC's ear. "No heat signatures at all in the Tudor Rose Museum on the second floor after the mezzanine. I'd wait there."

They left the hall as Yardley disconnected, then arrived at a public entry where the main staircase to the museum was. Hearing the footsteps of a security guard in the distance, they pulled off their shoes and raced silently up the marble steps.

The glass entry doors were locked.

KC squatted down to inspect the mechanism set into the steel frame of the doors. "It's just a regular bolt."

"Can you pick it? I can hear security on the mezzanine." Yardley's head was close to hers, and it spun KC's brain, still soaked with horny chemicals from their kiss.

"Do you have hair pins holding your hair down under your wig?"

Yardley rubbed along the lace edge of the wig, easing it off the crown of her braids. "How many do you need?"

"Two."

She handed them over. KC bent them straight and bit off the plastic tips, listening for the guard. She eased the two hairpin wires into the lock and explored the tumbler in her mind until she found a likely spot, pressed the tumblers open, and heard the lock click.

"Now if ASMR was like watching that, I'd fill my feed with it." Yardley's dimples were deep as they slipped into the foyer of the museum and immediately made their way to one of the hallways leading to an exhibit so the guard wouldn't see them through the glass doors.

"What is the Tudor Rose Museum, anyway?" KC crept down the passage with Yardley, the floor cold on her feet. It was lined with oversized panels printed with interpretations of small exhibits in glass cases. KC peeked into one that held what looked like a leather slipper.

"A child's shoe from the seventeenth century, found in the mud on the banks of the Thames and restored," Yardley read over her shoulder. "Riveting."

KC laughed.

"No, look! It *is* riveting! You can still see the wear marks from the child's foot." She spoke into KC's ear, her voice honeyed with simple pleasure. "Isn't it amazing to think that a real little kid wore this shoe all over London four hundred years ago, and you can still see how their big toe rubbed through?"

KC turned around.

She loved this woman so much, she felt her bones turn to sun-bright light, all at once. She had never felt this way, she was certain. She had loved Yardley, she had lost her, but she hadn't felt like this. Like everything was connected to everything else. Like she wanted to imagine that this little kid walking through London lost a shoe that sank into the Thames to be gently excavated by a reverent archaeologist and then restored by someone wearing a magnifying glass on a headlamp so that a docent could rest it on this pillow and they could find it in the dark, the whole world looking for them but safe for the moment, and KC could tumble down the exhilarating cliff of love.

"Oh," Yardley said. "Please keep looking at me like that."

KC took both of Yardley's hands between hers. She was trembling. "You're not too much," she said. "Don't ever believe it, even if your mama keeps telling those stories that make it sound like she was a saint for putting up with you." She reached up to wipe away the wetness from her cheeks. "You've always been exactly right, Yardley Whitmer, and I love you. I love you."

Yardley's eyes were wide and soft. "Does this mean you'll help me with my dioramas in the basement?"

"It does not. But it means I will admire every single diorama you make, take pictures of them, ask you a million questions, and send the pictures to any group chat we're a part of."

Yardley smiled. "In your fantasy, we're in a group chat together?"

"In my fantasies, we're in everything together. We're not alone anymore, remember?" KC looked around the empty hall. "Can we find a . . . chaise? A bench? Or a very sturdy wall?"

The question made Yardley's shoulders pull back into perfect posture. She tipped her chin up. "King Henry the Eighth and Queen Elizabeth were both born almost right on this spot. If I have learned anything at all about English people, I can promise you there is a reproduction Tudor four-poster bed somewhere on the premises."

They followed the shadowy halls, laughing as quietly as they could. KC had gotten briefly distracted by a gleaming executioner's ax painted with fake blood (she hoped it was fake) when she heard Yardley call out in a stage whisper, "Huzzah!"

Snorting with laughter, KC followed the direction of her whisper-shout and found Yardley standing behind velvet ropes in a life-size, well, *diorama*.

"Whoa." KC took in the pale blue velvet drapes hanging from an ornately embroidered frame attached to the ceiling, sheltering a carved wooden bed covered in a stack of embroidered quilts. "That's very . . ."

"Imperial? Indeed. Antique? No. It's a reproduction. Including the rather imaginative tapestries on the walls with their very juicy and naked subjects." Yardley sat on the end of the bed, then bounced up and down. "I don't think there was such a thing as Serta in the early modern era, but I'm glad it's not horsehair."

KC stepped over the ropes. "Or a wooden box shaped like a mattress."

Yardley reached out for KC's hands. "Are you going to cash all those checks you wrote in the banquet hall?"

"You." KC held her finger up to Yardley. "Shush."

It was important not to let her get sassy. In twelve hundred and one days, KC had learned *some* things.

She put her knee up on the bed beside Yardley's thigh. The wig was gone, sacrificed to the need for hairpins, and Yardley's dark braids had gotten mussed when she'd dragged it off. KC spied the end loop of a pin slid halfway from a braid and pulled it out, slow, not wanting to tug any hair.

Yardley shivered. And so KC had no choice but to find the remaining pins, one by one, and free them until first one heavy braid eased to Yardley's shoulder, then the other. There wasn't a sound except their breathing, a little faster than usual. The light was rosy, penetrating the hushed gloom of the curtained bed. KC settled her knees on either side of Yardley's thighs, and Yardley gripped KC's hips. She unbraided Yardley's hair with the entirety of her focus, threading her fingers between the weave, tugging every wave free and then stroking her hands over them until Yardley's hair made a curtain of black around her shoulders.

KC scraped her fingertips over Yardley's scalp, watching the twinkle of the diamonds swinging forward from her bent neck.

She tipped Yardley's head up and kissed her jaw, breathing in the scent of her skin. "Now you're not Max anymore," she said.

She kissed her neck. Softly bit her earlobe. Thanked every heaven.

"That's good, because I'm not sure I could keep up such a high level of sapphic dominance in the state I'm in." Yardley's voice was so low, her wit seemed sleepy. "What are you wearing underneath this crime of a dress?"

Her hand found KC's upper thigh, and her thumb dragged an arc over flexed quadriceps toward the juncture of her thighs, slow and with enough pressure to make it clear Yardley was feeling frustrated. The good kind of frustrated. KC pulled her hand away, ignoring the throb of protest from her clit.

Yardley laughed, but it was the laugh she always laughed right before things would get very, very serious between them—breathless and in her throat. "Tell me what to do."

"Tell me what you want." KC raked her hands through Yardley's hair and gently pulled.

"To feel what I do to you."

KC slid off Yardley's thighs. Her bare feet sank into the rug, a strangely intimate feeling for such a public space. She took in the hot flush on Yardley's cheeks and her serious blue eyes and how the bow of her upper lip had already swollen and lost its definition.

"Take off your disguise."

Yardley closed her eyes and let out a breath. She unbuttoned her trousers and lowered the zipper, turning her body to ease them off her ass. They slithered from the end of the bed, their satin lining sinking into them in a puddle at KC's feet.

KC thought of morning Yardley, belted into her robe in the kitchen of their house in Reston.

Yardley in that teetering pile of a wig in the back of the comm van after the Starbucks op.

Yardley in aviator shades and tight jeans, crossing the transportation bay at Langley.

They called her the Unicorn because she was singular. There was only one Yardley Lauren Bailey Whitmer the Third, and she belonged to KC.

"Keep going," she said.

Yardley unbuttoned the remaining two buttons of the tuxedo shirt, then the cuffs. The sound of the stiff oxford cotton snicking off her shoulders was loud enough to make KC wet. The shiny black strands of Yardley's hair curved over her collarbones to frame her full breasts, tipped in pale pink. She held her hands loose at her sides and dragged her heels over the quilt until her knees were bent. She looked exactly like a naked woman ought to look on the Elizabethan bed, begging with her eyes, every inch of her gorgeously corrupt.

"Your panties, too." Yardley must have heard the desperation in the command, because she started to smile, but KC shook her head at her. "No. It's serious what you've done to me. It hurts. I'm fucked." KC whispered this, giving Yardley what she wanted.

Showing her what she did to her.

Yardley dropped onto her back and lifted her hips, pulling off her tiny black panties. She lay in the darkest shadow of the bed, so that only her legs and hips had definition. It made KC feel like a voyeur, dirty in the best way, especially when Yardley dropped one of her knees open to show KC how wet she was.

KC crawled onto the bed at Yardley's feet and slid her hands up the outsides of her legs, smooth and shiny, a silken sensation that never failed to pull a hard hitch of desire from deep inside her.

"Please, please don't be nice," Yardley panted, the dusky light catching the restless movement of her hands she was holding over her head.

"Look at me." KC dug her fingernails into her palms, fighting for the control Yardley wanted. She rose on her knees to pull off her dress. As soon as the slithery material glided over her bare breasts and she met Yardley's serious eyes, she lost mastery of the situation.

She wanted to press herself against her, urgent, use her thigh, lick her neck. She wanted to come, and edging her body when it demanded she sprint toward delicious destruction was perfect and terrible, closer to an emotion than a sensation.

"Do you want to touch yourself?" KC pushed her hand into her thong and showed Yardley what she meant, her fingers immediately slick as the slightest pressure put her close enough that she had to bite the inside of her cheek to keep herself from taking it too far.

"*Fuck.*" Yardley's skin went pink everywhere, shiny in the dip between her breasts and throat. "Yes." She leaned up on one elbow, watching KC's finger move under her scrap of underwear.

"Don't look at me like that." Her smile bubbled up from her chest, effervescent and bright, throwing away whatever pretense remained that KC was in charge of what happened in the hushed space behind these velvet curtains.

Yardley smiled back, breathing hard. She hitched her knee up and touched herself.

KC's focus narrowed to one tight, throbbing ache—the woman in this bed with her, the ragged sound of her breath. Her heated skin on the thigh KC had reached down to hang on to was the exact temperature of KC's arousal. She knew it would be Yardley coming that made her come, because she could never last beyond the sound of Yardley's broken moans, her crying out. It had been too long without that. She hadn't realized how diminished she'd been without it.

She pulled her wet fingers from her underwear and caged her arms around Yardley. Their lips met at the same time she reached down and moved her fingers alongside Yardley's, urgent to take over, then slid inside her with an answering throb that KC felt in her toes. She savored the luxurious feel of Yardley's pussy, swollen, hot, smooth and rough, sweeping her tongue into her mouth and gasping when, between kisses, Yardley sucked her own fingers into her mouth.

KC didn't recognize the desperate noise her throat made. She needed more. She kissed her way down Yardley's body, alternating with small bites, and when she put her mouth over her, licking and sucking with no finesse, guided by the pitch of Yardley's rhythmic moans, she held her fingers still inside of her, not quite letting her get there. KC's hips started moving, searching, begging to find pressure and come, but she edged herself until she tasted Yardley and heard her coming, tightening around KC's fingers. Then all it took was one hard press against herself with a knuckle that made her come apart at the same time, clenching so hard her ears started ringing, both of their thighs shaking.

"Come here," KC croaked. Yardley reached her arms down to pull her clumsily up until their bodies aligned, skin touching skin from breasts to ankles.

KC curled around her, her face against Yardley's cheek. She felt her breath slow and her skin cool, their smell mingling with the dust from the quilts.

"I love you," Yardley whispered. "Now I have to kiss you."

She did, until KC's heart ached.

"I love you, I love you," Yardley breathed, and then turned her head. KC was looking into her eyes, their noses almost touching.

"Do you think you could make one of your tiny dioramas of what just happened here?" KC asked. "Make it historically accurate? Because I would cherish it."

Yardley let out a surprised laugh that wrinkled her nose, and made KC laugh, before they realized how loud they were and tried to shush each other while being unable to stop.

It wasn't a reproduction.

This was original, new love.

CHAPTER TWENTY

Yardley removed the large bandanna from around David Miller's eyes. They'd handcuffed him to a heavy, good English-oak chair, and Julia had turned the lights low to give him a chance to adjust to his circumstances.

Or to the existence of consequences for his behavior.

He squinted. His large, pale blue eyes focused on her where she sat in the Windsor-backed chair across from him. She'd buttoned up her tuxedo shirt and discarded the salt-and-pepper wig.

"Fuck," he said.

"You don't call, you don't write," she replied.

"I don't answer to you."

"You'd think that an agent of the United States of America would be eager to answer to their countryman and colleague in the wake of an arms auction of interest to the very organization they are undercover in. But definitely don't answer to *me*."

KC took the cue and walked into David Miller's line of sight. Julia had requisitioned a tutor's office on the campus of the old naval college. The tutor must have an association with the theater department, as bits and pieces of stagecraft in the corners and leaning against the wall provided an appropriately dramatic setting. KC's entrance was framed by a plague doctor's costume hanging on a peg and a teetering pile of prop books that looked like they belonged to a wizard.

"Hiya, Mr. Miller. Remember me?" She sat down with her legs crossed on a small chintz-covered chair.

"KC?" He said this under his breath, his head darting back and forth between the three women. He didn't seem to know whether to look at KC, whose appearance had slumped his shoulders, or at Julia, who made him sit up straighter and jangle the handcuffs.

"Have you seen the pictures of Emma's new baby?" KC asked. "She named her Amybeth, after your wife. Probably because Mrs. Miller has had such a fucking difficult year, what with her husband and the father of her children abandoning her with the liquid half of her life savings."

"I'm undercover," he said, a small fissure of anger in his tone.

"Are you, though?" KC asked. "Because there's a difference between being undercover and isolating yourself to keep from having to face the truth. I know a lot about that, actually."

KC's comment hit Yardley like an arrow whining through the air from above and then sunk heart-deep into her chest. They could have lost so much. *Secrets aren't the only way to keep a person safe*, Atlas had told her. *There are ways to share this work with a family or a partner. They aren't easy. There are no guarantees. Life isn't safe.*

Yardley had been doing the wrong hard things. She wouldn't make that mistake again.

"You can't possibly understand the delicacy of espionage at this level." David's voice had gone more than a little bit patriarchal.

"I mean, of the two of us, you're the one who's handcuffed to a chair. But please, tell me more about what I don't understand."

"Oh, I do like her," Julia said. "She's like a tiny jalapeño, Yards."

KC leaned back against the puffy cushion of her chair, pulling her sock-clad feet into a tighter crisscross. She was obviously more than okay. Fully in her powers and where she belonged. If anyone at the agency had ever thought to ask this woman what she wanted, they could've had all this talent in their global network years earlier.

Her and KC's crash course had taught them a lot about the power of a simple question. Yardley felt as though she'd plugged her heart into an electrical socket. Her love was neon-laced, electric pink, illuminating the world.

"My handler . . ." Miller said.

"Dr. Brown," KC supplied. "The worst traitor the agency's seen in a very long time. Maybe you missed the burn notice? Easy to do when you stop checking your work messages."

Miller went quiet. Yardley couldn't tell if KC had guessed right and Miller didn't know, or if this was what he looked like when he had an original thought.

KC tapped her finger against her knee. "Here's the bad news. With help from our friends at MI6, we have plenty of intel to indict you as a traitor. An extremely lazy traitor, granted, but if you're not spying, you're lying, so this is not the kind of situation where we answer your questions. This is the kind where it would be a good idea if you took this opportunity to unburden yourself of what you know about Dr. Brown, any new digital weapons, Swedish blackouts—really, whatever comes to mind. Doesn't even have to be linear. Pretty sure we can follow along."

Miller's long, aggrieved sigh reminded Yardley of her daddy when he picked up the stack of bills from the end of his desk and got his good pen out to start writing checks.

"Okay, boomer," KC said. "Give us a story."

"I haven't seen him for months," he said. "I haven't done anything but what I was asked to do." He clenched his teeth together and didn't elaborate.

"Cade, your son"—the hard edge to KC's tone made each word into a hammer blow—"had a garage sale where the only things he sold were what either belonged to you or reminded him of you. It was really something to see him put a fifty-cent sticker on a T-ball shirt because you coached the team when he was four."

Yardley was impressed. Psychological torture was tough to introduce into an interrogation, but KC was getting right in there. "If you don't like democracy," she said, "maybe you have a stock portfolio? Those really take a beating when an empire falls."

"My god," Agent Miller breathed.

"I want dates," KC prompted, frowning at him over her crossed arms. "Times. Conversations."

After a long moment punctuated by the ticking of the clock on the mantel, Miller lifted his chin. "He's better off," he told KC defiantly.

She went a little pale. Yardley might not have noticed if it weren't for the fact that it made her freckles stand out in stark relief against her skin. She looked ten years younger.

This man had known her then. Not ten years ago, but nearly twenty, when KC was a hot-tempered gifted kid and a friend to his daughter, curled up on his furniture or sitting with her arms around her knees on the carpeted floor, memorizing the moves of an MMA fighter.

A girl whose own father was never home.

"You mean Cade," KC said.

Miller nodded.

KC shook her head. She sounded more sad than angry when she said, "No. He's not. I promise you he is not. You know something about my situation growing up, so I'm going to offer you an insight. When my dad decided I was *better off* with my grandma while he was gone for work for weeks at a time, he might have thought it was my grandma who was parenting. She was, best she could. That's true. But what he didn't realize is that he was parenting me, too. He didn't explain why he had to be gone. He didn't reassure me that he loved me. His parenting taught me that I was on my own, and always would be, and even deserved to be. That is a lonely lesson for a kid to learn."

Miller cleared his throat. "Not everyone is equipped for it. I'm the type, right or wrong, better suited to this kind of work."

"Hardly working, though, are you?" Julia said mildly.

Staring at Miller, KC scraped her fingernail over the tender spot beneath her thumb. Abruptly, she stood and crossed to the chair where Miller was restrained. "I've heard that before," she said to Miller. "'Not everyone is equipped for every role.' 'You're well-suited to this type of work.'" The voice she used when she repeated Miller's phrases was, unmistakably, Dr. Brown's. She squatted down in front of Miller, her dress sparkling, her mouth grim. "You can make excuses," KC said solemnly. "But I promise you, your kids are not better off, regardless of how you feel, because the thing you need to consider is that the beginning and end of how *they* feel is not *your* feelings about them."

KC didn't look away. Miller, to his credit, didn't, either.

"It hurts," KC said. Her hand was on the arm of Miller's chair.

"It *hurts* to be abandoned. You hurt them. That is a fact. It's devastating when someone who's supposed to love you by default, who's supposed to be yours to guide you and teach you and cheer you on, can't be bothered. Because who are you then? What are you worth?"

Yardley had to close her eyes. She had to. Just for a moment, just until the surge of her breath-stealing revelation settled down.

She'd wanted to be a backstop against any harm coming to KC. From the moment they met, Yardley had tried to make her body, her life, into a bulwark against the hurt that was doled out so recklessly by the people in power—mostly, in all honesty, by the men, the Dr. Browns and David Millers of the world—telling herself the whole time that her decision to risk herself was what kept good people safe.

But seeing her incandescent, combustible KC confront one of those men with all the steely resolve and insight she'd earned for herself by walking through fire, Yardley knew she couldn't put herself between this woman and the world. It wasn't her job to make her body a shield against the world's danger. She couldn't love KC Nolan holding her breath, hoping nothing bad ever happened.

Her job was to honor what KC had made out of a lifetime of hurt. Even if KC never found a way to fix the pain her daddy, her mama, and her grandparents had visited on her by simply not showing up, *Yardley* could learn and do better, because a good part of loving this woman would be about showing up. Trying. Finding a hundred, a thousand different ways to remind KC that she wasn't going anywhere.

When Yardley opened her eyes, KC was watching her.

Yardley put her fingertip on her own sternum. She looked into KC's eyes and mouthed, *I love you.*

KC smiled. *I know,* she mouthed back.

She walked a few paces away from Miller, then returned. When she directed her attention to him again, he flinched. "Every decision you've made for a very long time," KC said, "has been about what you are afraid of. It's been about isolating and protecting yourself from what you know you actually want. You don't have to feel bad about that, because a lot of us do that. I've done that. But eventually we have to *try.* We have to risk."

Yardley watched him flush with hectic color and have to master himself as he looked out one of the dark squares of wavy glass fitted in the leaded windows.

KC sat back down. She leaned forward, her forearms stacked and balanced on her crossed legs. Her thinking pose.

Yardley crossed the room to stand next to the arm of Miller's chair. "What we need to know, in what you can imagine is an urgent manner, is where Dr. Brown is now." She offered this as a request softened with her native accent and relaxed posture. "It's so critical, and it would offer the kind of help that might help the agency understand better the . . . liberties you've taken with your cover."

"I'm not privy to that," Miller told her, his tone dropping into a more confidential register that told Yardley he liked not having to answer to KC. "It was my understanding he spent most of his time at headquarters."

KC shook her head. "He hates Langley. Always wants to work from the field if he can, or from a covert location if he can't."

Miller's brows drew together. "Not CIA headquarters," he said. "The black op's headquarters. In Leesburg."

Yardley's heart skipped a beat.

The black op's headquarters. In Leesburg. Which the agency *did not know about.*

"Leesburg, Virginia," she clarified.

Miller still looked confused. "It was in my report. Dr. Brown told me about it so that I could let him know if anyone in the London cell seemed to be interested in dealings with the op. I never heard anyone mention it, but I passed on that I was surveilling for mention of Leesburg in my report immediately following that visit from Dr. Brown."

"Date?" KC asked.

He closed his eyes. "August. Not last summer. Summer before."

"Filed how?" KC already had a laptop open.

"We have a secure channel."

"File drop?"

Miller nodded. KC typed furiously. She spun the laptop around and showed the screen to Miller. "This is the channel you use?"

"Yes."

Yardley crossed to put her hand on KC's shoulder. Her skin was as hot as a brick oven. "KC, you made this file drop channel for Dr. Brown?"

"That I did." KC had finished typing what looked like credentials into a login box. The display changed, and now Yardley was looking at long lists of encrypted file names. KC kept typing, then stopped and pointed. "Those are Miller's. Brown's been blocking them."

"I told you, I've done everything according to protocol," Agent Miller said smugly.

"If you don't stop lying, I'm going to unlock your handcuffs and *smack* you and have these two film me so I can share the video with your children." Julia said this in her poshest accent, with a smile.

KC was clicking through the files, skimming each one quickly, looking for something. When she found it, she spoke directly to Yardley. "No one else but Dr. Brown knows about this supposed black op headquarters in Leesburg."

Yardley felt the information snap into place as her hands curled into fists. "That's because Dr. Brown *is* the headquarters."

KC's self-satisfied smile boosted Yardley's confidence that they had this op in the bag. "Dr. Brown liked to reward me with little bits of personal information about himself, like treats," KC said. "He talked about the real estate market a lot. How he was trying to find the perfect place to relocate where he could entice his daughter to move, but her husband was tight-fisted with money. Leesburg came up a few times."

It was clear Dr. Brown had never imagined KC had thoughts of her own.

"Oh, for fuck's sake," Julia said. "Can I just say? Sometimes I get extremely weary that my enemies can't be arsed. Where's my Moriarty? I didn't think espionage would be so much about catching men with their hands plunged into the biscuit tin."

Yardley and KC both laughed.

"Most of the men I have been around these last years," Miller said, in an irritatingly defeated voice, "are only looking to find meaning."

"Well, can't these men take up woodworking?" Julia asked.

"My dad has really gotten into fermenting vegetables. Won a ribbon at his local fair. He was chuffed."

Yardley watched KC return her attention to the laptop, her hands flying over the keys. "You've got this to the team?" Yardley asked KC. "I can grab a comm set."

"No, we're good. Atlas just sent through that we're wheels up from RAF Northolt in ninety minutes." KC looked at Julia. "Give us a ride?"

"*Oh*." Julia put her hand on her chest. "Barely a day, and we're on ride-to-the-airbase terms. Come here."

Yardley laughed as KC smiled and stood up, grabbing Julia for a hug. "Thanks for everything."

Julia looked over KC's shoulder at Yardley. "This one has you locked down, I take it?"

Yardley smiled. "We've finally figured that out. Mostly. It's a long story. We moved in together, but—"

Julia gasped. "Fuck me, Yards! You didn't tell me all day that you're engaged?"

Yardley's neck went hot as she watched KC's posture stiffen. "*But*, I was about to say, we're not engaged." Yardley's voice choked over the final word.

Julia's brows furrowed. "You *did* tell me, didn't you, that you would never move in without a ring. That's right?"

Now KC was *looking* at her, arms crossed, eyebrows raised.

Yardley swallowed. "Yes, I did say that, but what I imagined was I would likely be retired. Or at least out of the field. But then there was KC, but I was still in the field, and she gave me a key and her mother's watch, which was incredibly romantic, so it just happened." Yardley would die of this blush. "It's a gold watch. It was her mother's."

"Yes, but is it an engagement watch?" Julia's nose wrinkled. "Maybe a watch is a queer thing, then. Or an inside kind of gift between you? Like you had to be there. But also, you can trade the watch for a ring."

"It's the only thing I have from my mother," KC interjected.

Yardley made herself breathe normally, her face flaming, her heart knocking.

"You didn't tell me," KC said. "At no point did you tell me that you would never, ever, ever move in without a ring."

"I didn't tell you," Yardley managed. "That is true. You didn't ask."

"I guess you're going to have to call the POD guy back and move out after all."

Yardley turned to stone. But before her rational mind had even caught up to what KC meant, her heart nearly leapt out of her chest with anticipation at what it knew KC *must* mean.

"Wait." Julia stepped forward. "Are you two breaking up? Are you? Because that wasn't a quick peck Jack told me about in the banquet hall." When Yardley looked at her, she widened her eyes. "What? I'm a *spy*."

"Because," KC said to Yardley, ignoring Julia entirely, "*you* don't live with someone until you're engaged. Ever. Never." Her eyes crinkled with amusement at the corners. She'd called Yardley out, and it *amused* her.

"My nan has always saved for me a beautiful mine-cut diamond in a darling setting," Yardley said. "I never thought I'd wear it."

"Such good intel." KC's elf smile washed away the last of Yardley's anxiety. "It's going to be so much fun to date you after I kick you out of my house."

Yardley was giddy.

Because she *was* that kind of old-fashioned, and she *did* love KC Nolan. It would be divine to be courted by her with all of their intentions stated right out loud, with the drama and lead-up and butterflies and delicious tiny mysteries and front-step kisses and sexting and learning absolutely everything about each other while talking about the future.

Their future. Their wild, unknown, started-all-over-again future.

Yardley kissed her beautiful girlfriend.

"It would be great if someone could unlock these handcuffs from the chair," Miller said. "If you're finished."

Yardley stepped away, laughing.

"You're the one who's finished," Julia said. "I hope you have a second career in mind in the event you don't end up sleeping in a steel bed welded to the wall of your cell."

The next eighty minutes were a blur of logistics, check-ins, and overlapping conversation. They handed Miller off to MI6 to be kept secure until the agency decided what to do with him, and then they had to rush to get to the airbase in time, rolling through the wrought-iron gates with Julia driving the borrowed van and bouncing it right off the paved drive and onto the airstrip behind it.

The Darkhorse was waiting for them, and so were Atlas and Gramercy, just emerging from a different black car with Kris and Declan. Yardley watched KC jog away from her to join them, her eyes bright, and exchange several shouted lines that were lost in the noise of the jet rumbling to life.

When KC turned back around, Yardley was still watching

her, her heart in her throat, her pulse pounding in her fingertips, her whole body singing.

"Mine, mine, mine," she whispered.

Life wasn't safe enough not to claim what she wanted.

CHAPTER TWENTY-ONE

Situation Room, the White House

Ada Williams, president of the United States, looked silently at the group sitting at the table in her Situation Room.

KC did her best not to fidget.

"Your plan"—the president crossed her arms—"turns my hair gray."

"Yes, ma'am." McLaughlin, the director of the agency, shuffled his stack of file folders. "There is some risk."

The president turned her attention to KC. Her merciless eye contact made it necessary for KC to remind herself that she'd voted for this woman in large part because she recognized the sovereignty and dignity of all people, and so President Williams was unlikely to send KC to a post in Antarctica to scan penguins for surveillance devices.

"I heard a lot from you in our first meeting," the president said, "but obviously not everything."

"I think who you didn't hear enough from was Dr. Brown." KC said this with as much confidence as she could muster. She *did* understand that the failures of Dr. Brown's leadership had led to her assigning total accountability for the device to herself, instead of to Dr. Brown, but it was difficult to integrate this perspective with the peril she, her colleagues, and civilians had been put in

due to her ignorance. Her thoughts still strayed to the twenty-
foot flames shooting from the propane tank on Mirabel's property, and to the sound of gunfire from helicopters raining down
around them.

No one wanted anything they did to come to that.

"If I may," Yardley interjected. She was leaning back in the
leather executive chair, her crossed arms echoing the president's
posture.

"Whitmer," the director warned.

"No." Yardley glanced at him. "This is important. The
president's right that this is a dangerous plan. Also, its meticulous
design, bolstered by literal reams of intelligence gathered by myself, Nolan, MI6, CSIS, and our asset, Kris Flynn, is backed by a
cavalcade of military on standby to descend by air, land, and sea.
This is a no-failure mission with a breathtaking level of resources
behind it."

"On civilian soil." President Williams's tone made her dis-
taste for this aspect of the plan more than clear.

Yardley leaned forward. "I have a reputation in the agency
for making my own rules." President Williams lifted an eyebrow.
"My reasons are the same reasons why you have consistently op-
erated by your own code." Yardley pointed down the long, shiny
table and circled her finger at the digital displays of the Situation
Room. "This is a room that never imagined people like us. The
agency is the endpoint of a system that prioritizes strict hierarchy
with inflexible protocols. Those protocols are in place to protect
mainly the people at the top. It's a system that enforces all of the
biases of the society we live in, ensuring that everyone at the top
looks like everyone else."

"Not like me," President Williams said.

"No. This office never imagined you. And how easy has it been?"

The president nodded in acknowledgment of Yardley's point.

"My power in this agency isn't that I know eight languages," Yardley said. "It's that I'm a woman and I'm queer. I make every decision with my experiences as a woman and a queer person behind me. That means I'm going to examine the variables a different way than they've been examined before, and that diversity of thinking in an agency like this—my perspective that considers angles and pitfalls and options and perspectives no one else might think of—keeps us safer. Safer still if there's even more of that diversity. It's exponential. What you're able to imagine for our country as a Black woman and our president is much different than the nearly three hundred years of leadership our country had previously."

President Williams nodded. "I like to think so. And, of course, I'm able to take into account their perspectives, too."

Yardley leaned forward. "Exactly. So now you can see why this entire situation, which we have had to design a dangerous plan to resolve, has been a clusterfuck from day one."

The president's expression of attentive listening didn't waver, even as Director McLaughlin looked as though he might like a trapdoor to open beneath him.

Then Yardley looked at her, and KC realized she was giving her the floor.

Far from being nervous, she liked it.

"It has been," she agreed. "Such a cluster. And that's not just because Dr. Brown recruited and sequestered me away for his own use. It's not just because so many of our mechanisms of reporting are easy to manipulate that he made us all believe he was somewhere he wasn't, or that those same mechanisms meant the United States effectively paid for an act of terrorism on Toronto perpetrated by one man"—here, McLaughlin winced—"and now we have to spend and risk even more to make sure it doesn't happen again."

"Tell me why you think it is, then." The president was focused only on KC.

"It's because we're protecting hierarchies and tradition instead of *people*," KC said. "Dr. Brown was protected by this agency to do exactly what he did. He used the system that was already in place. Our communication protocols, our forms, our methods."

There hadn't been anything out of protocol about her recruitment from MIT. Nothing officially wrong with Dr. Brown threatening her with arrest as a way of converting her into an officer of the CIA. So how was KC supposed to have figured out when he'd crossed the line that separated acceptable coercion from the self-serving deeds of a bad actor?

"What I've learned from Yardley," KC continued, "is that intelligence isn't really about secrets and power games. It's about people and the concerns people have. She's able to secure an asset because that asset wants people to be safe, or for their own family to be safe." KC thought of Kris climbing out of the wardrobe, tear-streaked, and how Yardley had stopped everything to make her a calming mug of tea and ask her, *How's baby?* "The asset trusts her because she cultivates a relationship with them, and that relationship is real. She's the Unicorn because she's Yardley, and, like she said, a woman and queer."

KC glanced around the table. She was gratified to see that Gramercy, Atlas, and Yardley were clearly very satisfied with how this meeting was going.

"I think what Yardley is asking," KC told the president, "is that once we complete this mission, we take the opportunity to prevent anything like it from happening again. And that we do that not with *more* protocol and consolidation of power, but by trusting that the agency needs more people like Atlas and Yardley and poor hacker girls from Reston."

The president covered her mouth with her hand, studying KC for a long moment. It was easy for KC to meet her eyes. She believed everything she'd said. She trusted her own judgment.

But most of all, she didn't have any secrets to keep.

"That's quite the speech," President Williams said.

"It's easy to learn when you care. Also, the agency might want to think about what it gained from withholding information from Yardley and me about each other. We fixed it for you, but the country is in more danger, not less, if two spies have to break up on a mission. I didn't even have sad music to listen to."

The president laughed. "Noted." She looked around the room. "No time to waste, then. The clusterfuck ends tonight."

Leesburg, Virginia

Dr. Brown's hideaway was the faux-rustic love child of a mountain cabin and an oil billionaire's mansion, six thousand square feet of rough-hewn stone, curving wrought-iron staircases, and unfinished pine paneling sitting on ten acres of pristine lawn and mature hardwood. He'd purchased it under a false identity from a local Realtor who cheerfully ID'd him to the agency and shared nearly a hundred high-resolution images of the home's grounds and interior that she'd commissioned for the listing. The agency had also located and interviewed the installation tech for the security company that wired the property.

"What a great corker of a house," Kris Flynn said in KC's ear. "I guess arms dealing isn't only about the bragging rights. There's a fair bit of coin in it, too."

KC and Yardley were presently crammed alongside Gramercy, Atlas, and three techs into the dark, airless interior of a twelve-foot-by-eight-foot POD container. It sat in the driveway of the home across the street from Dr. Brown's "headquarters," which turned out to be—as predicted—his two-and-a-half-million-dollar Leesburg pied-à-terre.

Kris Flynn's voice was being beamed to KC from the agency's actual headquarters, where she and Declan were safely ensconced and ready to help out in any way possible with the deployment of the countermeasure Kris had coded.

It was a clever bit of programming. Brilliant, actually. KC never would've come up with the solution Kris had found to shut down and annihilate her own invention, but Kris had cheerfully pointed out that she'd always been her own worst enemy, so it made sense that she'd be best equipped to identify and exploit the device's weaknesses.

The helpful Leesburg Realtor had been willing to install a SOLD sign at the end of the drive across from Dr. Brown's and back it up with a fake listing, which provided the cover necessary for them to drop the POD. It was the same Pack-On-Demand service container that currently sat at the end of the drive of KC's house in Reston.

Full circle.

You know your name will be in the history books, Gramercy had told her with a smile after the briefing with the president. *I can see that you don't know, which is why I wanted to say. And why I wanted to also say that I'm not at all surprised.*

It was nice to have a handler who believed in her.

KC switched her channel to audio sourced from inside the house, silencing any incoming chatter.

Dr. Brown had music playing, a country-western artist he'd once told her his dad loved. She could hear him walking across the wood floors, and she turned on the visual feed on her monitors. Yardley and Atlas were looking at the same feed. Gramercy sat in front of a different display that connected him to Homeland Security and the military.

The POD was quiet as they watched Dr. Brown enter the kitchen. He started a coffee maker and sat down on one of the leather stools at the island counter, pulling his phone from the holster he wore on his belt. The resolution from the feed was so sharp, they had all noted the shape of the micro drive bulging in his left trouser pocket. The computer where he was most likely to connect the drive was in his study.

"It's Monday night," she said, mostly to herself. "Nine o'clock. That means it's six in Flagstaff."

Yardley spun on her stool to look at KC. "Catch us up, Tabasco."

KC watched Dr. Brown swipe, tap, and then tap again. She watched his face break out in a smile and heard him say, "Hello, Sunshine."

"He's calling his daughter. He calls her every Monday night while she's making dinner."

"You want to pull in the audio?"

"No. This is it." She looked at him, the feed in perfect high definition. His mouth was smiling, but what KC bet no one else could see was that his eyes were sad, and when she watched him reach up and rub the bridge of his nose, laughing at something his daughter said, she turned to Yardley. "He'll deploy after he gets off the phone."

"Copy. Give me your go when you're ready."

No one asked KC why she thought so or if she was sure. The confidence loosened her muscles and quieted her thoughts to the task at hand. "I'll knock when he hangs up. I'm on the move." She hopped down from the back of the pod.

"Copy. Tabasco on the move. Cover in position."

It was a quiet night, the November air a little brisk as she ambled across the street.

The night she'd met Dr. Brown, when he showed up at her dorm room door, he took her to a wood-paneled seafood restaurant in Boston with a view of the harbor. At least three-quarters of what was on the menu she'd never tasted in her life. The prices ran to the triple digits.

That was where he'd threatened her with arrest and then bought her seventy-dollar pancakes and told her what she was going to do.

It was breathtaking to compare that to what she'd learned from Yardley in a cheap Swedish apartment and a banquet hall in London—with how many people they'd worked with, how many were their friends, and how much more interested she was in her own life than she'd ever been before.

KC walked up the driveway to the small porch over the grand front door.

"He's hung up his phone call," Yardley said. "The security system notified him of your arrival, and he checked the cameras on his phone. He's on his way to you."

KC knocked anyway. He opened the door before she had put down her arm.

"So you really came." Dr. Brown smiled. It looked like a real smile to KC, despite his red-rimmed eyes.

"I'd hoped you would take the chance on me in Lidingö," she said. "It would have been a lot easier. I wasn't sure I'd be able to surface long enough to be here and do this."

KC and the rest of the team had gone around and around about this approach. She was the only one who wasn't surprised when they got confirmation from Canadian intelligence officer Jack Tremblay that Dr. Brown remained certain KC was on his side.

It was like she'd told Yardley. She knew him better than he'd ever known her.

"After you." Dr. Brown opened the door and moved to the side. He didn't scan her for electronics or even look closely at the street behind her. KC's general impression was that, now that she had arrived, he was happy.

He wanted her to be impressed with him. He always had.

"My study." Dr. Brown smiled again. "I think you'll be pleased with what I've assembled. I have everything you asked for."

KC followed him into the room. It was crisp and dry from whatever environmental control he was using to cool the rack of servers alongside his desk. There were three monitors and a desktop CPU in a clear case, an extremely fast and expensive model. Beneath the central monitor was a row of unused ports. She did a quick scan as she sat down in the Herman Miller chair, then looked over her shoulder at him. "Do you mind if I confirm everything is as it should be?"

"After you." He smiled and pulled out another chair.

"We're locked in," Yardley said in her ear. "You're free to run the checks we planned."

KC got to work, supplying the agency with as much evidence as she could about his system, as well as giving Kris the heads-up in case there was anything she needed to know before KC deployed the countermeasure. As she discreetly sent data packet after data packet, she was chilled by how extremely prepared Dr. Brown was.

"I'm ready," she said, as much for the team as Dr. Brown. "Let's do this."

He reached into his pocket, and KC wondered again why she couldn't simply lay him out, snatch the device, and let the National Guard members stationed yards from his property take him into custody. It would be very simple.

Yardley's argument against it was that there wasn't any way to guarantee KC's life in that scenario.

The agency's argument was that they wanted to collect as much evidence as possible.

He stood, the green case in his hand. "You don't mind?" He gestured at her chair, inviting her to get out of it.

It took more effort to pull her body from the chair than KC had expected. She knew the next moments had been meticulously planned. She'd drilled for hours on every possible contingency.

None of which had any effect, in the end, on the fact that she didn't really want to watch him do this.

Dr. Brown took the chair. He set the tiny drive on the desk. It already had a cord attached to its USB-C input. Her heart rate must have spiked, because Yardley's voice filled her ear with a soft purr. "Easy."

The countermeasure was, literally, up her sleeve. An identical micro drive, but in a pale-yellow case—incidentally, the color KC had had in her online shopping cart all these months. Her pulse thrummed against it.

"It would be easier to monitor the spread and make sure it reaches its maximum effect if I could get back in there when you're done." She sounded normal. Interested.

"I'm not worried." He reached over, and KC kept her focus on the end of the wire with its small USB connector, forcing herself to breathe.

Then, he put a connector into the port.

But it wasn't the connector coming out of the drive.

She followed the cord, certain she must be incredibly wrong. It originated from the clear computer case of the CPU to the right of the monitor, the one running the stack of servers in the corner of the room. The case was whirring, lit up with colorful LED lights, and KC saw with a sick wrench of her stomach that there were four fat bricks of Semtex inside it, taped together with packing tape and snuggled against a simple LED detonator.

It was blinking. Powered, now, by the cord he'd just plugged in.

"Fuck," Atlas breathed in her ear.

"I'm sure you don't want to deal with the world on the other side of the interrogation table." Now, Dr. Brown snugged the micro drive into a second port.

"Look, I don't plan on being caught *or* dying today," KC said. "You must realize I got into this in the first place, when I was just a kid, to see what would happen." They only had seconds. The device was active. Unlocking doors. Taking control of systems. Moving like a dark whisper through the digital pathways that covered Leesburg, Virginia, and snaked outward to cross the entire Eastern Seaboard.

"I do know that," he said. "But you should know I'm not an arsonist like you. This isn't about me."

Bullshit, KC thought. *It's always been about you.*

The small light on the end of the micro drive began to blink at the same time she heard the first helicopter. She shook her arm, caught her own micro drive in her palm, lurched over Dr. Brown's arms, and plugged it in.

Its blue light illuminated, and then he was up, his body against hers, her arm bent behind her back.

She moved to a crouch to flip him over her, but he swept his leg at her knees hard enough that she lost her breath from the pain. KC threw herself at his side while he still had one leg up, toppling them both to the ground with her on top. The helicopters were loud now, their bright lights blasting into the small, high window of the room. She became aware of her own breathing and Dr. Brown's, louder even than the chatter in her ear.

The engines were roaring. KC could hear shouting outside. Dr. Brown dragged himself to his feet, his mouth set in a sour grimace. "I should have let you get yourself arrested."

She heard the shouts of soldiers at the front door, followed by the huge bang of a battering ram creating her way out.

She glanced behind her just in time to see Dr. Brown pull the USB cord on the bomb.

"*Fall back!*" she screamed, moving without conscious thought toward the sound of the battering ram as the detonator began to rapidly blink red.

Later, she would think a lot about what stopped her. About her complete lack of hesitation when she turned on a dime, ran back into the study, and—in a show of strength she could only thank her hours at the gym and pure adrenaline for—yanked Dr. Brown out of the room. They emerged onto the lawn to the sight of a line of National Guard behind blast shields. She pushed him past the line and fell behind it while actively questioning many of the life choices that had led her to this point.

The house exploded, and the world went silent.

When KC opened her eyes, she briefly panicked, feeling like she couldn't move her body, until she oriented to Yardley's smiling face—her eyes wet, the lights way too bright—and realized she was under a heated and weighted blanket in a hospital room.

Lights. Thank god.

She pulled an arm out from under the blanket. A hand slipped into hers. She turned her head.

Yardley.

So, so beautiful.

"You're so beautiful," KC said. She couldn't really hear. There was a far-away ringing that turned her voice into nothing but low vibration. Her heartbeat was loud. "Really beautiful. Like a goddess. Have I told you that before? That's what you looked like when I first saw you. You had a white dress. Maybe a crown. Did you have a crown?"

Yardley laughed, but KC couldn't hear it. "*Can you read lips?*" Yardley asked this with her mouth but not with her voice. KC wondered if Yardley would kiss her.

"I learned in training." KC pulled her other arm out and put her hand against her throat to feel if she was talking. "For the CIA. From being a spy." She dropped her arm to her chest and felt a painful pinch on her hand.

"*Careful, you'll pull out your IV.*" It was nice to watch Yardley's mouth, her cupid's bow, and how her dimples sank in on words like *you'll*. She tucked KC's arm along her side with the IV and straightened the tubing. There was a nasal cannula in KC's nose. Oxygen. KC felt a little sleepy, and it made her remember she'd woken up before now, looked at Yardley, and then fallen asleep again. She worked to keep her eyes open.

Then her heart started pounding. She remembered.

"Is everyone okay? Are there any injuries? Is anyone—"

Yardley put her hand on KC's chest. *"My gorgeous love, you're a hero. A real hero. You asked all this before. Zero casualties. We got Dr. Brown. We all got lucky. Flynn's code worked."*

As soon as Yardley reminded her, KC remembered asking. That's why she'd been able to fall back asleep. She looked around the room, saw her monitor and all her vitals, her IV pump. There was a whiteboard with her name and weight on it. It said she was a fall risk.

"Am I okay?"

"You're at Walter Reed. You have a concussion, but they don't expect complications. You have a bad ankle sprain. You may need some surgery on it. A lot of cuts, scrapes, and bruises. A burn that looks like a sunburn over your back from the heat of the blast, but that should heal well. Your hearing will come back slowly."

Yardley's fingers were in KC's hair, sifting, playing, twirling. It felt amazing. She looked amazing. Did she know that KC loved her?

"I love you," KC said. "Go on a date with me."

Yardley grinned. *"Very smooth."*

"I played it smooth the first time. This time, I'm just going to say it. Who cares if I'm smooth if I can love you? Let me love you. Let me love you until you move in with me again. Which you can't do yet."

"No," Yardley said. *"Not yet."*

"Yardley?" KC wished one of the monitors could show what

was inside her heart. She wanted Yardley to see exactly how big her love was, with a number. A number that meant no woman had been loved more on this earth than Yardley Whitmer.

"*Yes?*"

"I can't tell you, but it's not going to be very long before you can move back in with me."

She felt Yardley's cool hands on either side of her face. They put all of Yardley's love inside of her. All of her big, everything love.

"*Then I'll have to kiss you.*"

KC closed her eyes and fell asleep with Yardley's kiss gentle on her mouth, her cheeks, her forehead, glad they'd saved the world because Yardley was in it.

EPILOGUE

KC had taken Yardley to see the cherry blossoms on the Tidal Basin path by the National Mall, and they'd walked hand in hand, the unseasonably warm weather making the pink petals rain along the path like fairy magic.

The day had cooled down fast, though. Yardley was thinking she should go into Atlas and Marla's guest room and grab her cardigan to put on over her sundress, but she was so comfortable in a padded Adirondack chair, watching KC laugh at something Gramercy said where they stood by the grill, she didn't want to.

KC was slaying her in that minuscule cropped T-shirt and low-waisted shorts. She looked edible, freckles everywhere, her hair just long enough to curl disobediently.

She caught Yardley staring and gave her a wicked smile that Yardley felt in every bone in her body.

Dating Katherine Corrine Nolan should be illegal. If Yardley had known the first time around that this alternate, take-two version of their romance was an option, she would've quit the CIA and pursued a different calling a lot closer to what her mama had in mind for her. The sort of calling that involved a lot of baking and keeping herself pretty for a devastating suitor.

Her only complaint was that she couldn't have more of it.

More ecstatic moments when KC's voice came through on her apartment's intercom and Yardley buzzed her in, desperate to kiss her, desperate to convince her they didn't need to go out.

More long conversations into the wee hours of the morning on KC's back deck, wrapped in blankets, talking about everything and nothing, showing each other funny videos on their phones, dreaming about the future.

More surprise outings to a display of miniatures and models at the Smithsonian.

More vacations like the one they'd taken to a tiny, pretty resort in Mexico, where they'd barely left the huge bed, the doors that led to the ocean thrown open, late-night birria burning their lips.

But *more* was hard to lay claim to, because by necessity being a field operative took KC out into the field, and Yardley's hours at Langley as a handler were long. It wasn't ideal.

Still, having work they believed in was something they both wanted—one of those things they talked about for hours when they mapped their future and made goals. Yardley had an eye on even higher offices in the agency, and, while KC was enjoying her time in the field, she'd also talked to someone in Research and Development and told Yardley she saw possibilities for herself there. *Someday.*

"Finally got her down in the Pack 'n Play." Kris emerged from the patio doors. "But it was a near blessed thing. Thought I'd never get her off my boob. Declan thinks she's trying to teethe, but it's too early still. He's convinced his Corrine is advanced at everything."

Kris and Declan's baby was, quite simply, the most gorgeous infant Yardley had ever seen. That baby was giving her ideas. So far, those ideas also remained in the *someday* column, but she did have a lot of pictures of Corrine Byrne on her phone.

"Between you and me"—Kris leaned in, lowering her voice—"I think she takes after my sister and isn't destined for the Nobel Prize, if you know what I mean. But god, I love her."

"Phew."

Kris laughed. "I'm starved and going to get another hamburger. Can I get you anything, love?"

"I ate two, and potato salad, and a huge Rice Krispie treat from the pan KC brought, and I just finished a bag of chips. I can't move." Yardley stretched for emphasis. "Did I also have a long brunch on Capitol Hill after seeing the cherry blossoms? Yes. I did. There were poached eggs. There was gravy. Things filled with fruit, and fruit filled with cream. But I can't find my regrets anywhere."

Kris laughed. Atlas's solar party lights were just starting to blink on in the twilight. "Do you find the indictments that came in from the Justice Department to be what you anticipated?" Her voice had a hint of hesitation. "I thought they were . . . fair."

Yardley reached up and took Kris's hand, giving it a squeeze. "Yes. Fair." She studied her face. "How are you doing?"

Kris nodded. "Every day better and better."

"You start your internship in tech tomorrow. How does that feel?"

Kris's smile grew. "Can't wait, if I'm being honest. Corrine already loves the daycare we found. She'll be such a good American, scrabbling with the other babes. Maybe she'll meet all the Congress folks' babies and become part of one of your American political dynasties."

"I honestly hope for more for my goddaughter."

"We'll see. Did KC tell you Declan's work sponsorship came through at Sparkdesk?"

Yardley loved the excitement on Kris's face. "She hasn't had the chance. What a relief, huh?"

"It is. I'm all about doing everything by the book now, let me tell you. Look, here's your girl with our host and George Clooney."

Gramercy had tried very diligently to get Kris to stop calling him that, but she remained undeterred.

Atlas handed Yardley a glass filled with the pink lemonade Marla had made. "Too much party?"

"Maybe. I could rally, though. Don't count me out." Gramercy had just been embraced from behind by Lucas—rough-edged where Gramercy was polished, smiley where he was reserved, exuberant where he was watchful. But they looked at each other the very same way.

Her KC, who had been lifting with Lucas lately, and shared with him a sense of humor and inability to keep from calling a pig a pig, had nonetheless cultivated her deepest new connection with Gramercy. *He's always so glad when I'm confident I can do something*, she'd told Yardley. *Reminds me I'm allowed to be confident.*

Marla walked over, her long legs navigating the lawn in four-inch heeled sandals like she'd been born to it—which, just like Yardley, she had been. Her bright silk romper swished against her deep brown, perfect skin without wrinkling, shifting, or revealing even a quarter inch of bra strap. When she arrived at Atlas's side, a familiar hush came over all of them, stupefied by Marla's terrifying beauty. She straightened the fall of Atlas's crochet sweater, kissing them on the cheek in a way that made Yardley blush.

"Come with me." She pointed at Yardley with a perfect garnet fingernail. "Excuse us."

Yardley heaved herself from the Adirondack while looking around at her friends for a hint that might explain Marla's command, but they gave her nothing. Spies, all of them.

"Is your handbag in the guest room with your cardigan?" Marla's soft south Georgia accent floated behind her in the night air.

"It is."

"But you only brought that itty-bitty clutch." They'd entered the house now, and Marla closed the doors behind them. The noise from the party faded.

"I left my tote in the car."

"Well, go on and get it." Marla made a shooing motion with her hand.

Yardley, very confused, retrieved the straw tote she'd brought with her in case she needed anything for the long day and hustled back into the house. Marla led her to her master bathroom. It was as scrupulously clean as an operating room, but with trays of mysterious potions instead of instruments. Marla opened the tote and pulled out Yardley's brush, her little makeup kit, and a second, spare cardigan with rhinestones on it that Yardley had thrown in the bag just in case she and KC went somewhere fancy for brunch.

"Sit here." Marla pulled out a vanity stool. "Can I fix your hair?"

"Yes." Yardley sat obediently. "But why?"

Marla took out a barrette that had slumped to the side and started brushing. Yardley closed her eyes at how good it felt. Marla's strokes with the brush were as firm and no-nonsense as her mama's. "Because your girl's got a ring in her pocket, and you and I understand that these kinds of things cannot be a surprise. A woman needs some notice so you can focus on what's said to you instead of why you didn't get your nails done."

Marla picked up the weight of Yardley's hair and brushed up her nape.

"Oh, good lord." Yardley's chest felt tight. She stacked her hands over her heart and took a deep breath.

She'd known this would happen at some point. KC had not been even a little bit subtle. She'd left tabs open on the computer and even one magazine ad flipped so Yardley couldn't help but see it on the coffee table as a way to jump-start a conversation about what kind of ring Yardley would feel was suitable (a big one, mainly to make KC laugh, but there was a girlish corner of her heart that did shine with pure avarice), what kinds of proposals she approved of (no dancing, no Jumbotron, no strangers present), and whether it would be necessary for KC to speak to Yardley's father first (yes).

It turned out, however, there was a Grand Canyon of a difference between knowing it would happen sometime and knowing it would happen as soon as Marla finished making her presentable.

Yardley focused on her breathing.

"That's right, you pray." Marla opened a drawer, pulled out a parting comb, and deftly sectioned Yardley's hair. "You have an orange stick in your makeup bag. Work your cuticles while I finish with your hair."

Yardley nodded and got out her Tony manicure kit to freshen her nails, which, thank god, she'd just had done. She reviewed every single phone call she'd had with her nan lately, scrutinizing them for clues, because she *knew* Nan would know it was happening tonight. No doubt Yardley would receive a call from Nan first thing tomorrow morning to get the details.

She finished with her nails and studied herself in the mirror. Marla had put her hair into a half-up, half-down style accomplished with artful, careless-looking braids that actually had about a dozen hairpins holding them in their bohemian configuration.

"Here you go." Marla handed her a makeup wipe, which Yardley dutifully used to clean her face. Just when she'd lifted away the last shadow of mascara, she started to cry.

"Oh, no," Yardley choked. The tears weren't delicate little drops of tears. They were rivers that were swelling her eyelids and snotting her nose, blotching her face in great big red cabbage roses of emotion.

Marla pulled out another vanity stool and sat to face her, handing her a tissue that Yardley immediately needed for a long, embarrassing nose blow. "Tell me," she said.

Yardley looked at Marla's perfect, angelic eyelashes and the shining swoop of her cheekbones. When she opened her mouth, she just sobbed again.

"Never thought I'd see the Unicorn brought this low." Marla's voice was soothing. "To think of all you've been up against, only to be ruined by a ring."

But it wasn't the ring.

It was that when all the other little girls said they wanted to grow up to be elementary school teachers or veterinarians, Yardley Whitmer had made herself a sacred promise that she'd be a spy, just like her granddaddy. When all the other little girls debated with each other about whether they wanted a husband who was a doctor or an attorney, Yardley had known to a certainty that she wasn't ever—not ever, ever, *ever*—going to love any man besides her daddy and her granddaddy.

She'd been right on both counts. Although she had grown fond of Gramercy.

Now she was crying because she'd been wrong about absolutely everything else.

The tears were a soft clutch of her diaphragm, a gentle push that moved Yardley's old hurts out of her body and up to the surface so she could feel them.

She wiped at her eyes, gazing at herself in the mirror. "I thought I'd never fall in love," she said. "I thought it was up to me, which is absurd, and then I did fall in love, and I thought I'd invent a new and brilliant way to have KC in my life without blowing my cover, but that was a lie I was telling myself, because I wasn't trying to figure out anything at all. I was just lying and hiding and hoping it would work out."

She turned around to look at the woman who'd been kind enough to understand Yardley would need this moment, this space, to prepare herself.

"I ruined it, Marla. I absolutely and completely ruined it, and it's only by the grace of some very kind and benevolent god that I got a second chance. No one imagined this for me. Not even I could. If I had to guess, I'd say I'm crying because I'm not completely, totally convinced I deserve it."

"Maybe you don't," Marla said. "But maybe it doesn't work that way. Maybe love isn't something you can offer and withdraw at will, or something that's earned on merit or only belongs to the good or the straight or the humble or the perfect. Maybe you marry a spy and you have to tell your mama they travel for business while you worry yourself to a bloody knot on the inside.

Maybe your love comes to you when by no measure are you ready, and you lose it. Maybe you love someone the world tells you you're not allowed to and you die for it, throwing bricks at the police. It's not a pretty thing. It's a powerful thing. It will ask so much of you, including change and terrible grief." Marla patted Yardley's hands. "It would be more strange if you didn't cry."

Yardley could understand that. She let herself cry, and then she felt better, as though a storm had passed through and renewed her. "Will you make sure there's a good video? With decent lighting where you can see both of us in it?"

"Katherine is planning on taking you to our little pond by that big willow tree. Atlas already set up multiple angles of cameras and mics. They're motion-activated. Splash your face with cold water."

Yardley splashed until most of the swelling and redness had faded, and Marla whisked cosmetics over her face to take care of the rest.

Then, Yardley found herself focusing on the most unlikely thought of all: the moment when the front of Dr. Brown's house had crumbled with the explosion, and she'd watched every monitor go shaky and dark except for KC's contact lens camera. It showed her diving between the blast shields, but Yardley hadn't been able to see them, because what KC looked at—what Yardley saw—was how she had Dr. Brown gripped in her arms, saving him.

Yardley's entire heart had been lodged in her throat.

Gramercy told her later that she'd screamed KC's name, but she didn't remember.

It was a *moment* for Yardley, without a doubt. Not just because she'd only briefly had KC back, but also because it was a moment full of gorgeous awe at this woman who risked herself to save an enemy, simply because she trusted her feelings and acted on them.

Yardley could be as scared as she wanted, walking with KC to that pond. She knew KC Nolan wouldn't do one blessed thing, not anymore, unless she was *sure*.

"That's my best," Marla said. "The rest is posture."

"I know." She nodded. "Thank you."

When she left the house, the party had gotten louder in the gathering twilight, and more people had congregated around the chairs, the fire pit, and the coolers with drinks. It was easy to slip into the fray unnoticed, like she'd been there the whole time with perfect hair and kiss-proof lipstick. She found a scrum of Lucas's friends, people she knew casually from larger meetings with Homeland Security, and listened to one of them talk about a playset they'd just put together for their daughter, passing around their phone to show pictures.

Someone touched her elbow.

"Hey," KC said. "Can I borrow you for a minute?"

Praise be, KC was nervous. Her hand was cold in Yardley's, and she was talking about nothing too fast as she led Yardley away from the group, and so Yardley gave herself a second to look up at the sky and smile. Her nerves had melted away, leaving her feeling very hot and very powerful. Like the best prize. Like a lifetime of good things.

"So Atlas was telling me that this duck on their pond just hatched some ducklings, and I know how much you love baby animals."

"I do love baby animals." Yardley slid her arm around KC's

bare waist with a little shiver and an overwhelming pulse of *Mine. Yes. Mine.*

"But now that we're here, I'm realizing it's too late to see them and they're probably tucked under their mom's wing in their nest. If ducks sleep in nests. Do they? That seems like the kind of thing you would know."

Yardley looked at the crisscrossing strings of twinkling stars Atlas had hung up in this dark corner of the yard, taking note of several cameras quietly recording them from every angle. She put her shoulders back and smiled at KC. "I don't know where ducks sleep."

She leaned down and kissed KC, at first pretty, for the video, but then it got away from her somewhat. Yardley had not considered the nuclear impact of this proposal on her susceptibility to KC's prowess. She could understand now why first babies were so often "premature," their births dated roughly forty weeks from the moment of engagement, because she had never felt as ecstatically responsive as she did in this moment. She stroked her tongue against KC's, feeling her shoulders relax beneath her palms, and Yardley let out a sigh. When KC's hands came up to frame Yardley's face, it felt so good that Yardley forgot about her posture. She draped her arms over KC's shoulders helplessly, boneless with the first really good kiss she'd gotten all day. KC's mouth was perfect, and this kiss was horny and direct, sending KC's hands from Yardley's jaw to her sides, over her hips. She was ready to let KC do *anything.* This corner of the party was dark enough. Her thighs had burst into flames. Camera footage could always be erased, possibly after watching whatever it had captured over and over. KC was hardly wearing any clothes, her ridiculous microscopic T-shirt rucked up so easily, and then there was so *much* of KC between her breasts and her navel, the curve of her hips in those equally invisible shorts.

"Marry me," KC breathed against Yardley's neck, biting her just enough that goosebumps showered over her body in the space between that kiss and the next one over her bottom lip. "Marry me, Yardley Lauren Bailey Whitmer the Third."

"Yes," she panted. There was no way the microphones were picking that up, but KC's hand gripped the back of her thigh, right under her ass, and pulled her leg around KC's waist just as a deep, slick pulse of white-hot *yes yes yes* made itself as distracting as possible.

"God." Yardley couldn't breathe, as KC's hand found a place while her mouth found another. KC pulled away, just a little, and right when the cool night air was able to fit between them, Yardley opened her eyes.

KC was smiling, but she was also crying.

"Fuck," KC laughed, her tears rushing over her cheekbones. She looked up at the fairy lights. "I had a very classy proposal planned, for the record. I love you."

Yardley pulled down the skirt of her dress, laughing, too, and then KC was reaching into her pocket and taking Yardley's hand and sliding on a ring.

Yardley smiled so hard that it made her cheeks heat. KC had definitely appealed to the greediest debutante that resided in her heart.

"One more thing." KC held up a key tied on a ribbon. "Please move in with me. I don't want to get buzzed up to your apartment ever again. The bed is hard and small. You took all the throw pillows with you, and now there is nothing to lean on or nap on anywhere in our house. And it's not our house without you. It's fucking dire."

Yardley took the key, untied the ribbon, and retied it around her neck. "Yes. I will confess that I took the throw pillows on purpose. And I bought the worst mattress I could find for my apartment. In case you needed a push in this direction."

"You bought it on the internet." KC took a hold of the ring and gently pulled her closer. "You made me hike it up four flights of stairs."

This kiss was soft. It felt like saying *I love you*, over and over.

"Now," KC said, with enough authority to make Yardley's thighs clench. "Let's go home now."

"You don't want to celebrate at the party?"

"The northwest corner of Atlas's fence, just a few yards from here, has a gate. We can run along the side of the house with the hedges and make it to my car. At this time of night, we'll be home in fifteen minutes, tops."

"All my things are here."

"You won't need anything." The promise in KC's eyes lit Yardley's inner thighs on fire all over again.

She looked at her ring. "Everything else I own does seem a little shabby right now."

They ran out the gate, laughing in a very non-spy-like manner, and fell into the car, kissing before they could get their seatbelts fastened. "We're engaged," Yardley said against KC's mouth. "My mama is going to be a menace."

"Your mama already set up a Zoom meeting between me and her and the events manager at the country club. Nine o'clock to-morrow morning."

"Oh, you'll have to cancel that." Yardley kissed along KC's collarbone. "You can't let her get the upper hand."

"She has a whole vision." KC had managed to wiggle her hand beneath Yardley's dress, and now it was stroking hot up and over the top of her thigh.

"*No*," Yardley breathed. "Absolutely not." She set her hand on top of KC's. "You are going to have to take me home. I'm an engaged lady. I can't be compromised in a vehicle."

KC shook her head. "So many rules."

She started the car, and they drove home in the hushed dark, holding hands over the console. When they turned onto their street, Yardley watched the garage door lumber up. Light spilled through the cracks and out from beneath it, and even though she knew every corner of this house and had been here dozens of times since she moved out—had even spent the night at the end of more than one date with KC—it was transformed.

Probably it was silly for her to feel this way about a shift in the status of their relationship, she thought, caressing the ring on her finger. This engagement didn't change that Yardley was already and always going to spend the rest of her life with KC if she could manage to. Being engaged, being married, wouldn't make their relationship any better than one that didn't include a ceremony or a piece of paper filed with the courthouse.

But KC was right, Yardley had rules. Her own rules. Her rule when it came to Katherine Corrine Nolan was to put a ring on it, forever and ever.

She looked down at her ring in the bright light of the garage, where it came into full sparkle, and what she saw was a symbol of her choice to give her whole self fully to who she was, and to her partner.

She *was* glad it was big, then. And not just because that made it pretty.

When the car shut off, Yardley didn't even unbuckle before she kissed KC again, her fingers in her soft hair, heart in her throat. "Now I have to buy you a ring," she said. "So everyone knows you're taken."

"I want a watch," KC said against her mouth. "I liked Julia's mention of an engagement watch."

"You'll have your watch, then."

She thought they would float into the house in a pink haze, but KC unbuckled Yardley's seat belt to pull her closer, and that was unbearably, could-not-be-stood-for hot, so they tripped into the house kissing and shedding the small bits of clothing they wore. By the time they got to the bedroom, Yardley was fully naked when KC pushed her down to the mattress, banded her wrists over her head with her forearm, and kissed her, making Yardley's insides swoop like she was in the first car of a roller coaster.

She didn't know how they ended up on their sides, her leg between KC's thighs and KC's thigh over her hip, her palm against KC's clit, everything hot, but it meant KC was inside her, and it felt so full that even her bones were throbbing, and every inch of her skin was sensitized to every place KC's body touched hers—points of slick contact that felt like buzzing confetti settling over her body.

"Kiss me," she begged, and KC did, open-mouthed and filthy, her tongue sliding against Yardley's in time with the motion of her fingers, making Yardley dissolve into a gloss of sweat and taut, tightening thrusts of her hips.

With a broken moan, KC shifted until she was over Yardley, her muscled thighs on either side of Yardley's hips. She eased her fingers away. Yardley arched her back, protesting, reaching for KC.

KC leaned over and pulled open the nightstand drawer. Yardley stopped protesting and smiled at KC and her messy hair, red as the love bites Yardley had left on her neck.

"I love you," she said.

"Take this." KC handed her the smooth, pink vibrator known to be Yardley's favorite. "And let me hear you." She leaned down to give the order with a kiss, one that pulled Yardley's upper lip into KC's mouth and made the vibrator almost unnecessary.

Yardley had only just pressed it over her clit and turned it on, closing her eyes at how good it felt, when KC shifted, grabbing the headboard, settling her shins alongside Yardley's head, and then reaching down to trace Yardley's mouth with her finger, "I love you. Okay?"

Yardley reached up with the arm she had available and curled it around KC's ass, bringing her down to her mouth while pressing, pressing the vibrator against herself.

She let KC hear her, humming against her, overfocused on stroking her tongue alongside the rough point of KC's clit the way she liked best until Yardley's hips hitched up, right on the edge, and then surprised her with the sudden whiteout of the orgasm. Yardley came—forever, it felt like—and she was so glad KC was coming, too, because she was too replete, too full of love, and couldn't be coordinated anymore.

They didn't talk for a long time, until they had to crawl under the covers because they were getting cold.

"One thousand, three hundred and thirty-five days." KC yawned. "I don't want a long engagement."

Yardley moved into her arms. "No. I don't, either."

KC fell asleep, breathing soft into Yardley's hair, and Yardley let her. They'd both have to wake up early if KC was going to cut Yardley's mama off at the pass. They needed time to prepare a plan A, plan B, maybe a plan C, lest things get uncomfortable.

Though it wasn't comfort, really, that got Yardley out of bed in the morning. It wasn't faith, either, that the world needed her particular combination of talents and grit to keep good people safe.

It was that she had never stopped feeling like the world slowed down just a little bit when Katherine Corrine Nolan walked into a room.

She hadn't chosen to fall in love. Some benevolent force in the universe had pulled them together, a decision as far outside Yardley's control as her own heartbeat.

But she'd chosen to date her, knowing she shouldn't. She'd chosen to take her home to North Carolina to meet her family. She'd chosen to say *yes* when KC asked her to move in, *yes* when they found themselves in the toughest possible spot and had to work together to discover a way out, and *yes* to starting over without lies or compromises.

When the stakes were highest, they had made all the right choices.

It was always, always *yes*.

ACKNOWLEDGMENTS

There were reasons we wanted to write a Ms. and Ms. Spy book and set it on the world's stage, sending our lovers to multiple countries and dressing them in a wardrobe's worth of costumes and disguises and outfitting them with the best sort of secret tech-basement gadgets: Because, first of all, queer people have been all over the world in every profession, saving the world, for as long as there have been people. We didn't want to write a "gender-flipped" spy story, we wanted to write lesbian intelligence officers with their own strengths and challenges who were real people, in order to argue that the world we live in is better for all of the lesbians in it. Second, and perhaps more important, it was a way for us to honor all of the authors who have been writing queer fiction for generations, paving the way to this moment when two queer women can pitch a book like this to their editor and receive an email back full of excited exclamation points. This book is our thank-you—our *thank you, thank you, thank you*. It was so fun to write, and we're so grateful for all of the work, good trouble, and fierce fights of the authors and publishing professionals who came before us.

Thank you especially to our truly fearless editor, Alex Sehulster, she of the enthusiastic exclamation points, who made this book so much better that everyone who reads it should probably send her a thank-you note, too. She helped us find the joy in a story about a relationship in trouble, and she encouraged revisions that led us to more of everything good, fun, and romantic.

Our agents, Tara Gelsomino and Pamela Harty, remain fearless colleagues and champions, reassuring, advising, and celebrating with us over long email threads and interruption-filled conference calls. They have both made this journey fun and adventurous, and their confidence in our careers is infectious, which is exactly what authors want from their handlers. Thank you.

Our kids, August and James, are inspiring, funny, and the first to call us and the world out. Our gratitude to them is unending. They understand what it is we're trying to do and hype us and check us. Thank you for giving up the dining room table to our books and inviting us into your lives, thoughts, and hearts.

Susan Rogers is the best auntie and best friend ever. She will fly on a plane to a book signing, read our books multiple times, laugh at our jokes, spoil our kids, and in every way make it clear we must and should keep doing what we are doing. It means a lot to have someone who was there from the beginning be proud of you. Susan helps us stand back and appreciate this journey.

We couldn't have written our spies without Barb, Barry, and Austin Homrighaus, whose support is generous and loving and refuses to be questioned. One of the most fun activities in the world is tossing ideas and concepts back and forth with Austin. What a mind. Thank you!

Thank you to Vi-An Nguyen, our amazing cover artist and designer who created such a wonderful sister cover to the first book we wrote for St. Martin's Griffin. Thank you to Ally Demeter and her team at Macmillan Audio for a fantastic experience and for introducing us to the best audiobook performer in the business, Mia Hutchinson-Shaw. Thank you to Cassidy Graham, Ashley Quintana, Rebecca Lang, and Amelia Beckerman, who have been part of our team at St. Martin's, and for St. Martin's Griffin's continued support, excitement, and extraordinary author care. Mae Marvel is in the best hands.

Finally, thank you to the readers, librarians, and booksellers who have made us authors, shared your enthusiasm with us, made us laugh and cry happy tears, asked us amazing questions, and shared profound insights into our stories. We are here because of you.

ABOUT THE AUTHOR

Alyssa Lentz-Underwood

Mae Marvel is the alias of cowriters Ruthie Knox and Annie Mare, bestselling authors of over a dozen acclaimed romance novels between them. Mae lives with two teenagers, two dogs, one cat, four hermit crabs, and a plethora of snails and fish in a witchy century home in Wisconsin whose extravagant perennial garden gives them something to look forward to in the depths of winter. In addition to romance, they also write mystery novels and cannot promise not to branch into new novelistic territories at a moment's notice. They can be found online at maemarvel.com.